MID-CONTINENT

3 0003

D0561945

"Cute as a pink Persian... will keep the reader en... sex scenes, a bubble-gum-sweet but passionate romance, quick-moving action, and a variety of puns and riddle-making beasts."

—*Publishers Weekly*

"Fennell's sexy contemporary romp… takes its cue from Barbara Eden's indelible television role, but with enough original touches, careful research, and world building to make this tale pure fun."

—*Booklist*

"Absolutely delightful… will keep readers amused and completely enthralled in the cutest story ever. A stunning creation."

—*Fresh Fiction*

"A spellbinding flight into fantasy… Judi Fennell's breath-taking imagery and exquisite descriptions create a world that lures the reader in… Ms. Fennell's imagination, humor, and literary knowledge create a tale that shimmers, shines, sparkles, and sizzles with mind-blowing love scenes and world-rocking adventures."

—*Long and Short Reviews*

"Hilarious… goes from giggle mode to all out laughter in less time than it takes to snap your fingers."

—*Yankee Romance Reviewers*

Mid-Continent Public Library
15616 East US Highway 24
Independence, MO 64050

WITHDRAWN
FROM THE RECORDS OF THE
MID-CONTINENT PUBLIC LIBRARY

"Campiness galore… will amuse the reader to the very last page. Well done, Judi Fennell!"

—*Night Owl Romance*

"Campy yet clever, humorous yet tender… Welcome to a world of magic, adventure, sexy genies, and talking animals. Ms. Fennell blends pop-culture references and old world mythology… It's like Easter morning as you discover all of these little eggs she has cleverly written into her story."

—*That's What I'm Talking About*

"If you're looking for a magical romance, with quirky genie antics, a talking cat, humourous situations, and hot sizzling love scenes, look no further than *I Dream of Genies*… Spectacular!!"

—*Minding Spot*

"Magic… Fennell has a knack for combining zany characters with strange situations, mixing them up with a dash of humor and tossing in a bit of sizzling romance… If you're not careful you'll fall off your furniture laughing."

—*FangTastic Books*

"Judi Fennell has done it again! [Her] imagination never ceases to amaze me… This newest adventure will have you turning the pages quickly to see what comes next!"

—*Peeking Between the Pages*

"A thoroughly fun and enjoyable read… filled with the same adventure and compelling emotion as her previous series."

—*Star-Crossed Romance*

"Full of charm and adventure and characters that are unlike anyone else, let alone a world of magic that is closer than you think."

—*Book Reading Gals*

"Wit and humor abound... The love scenes between Eden and Matt practically sizzle off the pages. Fennell's descriptions... will make readers feel like they are on the magic carpet ride of a lifetime."

—*Debbie's Book Bag*

"Ms. Fennell brings charm, humor, exciting characters, and a fun story line... *I Dream of Genies* is a dream come true!"

—*Cheryl's Book Nook*

"Endearing... a terrific romantic fantasy."

—*Midwest Book Reviews*

"Hilarious entertaining... a fun, lighthearted read."

—*Drey's Library*

"A beautiful blend of humor, romance, and fantasy... The quirky humor and character antics had me laughing from page one. Bravo."

—*Author Kelly Moran's Blog*

"A wonderful blend of magic, adventure, romance, with a nice dose of mythology. I loved the humor."

—*Sizzling Hot Books*

Also by Judi Fennell

In Over Her Head

Wild Blue Under

Catch of a Lifetime

I Dream of Genies

Genie knows Best

JUDI FENNELL

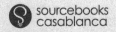

sourcebooks
casablanca

Copyright © 2011 by Judi Fennell
Cover and internal design © 2011 by Sourcebooks, Inc.
Cover illustration by Anne Cain

Sourcebooks and the colophon are registered trademarks of Sourcebooks, Inc.

All rights reserved. No part of this book may be reproduced in any form
or by any electronic or mechanical means including information storage
and retrieval systems—except in the case of brief quotations embodied
in critical articles or reviews—without permission in writing from its
publisher, Sourcebooks, Inc.

The characters and events portrayed in this book are fictitious or are
used fictitiously. Any similarity to real persons, living or dead, is purely
coincidental and not intended by the author.

Published by Sourcebooks Casablanca, an imprint of Sourcebooks, Inc.
P.O. Box 4410, Naperville, Illinois 60567-4410
(630) 961-3900
FAX: (630) 961-2168
www.sourcebooks.com

Printed and bound in Canada
WC 10 9 8 7 6 5 4 3 2 1

As always, to my husband and children.
For the magic you bring to my life.

And to Steph. I couldn't have
done it without you.

*Every wish comes
with complications…*

November 17, approximately 10:00 p.m.

SAMANTHA BLAINE HELD HER BREATH AND RUBBED the copper lantern on the desk in her father's office one more time. A little harder. A little longer.

But still… nothing.

No smoke, no genie, not even a dust bunny. She was being ridiculous; the thing was as much a genie lantern as Albert, her double-crossing, soon-to-be-fiancé—make that, her double-crossing, soon-to-be-*ex*-soon-to-be-fiancé—was Prince Charming.

Useless. Albert thought she, like this lantern, was useless.

"Trust me, Henley," he'd said during the phone conversation she'd inadvertently overheard not ten minutes earlier. "Daddy's little girl is clueless. Useless. On all fronts. Run the company? Her old man must have had another stroke back when he had that will drawn up. She's incapable. Inept. Hell, she doesn't even have a clue what I'm up to. She doesn't have a clue about *any*thing, so as soon as this memorial thing is over, I'll get my ring on her finger and my hands on the contents of that safe. Then you'll get your money."

Samantha flicked the edge of the letter with the

combination to the safe. Dad's attorney had given it
to her earlier. He'd said Dad had wanted her to have
it tonight during the funeral—no, during Dad's *life
celebration*. That was her father, always looking for
the good in everything, but what good had there been
in opening it now, in the middle of this party, just to
retrieve a souvenir from her parents' honeymoon?
She didn't really want a reminder of the happily ever
after she apparently wasn't going to have with Albert.
Without him. Whatever.

She traced the lantern's curved spout, thoroughly
appreciating the irony that Albert had been tearing the
house apart for weeks trying to find the combination to
the safe, yet *she'd* been the one to open it.

Useless, was she? Who was the inept one now?

She tapped the flame-shaped finial on the lid. Finding
this wasn't a victory though, because while Albert might
not have been Prince Charming material, she'd *thought*
he'd had some redeeming qualities, namely claiming
to love her for her. Not because of who her father was
or how much she'd be worth someday, or what great
merger-acquisition material she'd be like other corporate types she'd dated, but *her*. Not Samantha Blaine,
heiress, but Samantha, the woman who had hopes and
dreams of a long, loving relationship like her parents'
and the big family she'd never had. She wanted so much
to believe, so she'd let herself hope that, this time, it was
for real.

The troll had helped the illusion along not only
by offering to sign a prenup, but also by stepping in
and taking over the burden of running her father's
custom-car manufacturing company while she'd been

at Dad's hospital bedside these past six months. She'd been so grateful.

And now this. And tonight of all nights. The jerk.

She blinked back the tears, determined not to let him get to her. But, God, she'd been so trusting. So hopeful. Again.

And again she'd been disappointed.

Samantha tucked some curls behind her ears, plopped her chin in her palm, and ignored Wanda the housekeeper, who was calling her name from the foyer. Samantha wasn't up for seeing anyone right now.

Oh, not because Albert had just broken her heart. Sadly, deep down, she'd known he wasn't the guy for her. She'd known that. But he'd been the first—she'd *thought*—guy in her life who'd sincerely been interested in her. When Dad had had the stroke, Albert had been there. He'd helped out with the company and hadn't made any demands on her other than to sign paperwork.

That was when he'd started mentioning marriage, and Samantha had let herself go along with the idea because, more than Albert being her One True Love, she hadn't wanted to deal with the fact that when Dad was gone, she'd be alone in the world. Mom had died when she'd been a toddler, so it'd just been the two of them all these years. She'd never felt the lack of family more than she had when Dad died.

Albert had offered her a way out, so she'd given in to the hope that maybe, just maybe, he was the real deal. Stalwart, supportive, there when she'd needed something… That was what she'd always wished for, so she'd let him in. Trusted him. Believed in the fairy-tale ending.

And now he'd betrayed her.

She shook the long sleeve of the *djellaba* she wore over her street clothes up her arm and picked up the lantern, her reflection not distorted enough to hide the pain in her eyes at being betrayed.

Again.

Why was everyone always looking for handouts from her? What was wrong with her that she couldn't have someone want her just for who she was instead of what she had in her bank account or what she could do for them? It was sad really, how, with all the things money could and had bought for her, love wasn't one of them.

She ran her fingertips over the lantern's rounded side. Wouldn't it be perfect if this actually *were* a genie lantern? She could use a little magic in her life right now.

For her first wish, she'd turn Albert into a belly-crawling lizard. Then she'd bring Dad back, and then…

"And then I'd wish for the genie to take me away from all this, to some place where all my troubles would just disappear."

And, in a billowing cloud of orange smoke, that's exactly what happened.

Or… *was it?*

1

ORANGE SMOKE SURROUNDED HER, BURSTING FROM the lantern's spout like a boiling psychedelic tea kettle on hyper speed, and while Samantha's troubles weren't disappearing, the *office* was. And the desk *and* the chair *and* the safe and everything else around her.

Everything except the lantern.

The cloud grew thicker, and Samantha didn't know what to do except grab that lantern and hold on tight.

Her body tingled as if grains of sand were bombarding her, and an odd sense of speed surrounded her as if the world were rushing by while the wind swirled such thick, orange smoke all over her that she should be choking… but wasn't.

While she was pondering that, the wind and the world died down, and the orange smoke dissipated as quickly as it had appeared—and this time Samantha *did* know what to think.

First, the half-naked guy in front of her wearing only an orange vest and baggy white pants was way underdressed for a funeral. Second, she was no longer *at* a funeral, and third…

"Where am I?" Highly unoriginal, but then, clichés were overused for a reason, and she really didn't have a clue where she was.

The guy settled his fists on his hips and his orange

vest gaped open, showing off a six-pack that had nothing to do with beer.

"Izaaz," he answered, his voice skating across her nerve endings like smooth wine on fine chocolate—or maybe that was because his eyes were the color of said chocolate and oh my, were they fine. Warm and bone-meltingly delicious.

"Is what?" Knees a tad wobbly, Samantha reached around for the desk chair she'd just been sitting in. Except that the chair wasn't there. Neither was the desk. Or the office.

"Izaaz," said a high-pitched voice by her ankles.

Samantha looked down. A bat-eared Chihuahua smiled up at her.

There were so many things wrong with that sentence that Samantha didn't even bother trying to analyze it.

She looked back at the guy in the vest. Six-two with a set of shoulders that would make a linebacker proud, he looked like he'd walked right off a playing field. Or, in that outfit, a Hollywood movie set. Especially with the dark good looks of a leading man, a killer smile, eyes that made her think of hot desert nights, and thick, rich, mink-brown hair women would beg to run their fingers through.

And half-naked to boot.

Which still didn't explain who he was, where she was, and what the hell had happened to Dad's memorial service.

"I wish I had that chair," she muttered, trying to still her jittery legs and the butterflies in her stomach.

Those butterflies turned into helicopters when a chair *poofed* into existence beside her in a cloud of orange glitter.

"What's that?" Samantha squeaked, jumping backward.

"A chair," said the Chihuahua—which would have freaked her out except that when she'd jumped back, she'd hit something solid. And furry. And when she glanced over her shoulder, the furry thing there put the talking dog to shame.

Cousin Itt's cousin stood behind her. With dreadlocks.

"Hello," it said/mumbled/rumbled.

Samantha sidestepped away, her feet tripping over themselves. What the hell had happened to her sanity?

Half-Naked Hottie gripped her arm when she stumbled. "I think you better sit down," he said, motioning with his hand.

The chair *slid* next to her.

He didn't have to ask her twice. Samantha plunked her butt in the chair, then put her hands and the lantern in her lap.

"Are you all right?" Hottie asked.

Samantha nodded. Then she shook her head. Then she shrugged.

She didn't know what she was. Or where. She'd *thought* she was at Dad's Casablanca-inspired memorial service, with its large Moroccan tents and food and entertainment and costumes. Dad had specifically requested each of those items in his will since the city was where he and Mom had honeymooned.

That had been one of his happiest memories, and Samantha had gone all out honoring his wishes. And contrary to Albert's opinion of her competence—or lack thereof—if there was one thing she *was* good at, it was throwing a party. Even a funeral, if everyone's comments could be believed. Though, seriously, what defined a *good* funeral?

But this… This looked nothing like what David, the event organizer, had set up in the estate's backyard. Instead of the luxurious blue tents draped in silks and brass lanterns that she'd been standing under before going in search of Albert and that fateful conversation, she was looking at white paint peeling like shaved coconut off the oddest-shaped buildings she had ever seen.

A cross between Gaudi's buildings in Barcelona and Munch's *The Scream*, the multi-arched façades looked like a bunch of stone tepees that drooped to the left all honeycombed on top of each other, with pockmarks dotting every surface as if the place was a shooting gallery.

Dead plants draped over rusted balconies. Shutters hung lopsidedly off other abandoned-looking buildings, their gray-and-white-striped awnings torn, their edges frayed, and the median running down the deserted, dusty street had a long trough with what looked like fountain heads inside it, but not a drop of water.

"Hey, look!" said the dog with a bounce. "She's got your lantern."

He… *said*? The dog *talked*?

And she'd thought being congratulated for throwing a good funeral party was odd.

Then she looked around and knew what odd really was.

Aside from the dog, the furball, and the Hottie, there was nothing but white everywhere. Hard-packed sand beneath her feet, drab white buildings with dusty windows, a pale to the point of colorless sky above them… Even the palm trees lined up like bowling pins along the main thoroughfare, about three sizes bigger than any palm trees she'd ever seen, were white. And instead of the dark night sky that'd been above her L.A. home, here, it was broad daylight.

Then the dog's words registered.

"*Your* lantern?" She looked up at the Hottie. Then she looked him down. Oh, not in a check-him-out kind of way, though she obviously wasn't dead (she hoped), but yeah, she did check him out, and man-oh-man-oh-man... There definitely hadn't been anyone like him at the party tonight.

The sword swallower she'd hired had worn a similar outfit, but it hadn't looked anywhere near as good on him as it did on this guy. The long curved swords on their hips were the same, but other than that, there was no similarity. This guy's gaping vest had no chance of ever closing across that chest, and the gold sash wrapped around the top of his pants highlighted incredibly well-defined sexy lines by his hips.

And while the baggy pants that covered his long legs, the silver bracelets on his wrists, and the orange curled-toe slippers should have done serious damage to his masculinity, they actually enhanced it. Just like real men *could* wear pink, real hunks could pull off curled-toe slippers.

Though, honestly? Who did that?

The dog's next bounce jostled the lantern.

Samantha looked at it. Then back at the guy.

No. He couldn't be.

Could he?

She looked at the talking dog. What other possible explanation could there be?

She swallowed and forced the words out. "Please tell me your name isn't Aladdin."

One side of Hottie's mouth kicked back into a smile. If she'd thought he was hot before, now he was sizzling.

"Hardly."

Samantha blew out a breath.

So did the solid, furry thing behind her. "Ha!" it said, though the sound came out more as a smoker's hack than a laugh.

Then the dog piped up. "Aladdin? Of course that's not his name. After all, Aladdin wasn't a genie."

Which meant that the guy in front of her... *was*.

2

KAL WAVED HIS FINGERS, ROUSING HIS DORMANT magic to conjure up a glass of water for his newest—and last—master. Number One Thousand and One.

Yes, the number was ironic, given Scheherazade's nightly tales. But that number had haunted his existence: the thousand-and-one masters he had to Serve, the same number of wishes he had to grant each of those masters, the number of tiles in his bathroom floor, the divots in the lantern's lid, the songs on his iPod.

Probably even the grains of salt in his salt shaker, but he was beyond the humor at this point because Samantha was the beginning of the end of his sentence. The last of the masters he was to Serve to atone for ridding himself of the gold bracelets that bound him to The Service. At one time, he'd been proud to be the only djinni to have figured out how to get them off, but pride was a lonely bedfellow and a poor substitute for losing his magic. Thank the cosmos, the time had finally come. Now if only his Service to this last master would go by quickly.

If she were to die or someone took the lantern from her, it actually could. He'd gone through a few masters that way. But if either of those were to happen, he'd then be stuck in Service to that person and would have to wait (like the rest of the djinn world) until a trick of Karma set him free.

No, better for both of them would be for her to give him the lantern and wish him free, but in all his four thousand years of Service, not one mortal had even hinted at offering him his freedom, He'd learned to stop wishing for it, though the hope still simmered just beneath the surface. If only one of them would. It would only take one.

Unfortunately, however, he couldn't ask any of them for the lantern. Otherwise he'd find himself right back at square—and master—one, thanks to the convoluted stipulations of his imprisonment. He'd resigned himself long ago to playing by the High Master's rules.

Those rules would be some of the first things he'd change when he took over the job.

"Here. Perhaps you'd like something to drink?" After she took the glass, Kal shook the residual Glimmer of magic left behind from his hands and stretched his fingers. As a demi-genie—gods, how that term bugged the *kharah* out of him—he was permitted to use his magic only for his master's comfort, safety, and wishes. Six months shut up inside that lantern not only had him going stir crazy, but also had his magic bursting at the seams.

Then he got a look at her, a hint of ankle showing beneath the *djellaba* she wore, and something else was bursting at the seams.

It'd been a lot longer than six months for *that*, and she was none other than Monty's daughter, the woman whose image had kept him company on many lonely nights.

Soft curls the color of his lantern framed her face and caressed the hollow at the base of her throat, and her lips were moist from the quick dash her tongue had made over them. A dusting of freckles scattered over her upturned nose, and her eyes were so green that they outshone the emeralds one of his masters had given his harem. Samantha was stunning. Even her name was beautiful. If he could grant himself wishes, having Samantha would be at the top of the list.

"I wish I had an aspirin," she said, gulping down the water.

Aspirin was easy. Kal conjured up two. "Here you go."

She looked at him as if he had the same number of heads.

Kal hid his laugh. New masters. He'd seen that look before. Half the time they didn't know what they'd gotten into, and the other half... Well, Kal had never had any say in who his masters would be, but he found that Karma ended up giving most of them what they deserved.

And now maybe Karma had given him what he deserved. He'd certainly paid his dues through the centuries—dues he owed "thanks" to Faruq. That *ibn el-kalb* had stolen not only Kal's High Master's thesis and the job he'd wanted, but also his reputation. So instead of the promotion to vizier Kal had expected all those years ago, his name had been dragged through endless *jeribs* of worthless desert sand and buried so deep that even Mudd was a better name than his.

But now Faruq was the one confined to his lantern, awaiting his own sentencing for trying to double-cross the High Master, which left the vizier position up for grabs. Kal fully intended it to be his. Karma couldn't be that fickle twice.

Could she?

Kal shook his head, ending that thought before it could go any farther. Samantha was his last master, and no matter how often he'd fantasized about her, he couldn't allow himself to be distracted. Not when he was so close. "Where's Monty?"

"My father?" When Kal nodded, she set the glass in her lap and wrapped her fingers tighter around it. She didn't look at him when she answered. "He had a stroke six months ago and, well, his memorial service was today. Tonight. Whatever."

Zift. Kal hadn't wanted to end his Service to Monty this way; the man was—had been—a decent guy. He would have preferred that Samantha had discovered the lantern on her own and summoned him that way because Monty's death meant she was now alone in the world.

"I—" Kal cleared his throat when the words wouldn't come. It'd been centuries, but the pain of losing his family still struck a long-buried chord. He, more than most, understood what her father's death would mean to her, and he couldn't rejoice at the end of his sentence when it meant the beginning of one for her. "I'm sorry for your loss, Samantha."

"You know who I am?"

"Your father talked about you often." Which had suited Kal just fine. He'd been very appreciative of the photos of Samantha that Monty had had in his office. The ones of her in evening gowns at charity functions had sparked his interest; the one of her in a bikini on a Mediterranean vacation, which he was sure Monty had had no intention of him seeing, had sparked something else—and not because of the scenery. After all, most of the women he'd seen before her had been covered head to toe in *burquas* or Victorian clothing, so those seaside images had made an impression that even her *djellaba* couldn't squelch.

"So who are you?" she asked.

Right. The job.

Kal crossed his arms and gave her the standard greeting he'd given one thousand times before. "*Salam wa aleikum*. I am Khaled, the genie of the lantern. What is your wish, master?"

"Genie? Lantern? Wish?" She held up her glass. "I wish this was a lot stronger than water."

He'd heard that one before. "As you wish." Kal waved the fingers on one hand, his Way of doing magic, and turned the water into wine in a shimmer of orange Glimmer. Wish number four. Only nine hundred ninety-seven to go.

Samantha looked at him, then at the glass.

She took a sip.

Which she then spit out.

He'd seen that before, too. There wasn't much he *hadn't* seen or heard in his four thousand years.

"I was thinking coffee," she muttered, mopping the drops from her lap with the sleeve of her *djellaba*. "I wish I understood what's going on."

"Ooh, Kal can tell you that even without a wish," said Dirham, the magical-assistance assistant who'd been assigned to him for the duration of his sentence.

The fox was trying to be helpful, though hopefully not *too* helpful; the little guy did tend to get overzealous on occasion. Kal had had to interrupt Dirham more often than he'd liked because spilling the beans about Kal's sentence—or the fact that giving a djinni his or her lantern would set them free—would cause Kal to have to start over at master number one, as well as sentence the big mouth to life imprisonment. It was a good deterrent that had the added benefit of keeping Dirham quiet around new masters. He and Dir had learned through the years that rarely could a mortal accept a talking fox *and* the knowledge that Kal was a genie on the first go-round.

"How does your dog talk?"

And there; he was proven right again.

Kal cringed, waiting for Dirham's tirade. The fennec might be the most accommodating of beings, and quite clueless about a lot of things, but he did know when he'd been insulted, and calling him a dog was the biggest insult in Dirham's world.

Dir stood on his hind legs and rested his front paws on his hips. It was a ridiculous pose, but Kal had never had the heart to tell him so because the little guy was a sensitive soul.

"I speak the same way you do, with my mouth." The fox circled a paw around his snout. "And for your information, I am *not* a dog."

"Oh? What are you? A bat? A cat? A jackalope?"

Score one for Samantha. That was one Kal had never heard before.

Dirham fell onto all fours, his eyes as big as his ears. "A… a… *jackalope*? I don't have antlers." He veed his tiny eyebrows.

Kal had to step in. He didn't want Dirham getting any more insulted than he already was. The little guy took everything to heart, and no matter how many times they'd been through this, Dirham never understood why a mortal didn't believe them right off the bat. "Dirham is a fennec. A desert fox, native to the northern Sahara."

"Ah." Samantha set the glass on the ground and then stood up, his lantern still clutched in her hand. "Now I get it. I'm dreaming. Thank God that's cleared up since I don't remember going over any rainbow."

"That's because Kal ran out of mist-paint so I couldn't paint one," Dirham said, sniffing the glass.

"Rainbow?" Kal was glad these two knew what they were talking about because he didn't have a clue, and Izaaz was definitely not looking rainbow-ish. Matter of fact, it was looking damned sorry. What in the cosmos had happened here?

"You know," said Samantha. "As in Oz? Somewhere over the…?"

Kal raised an eyebrow. It never boded well when mortals quoted mythology to him; it just made it harder for them to accept what he was.

Samantha shook her head. "Never mind. What I mean is, the Sahara, the fox, you, my father, the memorial… I'm missing Dad. I opened the safe, and when I saw this…" She held up the lantern. "I thought I had a handle on his passing, but maybe I saw this and the memories overwhelmed me.

"And with Albert's crap, I probably put my head down and cried." She shrugged, talking more to herself than to him. "Wore myself out and fell asleep, and this is just a dream. An *Arabian Nights* kind of fairy tale." She cocked her head and looked at him. "So does that make *you* Prince Charming?"

He could be whatever she wanted him to be—and that was without the benefit of a wish. But, still, there were rules.

"Is that what you wish, Samantha?"

She chuckled. "Oh, yeah, right. *That's* what I wish. That you're my Prince Charming, come to kiss me awake."

Her wish was his command. Gods knew, he'd thought of little else since the first time he'd seen a picture of her.

Actually, he'd been thinking of a lot more, but he'd start with a kiss.

He tilted her head ever so slightly and kissed her before she realized what he was doing and wished him to stop. Kal didn't think he could stop. It'd been so long, and Samantha was just… tantalizing.

And her lips… He'd dreamed of them more than he should have, and now… Now, they were a dangerous combination of softness and sensuality. The hint of lilac that clung to her hair was a temptation to linger. And the feel of her in his arms… *jannah*.

It'd been so long since he'd held a woman in his arms.

Truly, he'd had no intention of kissing her. Interest, yes; intention, no. She was his master. His *last* master. He couldn't afford any distractions and she was one giant one.

Well, not so giant; she fit in his arms perfectly.

Kharah! No wonder it was said that the road to *Al-Jaheem* was paved with good intentions; Kal was already burning.

Then she made a tiny, soft sound at the back of her throat and the hell with his intentions—they were all good anyway.

And so was this. Kal swept her up in his arms so that she was at just the right height, her lips at just the right angle to be claimed, her arms at just the right spot to encircle his neck, and her breasts… ah, her breasts were perfect no matter where they were.

And when she gasped, the warmth of her mouth was just as perfect when his tongue slipped in to taste hers.

She tasted as sweet as he'd imagined. And imagine he had. Those pictures of her had gotten him through many a long and lonely night, and this kiss was turning his world upside down more than that last carpet ride he'd taken over the Himalayas.

Kal angled his head the other way, her curls sweeping across his cheek. He'd always liked lilac.

His hand slid to the small of her back and pressed her closer, her tongue dancing with his.

"Kal? Should I reserve a hoodoo for the two of you?"

Dirham. Leave it to Mr. Conscientious to be willing to help out by finding them a room.

Need played havoc with Kal's common sense. Her wish had been hypothetical, but by the letter of The Djinn Code, he was honor-bound to grant it.

And he'd wanted to. The minute he'd materialized in her father's office, saw that she was his new master and heard her wish, he'd started fantasizing about this.

Dirham cleared his throat. Kal was surprised that the troll behind her hadn't chimed in. Although, given Orkney's problem, he'd probably missed the entire thing.

Kal gripped her arms and allowed himself one last taste of her lips before breaking off the kiss. It took her a moment to open her eyes. And when she did, Kal saw the flash of desire in them.

But then he saw the confusion.

She ran a shaky hand through her curls, and Kal allowed himself to bask in the knowledge that he'd put that tremor there. A hundred and sixty-plus years of celibacy, and he still had it.

"I guess it wasn't a dream after all."

Orkney snorted, and a rope of his mud-brown dreads blew across the back of the chair to rest in the seat. "First time anyone's ever called me a dream."

Ah, so the narcoleptic troll *had* been paying attention.

Samantha spun around. "I'd forgotten you were there." She licked her lips. "What are you?"

Oh, gods, here it comes. Kal's ego and libido reined themselves in quickly. That moment was over.

"*What* am I? *What?*"

Orkney's ire made the ground tremble. Or rather, the stomp of a giant foot that was out of proportion to his height did. He said the reason he grew his hair long was to cover his feet, but, personally, Kal thought it had to do with the narcolepsy—the hair gave him an out when people accused him of falling asleep. But trolls as a race weren't narcoleptic, and they all had the same hairstyle.

"I am not a *what*. I'm a *who*, and I'll have you know that I'm a—"

"He's a blabbermouth, is what he is."

Kal groaned as Fritz crawled out of the listing drainpipe on Tia Pipa's Nut Shop. Talk about an end to whatever moment he and Samantha might have had... Where one gnome went, others were sure to follow, especially since many of them carried pint-sized friends beneath their pointed caps.

Surprisingly, this time, only six popped out. But they all had their pitchforks.

But then the shutters on McKeever's Pub opened and Seamus tapped the window with his shillelagh. His cronies raised their frosted mugs and flipped gold coins toward Seamus, who caught them in his green top hat with a wink at Kal.

So much for fulfilling Samantha's wish of making all her troubles disappear. From the way she was spinning around as the citizens of Izaaz crawled out of the woodwork—literally—Kal would bet (and from the looks of the leprechauns, *they* already were) that she was thinking her troubles were just beginning.

3

A GENIE.

A *genie*. No. That wasn't possible. Genies didn't exist. This had to be a dream. It was crazy. It was ridiculous. Insane.

Yet that kiss had been real. Samantha put her fingers to her mouth, the feel of her skin nothing like that of his lips.

She glanced at him. Why had he kissed her? And why wasn't she giving him hell for it?

She'd been about to, but then pitchfork-carrying, pointed-hat-wearing gnomes had crawled out of the downspouts, and… oh, yeah, that'd be why. It had nothing whatsoever to do with Albert's offhanded, metaphorical stomping of her dreams and self-esteem. Nothing to do with being blindsided yet again. Being used. No, nothing to do with that at all.

No, the reason she wasn't taking umbrage with that high-handed kiss was because the insanity of this situation was even more insane than some random guy kissing her.

Some random, half-naked, *hot* guy.

One of the gnomes tripped and his pitchfork went flying, landing at Samantha's feet.

Gnomes. Pitchfork-bearing gnomes. *That* was insanity.

Then the gnome picked up the pitchfork, tipped his hat to her, and army-crawled back the way he'd come.

She had to be in Oz. Or Narnia. Maybe Middle-earth. Or possibly the Addams family's neighborhood, because not only was she looking at gnomes, the likes of which she'd only ever seen on television commercials; but a dozen of Cousin Itt's cousins were shuffling out of one building, and a parade of men no taller than the back of that suddenly appearing chair were filing out of another. Dressed in green, the men had black shoes, black belts, and black bands around their green top hats, all with big gold buckles on them.

Yes, she'd definitely gone over some rainbow because this had to be Oz—and that guy at the head of the green-man brigade the mayor—because she'd planned Dad's funeral for November seventeenth *not* March seventeenth and she hadn't had even a sip of the *arak*.

"Top o' the mornin' to ye, lass," the mayor said with a heavy, deep brogue, putting the kibosh on Oz. Maybe she was in Brigadoon.

"All right, all right, stand back. Give the lady some breathing room." The fennec was running back and forth like a Border collie wannabe, as the parade fanned out around them. "She's still in the adjustment period. No one say anything to upset her."

Ah, her very own knight in shining fur. Pity he was too late on the no-upsetting thing.

Then a centaur trotted up behind the crowd, taking *upset* to a whole new level.

"Kal!" Half-horse, half-man, the creature fist-pumped the genie over the little people. "How's it goin'? You done yet? I figured, with the High Master all set to announce something big at the bash next week in Al-Jannah, you're finally getting that promotion."

Aladdin—no, *Kal*—shook his head. "Not yet, Wayne. There's still her." He nodded her way and the sword swung on his hip.

"Her... I mean, me?" Samantha squeaked. She stuck her hand behind her back and furiously pinched herself. *Wake up wake up wake up!* "What do I have to do with anything?"

"Oh lots," said the fennec, bouncing around. The guy could use some Xanax. "You're going to—mmmrph!"

Kal scooped up the fox and tapped his snout. "Enough, Dirham. Don't forget your job."

Job? The fox had a job?

Well, sure. Why not? Why not a feather boa, too?

That'd be because the boa idea had been claimed by the pair of sparkling white unicorns—literally sparkling and literally unicorns, horn and all—strolling down the sidewalk.

"I'll take that aspirin now, if you don't mind." Samantha held out her hand to Kal, then tossed the pills into her mouth sans water. Wine. Whatever.

Gulping them down, she grimaced at the chalky residue they left on her tongue. "Wish I had chocolate instead," she muttered.

And, voilà! A chocolate bar hovered before her eyes.

This time she sat without an invitation. "How... How is this happening?"

The gnome and the army of munchkins chuckled. Even Cousin Itt and his cousins cracked smiles beneath their hair, the upward curve of yellow teeth behind the dreads making them look like Rastafarian jack-o'-lanterns.

Dirham squirmed in the genie's arms. Nicely

muscled forearms that had been around her not five minutes ago—

"It's because Kal's your genie and he's here to do whatever you want."

Now *that* had some interesting possibilities…

Samantha shook her head. Apparently, betraying, soon-to-be-ex-boyfriends and strange dreams sent one's libido into overdrive. And let us not forget that out-of-this-world kiss. That definitely had gotten her libido going. Albert had never kissed her like that.

She didn't think Albert *could* kiss like that.

She touched her lips again. She'd liked it. A lot. If she needed any further proof that Albert wasn't the man for her—recent double-crossing, manipulative, lying, sack-of-shit status notwithstanding—the fact that his kisses had never left the kind of impression that one from a guy whose last name she didn't even know, ought to do it.

And then a gnome took off his hat and another gnome—an exact replica of the one who'd been wearing the hat, only smaller—popped out of it like one of a set of Russian dolls, and Samantha relegated everything to insanity, regardless of how wonderfully the guy could kiss. This place was just too much. Too surreal. Too unbelievable. She *had* to be dreaming.

Samantha pinched herself again, hard enough to leave a bruise, but… nope. She was still here. Still seeing things that shouldn't exist but somehow did.

Including the centaur who walked—cantered? trotted?—over to Kal. "Aw, man, Kal. I'm sorry, dude. I thought you'd be done by now."

Samantha was done, wholeheartedly, with whatever was happening here.

"Alad—Kal?" Samantha cleared her throat and stood. Not that her five-three gave her any advantage over him—over the munchkins, yes—but she was feeling at such a disadvantage that, if she could feel like the Jolly Green Giant around some gnomes, well then, she was going to take that advantage.

"Yes, Samantha?" All eyes, including Kal's warm, dark, melted-chocolate ones, turned her way.

There had to be some rational explanation for all of this. There *had* to be. Genies and lanterns and magic and gnomes just didn't exist.

"Um…" She shook the curls off her face and tried not to look at anyone but Kal. "Please tell me David put you up to this."

"David?"

She licked her lips, grasping at the straws lying haphazardly around her sanity. "Yes, David. Hughes. The owner of The Main Event." She'd recently sent David a slew of referrals for the event company she used for all her functions. He'd done an awesome job in converting the estate grounds into something out of *Lawrence of Arabia*; this had to be a bonus he'd come up with to thank her. His way of showing his appreciation for the business.

She wasn't quite sure it was appropriate, given the reason for tonight's party, but at least David was giving *to* her instead of taking *from* her. After Albert's little nondisclosure, she'd take the good where she could get it.

But this… She didn't know if she could take this. Albert's defection wasn't enough; now she had to deal with mythological beings, hairy sitcom creatures, and a devastatingly handsome, half-naked man who could kiss her right out of her *djellaba* if he so desired.

He could?

Samantha rewrapped her fingers around the lantern's handle, never more thankful for an interruption than for the fox with his squeaky voice, bouncing as high as her thigh next to her.

And if that didn't sound insane…

"Owner? There's another djinni around here?" Another bounce. "Cool, Kal! Someone for you to play with!"

The centaur laughed so hard he started choking. Cousin Itt whacked him on the withers until he neighed. Samantha didn't want to contemplate what that meant.

Kal looked at her. "I don't know anyone named David, Samantha. Not in this century anyway."

She'd had a feeling he was going to say that. Well, not the century part. And did she even want to know what *that* meant? Hell, no.

"So you're saying that you… and the fox… and the little green men—"

"Leprechauns." The mayor coughed the word behind his hand.

Samantha shot him a look. Of course they were leprechauns; she knew that—

What?

Samantha shook her head. In denial or to clear it, it was anyone's guess. "But you all can't be *real*."

Kal gripped her shoulder and that touch was definitely real. So were the electricity and goose bumps it ignited. "I assure you, Samantha, we are very real."

And if all of that wasn't enough to convince her—not to mention the tingle still going on with her lips from his kiss—something dropping out of the sky and landing on the road in front of her went a long way toward doing so.

Something that looked a lot like a dragon. An iridescent, purple-scaled, ridge-backed, frilled-neck dragon. With lime-green fingernails. Claws. Talons. Whatever.

Samantha shook her head. Again.

There was a *dragon* in front of her.

"What's your hurry, hon?" The dragon was chewing gum—at least, Samantha was hoping it was gum and not a leprechaun.

She stumbled back to the chair. David couldn't have had anything to do with *this*.

The dragon ambled closer, its long, pointed nose inches from Samantha's face.

Samantha held her breath.

"Kal?" asked the dragon—which was so much more *wrong* than a talking fox or people congratulating her for throwing a good funeral. "What'd you do to this one? She's looking a little green."

The leprechauns chuckled.

"I didn't do anything to her, Maille. She's still adjusting to the magic, and now you all come along and upset her. I haven't even had a chance to explain."

Upset… The word didn't *quite* convey what she was feeling, but Samantha had a feeling nothing would, so it was as good a word as any.

She licked her lips and then wished she hadn't when the dragon's eyes narrowed on her mouth. No need to give the giant lizard any ideas.

"You guys really don't have anything to do with The Main Event, do you?" Samantha was amazed she had enough air in her body to utter that question.

"The Mane Event?" the mayor asked. "Heinz's place? Faith, lass. Do ye think Orkney looks as if he's had a haircut lately?"

Cousin Itt—make that Orkney—shook his head with a weird, snuffling sound that Samantha was going to assume was laughter just for her own peace of mind.

"Oh, I don't know," said the centaur—Wayne. "I've seen Heinz's cuts, and I have to say, that's one of his better ones."

Another garden gnome ran out from between the dragon's front legs and poked Wayne's fetlock with a pitchfork. "Watch it, Hoof-and-Mouth. That's my cousin you're talking about."

The centaur pawed the ground. "Who are you calling Hoof-and-Mouth, you worm weasel?"

A colorful bird dove from the crooked spire of the highest building, its long purple-and-gold tail feathers skimming inches above the centaur's head. "Worm weasel! I love it!"

And then the bird burst into flame.

"Show-off," the dragon muttered, blasting the same spot with her own fire.

Samantha tried to move, but her legs weren't paying attention to her brain.

Neither were her eyes, apparently, because she couldn't possibly be seeing little gossamer-winged people flying off every balcony to the accompaniment of the peal of tiny bells with colorful ribbons streaming behind them. Though why they should be any more unbelievable than a dragon, Samantha couldn't fathom.

There was a lot she couldn't fathom.

The dragon sent a puff of lavender smoke at the beings. "Great. Just what we need. The do-good *peri* brigade."

"Hey, Maille, watch what you say about the *peris*. They're the bright spot in this place." The gnome who'd gone after Wayne now waved his pitchfork at the dragon.

"I'll say what I want to, *worm weasel*, and there's nothing you can do to stop me." She grabbed him by his collar and tossed him into the air.

He landed on his head, grumbling as he rolled over and grabbed his hat from where it had landed on the ground. He punched his fist into the tip—right *through* the tip—then hopped to his feet, pitchfork aimed like a lance. "You are so dead, Maille—"

"Fritz!" Kal got off one word before the dragon torched the gnome's hat.

"That could have been your head, *worm weasel*, so I'd step back if I were you." The dragon lowered her snout to the ground. Her eyes were as big as the gnome was tall. "Got it?"

Samantha had to hand it to Fritz. The little guy stood up to Maille—not that his was all that great of a height, but still, that took some balls. Which the dragon looked ready to fry.

Instead, she gave him a hotfoot.

"Ouch! Curses, you dirt-eating *amadán*!"

"Me? Dirt-eating?" The dragon shook her head, and the frill on her neck rattled. "Take a look in Seamus's shiny gold buckle, you twit. I'm not the one who lives in a hole in the sand."

"Now, now, there's no need t' be insultin', Maille." The mayor stepped forward and removed his hat to shine the buckle on it. "No worm weasel is going t' use me gold for anythin'. Especially no' a mirror."

The rest of the leprechauns' laughter was cut short by the river of gnomes that popped out of every drainpipe on the surrounding buildings and army-crawled across the sand faster than the leprechauns could run. But not faster than the unicorns, whose boas billowed onto a street lantern when they bounded over a row of empty white planters along the side of the road before fading into the background.

Literally fading into the background. Sparkles and all.

While Samantha was still processing that, the gnomes, en masse, raised their pitchforks.

And then all hell broke loose.

The leprechauns started dropkicking the gnomes, their curses in a brogue so heavy that Samantha couldn't understand a word anyone said. Then Orkney and his cousins started stomping the ground, which sent the fox into an apoplectic frenzy of bouncing, the phoenix *poofed* back into existence in a crackling burst of flames, the centaur pranced around the edges playing whack-a-gnome, and the dragon swung around to join in the fray, her long, sinewy tail almost slicing Samantha in half, if not for tall, dark, and genie-ish grabbing her out of the way.

Well, *grab* wasn't exactly the right word. Samantha wasn't sure what the right word was for what Kal did because he simply waved his hand and she went—

Flying across the sky!

4

ALBERT VIEHL FLIPPED HIS PHONE CLOSED AND,
with Henley's threats still ringing in his ears, barely refrained from throwing it across the biggest guest suite
in Samantha's home. He didn't want to have to pay for
wallpaper repairs when he moved in as soon as she accepted his proposal. That she would, he had no doubt.
He wished Henley wouldn't doubt it either—and he
wished Monty had died six months earlier so that this
nightmare would be over already.

Albert leaned against the headboard and dropped the
phone onto the pillow. No sense crushing it in his fist;
that would just be one more expense he'd have to cover.
His funds were a little low.

A *lot* low.

He eyeballed the phone. Henley was getting impa-
tient. With good reason. Albert owed him too much
money for it to be written off. If only he'd stopped when
he was into the thug for the first hundred grand…

Albert flung his forearm over his eyes. What the hell
was the combination to that safe? Monty had been the
sentimental sort, so Albert had tried every date that could
possibly be special to the man, but none had worked.

He needed that genie.

Albert stood up and shoved his phone into his pocket.
What a coup it'd been the day he'd gone looking for

Monty to ask for Samantha's hand in marriage. She was the quickest way to get his hands on a huge amount of cash, and if he didn't love her, well, hell, her bank account was an equitable trade, and her utter lack of interest in anything resembling business would give him carte blanche to plunder it. But then he'd seen Monty conjure up that genie and plans had changed.

He'd listened to the two of them chat while they'd played chess. He'd heard it all, how Monty and his wife had found the genie's lantern in the Moroccan marketplace and then discovered the genie inside, and how the genie's magic had made the company what it was today.

And now the lack of that magic was sending the company spiraling down the tubes. Just like Albert's gambling career and bank account. Jesus, he should have stopped months ago.

He needed that combination.

He headed into the sitting room. With Samantha occupied playing hostess, and the housekeeper, Pitbull Wanda, directing the staff in the kitchen, now was the perfect time to search the old man's office yet again.

He paused in front of the full-length mirror in the sitting room and adjusted his robe. Samantha's insistence that everyone dress in costume had been a boon; he'd sneaked inside the house without anyone noticing, and he'd go out the same way.

He reached for the fez he'd set onto the table beside the love seat—

Samantha's earring was on the cushion. It hadn't been when he'd put his hat there.

She'd been in this room. Had she heard him? Did she know?

Damn! Albert ran from the room and tore down the steps. He had to find the lantern before she did or he was going to be shit out of luck.

Outside Monty's office, cold sweat snaked down his back. The door was ajar. Dim light bled beneath it.

He listened but didn't hear anything inside. Good. Maybe Samantha was in her room crying because of what she'd overheard. Albert would be, too, if he wasn't so pressed for time.

The door swung open on well-oiled hinges— perfection that could be traced to genie magic. Probably how Samantha had gotten the drop on him upstairs.

Biting back the fear that his meal ticket had been fried to a crisp, Albert went inside.

No Samantha.

He exhaled, then caught his breath when he saw the safe. The door was open.

For a second—the tiniest, barest of seconds because no one would ever say Albert wasn't an opportunist—he stared at the open door as if it couldn't be real. And then he moved, practically vaulting the desk to get to the safe.

It was empty. Well, not completely empty: two bags were inside, but the lantern, the most important thing, was gone. Samantha must have found it.

Cold swamped his body. Could genies do invisibility? Were the two of them watching him right now to see what he'd do?

"Samantha? Honey?" He spun around, putting worry on his face. Not that he had to work at it, but he had to make it look like the worry was for her, not himself. "I don't know what you think you heard, but you obviously didn't hear the whole thing or you wouldn't have left. I love you, babe. This is just a simple misunderstanding."

Nothing. Not a single breath of anything fluttered the letter on Monty's desk.

"Samantha?" He listened.

Nothing.

The bitch had taken the genie. She'd grabbed that lantern and left him to fend for himself. Some fiancée she was.

And where the fuck was she? Walking around the party, or had the pampered princess gone somewhere else? St. Moritz? Monaco? The South Pacific? Christ, she could afford whatever she wanted even without the genie; what more could she possibly want?

Albert cursed. It wasn't fair. He'd been following her around like a lapdog, hoping for a few crumbs from the almighty Blaine table, and *she* ended up with the all-powerful being.

What the *fuck* was he going to do? Henley was going to kill him if he didn't pay up. He had to come up with something—

The bags!

Albert turned back to the safe. If Monty had locked them up with his prized possession, they had to be worth something. Maybe enough to get Henley off his back.

He removed one of the bags and dumped a six-inch, orange crystal obelisk onto his palm. Light from the desk lamp prismed through it, scattering tiny particles of orange in the air. He doubted it was a gemstone because the cut was one he'd never seen, and the fact that Samantha had left it here would support that idea. The woman did know jewelry—especially when one of her pieces had gone missing. That'd been the last time he'd taken anything from her seemingly endless stash.

He set the bauble on the desk, where it threw orange sparkles onto the blotter in a trick of the light. Then he removed the other bag and untied its strings.

A thick, gold coin slid out. As big as his palm, the weight alone would mark it as valuable, but the profile etched onto one side of a woman in an Egyptian headdress made it even more so.

This was an old coin. An old gold coin. A *big* old gold coin. And if that profile was who he thought it was… Had that genie given Monty some treasure from Cleopatra's coffers?

Giddiness trickled out in the form of a muffled laugh. Oh yeah, this could more than take care of Henley.

Albert sat in the old man's chair and set the coin on the blotter. He traced the profile. Cleopatra. Gold. He was rich. Beyond rich.

But he still wanted that genie. Monty had gone for small potatoes, wanting his company to be the best, never grasping his treasure's full potential. Albert sure did. With that genie, he'd be the most powerful man on Earth.

He lifted the crystal in his other hand. First, a priceless genie lantern, then the rare coin. There had to be more to this crystal than met the eye.

Rotating it caused orange sparkles to shimmer in the air behind the desk—orange sparkles in the shape of a man. Albert waved the crystal around. More sparkles formed a path in the air from the safe to the image, and Albert's pulse rate picked up. And then…

The outline of a lantern shimmered on the desk in

front of him, and Albert almost let out a whoop. He'd found the genie—or, actually, a way to track him.

Albert tucked the crystal and the coin inside the breast pocket of the suit jacket he wore beneath the robe, and patted them in place against his heart. Gold might be intrinsically valuable, but that crystal tracking device was, to him, even more.

She wasn't going to cut him off that easily. Albert Viehl did not go down without a fight.

His fingertips stroked the coin. Now if only he could find her... He wished he knew where the genie and Samantha had gone.

And, in a surprising *poof* of golden glitter, he was off to find out.

5

"WHAT THE—!" SAMANTHA GRABBED HOLD OF KAL'S arm when she landed next to him on a carpet that was a good thirty feet above the ground.

There was nothing good about being on a carpet thirty feet off the ground. Actually, there was something seriously *wrong* with being thirty feet off the ground on a carpet that was supposed to be *on* that ground.

"What just happened? What are we doing up here?" she asked, trying to catch both her breath and her balance, the latter made easier by her now-missing shoes that were probably back on Earth somewhere—if that's where she'd been to begin with.

"The natives got restless."

Two questions, one answer. It was a good thing that Kal had covered her hand with his to keep her from falling off the edge of the carpet, but with the impossibility of what she was seeing, not to mention the *flying* thing, plus the kiss, plus the fact that he was a genie, *plus* the dragons *and* the gnomes *and* the leprechauns *and* the unicorns *and* the—what was Orkney? An ogre? Or a troll? Which ones were taller?

Was she really contemplating a correct answer for that question? Why? What difference would it make if he was an ogre or a troll or even an island bum with that hair? None of it would make her feel any steadier.

And then Kal put his arm around her and tucked her against him.

Now *that*, on the other hand, would.

But then the fox flew by, dangling from the fairies' ribbons, and any steadiness went flying off with the breeze that had turned the little thing's ears inside out. Then her knees gave out from under her, and she sank onto the carpet. *The flying carpet.*

"Uh, Kal? Iph you woul-n-t mind…" the fox said around the ribbons in his mouth.

Kal drew his scimitar and cut the ribbons so that the fairylike *peris* could deposit Dirham on the rug. Samantha scooted out of the way—though not too far. The carpet wasn't that big, and she doubted the fringe would hold her.

That sentence would have made no sense a half hour ago.

Dirham bounced to his feet—the only surprise there was that he didn't bounce higher—and shook his head. His ears flipped right side out again.

Kal knelt down and tapped him on the snout. "Settle down, Dirham. I was just about to explain to Samantha what all of that is." He waved his hand toward the melee in the street.

"Ooh! Ooh!" There went Dirham bouncing again, one paw in the air as if he were in a classroom. "I know! I know! Let me tell her! Let me!"

Kal smiled, and Samantha's heart stuttered.

Sheesh… She rolled her eyes. This was neither the time nor the situation to find a guy attractive. Even if she was single. Newly single. So *newly* that her ex didn't know it yet. But definitely single—and Kal was definitely attractive. Combine that with his genie-in-shining-orange chivalry, and Kal was already light years beyond Albert in the Prince Charming department.

"So what happened is this." Dirham settled down with a halfhearted and half-heighted bounce. "Maille—the dragon—insulted the *peris,* and since *peris* are related to gnomes, Fritz took offense. Seamus did, too. Leprechauns are very particular about their gold, you know, especially because they think gnomes are beneath them." Another bounce had Dirham's tail flicking Samantha's cheek. "Actually, considering gnomes live underground, I guess that's true."

Samantha brushed a tiny fur ball off her eyelash. "I am *so* not in Kansas anymore."

Dirham cocked his head to the side. "But you weren't in Kansas before."

She couldn't help smiling at his earnest confusion. "I know. I was in my father's office."

The fox grinned—and there was so much wrong with just those three simple words, she ought to keep a running list of wrong things she and everyone else around her said. It'd probably end up being longer than that dragon's tail—

And there was another one.

"We were there, too, you know. We were inside the safe." Dirham stopped bouncing long enough to scratch one of his ears with his back foot.

"And *you* know that that's not a normal sentence, right?"

"But it's the truth." The fox looked confused.

Samantha patted him on the head. "So you guys live in the lantern?"

"Oh, not me. I just visit," said Dirham. "But Kal does."

"Not if I can help it," the genie muttered.

The tone was what surprised her. Didn't living in a lantern go with the whole genie gig? "You don't like your lantern?"

He glanced at her, then away. "It's not that. It's just that the outside world isn't as… solitary."

"And it's bigger," the fox added with a bounce. "Prettier." A higher bounce. "And the air is better." He almost landed off the carpet.

Kal caught him and set him in the middle. "That, too, Dir."

The "solitary" part struck Samantha because she knew exactly what he meant. With Dad gone, she was alone in the house, even with the staff there. The closest thing she had to a family was Wanda, the housekeeper who'd practically raised her. But Wanda went home to her own family. It just wasn't the same. Albert was supposed to have filled that void, but that obviously wasn't going to go as planned. Not that she wanted it to anymore.

But she did want someone in her life. Someone she could laugh with and make memories and a family and a future with. Someone who cared about her wants and needs because he cared about *her*, not because he wanted her to toss a bunch of stock shares into his portfolio. Looked like she was back to square one on that front.

A flame of purple smoke singed the tips of the gold fringe, grabbing Samantha's attention. She looked over the edge of the rug. Orkney's hair was singed, too. Or was that one of his cousins? She couldn't tell because they all looked alike. "I really wish someone would explain all of this to me. In terms that make sense." A definite pipe dream, but then, a girl could always hope.

"As you wish, Samantha." Kal waved his hand, and the carpet behind them folded itself to resemble a step. He removed his sword and laid it on the rug, then brushed aside the orange glitter that seemed to accompany his magic and sat down. "Please make yourself comfortable."

Comfortable? On a flying carpet? She raised her eyebrows but leaned back when he waved his hand again. The "step" gave way, contouring to her back and cradling her with just the right amount of support. She didn't even have any sensation of flying; if not for the wind blowing in her hair and the fact that they were thirty feet off the ground, she wouldn't have thought anything of it. But they were and she did, and oh God— they were *flying*.

"I have a feeling I'm never going to be comfortable again." She gripped the lantern in her lap with both hands.

"They all say that at first," Dirham said, his bounce somewhat subdued.

"They?"

"My masters," Kal answered, leaning back and stretching his long legs out in front of him.

"But then they start making wishes and pretty soon they're very comfortable." Dirham circled around and settled down, the tip of his bushy tail flicking like a metronome keeping time for "Flight of the Bumblebee."

"So." Samantha set the lantern on the rug beside her thigh. "You're a genie. Like Aladdin's."

Dirham squeaked and his fur bristled. "Kal? Like them? I think not."

Kal patted the fox's head. "Thanks, buddy." He scrubbed his jaw. "Aladdin's genies were women. That history got lost in translation."

"You mean the mythology did."

"Mythology?" Dirham hopped to his feet— nothing new there. "Mythology? You can say that? Take a look down there." He leaned so far over the edge that Samantha was afraid he'd fall off. "You call *them* mythological?"

Orkney howled when the dragon singed his hair again. Now he had a bald spot above the mullet he had going on behind his left ear.

"Good point." Samantha strummed her fingers on the carpet—something normal at last. Not common, but normal. Would wonders never cease?

And then a gnome went flying straight up in the air on a plume of purple smoke like a whale's spout, his little legs pinwheeling without a bicycle.

No, apparently they wouldn't.

"So how do you know the mytho—er, history is wrong? You didn't actually *know* Aladdin, did you?" Although… Kal had mentioned something about a century. When had Aladdin lived?

Had Aladdin lived? Wasn't he just some story Scheherazade came up with to save her life?

Samantha wouldn't mind having a story like that to save her sanity right now.

"No," said Kal. "Thank the cosmos, Aladdin and I never crossed paths. And before you ask, I didn't know any of the forty thieves either."

"What about Scheherazade?"

A tiny smile crept across his face. "Yes. I knew Sherry."

Something twisted in Samantha's belly. It made no sense, but that was the least of the things that didn't make sense right now.

He shook his head. "But that's ancient history, Samantha."

Really ancient. So ancient Samantha didn't even want to contemplate how ancient it was. Or how he could have known *Sherry*, and she didn't mean in the biblical sense, more the chronological one because she really didn't want to know if he knew *Sherry* in the biblical sense, thank you very much.

"For now, while my lantern is in your possession, you are my master, and I'm here to serve you. Is there anything you wish?" He waved his hand and a mug appeared in it. "Coffee?" Another wave had some breakfast pastries magically appearing. "Croissant? Or what about this?" A bowl of fruit was next, followed by a four-course meal.

Each one appeared in a shower of orange glitter and the blink of an eye as if they weren't there one second, then, the next, they were. Which actually was what happened, but that didn't explain why it happened or how it happened, and she didn't really think there *was* an explanation, which put the suddenly appearing food back in the insanity category again—

Just like the leprechaun that went flying on the dragon smoke this time, him going one way, his hat the other.

"I wish that guy could have his hat back."

Yes, that was what she wished. Not for unicorns or magically appearing biscotti, but that the mythological creature should get his hat back.

She had to be losing her mind. Had to be.

But if she was, then the leprechaun had to be, too,

because when he fell back to Earth, he had his hat clutched in his hands.

She watched him go all the way down. He slid off the phoenix's gold wing, landed on the centaur, who bucked him off like a bronco—which technically, she guessed, he was—then flopped sideways over the dragon's back, sliding down the tail to land on top of another leprechaun, and his hat went flying again.

She glanced at the half-naked hottie. The *genie.* "I thought that wasn't supposed to happen?"

Kal shrugged. "You only wished for him to get it back. Not keep it."

As if that made any sense. Samantha rolled her eyes. "Semantics? You're going to focus on semantics?"

"It's my job."

Everybody with the job thing. Like they were waiters or doctors or parking attendants instead of talking animals and fantastical myths come to life. She shook her head. "This is surreal."

"Tell me about it," said Dirham, curling his tail around himself at the corner of the carpet. "The place has changed a lot since I was here last."

She reached for a piece of the biscotti and then remembered that it had appeared out of nowhere and snatched her hand back. "Where exactly is *here*?"

"Ah." Kal crossed his legs and waved his hand. The food disappeared with a tiny crackle—or maybe that was the coffee mug clanking against the dinner plates as they flew off to wherever magically appearing foodstuffs disappear to—and an old map appeared on the rug in front of them. Kal lifted it to shake off the glitter.

"What's that? A pirate's treasure map?" She leaned

forward. The map looked more brittle than parchment, but there were decorations on the side, pictures of monsters undulating beneath the waves, and intricate drawings of strange plants and beings. No big red X, though.

She was buying into this whole fairy tale way too much.

You have another explanation for the flying thing?

Yeah, that was a problem.

"Pirates would give all of their bounty to get their hooks on this." Kal tugged the map closer. "No, it's a map of Izaaz."

"Is what?"

"Izaaz. Otherwise known as *Madeenat Al-saqf Al-zojaajey.* The City of the Glass Ceiling."

"Glass ceiling? Why would anyone name a city after an antiquated, sexist corporate structure?"

Kal raised an eyebrow. "Because we're under one?" He pointed up.

Samantha followed his finger. All she saw was sunshine. "I don't see anything."

"Try a pair of sunglasses."

"But I don't have—" *Any sunglasses* was what she was going to say, but before she could, he waved his hand and two display shelves full of designer glasses materialized out of thin air in a sparkle of orange.

Thin air. *That* was why she was having trouble catching her breath. The air was thin. That explained it.

Um… no.

She was half afraid to touch the glasses. Like gnomes and talking foxes, these shouldn't exist. Not floating in the middle of the sky. Then again, *she* shouldn't be floating in the middle of the sky, so what was one more thing?

"Go on, Samantha. Try some on," said Dirham.

Hesitantly, she took a pair and put them on, and instantly she got a perspective on exactly what Kal meant.

Off in the distance, walls ringed the city. Walls of sand that stretched to the sky, the tops of them in a perfectly straight line—

As if they had a lid on them.

A glass lid.

"Is that… You mean that's… It can't be…"

And then a huge bird flew overhead. It looked like a giant pterodactyl.

Not that she knew what a pterodactyl looked like, since they were, you know, *extinct*, but that was no ordinary bird. With tail feathers like a peacock on steroids, the claws of a lion, and the head of a dog, it made the platypus look like a beauty pageant queen. And when it skimmed that supposed ceiling, its dog head, long neck, and rounded back—not to mention its wings—all flattened for the few dozen feet it coasted along the glass.

Samantha looked at Kal, then pointed up. Words just weren't happening.

Kal conjured a glass of iced tea. He took one of her hands and wrapped her fingers around the glass. "Drink this."

She didn't even think not to drink it. Prehistoric dogbird? Glass ceiling? The sugary, minty beverage went down, if not easily, at least without choking her. "What happens if it falls?" And she could be talking about either the sky or the bird—that thing was no Chicken Little.

"It won't. The glass has been there for longer than anyone can remember. And considering I'm over four thousand years old, that's a long time. I think you're safe."

The glass slipped from her fingers, and she barely noticed that she and the lantern were now wearing sweet mint tea. "Four... *thousand*?"

Kal waved his fingers again, and she was once more holding a glass full of tea. Another wave of his fingers and the wet spot on her *djellaba* disappeared.

"Nice," she muttered. "I wish you could get rid of these extra ten pounds as easily."

"As you wish."

He waved his hand again, and if Samantha wasn't above imagining such things, she would have sworn the waistband of the skirt she had on beneath her *djellaba* slipped a few inches.

Actually, given what was going on around her, she *wasn't* above imagining such things, so she stood up. Her skirt fell down.

She almost did, too, but elected to gulp the rest of the tea instead. She gave half a thought to wishing for more of that water/wine he'd given her earlier, but figured sobriety was the better part of valor here. "Well *that's* handy."

Kal stood up and took the glass from her, *poofing* it into nothingness. "Your wish is my command, Samantha."

If only Albert had prescribed to the same train of thought.

No, not really. Samantha didn't want someone to be at her beck and call; she just wanted someone who wanted to share his life with her. Equally. Who wanted the same things she did.

Maybe she ought to wish for Kal to conjure up Mr. Perfect for her—though in that outfit, he was looking pretty perfect himself.

When something jostled the carpet and he grasped

her elbow with a "hold on to me, Samantha," *perfect* was exactly the word that came to mind.

"The wind currents are all over the place when Maille turns up the heat," said Kal, his breath warm beside her ear.

The dragon wasn't the only one turning up the heat.

So not what she needed to be thinking about thirty feet off the ground.

She adjusted her stance on the carpet that was shifting like quicksand beneath her feet, and almost kicked the lantern into that aforementioned thin air.

She looked over the edge of the rug. The leprechauns were still fighting the gnomes, and Wayne was having a tough time with four of the under-the-hat garden variety clinging to his legs, plus another two on his tail, and one with a double-fisted grip on the mane that ran down his back. The gnome was flopping from side to side while Wayne tried to shimmy him off.

Then a blast of dragon fire collided with the spontaneously combusting phoenix about ten feet off the front right corner of the rug, the heat forcing Samantha back, and, of course, thanks to the skirt at her feet, she tripped.

Right into Kal's chest.

She *would* like to thank her skirt. And Kal for zapping those ten pounds away. And the dragon for being oh-so-helpful in getting her into the vicinity of Kal's arms, and Fate for presenting the situation in the first place.

So much for not thinking about it…

Samantha fought for her balance. And her dignity. This was a mess—and she could be talking about the fracas going on below the carpet or the humming hormones above it. Or the fact that she was practically half naked beneath this robe.

"Samantha? Are you okay?" Kal's breath tickled her temple, causing her to shiver.

She was more than okay, and that definitely wasn't a tickle. It—he—felt good. Better than good. He felt so much more *more* than anyone had before. Plastered against her back, his warmth seeping through the *djellaba*, making her hotter. *Wetter*—

She pulled away. She was thirty feet in the air, for God's sake, dodging dragon fire. Practically naked from the waist down, and if not for this heat melting her brain, Kal and his magic fingers wouldn't be sidetracking her. She needed to do something about that.

She looked back over her shoulder. "Um, Kal? Is it possible… that is, can I get a new outfit? Something a little cooler that fits and covers all the necessary parts?"

"Sure you can."

He smiled and Samantha's pulse kicked up a few more ticks.

But his hand didn't move.

"Well?"

"Well what?"

"Are you going to?"

"Am I going to what?"

"Give me a new outfit?"

"Is that what you wish?"

Not exactly…

Her breasts tingled where she'd felt that fleeting touch and she wished he'd do it again.

Samantha held her breath, half expecting it to happen, but then she realized she hadn't uttered that wish out loud. Although… what if she did?

Another blast of hot dragon fire erupted off to the left,

and Samantha decided that was what had fried both her brain and her hormones. She couldn't actually be considering kissing him again, could she? She'd just gotten burned by Albert; did she really want to go down that road again?

Then again, Albert hadn't been all that interested in kissing her, or anything else for that matter, which probably should have been her first clue that he was more frog than prince, but with the strain of coping with Dad's illness, the house, the staff, the company, and everything else, she'd actually been glad of the reprieve.

Her hormones, however, apparently hadn't been and were more than willing to make up for lost time. Now, however, was *not* that time.

She shook her head, took two more steps away from Kal, and then turned around. "You don't have a girlfriend, do you?"

"I do." Dirham hopped to his feet with his perpetual smile, but then it faltered and he dropped his shoulders. "Lexy just doesn't know it yet."

Kal stared at her, then shook his head. "What makes you ask that, Samantha?"

She crossed her arms. "Your lantern, for one thing. You have to be a tad snug in there, given its size. I don't see how another person could fit in it with you."

"Lexy says size doesn't matter," chirped Dirham.

No one on the carpet said a word.

Wayne, on the other hand, shouted a very descriptive expletive from the street that was not only heard, crystal clear, above the din, but also actually had something to do with Dirham's malapropism.

Samantha tried to get that whole image out of her head. "And secondly, you obviously don't have a girlfriend because when a woman says she'd like something, it usually means she wants it."

"Ah." Kal nodded. "So you wish me to conjure up new clothing for you."

"If you could."

"Of course he can," said Dirham, bouncing again. "It's what he does."

Kal glanced at Dirham, then winked at Samantha. "As Dir says, it's what I do."

Samantha waited.

More expletives from Wayne filled the air, but Kal didn't do the hand-waving thing.

"Um... so?"

"So what?"

"Are you going to"—she swept her hand up and down in front of her *djellaba*—"you know, replace this?"

"Is that what you wish, Samantha?"

"Do I have to say 'I wish' any time I want something?"

Kal nodded. "I can't do anything to you unless you specifically wish it."

"That seems excessive. Why can't you just go with implied wishes? And aren't I supposed to only get three?"

Kal arched an eyebrow. "Don't believe the mythology. You get a lot more than three, and you should be thankful that you have to make a specific wish because that way, a genie can't do anything to the master that the master doesn't want. Just think if the genie didn't like the master. Or if a genie's magic got out of control. A lot could happen, so there are rules."

"You're going to have to go over those with me because you gave me food and wine when I hadn't asked for them."

"That's different. I can conjure up things to give you

comfort, but I can't do something to your person without your express wish."

She knew a few things he could do to her person…

So much for being burned by Albert; being burned by Kal was so much better.

Samantha cleared her throat and prayed he couldn't tell her face was burning. "Alrighty then. I wish you'd conjure up an appropriate outfit for me."

Kal waved his fingers again, but Samantha didn't have any sensation of her clothes disappearing or something new showing up on her body. One second she was in the *djellaba* and the next—

"Are you kidding me?" She fingered the yellow-green gauzy harem pants and half shirt. Typical guy.

She brushed the orange glitter away and glared at him—and tried not to notice that he was anything but typical. Heart-stoppingly devastating with the wind blowing through his hair, that same wind tossing the edges of his vest aside as he stood there, hands fisted on his hips, looking like something out of every woman's fantasy. Definitely a guy but definitely *not* typical.

"I wasn't attempting to be humorous, Samantha."

Good thing because she wasn't laughing.

No, she was mentally smacking herself upside the head. Leprechauns and gnomes, a dragon who could fry her to a crisp, Albert's betrayal… and she was obsessing over a good-looking guy? And not only that, but a guy who'd put her in *this*? Talk about sexist.

She shoved her hands to her hips, but the anger dissipated somewhat when she felt those missing pounds. She had to admit, that felt nice. But still… "Seriously, Kal. A harem outfit?"

Kal spread his arms. The vest gapped open again—thank you God and the wind—and his washboard rippled. "I'm wearing something similar and it keeps me cool. I didn't intend to offend you, Samantha. You asked for appropriate; that outfit is appropriate for Izaaz."

When he put it like that... She was going to have to watch what she wished for around him.

And then the dragon let loose with another blast of fiery hot air, and the fringe on the corner of the carpet ignited with a *whoosh!* and her outfit was the least of her concerns.

The rug lurched, throwing Samantha into Kal's arms again, and the two of them tumbled to the carpet while the lantern and Kal's sword went sliding toward the edge.

Samantha managed to hook the lantern on the curled part of her harem girl footwear, but the sword went sailing over the edge.

With Dirham not far behind.

Samantha had two seconds to worry after the fox's high-pitched "Kaaaaaaaalllllllll!" sailed away with the wind before the carpet started spinning out of control and her worry shifted to the here and now—

And the soon-to-come crashing around them, because she and Kal were going down!

6

SAMANTHA GRABBED HOLD OF KAL'S SHOULDERS and hid her face in his neck as the carpet spiraled downward. She didn't want to die like this.

She didn't want to die, period.

"I wish you'd get us out of this!" she yelled as the wind ripped through her hair and she prayed that was all it ripped through.

"As you wish, Samantha." Kal's voice rumbled against her ear, and for a moment she forgot they were in dire circumstances.

But then they landed, and even though the landing was gentle, straddling the branch of a giant palm tree while being half wrapped around a half-naked guy was a bit dire in and of itself. Especially since *she* was half-naked, too. And with her emotions raw and her ego fragile, this probably wasn't the best position to find herself in—though her nerve endings might disagree.

Samantha disengaged herself as quickly as possible and grabbed the lantern off her slipper. "This isn't quite what I was expecting." Which would be to find herself back in Dad's office. "But at least we're not up a creek. Though it sure feels like it."

"I can set you down in one if you wish." Kal brushed something off her cheek. Probably orange sparkles;

they went everywhere his magic did. "The palm was closer—and dryer—and you didn't specify."

"Semantics, I know." Trying to ignore the tingles from where his fingers had brushed her skin—and failing miserably even though they'd almost plummeted to Earth and died, but hey, apparently that was reason enough for her hormones to be on high alert—Samantha yanked her crop top down so she wasn't flashing any of the coconuts. And, no, that wasn't a euphemism, thank you very much.

Samantha adjusted her shirt again. At least Kal hadn't gotten an eyeful, though she thought he might have gotten a handful when she'd fallen on him. Her thighs went all quivery at that thought.

She readjusted her seat on the wide branch—because the bark was rough, not because there was any tingling going on *between* her thighs.

Okay, so maybe there was, but they'd only shared *one* kiss; why was she making it so much more than what it was? But oh, what it'd been...

Samantha cleared her throat again and glanced at the tree trunk. "So how do we get down? And why the tree? Why not the ground?"

"Have you looked at the ground?"

Samantha peeled back one of the fronds. The fight had escalated into a cartoonlike cloud of white dust with arms, legs, hooves, a couple of hats, and a shillelagh or two sticking out all over the place.

More troops kept arriving from every corner. Packs of gnomes and leprechauns. A bunch of beings she didn't recognize. More ogres. Or trolls. She hadn't gotten an answer to what Orkney and his cousins were yet, but they sure could shot-put a gnome.

One of the victims landed about fifty feet from the fray, jumped to his knees, yanked his pointed hat down over his ears, and army-crawled back in. "I'll show you, you... you... wig wannabe!"

Samantha winced when the handle of a gnome's pitchfork landed across the backs of a leprechaun's thighs, sending him crashing atop something small and furry.

"Is this a common occurrence?"

Kal shrugged. "Gnomes are always itching for a fight."

Another centaur bounded from one of the stone tepee things, along with something that looked a lot like that jackalope she'd accused Dirham of being.

Dirham! "Kal—where's Dirham? Is he going to be okay?"

Kal pointed to the sky. "Coming up on the right."

Dirham rode by on the back of the feathered pterodactyl, or whatever it was, waving and bobbing up a storm with a grin stretching along the sword blade he held in his teeth. When he was overhead, he dropped it to Kal.

"He seems to be enjoying himself," Samantha said.

"I'm sure he is. It's not every day Kismet allows someone to ride her."

The pterodactyl angled up and her head skimmed the ceiling. Dirham ducked.

"And that's a good thing because...?"

Kal's pecs flexed when he brushed his hair off his forehead. "Kismet is a Simurgh, the last of her race. She carries all the knowledge of the world on her shoulders. It's a heavy burden and, to carry someone else, even someone as small as Dirham, well, it's incredibly difficult for her."

"But very unselfish."

Kal nodded. "Kismet's a good egg."

The funny thing about that statement—besides the pun—was that Kal wasn't trying to be funny, so Samantha tried not to laugh. "So, um, how long are we going to have to stay up here? Can't we go somewhere more comfortable?"

"Sure we can. Where do you wish to go?"

Kismet took Dirham in for a landing on the outskirts of the fight, a nice, gentle landing. Safe and sound. Which sounded pretty good right about now.

Then a blast of dragon fire sent two gnomes howling into the sewer grate on the side of the road, and safe and sound sounded *really* good. "Can I go home?"

Kal nodded. "Of course. Whenever you want. All you have to do is wish it, and it will be so."

"No clicking my heels three times and saying, 'there's no place like home'?"

Kal's arched an eyebrow. "If you feel the need."

She smiled at that, but then the reality of her situation sneaked up on her. She should go back now because people would be wondering where she was. It was Dad's memorial after all, and she should be there. Although... Dad *had* wanted her to have the combination tonight; he had to have figured she'd open the safe. Maybe he'd thought something like this would happen. Well, not the dragon and incinerating carpet she was sure, but the whole genie experience. But would he have expected her to leave?

Knowing Dad, he might have. But Dad wasn't there to explain her absence to everyone.

"I guess we should go back. I've been gone at least an hour already, and if people haven't started wondering where I am, they will soon. They'll never believe this—unless you want to give a demonstration?"

"Most masters like to keep my existence a secret, Samantha. I've seen a lot of not-so-nice things happen when someone starts claiming to have a genie, from theft to attempted murder. You'd be best served not telling anyone."

Which explained why her father had never told her about the lantern. Understandable, perhaps, but she wouldn't have minded a little advance warning before the cloud of smoke had carried her out of one reality and into another. "But how will I explain my disappearance?"

"No explanations will be necessary. We'll return to the time that you left."

"You're talking time travel?" She almost did lose her perch at that. Although… since he could perform magic and travel through the air, why not time, too?

Kal squinted. "Not time travel, per se. Meaning, I can't take you back in time to a place where you didn't exist, like the 1700s. I also can't take you back to a place where you do exist because we don't want two of you there at the same time. That causes all sorts of problems with the world's axis, and there have been enough natural disasters lately.

"Unless, I drop you back into who you were at that point, but that can then negate everything that came after, starting you off on a cycle of redos. Given that, in all probability, you'd make the same decisions that landed you here in the first place, you could end up stuck in an endless loop, never moving forward, so I don't recommend that, either."

Her brain was on overload. What genies and time travel

and natural disasters had in common was beyond her ability to assimilate at the moment, and as for an endless loop... well, she sort of felt like that now. Especially when their tree swayed as more ogres or trolls stampeded from a structure that looked like a 1950s drive-in restaurant.

"I can, however, return you to a place where you aren't but could be," Kal continued. "If, for instance, you want to travel the world or take an extended vacation, I can return you to the point in time immediately after you left and no one will ever know."

"So if I decide I want to stay here for a while, it won't matter when I go back? People will think I was there all along?"

"Exactly."

Hmmm, that was something to consider because it wasn't every day that someone got to talk with gnomes and be insulted by leprechauns. Fly on a flying carpet. Almost die on one. Kiss a genie.

Lip-locks aside, if Kal employed his little semantical time-manipulation trick, she'd have time to not only explore this new world, but also figure out what she was going to do with the company she'd inherited and her penchant for attracting hangers-on and fair-weather boyfriends.

This journey had bonus written all over it.

"Okay, so let's say I hang out here for a while. Where are we? I mean, I know this is Izaaz, but where exactly is Izaaz? Are we still on Earth?" She shifted off the piece of bark that was cutting into her thigh.

Kal looked at her as if she'd asked him the size of his—well, as if she were out of her mind. But just because she might be didn't invalidate her question.

"Of course we're on Earth," he said. "Where else would we be?"

She started counting off on her fingers. "Mars. Venus. Some planet I've never heard of. Another dimension. A distant time. The future. How the hell do I know? I'm talking to a genie, for God's sake, on top of a palm tree on steroids, with gnomes and leprechauns and dragons fighting below me. You tell *me* where I am."

Kal put a hand on her arm. "Son of a Sumerian—"

"Well, okay then, *don't* tell me if it's that big of a deal."

"No, Samantha. Him." Kal pointed to a second dragon waddling out from the drive-in, only this one's scales looked like polished coal and it had two legs instead of four, and those looked like an eagle's.

"Who's he?"

Kal swung his leg over the branch and waved his hand. A classic Mercedes *poofed* out of nowhere in a shower of orange sparkles. A black, 1956 gull-wing coupe, if she wasn't mistaken, and very nice. Dad had had one for a while.

Probably *this* one.

"Bart's the baddest wyvern this side of the equator," said Kal. "The other side, too, though I won't say that to his face. His head's inflated enough."

"What's the big deal? Can't the other dragon take care of him?"

"That's a problem. Maille has taken care of him before. He's Maille's mate, and theirs was never a happy union. They've been separated for about fifteen hundred years, I think. Bart being here doesn't bode well. I need to get down there and make sure things don't get out of control."

Samantha looked at the jumble of body parts still tossing up dust, pitchforks, and the occasional gnome or two. Things could get worse?

The doors on the car raised, and Kal motioned for her to climb in. Then the car rotated in the air so he could.

"Any particular reason we're not using the carpet?" Not *how does the car hang out in midair*, or *did my father fly this, too,* just a question about the mode of transportation. Samantha tucked a few curls behind her ear. Well, she'd wanted to get away from all her troubles; she'd certainly done that.

Whether she'd inherited new ones or not remained to be seen.

"You mean, besides the fact that the carpet was torched?" Kal asked, waving his hand for the doors to close. Then he turned the steering wheel and the car angled *down*.

Samantha pulled on the seat belt in case this ride went the way of the carpet ride. "Don't tell me there's only one flying carpet in your world."

"No, but around Bart, it's a good idea to show some strength. The carpet's a little too flimsy. And flammable."

And a classic sports car was the perfect way to do macho. Kal might be a genie, but she'd been right; he actually was a typical guy.

Samantha clicked the seat belt. Obviously she wasn't going anywhere yet. And that was good for a few reasons, including time for her to come to grips with all that was going on in her life—current situation notwithstanding—plus, it'd give Albert the chance to wonder where she'd gone. Maybe worry a little. Panic even, because without her, he'd have nothing.

The corners of her mouth twitched upward. Panicking would do Albert some good.

7

ALBERT STARTED TO PANIC WHEN THE WORLD around him stopped spinning. First, because the world *had* been spinning; second, because Samantha knew the truth; third, because he *didn't* know where she and the genie were; and fourth, because when he tried to get his first look at where he was, he couldn't see a blasted thing.

Pitch black and windowless. Soundless and airless.

Albert put his hands out in front of him, scared to take a step for what he might trip over. Or into. Or down.

He fumbled with the robe he was wearing, looking for his cell phone. He had it on him somewhere, and the screen would provide at least enough light to see by. Good thing he hadn't crushed it.

Delving first into his pants pockets, then his jacket pockets, he finally found the phone in his breast pocket. His fingers brushed the coin there, and the fact that he bypassed gold for the phone showed how stressed out he was. Samantha and her damn charmed life were a pain in his ass. *She* was the one who'd gotten the genie. *She* was the one who'd gotten the first-class trip here— wherever here was—and he sure as hell bet the genie didn't have her languishing in some dark corner.

The screen light was dim, but at least it cut through the blackness. A foot behind him was a wall. He scanned it, looking for a light switch, but didn't have any luck.

He raised the phone toward the ceiling but couldn't see any light fixtures. Couldn't see the ceiling either.

The floor, however, was hard-packed earth. And no giant chasm loomed in front of him, so that was a plus.

He took a step forward, then another. He shone the light around, but all he could see were a haphazard stack of steamer trunks with the locks broken off, a pair of earthenware jars that came up to his thigh, and a pile of someone's laundry. Or bedsheets. He couldn't tell, and he wasn't exactly going to pick them up to find out.

Damn Samantha. If she'd married him months ago, he wouldn't have needed to go after her. But no bank manager would let him touch a penny of Blaine money without a marriage certificate even though he'd been running the business for months.

Albert hated being at anyone's mercy and that's all he'd been since he'd started losing at the tables. Cold fear slithered up his spine. Henley hadn't given him much more time. He needed to find Samantha, get his ring on her finger, and more importantly, his name on the joint signature card. Or find the genie.

He took another step, listening for something, some sound to tell him what was going on, but… nothing.

On the left was a weathered table that looked as if it'd been hand carved, and not in any antique way. It had no lamp on it, nor a phone. He flipped his cell over and looked for connection bars. No service, dammit.

He took another step and finally saw something: stars. Son of a bitch. He'd smashed into a wall.

His hands shot out as he started to fall back, and they latched onto something with enough surface area for him to grab hold of. A doorknob.

Both hands wrapped around the knob, Albert regained his balance, then looked around for his phone. It'd landed face down so its light was faint but enough to locate it. He dragged the phone toward him with his foot, giving a moment's thought to the trashing the screen was going to take, but no way was he letting go of the knob.

Phone in one hand, Albert turned the knob with the other, wincing when the tumbler inside squeaked. He opened the door slowly, and the dim light in the room beyond blinded him for a few seconds until his eyes grew accustomed to it.

But how long would it take him to get accustomed to what he was seeing?

Holy shit.

Albert shoved his phone into his pants pocket, rethought that, then shoved it back into his breast pocket with the coin. He needed room in the bigger pockets because he was about to become rich beyond his wildest imagination.

Well, no, that wasn't true. He had a damn good imagination, and it'd take a lot more gold and jewels than what were lying chaotically around what looked to be a pawnshop. The stash was damn impressive, though. A man could retire on this kind of loot.

Without a rich girlfriend.

He wedged himself in the door opening, checked the immediate vicinity, didn't see anyone, then slid through the doorway and along the wall like a shadow. A shadow with pockets, that is. And grabby hands that shoved as many priceless objects as he could fit into those pockets.

The emerald on the face of a small vase would be enough to keep him in luxury for at least the next twenty years. Coupled with a dagger with a ruby-encrusted hilt, the treasures should enable him to live the rest of his life in luxury.

But his pockets—and his greed—were bigger than that, and he worked hard to fill both.

A crash and shattering glass outside the shop left his pockets half empty. Albert ducked and ran to the window at the front of the store. He wasn't stupid; better half-full pockets than nothing. He plastered himself to the wall beside the window and dusted a smudge of grime from the glass.

Holy double shit.

It was chaos outside the shop, too. Utter and beautiful billionaire-making chaos. The hell with the trinkets in here.

He swept a bigger slice of dust away. Look at all those mythological creatures. One of them alone would earn him enough in sideshow admission fees to pay off Henley ten times over. Two of them would be twenty. Three, forty.

Albert's brain was doing the math as fast as the bald leprechaun was stacking gold coins on the ground—a gold-counting leprechaun! He'd hit the freaking jackpot. But where was the genie?

Albert removed the crystal from his pocket again and waved it in the air. No glitter anywhere. Damn.

A ray of sunlight hit the crystal and prismed off at an angle in a solid beam of orange. The padded lid of the jewel-encrusted box it landed on burst into flame.

He changed the angle, and the beam hit a tiny Chinese gong with a *clang*, then bent in an undulating wave toward an intricate blown-glass vial. The liquid inside the vial started to boil.

He changed the angle again, and the light stretched out toward a large mirror—which cracked with a loud *pop*.

Not a good thing. Albert wasn't superstitious, but the noise alone could do him in. He shoved the crystal back into his pocket where it was warm enough to burn a hole through it. Ah, the irony.

He backed up against the wall beside the window. The dragon was tossing gnomes into the air like a sea lion with its dinner. More gnomes were trying to catch them when they fell back to Earth. The centaur was trying to kill as many of the creatures as possible—that had to stop; those were his retirement plan!—and the leprechauns were falling over themselves tossing money at the bald one. Probably their bookie.

He liked those guys. He'd like them even more when people were tossing money at *him* to see them up close and personal—if he could just figure out how to get home from wherever the hell he was.

"Hey, guys! Cut it out! We have a guest!" something yelled, bouncing in front of the window. It looked like a yippy little dog with ears like a bat, but it had *yelled*. Not *barked*. That had to be worth a few mil at least.

He was going to be so rich if he could get out of here with one of them, but—

The thing bounced again, its face turned right toward the window. Shit! Had it seen him? Albert ducked. No need to be found and in the dragon's firing line. He'd head toward the other side of the window.

"Seriously, you guys!" The dog kept bouncing while Albert timed his run to happen on the downstroke. "Samantha's not going to want to hang out here if you're acting like this."

Samantha. The dog hadn't been talking about him.

Albert stopped mid-run and took a deep breath—and then another when he realized what else the dog's words meant. She was here. Which meant the genie had to be, too.

Suddenly, all those mythical fairy-tale creatures and gold coins were no longer interesting. Albert stood up in the shadow on the other side of the window and raised himself onto his toes, just able to make out what he thought was the back of a human head beyond the dragon's ridged back. It could be the genie—or it could be an ogre. With the looks of this place, anything was possible.

And then he saw Samantha.

Son of a bitch; she'd never dressed like that for him. The one time she'd tried, he'd had to make her change—not a good idea to put her on display when his ring wasn't on her finger. But, hell, she'd never looked like that around him. Slim. Curvy. Half-naked. Sexy.

The genie must have bewitched her. That was a handy ability. Albert would be sure to take advantage of that little trick in the future. He'd be able to have any woman he wanted. Albert almost wrung his hands in glee, but first he had to capture that genie.

He crouched again and worked his way toward the back of the shop, picking up another trinket or two—okay, seven—along the way. He was going to need to keep a low profile and figure out some way to get that genie.

But get him he would. And if Samantha got in the way, well, that wasn't a big deal. She was useless to him at this point anyway.

8

SAMANTHA TOOK KAL'S HAND TO GET OUT OF THE Mercedes as the second dragon—the wyvern—waddled into view. She was glad for Kal's strength and magic because, while dragons might be second nature to him and the talking fox, she hadn't quite jumped on the mythological-creature bandwagon. It was all too fantastical, which was probably why the arrival of neither a second dragon nor a flying car was of enough interest to stop the fracas.

Neither was poor Dirham.

"Guys!" he yelled, still bouncing, this time on the sidewalk beneath a tattered awning. "Come on! Stop this! This is really immature of you. We've got company and—uh oh!" Dirham's last bounce ended with him landing with a *splat!* on the ground, his legs splayed out to the sides as he glanced at the newcomer.

The wyvern spit out the large toothpick he'd been gnawing on. At least, Samantha hoped it *was* a large toothpick and not someone's femur. The object landed on a leprechaun—the bald one counting his coins.

"*Loscadh is dó ort*, Festwick. Can't ye see I'm countin' me gold?"

"What I see is that you're looking a little plumper than when I last saw ya, Seamus." The wyvern's tongue snaked around his beak in direct counterpoint to the swish of his tail, and neither looked good for the frazzled Seamus.

The leprechaun bounded to his feet, his gold scattering. "Yer not Festwick."

"At least your eyesight's not gone, though your brains are. Perfect for a dunghill, I'm betting. Oh, wait. That's your area of expertise, isn't it?" The wyvern flicked a coin with his talon and it landed in the middle of the fight.

"Here we go," Kal groaned.

"What do you mean?" Samantha slid a little closer.

"If there's one thing that gets leprechauns' attention faster than a good fight, it's a piece of gold they don't have to work for." Kal guided her back behind the car. "Watch."

Sure enough, the leprechauns who'd been holding back a band of gnomes turned tail and leapt into the fray, bodysurfing over that rabbit thing with the horns and the dozens of hairy whatevers. The fight escalated, Gaelic being hurled even louder than Orkney and company's grunts, and more hats, shoes, a shillelagh or two, and someone's belt buckle went sailing onto the sand.

And then Maille rose to her back legs, her gaze locked onto the wyvern like a heat-seeking missile. "You!"

Kal cursed, then waved his hand. A shield appeared in it. "Duck!"

He pulled Samantha down with him, but she needed no urging. A roar roiled through the air, the dragon's fire sucking every bit of oxygen from it, and the shield lit up like a beacon.

Gnomes and leprechauns scattered everywhere, most of them, it seemed, determined to get under the shield with her and Kal.

A loud crack was followed by a *thwack*, and glass shattered somewhere.

"Nice, Maille," sneered the wyvern. "Bad enough you can't keep our dwelling clean, but now you go clutter up the town. Such as it is."

"Don't get all high and mighty with me, you sniveling wyvern. What are you doing here, Bart? Last I checked, I had a restraining order against you."

"Which expired as of three a.m. Greenwich today, so here I am. We've got lots to discuss, so why don't you come give us a kiss, sweets."

"Over my dead body."

"That can be arranged."

Kal handed the shield to Samantha. "Hold this. And don't come out until I say it's safe. I don't want anything to happen to you."

Hung up on that last part, Samantha needed a few seconds before she could respond. But what was the right response to that statement anyhow? *Okay, but don't get burned by dragon fire? Don't let it crush you in its beak? Watch out for the talons?*

Thanks for caring about me?

Samantha shook her head. She shouldn't read anything into what was a normal comment; no sane person wanted to get caught in dragon crossfire.

Except, apparently, Kal.

He marched between the two dragons, who had squared off like gunfighters at the O.K. Corral, as if he were fireproof.

Samantha hoped, for his sake, that he was, but she wasn't especially looking forward to finding out.

"Enough, Maille. Bart," Kal said.

"Get out of here, djinni. You've done enough damage, and this is none of your business."

"When it puts my master in danger, it is," said Kal, much more calmly than Samantha's pulse rate. "You two need to take this someplace else."

"I'm not going anywhere with him." Maille crossed her arms, her green talons tapping her scales.

"Trust me, sweets, I'm not all that keen on it, either. I'm here for one reason only." Bart spat, barely missing the back end of a gnome who was sticking out from under a twisted hunk of metal that looked to have once been a mailbox.

Maille exhaled a stream of smoke that dried up the spittle but also sparked the gnome's pants. "I have no idea what you're talking about."

"Ow! Put it out! Put it out!" The gnome, hopped around, swatting at his butt with his pointed hat, and his Mini-Me leapt off his head.

Wayne kicked some sand onto the gnome and his little doppelgänger to put out the sparks.

"Sure you do, sweets." Bart swaggered down the street. "And might I suggest you clean up that mess? Oh, wait. You don't clean. Half the reason I moved out in the first place."

Maille didn't budge. "And the other half was Laverne. Don't give me your holier-than-thou crock, Bart. Your conscience's as black as your scales. And your name."

Samantha groaned. Black Bart. For a dragon. Maybe this *was* the genie version of the O.K. Corral after all. The dry, dusty road could definitely pass for a cowboy town, well, except for the white sand instead of dirt. The drooping white tepee building took the place of a swinging-door saloon, and rather than a general store or local jail, vacant storefronts with shattered glass were the norm on Main Street.

The bundles of loose sand and debris that rolled by could pass for tumbleweeds, and the unicorns were this reality's version of cowboys' noble steeds. All this place needed were hitching posts, a couple of outlaw WANTED posters, and an assayer's sign to look like an old-time Wild West town. Or, with all the white, dusty, dilapidated buildings, a ghost town.

And considering everyone who lived here, Samantha wouldn't have been surprised to see a few ghosts—though the satyr trotting out of a building through the bottom half of a set of swinging doors was a bit unexpected.

"Khaled!" The satyr skidded to a halt in front of them and adjusted the hat on his head—a cowboy hat. Seemed to be a theme: he wore a holster around his waist—if a goat *had* a waist—and a silver star hung from a ring of laurel leaves around his neck. "Boy, am I glad to see you. It's been a long time—"

"Oh, puhleez." Maille huffed another puff of lavender smoke. "Give it a rest, Stavros. We've had it with you and your orders. That badge is strictly for show."

"Now see here, Maille—"

"Enough!" Kal nodded at Orkney, who slammed his foot down. The ground shook—at least a five-point-six on the Richter scale—and everyone bounced a good ten inches off the ground. The gnomes went higher.

Samantha shook her head when it stopped rattling. What had happened to her nice, safe little world? Sadly, she knew what had happened to it: it'd been more of a fairy tale than this place, and she'd closed the book on it without reaching the happily ever after part.

"You two need to sit down and discuss this like rational adults," said Kal.

"That'd mean he'd have to be both rational *and* an adult," said Maille, pointing her pointed snout in the air, "and *brat's* nothing but a whiny little hatchling."

"This from the female who'd cry big ol' dragon tears when she didn't get her way." Bart bared dagger-like teeth that had nothing shiny about them, as if he used them for the very purpose Samantha had a sinking feeling they'd been designed for—as evidenced by that toothpick she suspected hadn't been a toothpick. "Let's talk about mature, *Mailleficent*. And hatchlings, too."

Maille blasted him with an UZI-like succession of fireballs, but Bart managed to leap out of the way.

The building behind him wasn't so lucky. The first spinning ball of fire hit the left front corner, and the structure that had already been listing to the right now groaned to the left. The next half dozen took out the orange roof tiles, which slid off and crashed to the ground, the shards breaking the front windows and making everyone near them dive for cover.

But not Samantha. She stood up. This was B.S. If she'd wanted domestic drama, she would have stayed home and confronted Albert. She'd wished to get away from all her troubles and Kal had been good enough to oblige her. No way was she going to spend her time in this magical place listening to the marital woes of dragons. What good were genie wishes if she didn't avail herself of them?

She left the shield in the care of the rabbit thing. Miraj, someone had called him. She could see when, with those antlers, he might seem to be a mirage if he was seen hopping around, out of context, in the desert. Here in Izaaz, however, he was just part of the scenery.

"Samantha, no!" Dirham hopped to his feet and bounced along the sidewalk.

Kal spun around. "Sam—"

"It's okay, Kal. I just wanted to say that I wish you could make these two sit down and talk things out."

"I like the way you think." He smiled at her, which warmed her in a far better way than the way the dragons were looking like they wanted to.

"You didn't." Maille's eyes were so black that Samantha thought she ought to feel cold, but with a fire-breathing dragon glaring at her, that was next to impossible.

"Ha! Kal's actually got himself a smart one. I like that." Bart hacked out a laugh, then ended up choking. Not surprising, given his blowtorch imitation a few minutes ago.

"See how much you like it when we're stuck at a bargaining table for eternity, thanks to her." Maille's beak curled back in the center, those shiny white teeth now as menacing as Bart's yellowed ones.

And then Bart's face turned yellow. His mouth dropped open for a second, then snapped shut. "Oh, *imigh sa diabhal*! She didn't!"

Kal laughed. "You heard the lady."

He waved his hand and the two dragons disappeared in a trail of orange glitter.

"You didn't put them in the Forum, did you, Kal?" asked Orkney. Samantha still needed to find out what he was.

"What's wrong with the Forum?"

"Ooh! Ooh! I know! I know!" Dirham bounced over

like a gazelle on a pogo stick. "Maille blew the roof to bits a couple of months ago."

Orkney didn't say a word.

"You're not fooling me, Ork." Kal shook Orkney's shoulder. "Wake up and answer the question."

The ogre let out a little snore.

The satyr hiked his holster. "We haven't, er, gotten around to fixing it yet."

Kal glanced at the lopsided tepee building. "Like a lot of things around here."

"Well, uh, things happen, and people, they don't want to pitch in." The satyr shrugged. "Pretty soon they're all too busy."

"Too busy or too lazy?"

Samantha had been aware of a low hum behind her, and when she turned around, she found, interestingly, that everyone had disappeared. Probably went back into whatever hole they'd crawled out of.

Stavros looked like he wanted to join them. "It's difficult to explain."

"Try." Kal's voice brooked no argument.

The satyr scratched the sand and the spurs on his hooves rattled. "Apathy," he said.

"Appetizers?" Dirham's ears perked up. "Cool! I'm hungry."

"Apathy, Dir, not appetizers," said Kal.

The bounce went out of the fennec. "Oh. Bummer."

"I'll see what I can rustle up for you, little guy." The satyr patted Dirham's head. "Unless you're in a hurry?"

Dirham's big brown eyes couldn't be any more pathetic as he looked at Kal. "Please, Kal? Just a little nibble? You know how much I need to keep my strength up."

Bouncing as much as he did had to use up a lot of energy.

"I'm not the one you have to ask. Sam's calling the shots."

Sam? No one called her Sam. Her father's stipulation when her mother had wanted to name her Samantha had been that no one was to shorten it to Sam because Sam was "a boy's name, and I didn't have a beautiful daughter to give her a boy's name." But she liked how it sounded coming from Kal.

She was beginning to like a lot of things about Kal.

"Samantha?"

Ah, well, it'd been nice while it'd lasted. She nodded. "You said we have all the time in the world, so sure. Why not?" She nodded at the satyr. "Lead on, MacDuff."

"You mean Stavros, Samantha," Dirham piped up. "That's his name."

Samantha didn't answer. Semantics. Her whole new world was being governed by semantics.

9

STAVROS LOOKED ANYTHING BUT HAPPY AS HE LED them through the administration building toward his office, which, combined with the looks of the city, had Kal on edge. If they hadn't dropped into the middle of one of the gnomes' melees, he would have addressed the issue then, but he'd been more concerned with keeping Samantha out of harm's way than with the state of the union here.

But all was definitely not right in the state of Izaaz, a fact that had been brought home when he'd seen Bart. The wyvern was always trouble, and Kal would have whisked Samantha out of there, except that she'd decided to stay. Unless one of the dragons aimed deadly fire at her—or she made a wish to the contrary—they were staying put.

"I could go for some of Aleka's *baklava*, Stavros." Dirham hopped beside the satyr. "Or what about the *tsoureki*?"

"No, my little friend. No more *tsoureki*, and we're all out of *baklava*. Aleka's is closed."

"What?" Kal asked the question at the same time that Dirham squeaked it.

Stavros held up a hand. "And Martina's, too."

"Why?" Kal opened the door—the upper portion to Stavros's lower one. "What happened? Martina has made the best chicken Florentine ever since da Vinci designed her ovens."

"She said she was tired of cooking." Stavros scratched his eyebrow. "Imagine. A cook who doesn't like to cook. This place, it's not the same."

"So where can we get a bite to eat?" asked Dirham, landing on a chair. Which broke, but the fox picked himself up, his perpetual smile firmly in place. "Palm Street looks all closed up. Is it a holiday, or is everyone on vacation?"

"Something like that, though Seamus and the boys keep McKeever's open. But I wouldn't recommend trying to get something to eat there. It's become their hangout, and the barkeep left a long time ago."

Kal didn't like the sound of this. He didn't like the looks of everything, either. Granted, he hadn't been here for a while, but the last time he'd been in Izaaz, the city had rivaled the Djinn capital of Al-Jannah for beauty. It had been full of color and life, the complete opposite of this dried-up husk of a town.

Plants and flowers had grown like wildfire, and blankets of poppy fields had bordered lush lawns. The palms had been full and green, their coconuts the color of gemstones. The smell of hyacinth and jasmine had sweetened the air, and the buildings had been painted in pastel colors so that when he'd stood at either end of the street, he'd seen those rainbows Dirham was so fond of. Even the sand had been a, well, sandy color, not bleached white, and the stained glass, cut gemstones, and mosaic tiles that had decorated everything had made the city sparkle. It was why he'd thought to bring Samantha here.

Something drastic had to have happened to leach the color from everything. And when he stepped into Stavros's office, he realized that more than just the color had been leached out: motivation, purpose. *Hygiene*.

Clutter was everywhere, and not the normal workday paper filings and messages tacked all over the place. Boxes of takeout—from Martina's—were stacked in a corner. A rotary fan with a blade missing *thwumped* on top of a filing cabinet that was missing a drawer, its cord frayed at the outlet. Grime covered the window, making it seem to be dusk instead of almost noon, and the coffee in the mug on the desk resembled the La Brea tar pits. Stavros had been working behind that desk for at least as long as Kal had been alive so it very possibly could be.

About the only thing that was in good condition was the frame around Colette's picture. Stavros had adored his wife.

Kal held a swinging electric cord out of Samantha's way, the sparks zapping between the wires at the frayed end making it as dangerous as dragon fire. "What happened here, Stavros?"

Dirham bolted toward the stack of boxes, his pointed little nose twitching, while Stavros leaped onto his chair. A wheel cracked off, and the chair listed sideways as it spun to the right. Stavros stood up and dragged it the chair across the chipped, mosaic-tiled floor until it banged against the desk. The picture of his late wife fell over.

"Nothing's happened here. That's the problem." The satyr stood the photograph up. "Ever since Faruq got himself arrested, no one cares. Now it's just me and Tarek, and you know how he likes the ladies. Time was I liked them, too. Then, Colette, ahh." He stroked a finger along the frame. "They don't know what to do with themselves."

They... or Stavros? Kal had a feeling he knew what the true answer was. You couldn't put a bunch of magical beings, each with different powers, together and not expect pissing matches. It took a strong leader to keep everyone in line. Faruq had used fear as his motivator, but Stavros? The state of his office and the rest of the town spoke to his lack of success.

"I'm sorry for your loss, Stavros," Samantha said, brushing between Kal and a large steamer trunk. The tarnished lock snagged her pants. "How long were you and your wife together?"

Kal couldn't read the lettering on the trunk's faceplate, which was probably a good thing. Izaaz housed its share of important artifacts, and to see the place disorganized like this, well, he just hoped none of those artifacts got into the wrong hands.

"Colette and I were together for three and a half millennia come next Tuesday," Stavros answered.

Kal gripped Samantha's elbow when she stumbled, as he'd known she would. She was handling this situation a lot better than he'd expected, but realizing someone had been married for more than thirty-five hundred years would test any mortal's mettle. "Sam? Are you okay?"

She blinked, her green eyes wide. "I really wish I hadn't asked that question."

"As you wish, Sam." Kal waved his hand and hoped Dirham was keeping tabs on the number of wishes he was granting. One thousand and one, and he'd be home free.

She stumbled against the trunk again. Her pants

caught a second time. But this time when she freed the fabric, enough dust came with it that Kal could read the inscription.

Kharah! That was Pandora's box. So *that's* where it'd gotten to. Contrary to popular belief, the reason Pandora hadn't let Hope out was because the box had gotten caught up in the whirlwind of the chaos she'd unleashed and had disappeared before she had the chance. Her publicist had concocted the other story to keep the truth from coming to light and causing widespread panic, but Kal had run into Pandi in a bar one night when she'd been too far into her cups of ouzo, and the story had come out.

No wonder Izaaz looked the way it did; its citizens had no Hope—because it was locked up and forgotten in Stavros's office.

Apparently, the satyr had no idea what he had, and given Stavros's state of mind right now, Kal wasn't sure telling him would be the best thing. One crisis at a time.

"I'm sorry for your loss, Stavros," Samantha said, oblivious to what she was standing next to—*and* what had just happened. She was looking a little confused, though.

"Déjà vu," Kal whispered. Since she'd wished she hadn't asked the question, he couldn't explain to her why she thought she was reliving the scene. Déjà vu was a handy excuse, and one all djinn learned in Wish Fulfillment 101. It worked on people their masters interacted with, too.

"*Efharistó*, Samantha," Stavros said, as if the re-do hadn't happened. The citizens of Izaaz weren't fazed by genie magic, but sadly, neither they nor the town seemed to have seen any magic in a lot longer than the time Faruq had been incarcerated.

Kal put Izaaz's magical updates on his mental to-do list for when he was in office. He'd be cleaning up a lot of messes, Faruq's and otherwise.

He started with the mess on the chair in front of Stavros's desk, magicking the clutter into the drawer he restored on the file cabinet, all under the rationale of providing Samantha with a place to sit. For himself, he brushed a pile of stuff away from the end of the desk and leaned his hip against it.

Something crashed to the floor, eliciting a yelp from Dirham when it clipped his hind end. The fox raced out the door, scattering papers all over the place.

Stavros shook his head when Kal went to straighten them up. "Don't worry about them, Kal. One more mess won't change things here."

Definitely the wrong attitude. No wonder the place had gone down the tubes.

Kal grabbed an old paper bag and an issue of *Izaaz Weekly* that had landed on the curled toe of his left *khussa*. The newspaper was dated ten months ago. Shaking his head, he grabbed the carburetor that had fallen as well and set them all on the top of the file cabinet.

"It hasn't been that long since Faruq was arrested, Stavros. How did this place go downhill so quickly?"

The satyr rested his elbows on the desk. A sweet potato chip crunched beneath one. "It was as if we had a blackout. News hit town and that was it. No one has done anything since that day except sit around and play chess or start a fight. And half the time the chess matches end up in fights so I have to referee. I swear, I'm going to turn this badge in for a whistle."

He lifted the coffee mug and swirled it around. Kal would swear none of the liquid moved even a bit.

"Once upon a time," Stavros continued, "my job, as Maille pointed out, was basically ceremonial. But now? I've tried to organize everyone. Round them up. Make them care. Hades, the ceiling hasn't been regulated in months; you can see what the sun's done. I'm worried that mortals' satellites are going to find us soon.

"Although, ironically, deregulation actually helped with that because every plant from here to the Weeping Wall has been fried, camouflaging us against the rest of the desert. But no one seems to care that we're living in less than ideal circumstances and could be discovered at any time."

"But how do they live? How do they eat? And a weeping wall?" Samantha slid a pile of poker chips aside and set the lantern on Stavros's desk.

"Izaaz's magic provides for the citizens," Kal answered, having done a study of it for the new High Master's thesis he was working on since Faruq had gotten his mitts on the old one. And this situation proved his point: magic wasn't the be-all everyone thought. A three-wish limit was a better course of action.

"Pegasus struck the sand with his hoof at what is now the Weeping Wall, creating an unending waterfall that formed the oasis that became Izaaz. Eventually, as the town grew, it became a landing place for displaced beings. As your world loses its wonderment, its belief in the impossible, as it becomes more information-driven, more reality-based, and the population grows and infiltrates so-called mythical beings' environments, those beings migrate here. Where they can be themselves and not have to hide their powers from mortals. Where they can be who they are and live life as they were meant to." At least in theory. In practice, though, that obviously wasn't the case.

"But if they have powers, why can't they fix everything?" Samantha asked.

"No one has the kind of magic you're talking about," said Stavros. "Not like Kal's. Ours is specialized. Dragons used to fill the skies, keeping the peace and the balance with mortals. Dwarves managed the earth and its minerals, fairies the forests, gnomes the land, Kismet and her flocks of birds the skies. Nature entrusted the balance to all of us.

"But through the advancement of your civilization, our magic lost the awe and respect we'd always had in the outside world. Spells and other magical mishaps that, in centuries past, would have frightened mortals, now no longer do. Dragons were decimated by knights in shining armor, which put the dwarves' union on strike—and rightfully so since they need dragon fire to fuel their forges." Stavros set the mug on his desk, and again not a drop sloshed inside. "Then the Industrial Age came along and put the elves and gnomes out of business, so they came to Izaaz."

Samantha glanced inside the mug and wrinkled her nose.

"Faruq kept everyone in line, but now that he's gone, there's no incentive to take care of the place or do anything. Seamus fancies himself the next head of state and has tried bribing everyone into following him with the leprechauns' gold, but that not only doesn't go over well with the leprechauns, it also hasn't tempted anyone *except* leprechauns because gold isn't the lure to others that it is to them. So that results in *more* fighting. Then the gnomes get involved; they just love to tweak the leprechauns' beards, and it's a never-ending cycle."

Stavros blew out a breath and his shoulders slumped. "And Maille and her cronies don't care what they torch. They've destroyed pretty much everything the gremlins had their fingers into, and you know what happens with disgruntled gremlins. Then there's poor Kismet who's so disheartened by the apathy that she's threatening to go into the Light and take all her knowledge with her. That would be the biggest shame of this whole thing, but I just can't get anyone motivated to do anything."

"Izaaz sounds like the island of misfit toys. No one has any purpose." Samantha moved the cup of primordial ooze to the overflowing trash bin.

Stavros hopped to his hooves, the action spinning the lopsided chair drunkenly. "There's an island? Why wasn't I informed? Where are these misfits? What do they do to keep themselves occupied? Can we set up a conference call and brainstorm some ideas? Maybe some kind of exchange program? Do they Skype?"

Kal stopped the spinning chair. "It was just a figure of speech, Stavros. There's no such island."

He knew what Samantha was referring to because he'd kept abreast of current culture while confined to his lantern, surfing every television channel there was when cable had come to the Djinn world. Great invention that, and it had actually given the gremlins jobs. They'd thrived with their new careers, sabotaging cable connections left and right. When that worldwide Kournikova computer virus had hit back in 2001, Kal had suspected that the gremlins had moved on to computer hacking because Sneek, the gremlin prime minister, had had a thing for Anna Kournikova, though he'd never admitted to it.

Samantha uncrossed, then recrossed her legs, and Kal admitted he might have a thing for *her*. Then she smiled at him, and there was no *might* about it. All those fantasies he'd had during the long lonely nights in his lantern… He definitely had a thing for her. One their kiss had only heightened.

His cock hardened and he grabbed something off Stavros's desk to hide the evidence. *Kharah*, here they were, discussing urban blight, and he was thinking with his dick.

But it'd been too long since he'd held a woman, let alone one as beautiful as Samantha. Her smile lit up the place in a way the sun with its brutal intensity couldn't, and made him burn even more. And with the way Monty had talked about her, Kal felt as if he knew her.

She tapped the desk with her fingernails. "It's a shame what's happened here. I wish there was some way to make this town what it once was."

Stavros caught his breath.

So did Kal. It was a brilliant solution, and one that would have her going through a thousand and one wishes in no time. He'd break his previous record of three days. That master had been a seven-year-old who'd gotten the lantern for his birthday. The kid had barely slept for getting all his wishes out. Then he'd barely slept while playing with everything he'd wished for.

The parents would have been better off keeping Kal's services for themselves and giving the kid a few things, but those maharajas… They liked to do things in a big way.

But Kal hadn't complained, and master number four hundred and forty-three had come and gone in three days. He didn't want Samantha to go in three days.

Though he wouldn't mind her coming…

Kal pressed the metallic thing harder against his groin, hoping it'd cool him down. But heat seared him as he imagined Samantha naked beneath him, writhing in pleasure as he traced his fingers and lips all over her body, bringing her to her peak. Her skin would be damp, moist from passion smoother than silk, with that lilac scent of hers as potent as any aphrodisiac a mystic could concoct.

He shifted his stance, trying to hide the evidence of his thoughts, but when his sash snagged on the thing in his hand, it brought that whole area into focus. Especially when he realized what had caused it, what he held, and where it was situated.

A vegetable slicer.

Kal practically threw it across the room. *Son of a Sumerian!* That thing was dangerous.

"Kal?" Samantha put her hand on his knee. "Are you okay?"

Definitely not. And with her hand where it was, so close to where his body was screaming for it to be, even less so. *Zift*, Samantha was more dangerous to him than the slicer. Forget about keeping her longer than three days. He'd be better off in a lot of ways if they broke his record in the next three *hours*.

"I'm fine, Samantha. But I can't just wave my hand and grant that wish. You need to be more specific."

Then she cocked her head and nibbled her bottom lip—the one he'd run his tongue over and had gently drawn between his teeth—and he realized he was only kidding himself. There she was, concentrating on servicing the community, and he was concentrating on servicing *her*.

She'd tasted so good. Had felt even better. That little gasp she'd made in the back of her throat when he'd brushed the side of her breast—and don't think he hadn't wanted to cup her. Stroke her. Feel her nipple pebble between his fingers and beneath his tongue as he took his time exploring all her hidden secrets, bringing them both to the pinnacle over and over, only to back off at the last minute to savor the sensation, that heightened sense of being before they both tumbled over the edge—

Maybe he should have held on to that slicer.

Kal shook his head. Enough already. For the past two thousand years, he'd done nothing but try to hurry things along, and now, when he was so close, he wanted to make it last? Savor it? Savor her?

Kal gritted his teeth and shifted his legs to dislodge her hand. He had to keep his focus on the ultimate prize—and Samantha wasn't it. She couldn't be. Genies lived forever and Kal knew, firsthand, the pain of watching someone he loved die. He'd lived—barely—through the death of his parents and brothers and sisters. Even the baby, Noor. He'd been young when he'd been Chosen to enter The Service, an honor his parents had been so proud of. He had, too.

But none of them had realized the consequences of immortality. Of what watching them grow old and die would do to him. How it'd leave him alone and, with his jail sentence, without support. Without anyone left to care about him or believe in his innocence. No one to be there when he got out.

Well, except Dirham, of course, but as supportive as the fennec was, it wasn't the same.

And Samantha couldn't be. She was his way out, and the quicker it was over, the better. He had to focus on clearing his name and getting his life back, not the sexy hint of her tongue as she pulled another little bit of her bottom lip between her teeth, or the sparkle in her eyes, or the way her shirt lovingly cupped her breasts, the dip in her navel that he'd like to taste, the flare of her hips with the low-riding harem pants—

Kal cleared his throat and dragged his mind off that delectable image. He wasn't an animal, for gods' sakes. "So where do you wish to start, Samantha?"

Her earlobe would be a good spot, followed by the soft hollow beneath, the graceful curve of her neck, down between her breasts—

So much for not being an animal. Kal raked a hand through his hair. Could he just keep his focus—and his dick—where it belonged already?

"What about we start here? With this office and then the buildings around it? Sound good, Stavros?" Samantha's fingers threaded through her copper curls, and Kal couldn't help noticing the way the diffused sunlight flashed golden fire on the strands. Couldn't help wanting to feel those curls slip through his fingers.

Over his chest.

Along his abs.

Lower.

"Sure," said Stavros. "And then I'm thinking

storefront revitalization. A whole spectrum of colors. Maybe neon; it is the twenty-first century after all. The road could use some sprucing up. A few spruces wouldn't be amiss, either. A whole new landscape, too. The dodos have been asking for their own fruit-tree grove, and the phoenixes really need a new aviary. They keep lighting theirs on fire and then moving on to someone else's, and pretty soon we have all the birds laying eggs atop the street lanterns. Ever get hit on the head by a huma egg?" He rubbed his head. "Suckers hurt. Not to mention, lost eggs decrease the population."

Samantha turned a brilliant smile Kal's way. "Can you do that, Kal?"

Oh he could do it all right. And her. Whatever she wanted. And that'd be only the beginning. Then he'd—

He felt both her and Stavros's gazes on him. Ah. She'd meant her wish. He willed his blood to cool. "Yes, Samantha, I can."

One more wish coming up. One step closer to losing her.

Kal's chest tightened. What was wrong with him? He'd been without a woman for long periods of time before—part of the whole genie thing—but this… He needed to get away from her. Find a willing woman somewhere. Take the edge off. Then he could focus on what he'd been striving for for the past two thousand years—and that *wasn't* Samantha.

"Kal?"

Samantha's green eyes sparkled in the way the gems of Izaaz used to and called attention to the sprinkling of freckles across her nose, so light no one would know they were there without getting up close. But he knew. He'd been up close—and very personal—and just the memory of how personal held him immobile for a few seconds.

Luckily, she took his silence to mean something else. "Oh, right. I wish you'd fix Stavros's office."

"As you wish, Samantha." Kal cleared his throat and waved his hand, on his way to fulfilling wish number sixteen. At this rate, they'd blow through the other nine hundred and some in no time.

He should be happy about that. And he would be. In a minute or so. Or a century or two.

Then an explosion rocked the town and purple hellfire rained down from the sky and Kal couldn't afford the luxury of time.

Bart and Maille had left their building.

10

THE SCENE IN THE STREET REALLY DID LOOK LIKE a pair of gunslingers had come to town. Maille was blasting awnings to a crisp, and Bart was searing destructively beautiful calligraphy onto the walls with a laser beam of firepower like a graffiti artist on acid. Smelled like acid, too. Of the sulfuric kind.

Another explosion rocked the town, and the gnomes popped back into their drainpipes like sea anemones on the sea floor, while the fairies took off for parts unknown like a flock of hummingbirds.

Another blast of purple sparks followed Maille to the ground, encircling a palm tree in a ring of fire, torching it and turning it to ash in no time flat. At this rate, the town would be in cinders by dinner.

Samantha strode across the dusty road, her mind whirling like the scene in front of them. She didn't have any experience in renovations other than a week on a Habitat for Humanity project, but taking Kal up on his "wish is his command" directive would solve that problem.

Samantha walked around a leaning pole with a genie lantern on top. "Kal, I wish you'd fix that."

Kal waved his hand, and orange glitter seemed to spout from his fingers as the pole went erect really quickly.

That was *so* not a word she needed to be thinking

about. She'd noticed his reaction to her touch back in Stavros's office—and she was well aware of her reaction to him charging across the street toward the two dragons. Kal, in full-on genie glory, was definitely not a typical guy.

Bart seared the spire off a building with another blast of fire, torching a window into a molten lump of glass that cooled as it fell, only to shatter when it hit the sidewalk below it.

Maille's neck frill ruffed up like a medieval queen's best court finery. "That's it, you self-important sauropod. I told you to leave me alone. This town isn't big enough for the both of us."

"You've got that right, Maille." Kal waved his hand, and sparkly orange muzzles appeared on the dragons' snouts. "I sent you to the Forum to work things out. What are you doing back here?"

Maille crossed her dragon arms—something Bart wasn't able to do since he didn't have any—and pointed one long, lime green claw at the muzzle.

Samantha didn't want to be out in the open when that came off so she slid behind Kal.

Kal waved his hand, and the muzzle disappeared. "No fire or I put it back. I'm not going to risk Sam."

Maille blew the sprinkles off the end of her nose. "Sit down and talk it over? Yeah, we did that. Done. Check. Mate. Or rather, *stale*mate. Which is what ol' brat is. A stale mate."

"And you're a lying, heartless witch, chain-Maille!" Bart scratched the sand like an angry bull preparing to charge—which he then did, his run turning into flight so fast that anyone else would have ended up in his

vicious talons, but Maille took to the air and outma-
neuvered him.

Kal sighed and crossed his arms. "This is getting
us nowhere."

Samantha came out from behind him, one hand
shielding her eyes from the sun the dragons had flown
toward. "It'd be so much better if they couldn't blast
each other."

Kal turned his head slightly, a devilish smile on his
lips. "Is that what you wish?"

Samantha smiled back. Nothing like being on the
same page. "You know? It is. I wish they couldn't blast
each other. Or fly, either."

"As you wish, Sam."

Two seconds later, Maille and Bart—at least she
thought they were Maille and Bart—floated down from
the sky amid a shower of sparkles.

In human form.

"You didn't! You couldn't!" Maille screamed, fire
threatening to erupt from her eyes. Better there than
her throat.

The same height as Samantha, Maille was full of muscle, with a purple stripe bisecting sleek, black hair that
hung to her knees, and almond-shaped eyes that tilted up
at the outside corners—and not because she was smiling.

Far from it.

"You cursed brat, and I don't mean my idiot ex.
Seriously? You wished this on us? Where are my scales?
My beautiful scales?" Maille twisted to look at her back,
now covered in a replica of the outfit Samantha wore but
in red. "And my wings? You got rid of my wings? How
could you?"

"Chill out, hothead," said Bart in a surprise move. Balding and about a foot shorter than Kal, Bart was a beanpole whose vest and billowy pants hung on him. And he, unfortunately, could *not* pull off curly-toed slippers. Especially fuchsia ones. "Girl's got a point. You can't go around destroying the place."

"Me?" Maille lunged toward her mate, who, even though he had arms now, seemed to forget that fact as he leapt out of the way with all the speed his dragon self had had. "You should have thought of that before you went out 'bowling' all night with Laverne."

"I'd wish they'd stop talking for a minute, Kal," Samantha whispered.

Kal chuckled and waved his hand. The dragons' mouths clamped shut, and a giant stopwatch appeared in the air behind their heads. "As you wish, Samantha."

The air suddenly got a lot clearer, in terms of dragon smoke and noise pollution. But the two dragons looked like they wanted to blast *her* with fire.

Samantha mentally kicked herself as the seconds ticked down. She shouldn't have added the time stipulation. *Semantics*.

"Now, let's try this again, you two." Kal walked toward them.

"I can't believe you did this, Kal." Maille said when the second hand hit zero and the new muzzles disintegrated in a shower of orange dust. She flung her arms and stomped her feet. "We haven't been in this form in, what? Five thousand years? We evolved beyond this, for gods' sakes. All our training, all our study, and you reduce us to this?"

"All your training didn't make you any more

civilized, so I suggest you get over it. Work out your differences in this form before you destroy Izaaz more than it already is. The place is supposed to be a haven, but you two have turned it into a hellhole."

"You can't blame that on us," said Maille, the fingernail she was pointing at Kal still lime green and long enough that it was starting to curl. "Have you seen the usury the leprechauns are putting out there? And the gnomes are threatening to tunnel under all the buildings and make them unstable unless they get some payola. And let's not forget the *peris*. Oh, no. Everyone thinks they're so sweet and lighthearted and beautiful, spreading happiness and good cheer wherever they go, but it's enough to make you puke. And where's their glitter? Their sparkle?"

A gnome popped out of a drain spout. "I'll tell ya where it is, you bigmouthed Gila monster. It's buried under all the rubble you and your friends keep heaping on us. Can you blame them for not wanting to waste any more of it? I wouldn't if I were them."

"And you, Maille," the wyvern sneered—which would have had much more impact if he still had a beak full of pointed teeth. "Shall we count the ways you're so blameless? Let's start with the hatchlings. When were you going to tell me?"

The leprechauns showed up next and Samantha felt as if she were in a three-ring circus. Then a pack of furry little creatures with pointed ears and mouths full of spikes as nasty as Maille's showed up, and it became a four-ring one. Five when the unicorns trotted back out. Six with the centaurs.

And then Samantha lost count as hundreds, if not

thousands, of creatures filed into the streets, hurling insults and clumps of sand all over the place.

Kal kneaded the back of his neck and looked at her. "Anything else you want to wish for?"

Samantha straightened and rolled back her shoulders. No wonder the place looked like it did. "Yes. Let's take care of a few things." She rubbed her hands. "First, I wish you'd make all of them immobile and quiet."

"Done." He made a karate-chop move with his hand and peace reigned as the glitter settled onto the street. It was a big improvement.

"Next, I wish you'd shore up those buildings."

"Gotcha." He waved at the droopy buildings lining the street, making them perk up. The way his abs rippled, framed by his orange vest and highlighted by glitter, made *her* perk up.

Samantha shoved that image from her mind. She had a job to do. "And the trees. I wish they were orange—er, green."

So much for the job.

"Absolutely." Another wave of Kal's hand, and the landscape got prettier—though more of an orangish-green than full-on green, but if she had him change the trees back, she'd have to come clean about why. Bad enough her subconscious was duking it out with her libido, she didn't want to have to come out and admit something like that.

Kal waved his hand again, and the coconuts turned into sparkling gemstones. "Anything else you want to wish for, Samantha?"

She started counting tasks off on her fingers. "A better road surface. New paint on the buildings. Water for the fountain. Trash cans. A working café with outside seating. How about a monorail-type system? Good for the air and less flammable than carpets. Oh, and the fruit trees. That aviary. What else? Where's Stavros? He'd know."

Kal grabbed her hand. "Whoa there, Bob Vila. You have to make wishes. I can't grant off a list."

"Oh, right. Okay. Here we go." The *I wish*es flew out of her mouth, and the long, crumbling staircase at the far end of the street—à la Rome's Spanish Steps—rebuilt itself, chunks of marble that had broken off onto the steps below flying back into place as if she were watching an earthquake video in reverse.

The dull, gray stone structure ringing the platform at the top became shimmering amethyst quartz that extended from the wall of sand behind it, down the stairs, to the new road. Made of malachite bricks, the new surface slid over the old like spilled milk on hardwood flooring. As the road turned to color, jets of water in the dry fountain that ran the length of the median erupted into gravity-defying patterns. Grass grew so green it was almost emerald, and mosaic tiles bloomed along the sidewalk. All of this slid beneath the frozen citizens in a reverse magician's trick of yanking the tablecloth out from under the dishes.

The buildings Kal had shored up got a new look, too. Jewels popped into the pockmarks like popcorn, and the balconies lost their rust and gained a white coating. Trumpet vines and enormous honeysuckle grew in place of the dead leaves, and like the brigand of *peris* she'd seen earlier, hummingbirds darted from behind the buildings to claim the new flowers.

Overhead, sand sifted onto the glass ceiling, proving it really was there, and providing some much needed shade to parts of the city.

Kal brushed his hands to sweep up all the glitter when she stopped to take a breath. "We're going to have to think about that monorail system, Sam. It's a good idea, but maybe we should set the rest of the city to rights before we start any additions."

"Good point. I think we've done enough for now. You want to set them all free?"

"It doesn't matter what I want, Samantha. What do you wish?"

She wished he'd kiss her again—and even if that was inappropriate, it was understandable.

Samantha tucked her curls behind her ears, hiding her face that was probably as red as the rubies over the Nut Shop as she did so. "Um, yes, Kal. I wish you'd let everyone go back the way they were."

Kal waved his hand and life returned to normal. Well, as normal as this place could be.

Sort of.

A collective sigh happened, but no one moved. They just stood there, blinking. Shock. Surprise. Maybe some awe? That might just be hero worship in Miraj's eyes.

Kal squeezed her shoulder. "Good job, Samantha. You've made them speechless. Let's hope appreciative, too. But in my experience, they're about to get very greedy. I'd suggest we head somewhere else until the initial shock wears off."

Samantha knew all about greedy. Knew all about people wanting things from her. But, here, in this place, she understood it. These people—er, beings—needed something to motivate them, and hopefully, what she and Kal had done would be that impetus. Though human nature—and troll and dwarf and fairy nature, too, presumably—would want to take the easy way out.

She knew all about that, too.

Unfortunately, the shock lasted only a few seconds. Then everyone and their brother began rushing toward Samantha, shouting out their wishes like dragons with fire bolts.

Samantha felt like a translator as she listened to someone's wish, then parroted it to Kal in her own words. Clothing started to appear in the shops, nice cars along the side streets, even an Xbox in someone named Newton's newly renovated king-sized bedroom. Self-serving ovens, self-sweeping brooms, forever-flowering fruit trees... the citizens of Izaaz had a better imagination than the crew at Disney.

"Rain, lass. Make it rain."

"No, make it snow! We've never had snow in Izaaz!"

"Snow? Are you out of your cotton-pickin' mind? We're not prepared for snow!"

"So wish for a snowmobile."

"Or a snow blower."

"Or skis! Yeah, let's go skiing!"

"Then we're going to need a mountain. Can you wish us the perfect ski mountain?"

"With bunny slopes," hollered Miraj.

"And a lodge with a big stone fireplace," said the phoenix, bursting into flame again.

"And a Matterhorn cliff," said Stavros, getting into the act.

A mountain? Cliffs? Ski lodge? Snow? Samantha

shook her head. The wishes were getting out of control. And so was the mob. They had formed tight circles around her and Kal, and were pressing in.

She moved closer to him. "Um, Kal? About your idea to get out of here. I think now would be a good time to take you up on that offer. Where can we go?"

"Anywhere you'd like, Samantha. What appeals to you?"

If she were home, she'd head to Antoine's Day Spa. "This place doesn't have a spa, does it?"

"It has whatever you wish it to have, Samantha, but in this case, you're lucky. The thermal pools here are the perfect reason for a spa. And since it is my job to see to your comfort, you don't even have to wish to go there. I'll take you. A gimme, if you will. A simple yes is all you need to say."

Kal looked at her with those warm, chocolate eyes, and his arm brushed her breast. His breath was warm against her temple, and saying yes to him became anything but simple.

11

ALBERT SLIPPED INSIDE THE DOMED BUILDING a few blocks from the scene of the street fight, managing to make it there without garnering any attention—but also, unfortunately, without capturing the genie.

He'd been so close that if he could have done something about it, he would have, but with the genie doling out magic left and right, Albert had erred on the side of caution.

He'd thought he'd been found out when he, and the entire scenario, had been frozen in place. Luckily, he'd been behind one of those walking carpets because the genie had been *right* there, so close that Albert could have reached out and grabbed him—*if* he could have reached out. He couldn't wait to get his hands on that genie and the badass car he'd driven in on. That'd be one of the first things Albert would wish for when he caught him.

But what had Samantha wished for? Albert couldn't believe it—or maybe he could. After all, with her charmed life, what did it matter to a woman used to having everything handed to her on a silver platter to use genie wishes for *urban renewal*? She'd *never* appreciated what she had. What her father had had. But Albert would. Oh, how he would.

He'd wanted to run into that street, pick her up, and

shake some sense into her. God, what it must have been like to grow up as she had, every wish granted with one little smile at her father. The man had been a pushover for Samantha, and it had sickened Albert to no end to have to play along while the guy had been alive. But Albert would do anything to get his hands on the kind of money Blaine had, so he'd sucked it up.

But to have to stand there and watch Samantha and her do-good magical lackey spruce up the town… The woman really was clueless.

Albert had thought for sure that the adrenaline and anger boiling up inside him would spill over and free him from being a human statue when, all of a sudden, he'd been able to move and that car had taken off— upwards. It'd hovered above them like some damn flying saucer, rotating silently before blasting off for parts unknown. And he'd lost them again.

He shoved off from the heavily carved wooden door inside the dark building. An arched entranceway led to a large chamber where an enclosed stone staircase circled upward in the middle, the room supported by stone pillars whose tops and arched supports were painted in red bands. Daylight filtered through thin slits high on the walls, but the shadows were growing longer by the minute as he tried to figure out what he should do next. He was running out of time, and now, with Samantha and her genie flying off to God-knew-where, he was running out of chances.

Feeling for the coin yet again, Albert replayed his wish to find them for the thousandth time. He didn't know why the coin wasn't working, and he was seriously worried that he was going to be stuck here.

How many different ways could he say that he needed that genie?

God, he was tired. He'd been up for hours, and it'd been nighttime when he'd found the safe open. The mass exodus of adrenaline from finding the safe and following them here was leaving him exhausted. He needed some place to rest. To recharge and refocus. To come up with a plan.

Albert climbed the circular steps in the narrow tower, trying for perspective on both where he was and what he was facing.

He reached the small platform at the top and realized he didn't have a clue as to what he was facing. The building and he—the entire *town*—were underground.

Long rays of the sun stretched out across the city and hit a wall at the far end. A wall that encircled the entire place. A wall of sand. Albert leaned out from under the roof that covered the platform and looked up. The sky was covered in sand, too. How the hell was *that* possible?

Claustrophobia set in. Forget cement shoes or getting whacked; Henley wasn't going to have to set his goons after him if Albert didn't deliver the money because Samantha and her damn genie were going to bury him alive.

Then he saw something black and bug-shaped off in the sky. The car! Samantha and her genie were still here! He still had a chance!

Albert raced down the stairs and out into the street, pulling back against the wall when a two-legged, unusually large-sized rodent turned the corner at the end of the street.

He couldn't be seen now; he had a genie to catch.

12

IF KAL THOUGHT THIS WAS SEEING TO HER COMFORT, then he definitely didn't have a girlfriend.

The Mercedes landed in front of a tall, dilapidated, gray wood fence covered in white roses. Dead white roses.

With the dull *blah* of the sand walls in the distance behind it and the withered vines covering the structure beside it, the place looked about as inviting as Macy's after a Black Friday sale.

"Um, Kal?" Samantha climbed out of the car and crossed her arms, wincing when the lantern dinged her funny bone.

Kal walked around the back of the car. "A little bit of magic, and you'll see what I'm talking about."

When he put his hands on her shoulders, she had to wonder what kind of magic he was talking about. But then he swept a hand in front of her, and the scene seemed to unfold from the upper left in a shower of glitter like wallpaper being peeled from a wall, except that color filled in the drabness, as if it were an enormous paint-by-numbers picture.

All but the roses. Those remained white, but they did spring to life like a nature movie on fast-forward. Atop a deep plum fence, their petals turned as pristine and sparkly as the unicorns, but sprinkled with more of Kal's magical glitter. Soft harp music wafted with the scent of anise and patchouli from the courtyard behind it, where the vines regrew *backward* on a Mediterranean-style tiled roof atop a yellow adobe building. Broken panes in the arched windows rebuilt themselves in beautiful stained glass patterns, with the shutters matching the color of the fence.

Kal walked past her and pushed open the gate to where a yellow brick path led inside. He cocked his head. "Shall we?"

Shall we what?

Samantha kept her mouth closed, her eyes forward, and her concentration on the beautiful courtyard ahead of her. Until his fingers brushed her waist as she passed him.

Then she couldn't focus on anything but what his touch did to her, how good he smelled, and how tall and broad he was. How feminine she felt next to him. How much she wanted to be held by him. Wanted to hold him.

Obviously, she was over Albert. Hell, with what Kal could do to her with just one look, she'd obviously never been *into* Albert.

Funny that what should be one of the worst nights of her life was turning out to be one of the best. Was that why Dad had told his attorney to give her the letter at the memorial? To give her something to focus on besides losing him? Had he wanted to ensure she'd have someone in her life who'd see to her safety and comfort as he had? She wished she could ask him.

Wait. *Could* she ask him?

"Um, Kal." Samantha turned around in front of another gate, this one white wrought-iron, the adjoining fence covered in purple roses. "You're going to have to explain the rules to this genie/master thing. Everything's happened so fast that we haven't really had a chance to talk about it. What can I do? What can you do? Can we bring my father back?"

Kal took a step closer than he needed to—not that Samantha was complaining. "For mortals, Samantha, there aren't many rules. You already know you have to be specific and wish for something before I can grant it. But, I'm sorry." He ran the backs of his fingertips down her cheek. "I can't bring your father, or anyone, back from the dead. I can't cure illnesses or injuries, though I can conjure the medication that will help them if it exists. And because Karma plays a part in the checks and balances of The Djinn Code to keep us on task and honest, since I can't bring anyone back from the dead, I also can't kill anyone."

She'd figured that was the case, but it didn't make it any easier to hear. She'd so hoped to be able to have her father again. But she had to admit that the word *honest* took away the disappointment. Aside from her father and Wanda, Samantha couldn't name one other honest person in her inner circle.

But now there was Kal. And that honesty made him more attractive to her than his looks or his kiss or what he could do for her combined, because, after all, he was a genie; there was nothing she could possibly do for him or give to him that he couldn't do or give to himself. He had no reason not to be honest with her, and luckily this Code of his demanded it.

And that, more than his fingers on her cheek, put a little hitch in her breath. A little swirl to her tummy. A little zing beneath her skin.

Sure, the chemistry was there between them, but the

look in his eyes—warm and gentle and, dare she say, compassionate?—was what turned her knees to mush and made her yearn to lean on him. To wrap her arms around him. To share this moment in time with him.

She was about to take that infinitesimally small step into his embrace when a door slammed open nearby, shattering both a window and the moment. Though she knew she should be happy for the interruption, given the upheaval going on in her life and the fragile state of her emotions at the moment, Samantha wasn't so sure she was.

"*Välkommen*." Blue eyed and tan, with blond hair to his shoulders and looking like the mountain he had to have been carved from, the "interruption" walked toward them in a white wraparound robe with a blue sash, Japanese wooden flip-flops, and carrying an armload of white towels. "I am Sven. You vish for massage, *ja*?"

Did it have to be from him? Most women might find Sven the stuff dreams were made of, but Samantha had had better luck with wishes than dreams lately, and Kal was the main reason.

She glanced at him. He was dark to Sven's lightness, and she couldn't stop the excited flip in her belly when their gazes met. So much for fragile emotions and significant moments; that chemistry was alive and well between them and on its way to full-on combustion.

"Sam? Would you like a massage?" Kal asked.

She would actually, but only if Kal was the one doing the massaging. Given her recent thoughts, now probably wasn't the best time to answer that question. Especially with Sven as an audience.

She shook her head and walked toward a stone basin

that was filled from a waterfall flowing over a rock wall beneath a flowering mimosa tree. The tree's feathery, pink flowers swayed in the steam rising from the water. Beside it, on an alabaster pedestal, a self-strumming ebony harp's harmony mingled with the melody of the gurgling water. On the other side stood Sven's massage table beneath a bamboo pergola covered in purple morning glory.

She fluttered her fingers in the water. Too bad it was warm. She'd been hoping for ice cold, but then, the water would have to have come from a glacier not a thermal pool, and with the way Kal was looking at her, she wasn't so sure even a glacier would do the trick of cooling her down.

"I think I'll park myself here." She sat in one of the white rattan lounge chairs in front of the hot tub, set the lantern on the table beside her, and fluffed a cushion behind her head. "I could use a nap since I'm still on California time. It's pretty late for me." And she could give her brain and her hormones a time-out.

Kal conjured up a daiquiri on the table next to her then nodded toward the basin. "What about a soak in the thermal pool?"

Yes, that's what she needed: to get drunk and naked in hot, frothing water around him. She brushed the glitter off the tabletop. "No thanks. The nap will do."

"There's food in the next room. Whatever you want."

"Seriously, Kal, I'm fine. I ate a lot earlier tonight. Today. Whatever."

"You're sure? All you have to do is make a wish."

She *knew* that. That was half the problem. "Actually, Kal, I do wish for something. I wish *you'd* get the massage." Hmm, semantics did have their uses. That ought to put an end to his questions.

Only… it raised more when Kal walked out of a dressing room—or rather, the *un*dressing room—a few minutes later clad in only a towel: namely, *Albert who?* and *What had happened to her tongue?*

Samantha took a sip of her drink, trying to cool down while his hard, cut muscles flexed and contracted as he climbed onto the table to lay on his stomach, and the hot tub behind her bubbled its invitation to get naked—which Kal already was, and only by a few judicious towel adjustments did he remain decent while her thoughts were anything but.

"You doing okay, Sam?" Seeing him with his arms crossed beneath him, his shoulders bulked up more than they already were, and his smile just this side of come-hither, Samantha was definitely okay and moving right along to rapturous.

She nodded and took a big gulp of the daiquiri. Ouch. Cold headache. But at least it got rid of the fire burning through her.

Samantha closed her eyes and laid her head back. She had to remember that: A) she was exhausted, emotional, and had been transported so far outside her comfort zone that unless she had Kal with her, she wouldn't have a prayer of ever seeing her comfort zone again; B) the guy she was depending on for her comfort was a genie; C) this fascination she felt for him wasn't real—oh, it was real in the sense that she felt it, but he was a *genie*; and D) she couldn't have a future with a genie.

Who says you need a future with him? What about a few hours? A week? A guy who needs nothing from you and can give you whatever you want; what more could a girl want?

Clarity. Sleep. A cold shower.

She made the mistake of opening one eye just in time to see Sven working oil into Kal's back. Make that *two* cold showers.

She drained the daiquiri, glad that Kal was face down on the table so he couldn't conjure up another one for her *comfort*. She'd never been into the idea of two men, but the sight of Kal being oiled up was making her so not comfortable right now. Not *un*comfortable, just *not* comfortable.

Wiggling in her chair, Samantha tried to *get* comfortable, but with him half naked—or more—on the table in front of her with slick, oiled muscles and that gorgeous head of hair her fingers were clamoring to run through, that wasn't happening.

She'd never had this kind of chemistry with anyone before, and Samantha was finding it hard to remember that she'd just met him. And he was a genie, for Pete's sake. A *genie*. Magical, mythological. Here to see to her every need and desire.

Honest.

An utterly dangerous combination on a good day, let alone in her frame of mind.

Samantha rolled onto her side and felt for the mechanism that would lower the back of the chair, hoping to put him out of her line of sight and then her thoughts, but she couldn't find the damned thing.

She moved again, inadvertently knocking the lantern off the table, but she caught it before it smashed onto the terra-cotta tiled floor. Damn. She could *not* get comfortable. Huffing, she set the lantern on the tiles and felt around again for the lever. Her fingers had just closed over it when the chair back lowered as if by magic...

She opened her eyes, her startled gaze meeting Kal's intense one as his fingers were just finishing the movement. She didn't even have to say anything before he gave her that sexy half smile she so liked.

"It *is* my job to make sure you're comfortable."

He wasn't talking about the chair.

Samantha gulped and reached for the daiquiri—which was now full again. She could use the cold headache.

As Sven worked up Kal's back, Samantha gave serious thought to dumping the drink over her own head, but instead, she slammed her eyes closed. She wasn't into voyeurism, and needed no more encouragement to project herself into the events on that table.

She needed a nap big time. With the memorial service, Albert's betrayal, finding out her father had had a genie locked in his safe for thirty-five years, the trek to Izaaz with all its attendant issues, the events of the day, and the feelings Kal evoked—not to mention the sight of Sven and Kal—she was pretty much done in. Nothing a nap wouldn't cure.

She hoped.

Blowing out a breath, Samantha crossed her arms and focused on the soothing trickle of water, willing herself to relax.

———

Kal was trying to relax, but he kept imagining Samantha's hands on his skin. *Wanting* Sam's hands on his skin.

He peeked beneath his arm at her on the chaise.

He'd planned for her to get the massage, but then she'd wished for him to, and well, her wish was his command.

Kal grunted when Sven hit a knot beneath his shoulder blade. The ironic thing was that he wanted Samantha's wishes to be his commands—and not in any way that had to do with The Service or his sentence. She'd looked so adorable making her rundown of wishes, and Kal had felt sick to his stomach as he counted at least seventy-two of them. In the grand scheme of things, seventy-two weren't that many, but she'd just gotten started and Izaaz needed a lot of magic. It'd been a stroke of demi-genie genius to fix up this part of the spa under the guise of seeing to her comfort, but he couldn't do the same thing for the rest of Izaaz. She'd have to use her wishes.

He didn't want her to. And that worried him.

Samantha shifted in her sleep, a soft murmur on her lips. He wished he could hear it, but unfortunately, his wishes didn't count for anything—and if he wanted them to, he had to keep his eyes on the final prize and *off* Samantha. Already, she meant more to him than any other master he'd had before. Not wanting her to make wishes? Coming up with an excuse to prevent her from making a wish? He had to be out of his mind.

She couldn't—*shouldn't*—be anything more to him than a means to an end. A way out. The way to regain his reputation and secure the job that should have been his two thousand years ago. He couldn't risk any of it because of this growing attraction she held for him.

But, gods, did he want to hold *her*.

Sven hit another nerve, and Kal sucked in a breath.

"You're tense, *min vän*," Sven said softly. "Is it because your sentence is almost complete and you will be able to seize your destiny, or because you don't know what that destiny is?"

The mystic powers of Nordic elves were legendary, and Kal would have loved to ask Sven what the future held, but he wasn't sure he really wanted to know.

He exhaled and it had nothing to do with Sven's massage techniques. Always, he'd been certain that once he was free, he'd recoup his loss and take his rightful place in the Djinn hierarchy. Why wasn't he so sure now?

Samantha shifted again, and Kal knew why. But he didn't want to admit it because admitting to feeling something for her, something beyond the master/genie relationship, was tantamount to giving up all he'd worked for. A genie who fell in love with his master risked it all: honor, position, magic, immortality. Three simple words took it all away. Kal hadn't come this far to give it all up now.

Samantha curled her legs up and tucked her hands beneath her cheek like a child, and Kal wondered what her children would look like. The thought slashed into him deeper than the sharpest *jambaya*. He exhaled again, allowing Sven to think it was from the knot he'd just released, although, knowing Sven, he probably knew the truth.

Zift. Kal had spent lifetimes with his masters, had watched them marry, have children and grandchildren, all things he'd never have. Before Faruq had yanked the *killim* out from under him, he'd been fine with it; the honor of his position and the career he would've had had filled any void.

But after watching it happen again and again, knowing he was so far from anything he wanted... it'd been rough. And now, imagining Samantha carrying someone's child... Gods, that hurt in a way that made Sven's deep-muscle massage seem like a feather over Kal's skin.

Samantha snuggled into her hands, and Kal wanted her to do that against him so fiercely that he waved his fingers so the robe on the other divan floated over to cover her. Lying there in that outfit, she was sexier than when he'd first magicked it onto her, and seeing her in it took this torture to a whole other level. What had he been thinking?

He hadn't. After a hundred and sixty years of celibacy and with Samantha and freedom within his grasp, Kal had wanted it all.

As she tugged the robe over her shoulder and snuggled into it, Kal realized that now he was close to *risking* it all.

13

SAMANTHA WAS IN THE HALF-WAKEFUL STAGE BE-
tween dreaming and reality and was hoping to hold off
on reality for as long as possible because, in her dream,
she was the one oiling Kal down.

Her fingers twitched, and she wanted to run them
over his shoulders. Down his arms. Over his abs. Feel
the strength in his muscles, feel them contract when she
touched him.

"Samantha."

Of course, if he said her name like that in reality, half
whispered with a hint of yearning, she might just wake
up and let reality in.

"Samantha," he whispered again.

She tried to answer him, but she couldn't utter the
words. Her lips were too dry, and with the way her
breasts were tingling, all she'd probably be able to get
out was a moan.

Not a good thing, moaning in your sleep when the
two guys not fifteen feet away would be witness to it.
So much for the curative effects of a nap. She shifted on
the bed. Chair. Whatever.

"Samantha." A little louder now.

Samantha opened her eyes. Had he really said her name?

But… no. That couldn't be. He was still face down on
the table and Sven was working on his shoulders, but,

man, the guy sparked some extremely realistic dreams. Or maybe that was wishful thinking.

Her face—and the rest of her—burning, Samantha shifted in her chair again. She could *not* get comfortable, and it was all Kal's fault. His job might be to see to her comfort, but he was also responsible for her *dis*comfort.

Why'd he have to be so nice to her? So protective? So unselfish?

So... *honest*.

She looked at him. Hot, too. Couldn't forget that. Hell, she wouldn't be female if she forgot that.

Not that it—he—was all that easy to forget. Broad shoulders and supple, sleek, well-defined biceps, strong enough to lift her to just the right height, rippled beneath his skin when Sven kneaded them. Long, muscular legs and the tight mounds of his butt beneath the towel. A glimpse of toned flank when he shifted... mouthwatering.

If he ever decided to give up being a genie, he could change his name to Adonis and no one would bat an eye. Well, actually, she'd bet women everywhere would bat an eye. Swish their hips or shimmy their shoulders just to get his attention.

And he was all hers.

Despite the thick robe, Samantha shivered. He *was* hers, her genie, and there'd been no mention in his rules about not fraternizing. All she had to do was wish, he'd said. She was wishing all right. She wished to be the one stroking his back. To thread her fingers through his hair. Massage the oil into his skin.

Her breath fluttered. So did her tummy. Could she? *Should* she?

She held her breath. The water gurgled behind her, and the feathery pink flowers floated above her. Sven's fingers still kneaded Kal's back, but no magical answers rained down from the sky. No letters magically appeared on the cushion in front of her, telling her what she should do. The only way that would happen was if she wished them to, and since Kal would be the one granting that wish, it seemed kind of pointless to wish for something when doing was so much better.

Samantha set the robe on the chair next to her and walked to the table, pantomiming to Sven that she wanted to take over. Some wishes didn't have to be spoken to come true.

Sven's blue eyes twinkled when he smiled. He nodded, allowing Samantha's left hand to replace his, then the right. With a quick squeeze on her shoulder, Sven disappeared through the wall of morning glory, no magic involved in that at all.

When Samantha's palms flattened on Kal's back, however, magic poured through her.

His skin was perfect. Smooth yet rough. Masculine. Stretched tight over sleek muscles yet with enough give that she knew it'd be perfect to rest her cheek against. She knew how it smelled, wished she knew its taste—and couldn't condemn herself for wanting to know.

No, the only thing she'd condemn herself for was if she didn't find out. And this time, she knew going in that it wouldn't be forever. This wasn't the fairy tale. Not with a genie. But it just might be magical.

She ran her palms from the base of his neck out to his shoulders, her fingers tracing his collarbone. His pulse throbbed there. So did hers.

"Samantha."

It wasn't a question.

She traced her fingers along his spine, massaging the muscles on either side, and traced around his shoulder blades, her fingers gliding over the coiled muscles. Kal groaned, the deep longing causing an ache to start between her thighs.

She slid the tips of her fingers along his back and down his obliques to his waist, every solid muscle contracting at her touch and causing an answering contraction in her belly. Just touching him turned her on, and the memory of what it'd felt like to kiss him made her hotter.

She wanted to kiss him again. Wanted him to kiss her again. Wanted to feel wanted and desired by the one man who wanted nothing from her but that.

She changed the angle, her palms now resting against his skin, and she pressed upward. Kal inhaled long and deep, then released it even deeper. Her fingers danced along the sides of his rib cage, and she felt the quick hitch of his breath.

"Sam. Please."

Oh she pleased. She slid her hands beneath his arms, stroking them over his chest, but the table got in the way.

"Roll over, Kal."

He exhaled a shuddering breath.

"Are you going to make me wish for it?"

He turned before he even answered her, grabbed the back of his neck before she registered it, and kissed her senseless before she had to ask for it.

Samantha fell into the kiss. Plastered across his chest, her outfit, so flimsy and nonexistent, felt as confining as the *djellaba* she'd worn earlier. She wanted to be free. Wanted to feel his skin against hers.

His tongue plunged into her mouth, and Samantha angled her head to take him deeper. Danced hers against his, stroking it, tasting him.

A groan rumbled in Kal's chest and, oh, what that did to the tips of her breasts. The material chafing, Samantha rubbed against him, the friction of the fabric a poor, but necessary, substitute for his skin.

God, she wished he'd touch her.

And then, suddenly he was. Had she uttered that wish out loud or could he read minds?

Samantha didn't know, and, oh God, she didn't care. She wanted this.

His fingers stroked along the sides of her aching breasts, his thumbs circling on her nipples as his tongue did the same thing to hers. Samantha's legs gave out, and she had to brace herself on the table so she wouldn't fall on top of him—which would be a tragedy only because he'd have to stop doing all the delicious things he was doing.

He tweaked the pebbled tip and a straight shot of desire down to her core.

"Kal," she panted against his lips.

"Yes, Sam?"

"I want you." She surprised herself with that, because it wasn't like her to be so up front, but oh God, with him… She really did want him and saying it seemed like the most natural thing in the world.

So did the nip he gave her jaw. "Good. Because I can't get enough of you."

Yeah, she got that. Samantha dug her hands into his

hair and captured his lips, then ran the fingers of one hand down his chest, playing with his nipple every bit as torturously deliciously as he'd done to hers.

He groaned and fell back onto the table, pulling her with him, and kissed her, catching her bottom lip between his teeth.

Samantha's eyes flared open—and she saw him watching her, twin flames of desire burning eyes so dark they were almost black.

She flicked his nipple again and was rewarded by his groan. She slid her lips to his throat, the musky, damp taste turning her legs to jelly.

Kal's palm found her butt, and he helped her stay vertical.

"It's like you can read my mind," she breathed against his skin.

Kal flexed his fingers. "No, that's Sven's talent. Mine is knowing how I want to touch you." One finger slid between her legs, and Samantha moved her hips just enough that it'd find the place she so desperately needed it to. "Gods, Sam, do you know how long I've imagined this? How long I've wanted you?"

She shook her head, running her teeth along his collarbone. He hissed.

"No, Kal, I have no idea. I didn't know you existed before today." A serious shame.

"But I've known all about you." He slid the backs of his fingertips along her arm, capturing her hand and intertwining his fingers with hers. "I've wanted you for years."

Butterflies did the polka in her belly, fluttering away any reservations she had about any of this. She propped her chin on his chest and met his gaze. "Now's your chance."

The gurgle of water punctuated a silence broken only by Kal's harsh indrawn breath. "You're sure, Sam? No question?"

She shook her head and threw caution—and her normally conservative scruples—to the wind. "The only one I have is… are we going to do this here?"

Kal smiled that half smile that turned her insides to mush. "No, Sam. The question is, where shall I put the bed?"

She let her fingers trail over his abs. "I like the way you think."

"That's my line."

"No lines, Kal." Her voice was serious.

Kal's eyes lost their good-natured twinkle and grew just as serious. "That's right, Sam. No lines. No pretenses. Just you and me and what's between us."

She wished he'd kiss her already.

And then he was. If he wasn't reading her mind, she must have uttered that out loud, and frankly, she didn't care.

He wrapped one arm around her back, pinning her to his chest, then spread his other hand over her backside and lifted her so that her legs were between his.

Oh he wanted her all right.

Samantha wiggled against him, her body completely aware of where this was leading, her mind in full agreement, and her hormones singing the "Hallelujah Chorus."

Kal drew his fingers up the crease of her backside slowly, the gauzy fabric heightening the sensation, the action pulling her thong just a little snugger against her. Samantha could feel herself growing damp, could feel the ache growing until she wanted to straddle him.

But Kal wouldn't let her. He hooked one leg over hers and repeated the action.

She panted against him in sweet torture. "Kal…"

"What is your wish, Sam?"

She shook her head. "Not a wish. A desire. I have to do something. Touch you. See you. *Move*."

"All right, Sam—"

"Not here, Kismet! In that courtyard over there!"

The high-pitched voice could only belong to one person. Er, thing. Being.

Fox.

Not that it mattered who it belonged to—Samantha shot up as if she'd been electrified, flung herself off Kal, and only by the grace of God—and Kal's woman-catching ability—did she not take a header onto the floor, somehow managing to make it to her feet and over to the pedestal with the harp before the fox and his mode of transportation soared into view.

"Hi, guys! I mean, lady and guy! Hi, Samantha! I didn't know you played the harp."

Dirham waved from Kismet's back while Samantha tried to catch her breath—and make sure all pertinent parts were covered. The *one* time she let her libido take over…

"Kal, can I come down there? I don't want to take advantage of Kissy's hospitality. She's a double hero, you know. Saved me from a fiery death twice today."

Kal glanced at Samantha and she nodded. As if she could say anything— both literally and figuratively because her breath was still AWOL, and as for her tongue… it was still tied.

"Sure thing, Dir." Kal sat up, and Samantha almost lost

her ability to think with the ripple of his abs and the contraction of his thigh muscles as the towel slid along his leg.

Dirham leapt from Kismet's back onto Samantha's chair while Kal raised an eyebrow and slowly—reeeeally slowly—dragged the towel onto his lap.

Samantha's mouth was as dry as the desert around them by the time it was back in place.

Dirham crawled out from beneath Samantha's chair with Kal's lantern in his mouth. "Hey, you don't want to lose this, Samantha. Lose it and you'll lose Kal."

She was losing something: her mind, her inhibitions, and now Kal's lantern. Losing the lantern would be the worst part.

She felt Kal's gaze on her and looked up to find his dark eyes so intense that they went beyond warm and chocolaty to twin pieces of coal with all the accompanying heat, and she shivered.

"Is there anything to eat around here?" Dirham hopped onto the table next to Kal, his paws pulling the towel dangerously to the side again. Dangerous for both the fox's modesty and her libido. She didn't think Kal would complain at all.

"There's food through that door, Dir," Kal answered, his voice husky, the quick grin he gave her proving her theory. "Help yourself."

He wasn't talking to the fox.

Dirham leapt off the table and was halfway to the door when he stopped—which was probably a good thing since, thanks to Kal's gaze being hot enough to sear straight through her clothes and ignite every nerve ending she possessed, there was no telling what Dirham might interrupt when he came back.

"Oh, darn, I can't. I'm supposed to tell you that you guys have a command performance downtown," Dirham said. "Someone big wants to speak with you."

"How big?" Samantha was thinking ogres. Or trolls. She still didn't know what Orkney was and which was bigger. Or were there giants here, too?

Oh, yeah, that's right. She'd forgotten for a moment (or several) what lay beyond the fence. The strange and wondrous world he'd brought her to.

Of course, it was a wondrous world on this side of the fence, too.

"Who wants to speak with us, Dirham?" Kal tossed a fig at the fox.

Samantha looked around—where had that come from?

The fox pounced on the fruit like a cat with a toy, then balanced it on the end of his nose, spinning it with a paw like a basketball. "Stavros didn't say. He just told me to tell you guys to get back pronto. 'For a history-making visit' is what he said." Dirham flipped the fig into the air and caught it between his teeth, then munched on it. "Coming?"

Not yet…

Samantha made the mistake of looking at Kal, who did his magical nonmind-reading thing again and winked at her.

"We'll be along shortly, Dir." Kal swung his legs over the side of the table and Samantha had to work really hard not to stare at his naked back. God, he was magnificent. "I have to get dressed."

Oh, no he didn't.

"Okay. But I don't have a ride back. I thought I'd go back with you guys."

"I guess that'll work." Kal tossed another fig to the fox and stood, knowing full well the view of his backside Samantha was getting. She could tell from that half smile and the quick glance he sent her.

Tease.

He winked again. That had all sorts of possibilities — one she planned on taking full advantage of as soon as they got to town.

And then they got to town.

14

SAMANTHA WOULDN'T BE TAKING ADVANTAGE OF anything any time soon.

Kal flew them back in the Mercedes, heading in for a landing on the oval marble platform at the end of the main road simply because there was no other place to land.

A parade was in full swing down Main Street, er, Palm Street, and thousands of Izaaz's inhabitants lined it, waving colorful banners as if they were the Munchkins awaiting Glinda's arrival. Matter of fact, one group actually did look like the Lollipop Guild.

Dirham, as usual, was bouncing. On the dashboard in front of her, then onto the space between the seats, then to the luggage shelf in the back; the fox was all over the place.

"Didn't I tell you? Didn't I? Do you like your surprise? Look how great this place looks. See that building over there that you fixed up? That's where my friend George lived before he went off to slay that crocodile. Then you know how that story somehow converted the croc to a dragon? Well, he had to go away to hide from all the celebrity. And Maille, too. She wasn't all that thrilled, no matter how much we tried to explain the misunderstanding to her. But we had some good times there in the old days, me and George."

George? Dragon? Samantha didn't want to make that connection or even try to understand what Dirham was talking about.

"And over there in that courtyard? That's where I saw my first-ever manticore. They're rare, you know, Samantha. They don't like large crowds. And over there, me, Remus, and his brother found one of Mayat's amulets lying on that bench. We took it to Stavros, of course. He gave us some *baklava* as a reward." Dirham's tongue circled his snout. "I love *baklava*."

"I'll put that on my next wish list," Samantha said, patting him. "Matter of fact... Kal? I'd like to wish for a *baklava* bakery for Dirham."

Something—a grimace?—flashed across Kal's face so quickly that Samantha wasn't sure if she'd imagined it or not. But he was smiling now, even had a little chuckle going as he waved his hand and glitter sprinkled the car. "Sixth and Acanthus, Dir. It even has a fox door around back."

Samantha did a double-take at the *fox door* but let her comment go when she heard what the crowd was chanting: "Sa-man-tha! Sa-man-tha!"

"What's going on?" It was more than a little unsettling to have a crowd of thousands calling her name. They'd already thanked her for fixing up the place; what more could they possibly want?

That they wanted more was a given.

Call her jaded—she was—but she didn't open the door to find out, preferring not to know. Unfortunately, Kal did it for her with a wave of his hand. Having a genie to see to your every whim, presumed or otherwise, wasn't necessarily all it was cracked up to be.

"Your public awaits, m'lady," he said.

"Sa-man-tha!" Their chants ratchetted up to full-on scream when the door swung upward. "Sa-man-tha!"

"That's a good thing?"

"'Course it is!" Dirham bounded onto her lap, then out of the car. "Come on! Let's go enjoy your parade! Look at all the pretty colors!"

Colors were not Samantha's focus as she climbed out of the car. Kal was right there to help her, but surprisingly, even *he* wasn't her focus. Nor were the unicorns, centaurs, ogre/trolls, gnomes, leprechauns, satyrs, or any of the other beings that were now normal to her.

Even the new creatures: birds as large as Kismet, half-bull/half-human creatures, Pan and his family, walking, talking Sphinxes, other birds that looked like dodo birds she'd seen in books, a bunch of yetis and Bigfoot— Big*feet* maybe. And a pair of three-headed dogs—did that make them a six pack? And goblins and gremlins and gorgons, oh my. And all of them were repeating her name and flourishing banners as if she were visiting royalty.

But she wasn't. No, the reason they were excited was because of what she'd done for them. And what *more* she could do. It was the same thing all over again. Different place but still the same. And this time, her name shouldn't even be attached to it because they were cheering her for something Kal had done.

Oh, sure, she was the one who'd wished it, but as Stavros had said, only a genie could have pulled the whole thing off. She was merely the vessel through which Kal worked his magic; anyone else could have done the same. She really *was* useless. Just like Albert had said.

Kal flicked his fingers, and the car disappeared in a shower of orange glitter, eliciting another roar of approval from the crowd. Then he intertwined his fingers with hers and Samantha tried to muster a smile, but the truth was hitting her hard.

All her life, she'd been the window dressing. The gatekeeper to the Blaine vaults. Easy access to her father. The so-called friends who'd always been up for the next party or vacation—as long as she picked up the tab. The boyfriends who'd been after only one thing (and *not* what most mothers warned their daughters about). Albert. He'd been the biggest offender. Not only was she useless, but she *was* clueless. Just like he'd said.

One of Pan's fauns trotted up the steps on pink-polished hooves, pulling a suit jacket over her white tuxedo shirt, and taking a pad and pencil from the breast pocket. She palmed something that looked like a hair-brush from took pocket and stuck it in Samantha's face, bottom end up, like Samantha used to do as a teenager in front of her bedroom mirror with a Walkman blasting in her ears.

This scenario was just as fake.

"What's next, Samantha?" the faun yelled above the noise. "What can we expect to see in the coming days? Do you have any more plans?"

Samantha stepped back. Plans? Right now she was dealing with the here and now and the demoralizing realization that she didn't seem to have a purpose to her life, a fact she probably had known but had repressed, since that knowledge almost cut her in two.

Samantha slid her hands around her waist, the lantern dinging her hip. The microphone hung there for an uncomfortable silence until Kal whispered something to the faun that got her to remove it and trot back down the steps.

He slid his hand beneath Samantha's elbow. "Are you okay, Sam?"

Never let them see you sweat. She hadn't let Albert see her break down, and she wouldn't let the citizens of Izaaz.

Or Kal.

She plastered a smile on her face and nodded. "I'm fine, Kal. Let's go greet your public."

Kal looked at her strangely but didn't have the chance to say anything as a group of fairies as tall as four-year-olds (but who definitely didn't *look* like four-year-olds in the flimsy, filmy toga-like things they wore) flew up the steps with leis of beautiful orchids in their hands.

Samantha bent down to accept the delicate gift, her emotions just as fragile. "Thank you," she whispered, her throat clogged with those emotions. She was a fraud. Window dressing yet again.

Oh, she knew no one cared; as long as she gave them what they wanted, they were content. But she wasn't. She didn't want to be arm candy, an ornament accepted only because she looked the part or had the money or magic behind her. She wanted to *be* the part. But without Kal, she had as much chance of that as Dirham did of besting a dragon.

The crash of cymbals accompanied by a quick tempo of drumbeats put an end to that thought none too soon. The last thing she needed was to fall apart in front of the entire population of Izaaz.

Kal moved next to her, and Samantha took a

shuddering breath as the sea of people below them parted. She would get through this; she'd had lots of practice.

A parade came down the street. Miniature blond horses like Lipizzaner stallions with lion-headed, monkey-like tamarins on their saddles and a herd of antelopes with bells on their twisted antlers led the way, followed by a bevy of belly dancers, the finger cymbals and silver bangles on their swishing hips marking the drums' downbeat in time with the crowd's clapping. Several dozen musicians strummed rounded guitar-like instruments or blew into long reed ones, and others shook U-shaped pieces of metal with jangling rings like tambourines.

Behind the musicians, dozens of people followed a palanquin carried by six centaurs, its occupant shielded from view by layers of pastel chiffon veils. A pair of servants held ostrich-feather fans over the procession in a showy display of grandeur, but they were too far removed to be effective.

Samantha could so relate. Without Kal's magic, she'd be just as ineffective. Just as obsolete. Without her wishes, she'd be nobody.

The parade stopped at the bottom of the stairway. The centaurs rotated the litter to the side, then knelt on their front legs. The fairies who'd greeted her and Kal flew down to peel the veils from the seating area of the palanquin.

A tanned, gnarled old man dressed in silk robes and a turban climbed from the interior, and the crowd segued from Samantha's name to, "Ber-o-sus! Ber-o-sus!"

The old man clapped his hands, and a dozen dwarves dashed out of the building closest to the stairway, each carrying a stone. In no time flat, they'd constructed a bridge so he could reach the stairway without having to step foot on the ground.

Samantha took a step forward, but Kal gripped her shoulder. "It will be an insult if you meet him halfway. We should wait here."

She stayed. Bad enough she was a fraud; she didn't want to be an inconsiderate one. "Who is he?" she whispered.

"Berosus," Dirham answered, the "duh" unsaid, but not uninflected.

Kal, however, sucked in a breath and answered, "The Oracle," almost reverently.

"*Oracle*? As in Delphi? Seer of the future? Prognosticator? He who sees all?"

"Not Delphi, Samantha," said Dirham, his tail twitching madly. "Izaaz."

Wherever he was from, an Oracle was an Oracle. Would he see her for the fake she was?

15

KAL COULDN'T BELIEVE BEROSUS WAS HERE. ORACLE revelations were a great honor and rarer than genie magic in Izaaz. Kal should know; he'd petitioned Berosus to reveal the truth about what Faruq had done to clear his name, but his request had been postponed until some gods-knew-when appointed moment that Berosus divined would be the most effective use of his powers.

Maybe that time was now. A little late, given that Kal was on his last master and the High Master was all set to make an announcement, but Kal wouldn't look a gift unicorn in the mouth.

Then Samantha licked her lips and Kal found himself staring at *her* mouth.

Stop it! Kal gripped his hips, his fingers biting into his flesh. He'd been all too focused on Samantha once Monty had explained how he would leave instructions for her to find the lantern after he was gone. Kal had known she would be his last master, and the thought of meeting her, talking to her, touching her, had tortured him whenever Monty had talked about her.

Having done those things, having held her and kissed her, he needed to stop having these kinds of thoughts. They were dangerous not only to his ultimate goal, but also to his heart and the rest of his life, because a genie falling in love with a mortal was not only foolish, but suicidal. Kal already felt more than he should for her, but he hadn't worked through the past two thousand years to give it all up now for something as fleeting as a mortal life.

The animals climbed the steps and leapt onto the amethyst wall, one line to the right, another to the left. Kal tugged Samantha's hand so she'd move to the middle of the platform; he'd witnessed a few Oracle visits and knew the pomp and circumstance mystics expected. Berosus was always good for a show, and Kal was more than willing to indulge him if it meant he'd learn he was pardoned or, better yet, had been appointed vizier.

Belly dancers paraded onto the platform, fanning out in front of the wall and, with a final swish of their hips, sank onto the marble, curling their legs into the lotus position. Amita, an old friend on the end, smiled at him as if she knew what was in store, giving him hope—except that hope was locked up in an old trunk in the corner of Stavros's office and no one but him apparently knew it.

Kal felt for Samantha's hand—merely to calm her nerves; it wasn't every day that a mortal met an Oracle.

That was his story, and he was sticking to it.

However, her fingers still bore traces of the oil she'd rubbed into his skin and there was no way he could deny that he wanted to touch her for any reason other than he hadn't gotten enough of her back in Sven's courtyard.

Kal kneaded his neck muscles with his other hand. *Kharah*, what had he been thinking back there? He'd spilled his guts—"Do you know how long I've wanted you?" Thank the gods he wasn't in love with her, or he might have spouted off about that, too, and then where would he be?

Stuck in the middle of the Arabian Peninsula with a mortal and a pair of angry dragons. Nothing about that was optimal.

Then he got a whiff of that lilac scent of hers, and his body went left while his common sense went right.

Kal dropped her hand. This was not the time, nor the place, to head down the path that'd make him hotter than the desert at noon. He needed to stay focused and hear what the Oracle had to say.

He shifted his stance, thankful for the baggy *sirwal* he wore—until he made the mistake of glancing at her. Then he wished for a camel blanket—the thick, scratchy kind—because that would be the only thing that could take his mind off the fact that she was nibbling her bottom lip. The one he'd licked and sucked and kissed.

Yeah, the pants weren't going to cut it.

"Are you okay, Sam? Is there anything you wish?" Like whisking them out of here. Even Oracles were subject to mortal wishes—or, rather, Oracle revelations took a backseat to any wish Kal was honor-bound to grant.

"No, that's okay." She blinked and her breath hitched. "I'm fine."

Right. And he was a griffin's uncle. Beneath that serene exterior, she looked done in. Fragile.

Kal bit back a frustrated sigh. He'd forgotten what the time change could do to a mortal's system. She had to be physically exhausted on top of all the mind-bending things she'd seen—not to mention what'd been going on when Dirham had interrupted them in the courtyard— yet there she was, valiantly trying to mask her fatigue.

If Berosus were anyone other than the Oracle, Kal

would have postponed this ceremony regardless of what it meant for him personally, but one didn't diss an Oracle without very good reason.

Berosus reached the platform, and the music crescendoed to an abrupt halt. It was probably too much to hope that he'd impart his news just as quickly so that Kal could take Samantha to bed. Not in the carnal way, of course, but just get her *into* bed. To sleep.

Yes, that was the reason he wanted to get her into bed: to sleep.

One of the antelopes snorted. He was kidding no one.

"Welcome, most revered guests." Berosus bowed toward them, then clapped his hands. Half a dozen men in pale yellow *thobes* broke rank from the parade and strode up the stairs carrying a pair of small tables, three upholstered *poufs*, a pillow, and a tea service that they set up in the middle of the platform.

Tea. So much for this being quick.

On the plus side, he now had the chance to get certain body parts under control and cool down.

Then Samantha swayed and Kal put out a hand to steady her, and a certain body part let him know it had no intention of cooling down.

To hide the evidence, Kal bowed lower than he normally would. "It is our honor, *saahbey*. May I present my master, Samantha Blaine?"

Berosus clasped her hands, a great honor and one that meant this audience had nothing to do with Kal.

The thought crossed Kal's mind that, at the very least, he ought to be frustrated that he wouldn't have his request granted, but he was more concerned with getting this over with so Samantha could lie down. The end of his sentence would come regardless, and if that was later rather than sooner, he'd live with it.

Because he'd be living with her.

"I am Berosus, the Oracle of *Madeenat Al-saqf Al-zojaajey*. Welcome to what was once a fair city. Now that you are here, it will be again. It is my honor to thank you for that on behalf of the citizens."

"Thank you for welcoming me," Samantha said, her voice soft and controlled, as if she were at one of those society functions Monty had told him about, except that she wasn't wearing an evening gown, and her bottom lip trembled. Slightly, but Kal saw it. By the gods, what he wouldn't give to be able to take her in his arms and make that look go away.

What he wouldn't give to be able to take her in his arms, period.

Then Berosus swept his hands toward the seating arrangement and that thought got tabled.

For now.

Kal shook his head and offered Samantha his arm as they walked over. It was one thing to want to take her to bed to ease the ache a hundred and sixty years of solitude had created, but a far greater thing to want to take her in his arms and offer her comfort.

More than the physical attraction, he was coming to care for her—and *that* was a thought that needed to be tabled not only for now, but forever.

Dirham bounced ahead of them, landing in the middle of the red cushion on the platform between the *poufs*. The fennec circled around a few times, then lay in the depression he'd created and curled his tail around himself.

Kal didn't have that luxury. All he could do was sit on

the cushion and cross his legs, draping the baggy material of his *sirwal* over his recalcitrant body part.

Four women in long, diaphanous skirts sprinted lightly up the stairs, their movements seductive in the way of *chiwaras*—bipedal half-gazelle/half-human women who were the most innately graceful beings on the planet. But today, they left him cold. Nothing could match the soft brush of Samantha's skin against his, or the flash of fire in her emerald eyes when she smiled.

She wasn't smiling now, and that flash had burned itself out. *Samantha* was on burnout.

He needed to get her out of here, pronto. If only she would wish it, but he had no time to lead her down that train of thought as Berosus levitated onto his cushion with the full pageantry of his role. Kal could only hope this would be quick.

Except hope was still locked up in Stavros's office.

Two of the *chiwaras* brought a *tas* toward Samantha and him. One held the basin, the other a ewer of rosewater and hand towels. Together they stood before him first, then Samantha, for the ceremonial washing of hands. Even Dirham washed his paws and accepted a delicate drinking bowl from another woman who handed Kal and Samantha matching glasses.

A fourth woman carried the teapot from the table to pour sweet mint tea with an impressively long, backward arc that was as beautifully artistic as any he'd ever seen, both the pour and the woman, yet he still found himself wanting to stare at Samantha. *Chiwaras* had held men spellbound for generations, which was why they only served Oracles, one of the few races strong enough to resist their allure.

And now Kal was another.

Seven courses were passed, much too slowly for Kal's liking. He hardly registered the tastes, eating enough to be polite for both of them because Samantha barely had any.

Kal's concern increased by the minute, so by the time the *baklava* was passed—Dirham making sure he got an extra large piece, of course—Kal was looking for any excuse to whisk her away.

Unfortunately, though, Berosus took far too much time, pomp, and circumstance to share his revelation.

After a hookah had been smoked—Samantha declining and Kal accepting only because he figured it'd go quicker that way—Berosus held up his hands. The crowd quieted. He flicked his fingers and the servers retreated to the perimeter wall, leaving the three of them and Dirham center stage.

A rotation of his right wrist conjured a ram's horn which Berosus then spoke into. "As you can see from the masses before us, the citizens of Izaaz are singing your praises, Samantha Blaine. I have always known a great lady would come to their aid, but the Mists and Chaos did not choose to reveal her name nor when she would appear. It was the sound of the citizens' exclamation, the surprise and celebration in their voices, that brought me the truth of who you are." Berosus tapped her on the knee, a blessing in the eyes of the Djinn.

Samantha sucked in a quivering breath and blinked.

Gods, she really was exhausted. Kal felt like an ass for not recognizing it sooner. He should have insisted she get the massage—

Not the place to go at the moment.

"Ah, you mustn't cry, *haanim*," said Berosus. "It is the citizens who should weep for your largesse." He raised his tea. "I toast you, Samantha Blaine, for giving the citizens of this city hope."

Kal refrained from mentioning Pandora's box.

"Their eyes have been opened to the mistakes of the past, and it is a foolish being who does not learn from those mistakes, for they are destined to be repeated unless one does. Changing one's history changes one's destiny."

Berosus sat back, a serene smile on his face, as if the allegory were easily understood.

Kal didn't understand any of this. The logic made no sense—as Oracle revelations were wont to do. Parables and allegories, cryptic at their best, indecipherable at their worst. Kal had never had so much riding on one as he did on this one—and he didn't understand a single word. Samantha hadn't changed anything about the past in Izaaz, merely where they'd go from here.

But people not only didn't diss an Oracle, they also didn't question him.

"And to show our appreciation, we wish to present you with this." Berosus clapped his hands and a trio of trumpeters sounded their rams' horns as another servant carried a gold-braided cushion on an engraved silver platter over to them.

Dirham leapt onto Kal's *pouf* and stretched his neck to see what was going on, his claws digging into Kal's knee.

Berosus stood and took a silver chain from the cushion, dangling an orange gemstone fashioned into the shape of an eagle in front of Samantha. Then he placed it over her head.

"Please wear this as a sign of our appreciation and

know that the knowledge you need is always in your heart," he said while Dirham let out a "Cool!" and started bouncing again.

Kal didn't know how cool it was. The eagle was a symbol of knowledge and the orange gemstone representative of his personal carnelian. What those two had to do with the so-called revelation, Kal didn't know. And what he didn't know worried him.

"And now," said Berosus, patting Dirham on the head, then sitting back on his *pouf*, "we will celebrate with a dance."

Kal almost groaned. Celebratory dances could last for hours. He wouldn't mind if Samantha made a wish right now—any wish—so that they could get out of here. Then he'd have the chance to figure out what Berosus was talking about. There was a clue in there somewhere, as was typical of Oracles, because if the revelations were too easy to understand, anyone could fancy himself an Oracle.

Kal didn't care who fancied what. All he wanted was some sign from Samantha that she was about to make a wish so they could take off.

A tear trickling down her cheek worked just as well.

Kal levitated and uncrossed his legs from the lotus position as he hovered above the *pouf*, uncaring that he was breaking every protocol there was in dealing with Oracles. His master's well-being came above all else, and Samantha needed his care.

He held out his hand. "Sam?"

Her tongue flicked out to lick her bottom lip and her eyelashes fluttered. Twin pools of glistening emerald blinked up at him. "Yes?" Her voice was husky as she dashed the tear from her cheek and placed her hand in his.

Berosus waved off the servants who'd started forward at Kal's gross misconduct, just as Kal would expect. The Oracle knew The Code of Djinn Conduct as well as he did. Probably better since Berosus had had a hand in crafting it, though The Code read like an elementary school primer compared to that allegorical mess the man had just spouted.

"Sam, would you like to make a wish?" Kal asked.

Samantha cleared her throat and curled her fingers over his.

Did she want to make a wish? Dear God, yes. Every word this man had spoken had been another lance to her self-esteem. And the gift? Another jab at the farce this scene had become, and she had no idea how to put an end to it.

Her. Giving them hope. Changing history. Changing destiny. She was a fraud, for God's sake. Was she supposed to come out and tell everyone? Stand up and shout from the rooftops that she'd had only the smallest part in fixing things? That without Kal she was useless? And that their supposed all-knowing Oracle didn't know a thing about her?

She touched the stone hanging between her breasts. Dirham was wrong; it wasn't cool. There was some warmth to it. She was the one who was cold.

Thank God Kal had given her a way out. "Yes, Kal, I do want to make a wish. Everything's catching up to me." That was a way to phrase the fact that Albert's betrayal had nothing over her own self-doubt, and this guy, this supposed Oracle, had only shredded it even more. "I wish we could go somewhere and rest."

"Ooh! Ooh! I know where you can take her, Kal!" Dirham bounced on his cushion. "There's a hoodoo with your name on it. Well, not your actual name because, you know, that's going to take a little while to carve and no one thought to wish for that, but the *peris* spruced up one of the vacant ones just for you guys, making it all nice and cozy inside. And there's some food and pomegranate juice and even a shower. You should see it, Samantha."

Dirham shook himself. "Oh, I guess you will when Kal takes you there. Is that okay, Berosus, I mean, Your Most Supreme Oracle? Kal wouldn't have interrupted if it weren't important, and he's right. Samantha has been up a very long time. You're okay with that, aren't you? I mean, she has Kal's lantern and received your revelation so she's all set to go, right?"

Samantha didn't know whether to kiss Dirham or muzzle him. Kal, too.

Then Kal linked their fingers and, scratch that; she knew exactly which she'd choose for him. He waved his other hand, and a plume of orange smoke clouded the Oracle's smiling face as he waved good-bye to them.

That rushing feeling came over her again. Her body felt as if grains of sand were pinging it as she traveled on an air current at the speed of light, the analogy to her life sadly illuminating.

But as quick as she'd thought it (the flying thing, not her life story) the rush was over and the smoke drifted away to reveal a tall, cone-shaped, Dr. Seuss-like building with a flat, round stone covered in mosaic tiles standing on edge atop the chimney. A pair of crooked, barren trees straight out of Whoville graced either side of the funky arched door that swung open with another wave of Kal's hand.

Inside, vibrantly dyed silk panels covered the walls above a mahogany dresser inlaid with gold filigree, and a matching pair of night tables sat on either side of the silk-covered bed that invited one to do anything but sleep.

Part of her was up for that. The other part wasn't up at all. The nap hadn't even taken the edge off her fatigue; the rest of the day's events had only added to it.

"Samantha? Are you okay?" Kal asked, holding the door open so she could enter. He must have *never* had a girlfriend to ask that question.

She removed the eagle necklace. It'd be more true to life if it were an albatross.

She set it and the lantern on the dresser. "If it's all the same to you, Kal, I just wish to be alone for a little while."

16

Nothing like tying his hands. And not in any way that had to do with the silver cuffs that bound him to The Service.

Kal sat on the end of the bed and looked at his hands as they hung between his knees, the image of Samantha tying them—preferably to the bedpost—front and center in his mind. She was tying him in knots, too.

She'd wished to be alone, not revisit what had happened between them at the spa. He would put her mood down to being exhausted, but the tear and her wish said it was more than that. Thankfully, though, she hadn't put a longer time frame or location on that wish, but even a few minutes was too long when she was so sad.

He looked at the door to the bathroom with half a mind to drag her out to talk to him, but the Roman plumbing came on, and the image of Samantha in the shower not only nailed him to the bed but had him wanting.

The memory of her hands on him had him aching.

The taste of her had him longing.

But the tears in her eyes had him worrying. Which meant he had work to do. After all, with or without his magic, his job was to see to her well-being. His mental musings would be far better used in figuring out the cliché platitude wrapped around an enigma disguised as a profound revelation Berosus had given them instead of trying to figure out what was bothering her. She'd tell him when she wanted to.

The bigger issue was what in *Al-Jaheem* Berosus had meant.

Kal picked up the eagle necklace and ran his fingers over it. As far as knowledge went, the eagle was imparting none.

He closed his eyes and tried to summon the power the carnelian held. Djinn were tuned in to the properties of gems; the stones enhanced magical powers like a life force and became the Glimmer their magic released, but this one was doing nothing for him.

Sighing, Kal opened his eyes and his fist. The stone looked exactly the same, no light inside it as in others he'd held, and he was no closer to the answer than before he'd held it.

He set it on the side table, cranked the skylight open, then lay back on the bed's silk coverlet, replaying Berosus's riddle. What did it mean? What were they supposed to learn? To know?

Kal tried translating the words into other languages to see if there were different meanings, different interpretations, but nothing came to him.

Kharah! How was he supposed to take care of Samantha if he couldn't figure out what the Oracle had been trying to tell them?

He couldn't let Monty down. Monty had kept his lantern in that safe, locked away except for when they'd played chess, to ensure that Kal would be around to look out for Samantha when Monty wouldn't be. That was the promise he'd demanded of Kal. Not wished, but demanded. He'd given Kal a choice, though as far as Kal was concerned, there had been no choice. His job was to look after his master, so look after her he would. But he'd given Monty his word as a man, not a genie.

And now he was failing both his last master and his job.

Kal pinched the bridge of his nose. There had to be something. Some key to figuring out Berosus's riddle.

He tried to will his mind to go blank. To stop thinking and let his subconscious work it out. Sometimes intuitive reasoning could come up with the answer the conscious brain couldn't. He'd learned the technique from his sixteenth master. Tansar had been a high priest and a scholar; getting him to make wishes had been harder than milking a camel—and Tansar hadn't let him do even *that* by magic.

Kal closed his eyes and took several deep breaths. He focused on the blue sky above Izaaz, and imagined the flow of water over the Weeping Wall, the lush palms that lined its verdant shoreline. Peaceful, serene, floating wherever the water and his thoughts took him.

He opened his eyes and looked up. The sky was no longer blue; the open capstone allowed the beginnings of the pale-pink evening sky into the room. Pale-pink sky that would lead to the darkness of night. When he and Samantha would be here, sharing the hoodoo.

The shower cut off and Kal's imagination went into overtime. More so when the towel rack jiggled and the mental image of Samantha wrapping a towel around her damp, naked body followed.

Kal cursed in Akkadian, the only language that had

just the nuance he needed, and one unused enough to make him have to think about it and not Sam.

So much for meditation. He actively—forcibly—turned his thoughts to the revelation. Something, *anything* to get that image of her out of his head, because *that* had never been part of Monty's plan.

His own, on the other hand… Kal shook his head. *The revelation. Focus on the revelation.*

The part about changing history bugged him the most. Oracles chose their words carefully, each one wrapped in a layer of meaning like an onion wrapped in its transparent yet strong skin. Berosus couldn't possibly mean Samantha was to undo Faruq's arrest, could he? Did he want Kal to transport her back to that point so they could do something to prevent Faruq from getting himself arrested, which would then ripple down through time so that the citizens wouldn't abandon the town? And if so, what did that mean for him personally? Was that why he still had no clarification on his own request?

Frustration clawed at him—on many levels. Was he going to have to give up the chance at the job he wanted for Samantha? Gods, he hoped not. He was so close he could touch the title. To have to give it up for a master…

Not just any *master*.

And that was the problem. Sam *wasn't* just any master. But she was still a master and a means to an end, and if she wished for him to do something about Faruq, his hands were tied.

It came back to that.

And when she walked out of the bathroom in just the towel and damp tendrils of hair clinging to her neck, he was still tied in knots.

He jumped to his feet, then sat on the wrought-iron chair at the table beside the door. The bed was the last place he should be with Sam in the room.

"Kal, what's going on?" She nodded at the necklace. "What does he want from me?"

All sorts of answers lined up to be voiced, but they were what *Kal* wanted from her, not Berosus. And if he knew what Berosus wanted, Kal could skip the vizier post and go straight to High Master. "I don't know, Sam. Oracles are typically obtuse. I say we sleep on it. Things are bound to look better in the morning."

Then her towel slipped a half inch lower, and he didn't see how anything would look better than that.

"Would you like something to sleep in?" *Please, gods, say* yes, *and not a bed covered in rose petals and surrounded by candlelight.*

Although…

"A nightgown would be nice, yes. Thanks."

Kal waved his hand. That was what he'd meant, but covering such perfection was a sacrilege. Just as it would be to sleep in this room and not touch her.

He didn't know if he *could* not touch her.

That decided it. He was going to spend the night in his lantern, which showed how dire their—no, *his*—circumstance really was. Voluntarily sequestering oneself in one's lantern wasn't done without careful thought and consideration, but it was a better idea than spending the night out here wanting what he shouldn't have.

"The robe's a nice touch. Thank you."

Kal opened his eyes. Sea green, the plush robe brought out the color of her eyes and covered her better than that *djellaba*. Saved his sanity, too. Barely.

"My pleasure."

She started to say something but ended up nibbling on her lip. Gods. That was an image he'd take with him into the lantern where he'd have to do what he'd done over the past one hundred and sixty years to relieve his frustration.

He adjusted the waistband of his *sirwal*, redistributing the fall of the fabric. "If you don't need anything else, Sam, I'll be going."

Question was, how was he going to get to his lantern without walking past her? Climbing over the bed wasn't a better idea.

The situation got more complicated when she walked around that bed and put her hand on his arm. "You're leaving me?"

Not in a thousand years. Hell, it'd taken him two thousand to find her.

"I thought I'd spend the night in my lantern." Him and his good intentions...

"Oh. Is that what genies do? I thought you didn't like being in there."

Normally, no. Tonight a lot of things were different. "It's okay, Sam. It's comfortable in there. I have a kitchen and a den, some workout equipment, a bed."

A very big bed. A very big, comfortable bed. A very big, comfortable, *lonely* bed.

"Oh. Okay. Well, I guess I'll see you in the morning and we can figure all of this out. What should I do with your lantern? Keep it here on the table or somewhere else?"

On the pillow was too corny of an answer. And too tempting.

Not that he would be able to do anything about that once he was inside. Which, with the way the water from the shower had dewed on her shoulder, the way that tendril was drying and springing to life right in that soft spot beneath her ear, and the way that hint of cleavage at the vee of her robe was beckoning him, was a really good thing. The only way he would be able to leave the lantern was if she summoned him, so they'd both be safe—her from him and him from himself.

"That's fine, Samantha. I'll be right here if you need me."

And with that, Kal summoned his smoke cloud and whisked himself inside the lantern and out of temptation's way.

Kal disappeared before her eyes, and Samantha felt the loss immediately. If she needed him? God, he didn't know how on target he was with those words.

Was it wrong to want to wish him to hold her? Just lie next to her and hold her all night and tell her that it was all going to be okay? That it was okay if everyone thought she was something she wasn't? That it was okay to use him for his magic so she'd look good in the eyes of the citizens of Izaaz and the Oracle?

That she wasn't totally useless?

Samantha pulled back the silk bedcovering and climbed between the cotton sheets. Fifteen hundred count, if she wasn't mistaken. Heh. There was something else she was good at: picking out good bedding. Not totally useless.

Samantha flopped back onto the pillow. She was

wallowing and that wasn't like her. And she wasn't use-less. Not really. So she couldn't fix this place without magic; big deal. No one but Kal could, either—and they *had* magic. Besides, it wasn't as if they thought *she* was the one doing the magic; they expected her to use Kal's powers to their benefit. That's how it worked.

So why was she upset about it?

They needed help, and she could provide it. No one expected anything different. She, however, did. Albert's words stung. The truth in them. So she'd seen a chance to help out and she had; how was that any different than what she did with the charities back home? There was a need for her services, and she fulfilled it.

But she wanted to be more than that. Wanted some-thing she could be proud of—she wasn't very proud of herself for allowing Albert to run Dad's company. She should have stepped in. Should have manned up, as the saying goes, and taken the responsibility. But it'd been easier not to. Easier to allow Albert to do it while she sat at Dad's bedside.

Well, she didn't have that excuse now. Dad was gone, the company wasn't, and Albert would be as soon as she got home. Then it would all be up to her. The question was: Was she up for the challenge? Was she up for more than just being a mouthpiece?

She punched the pillow, trying to get more comfort-able, but sadly, not only didn't it work, but she didn't think anything would make her more comfortable.

Saying she was going to take over was all fine and good, but if she'd thought Albert's learning curve had been steep, hers was going to be almost vertical.

Then again… she had a genie to help her.

But was that what she really wanted? How did using Kal to do her job make her any less useless than she was now?

She flopped back onto the pillow. She'd think about that tomorrow; today had been enough to wrap her brain around.

Samantha pulled the sheets up. The skylight was open and it was getting chilly. She was about to close it when a shooting star arced across the sky in the center of the opening and she decided to keep it open. Maybe she should make a wish.

Samantha snorted. Make a wish. That's hadn't solved any of her problems yet, merely created new ones.

She ran a finger along Kal's lantern. He was in there. What did he see when he looked out? What was it like looking at the inside of a lantern day in and day out for years?

Four thousand of them.

She rubbed her forehead. She had to stop thinking. Her emotions were getting the best of her. She needed to get some sleep. She'd been up for over twenty-four hours; no one thought clearly after being awake that long, especially with all the upheaval she'd been through. Kal was right. Everything would look better in the morning.

Funny how he turned out to be right about that—but not in the way either of them had thought he'd meant. And then, only for a little while. A *very* little while.

17

KAL TOSSED FOR THE EIGHT HUNDRED AND TWELFTH time. Counting had become second nature over the centuries and tonight was no different.

He just hoped he didn't get to one thousand and one.

Between Berosus's riddle and Samantha in that towel, he made it to eight hundred and seventeen before he finally got out of bed. Naked, he stretched the aches and stiffness out of his back. He'd fallen asleep for forty-five minutes after relieving himself of pent-up desire. Sadly, that relief had lasted all of about ten minutes. Not even an hour's reprieve.

If only she'd offer him the lantern and his freedom, he wouldn't have to suffer like this. He could fly out of here and focus on the rest of his life.

But now all he could focus on was her. He kept visualizing her in that towel. That damn towel. A three-foot-long piece of plain, white cotton fueled his imagination in a way that even the outfit he'd conjured up for her couldn't. Being with Samantha until this Servitude was over was going to be rough.

That thought—of it being over—socked him in the gut enough to double him over. And before he had a chance to analyze it and try to talk himself out of the logical conclusion he'd eventually come to, something *else* socked him in the gut harder than that thought.

Samantha was crying. It was soft and it was faint, but it was definitely a sob. And there wasn't a damn thing he could do about it.

Her face must be right there next to the lantern, her lips so close he'd be able to touch them if not for the thin copper between them, but she could have been on the other side of the world for all the good it'd do him.

There was nothing he could do for her. He was stuck inside the lantern. Gods, what had made him think spending the night in here would be a good idea?

When she sobbed again, the wrench in his heart reminded him why—and mocked him at the same time.

Kal strode to the lantern wall and waved his hand, the habit still ingrained despite the fact that his magic hadn't worked in here in two thousand years. Frustrated, he yanked the pull string on the copper shade that darkened the inside of his prison cell, and it retracted into the slot in the ceiling.

Not exactly a window, this section of his lantern was transparent from the inside, but the special alloy kept those outside from seeing in. Only Dirham's rainbow paintings created enough light to penetrate to the outer world.

He was seeing anything but rainbows right now.

Samantha's face, twitching as she fought whatever bad dream she was having, was so close he could almost reach out and stroke her cheek. A tear traced across the bridge of her nose, and Kal put his hand against the cool copper surface, trying to wipe it away.

"Wake up, Sam."

She sniffled and her tongue wet her lips.

"Samantha! Wake up, sweetheart." The endearment

slipped out, and Kal let himself enjoy it for a moment—until another tear tracked down her cheek. This one she swatted away, her fingers jerking against his lantern, toppling it onto the bed with her.

Kal groaned as he braced himself against the movement. As it was, the beer he'd taken only a few swigs of earlier fell off his bedside table and banged him on the shoulder, frothing all over his bed. Well, he hadn't been getting much sleep there before; what did it matter now?

She sobbed again.

Kharah! That was a sound he couldn't stand. "Samantha. Wake up, honey. Wish me out of here."

She shifted again, her hand stroking across the lantern—just enough to open the lid.

Kal was out of there before she took another breath and accidentally closed it. Which she did with the next sob. This one was accompanied by a little moan.

Kal materialized from his orange smoke into the bed beside her, wrapped his arms around her, and rolled her toward him, cradling her face against his shoulder. "Sssh, sweetheart. Don't cry. It's just a bad dream." She smelled so good. Lilacs had become his favorite flower.

She shifted and her cheek was soft as it brushed against his lips, her hair silky beneath his fingers, her nightgown sensuous against his body—

His naked body.

Kal realized his predicament right before it got worse—or better, depending on your take on the situation, but the situation was that Samantha had curled into him and wrapped her arm around his waist.

He had every intention of untangling himself to find that damned towel and put some kind of barrier between them. That silky negligee he hadn't been able to resist conjuring for her was nowhere close to being called a barrier, and even the towel would be doubtful, but at least it'd be thicker than silk.

But then Samantha murmured his name and Kal's intentions went on hiatus.

She snuggled into him, her breath moist and warm against his throat, and completely new intentions showed up.

Desire swamped him. He wanted to pull her atop him, plunge his tongue into her mouth, his cock into her warm, tight wetness, and give them both the best dreams they'd ever had. But if he did, he'd be the biggest ass any genie had ever been.

She rubbed her cheek against his chest, and Kal shuddered. Gods, what she did to him.

"Sam? Honey? I don't think this is a good idea." Well, actually he did, but it really shouldn't be. He needed to find out what was bothering her. They needed to talk.

She sighed against him, and when she turned her face just a bit to the left—atop his heart—Kal knew there wasn't going to be any talking.

He'd thought the sound of her sobs socked him in the gut? That had nothing compared to the feel of her lips against his skin. He palmed the back of her head, resisting the urge to run his fingers through her curls.

Almost.

"Samantha. Please. Sweetheart. Wake up. This isn't a good idea." His good intentions tried to come to the rescue, but then her head lifted of its own volition and green eyes opened slowly. Watery green eyes.

"Kiss me, Kal."

"Samantha, I really don't think—"

"Kiss me, Kal. I wish you'd kiss me."

When she put it like that—

Kal kissed her. And he wasn't kidding himself that it had anything to do with the fact that she'd wished it—because he would have done it without the word *wish*.

He speared his fingers through her hair and deepened the kiss. He couldn't help himself; it was as if he were starving and she the only sustenance around.

Samantha slid her hand down his back, over the curve of his ass, and he couldn't stop the thrust that happened naturally. She groaned and it undid him.

He changed the angle of his head, and his tongue danced with hers, the fire sweeping over him so fast it was as if dragons were feuding around them, but Kal had no intention of dousing it.

Samantha's hands were everywhere, sliding up his spine, fanning out to trace over his hipbone, stroking down toward his groin, stealing his breath as her fingers came so utterly close to his cock, only to tease him at the last moment and flutter along his thigh. Then they slid over his hip again, spanning his cheek, and she pulled him against her.

He went willingly, his achingly hard cock pulsing against her. Kal wanted to rip that gown from her body and plunge inside her. Instead, he contented himself—as much as possible—with tasting every part of her mouth, eating at her lips, the contact fast and furious and almost beyond his control. She shifted, and, oh gods, the sweet, undeniable torture that ran along his entire length.

Kal groaned into her mouth, unable to stop it. Uncaring that he couldn't.

She kissed him. Wilder than before. Wetter.

Kal couldn't take the torture. "Touch me, Sam," he groaned, dragging his hand from her hair down along the column of her throat and over her shoulder to find the sweet perfection of her breast cupped so lovingly in that flimsy piece of silk and lace.

He stroked his thumb over the nipple. Samantha stiffened for a tiny second, then melted against him, thrusting her breast against his fingers. Against his chest.

Her leg slid along his.

Her hand skimmed lower.

This time she didn't tease him. She found the head of his cock, her fingers circling in a motion that drew panted gasps from him. Had him jerking for more, and he felt the moisture seep from the tip.

"Gods, Samantha. What you do to me," he growled against her throat, inhaling the soft, musky scent of her arousal intertwined with the lilac.

She wiggled closer, freeing her leg from the gown. He should have made it a short one, dammit, but he'd been trying to be conscientious. Responsible. Not a lech.

Kal raised his knee, hiking the gown higher on her thighs, brushing the dampness at their apex. So much for that. And he didn't give a damn.

He nudged her onto her back, cradled between the side table and the pillow. His lantern was probably caught somewhere beneath her, and he didn't give a damn about that, either.

He cupped her breasts, his thumbs playing over her nipples, his fingers stroking the sides, and he felt the sweet tightness in them, saw the evidence of how much she was enjoying it.

But he had to ask. Had to know. Had to hear her say it. "You like that, Sam?"

She licked her lips and nodded, her breath coming in short gasps, her eyes so dark that they were blending in with her dilated pupils.

"Say it, Sam. I want to hear you say it."

"I... like it—oh, God, yes. Do that again."

He rolled her nipples between his thumb and finger.

She pressed against his knee. "Oh, God, Kal—"

He brushed his thumb over them.

"I wish... Oh, I wish..." She arched into his hands as he swept his palms over the silky fabric covering her nipples.

"What, Sam? What do you wish?"

"Please... God, please..."

He'd please her all right. "Say it, Sam. I want to hear you say it." *Needed* to hear her say it.

She groaned and wrapped one leg over his, grinding herself against his knee. "Taste me. Lick me. Oh, God, yes."

She didn't have to wish it. Kal yanked the fabric down, baring her to his gaze for all of two seconds before those tight, hard nipples tempted him beyond reason and he swirled his tongue around one of them, then sucked on it.

She arched against him, grasping his shoulder with one hand, the sheet behind her head with the other—all the more perfect to fit her perfectly inside his mouth.

"Do you like that?" He pulled back a little, her nipple still between his lips.

Samantha's eyes flew open and she gasped, her gaze riveted to what he was doing to her.

Kal's gaze was riveted to her face. Flushed with passion, her eyes deep and dark and green, intent upon the sight of him on her body. With her lips parted and moist, she was every fantasy he'd had for the past century and a half.

He smiled around her. "Like that?"

This time she could barely even nod.

He smiled wickedly and swept his lips to the other breast, his fingers using the wetness he'd left behind on the first to glide over her nipple, and Samantha ground herself against him.

"I want…" Her head tossed to the side. "I want to feel you against me, Kal."

He knew what she meant, but he had too many years of longing to make up for and his control was nonexistent. He had to make this last—or *he* wouldn't. He flicked his tongue on her nipple. "I'm right here, Sam."

She speared her fingers through his hair and pressed him into her. "Naked. I wish I were naked."

Thankfully, it only took a slight wave of two of his fingers to fulfill that wish since his other ones were still busy tormenting her nipple.

He kissed his way from her breast up to her collarbone, nuzzling in the hollow at the base of her throat, then up along the pulsing cord of her neck. Her breasts slid against his chest, the pointed tips setting off more fire along his skin, as if the rush of blood pounding through his veins wasn't enough.

Kal didn't know how much more of this he could take, but he was willing to test the limits of his sanity. And hers.

Samantha writhed beneath him as he nipped along

her jaw to her earlobe, taking it into his mouth and then swirling his tongue along the shell of her ear. She raked her nails on his skin—one hand up his back, the other down his ass, and she grabbed hold.

"You like that, Sam?" He blew softly in her ear, and she shuddered her answer.

"Ah… yessss."

He smiled, changing the direction of his kisses, moving along her cheek toward her mouth, nipping once at her bottom lip, and leaving her panting as he retraced the path he'd taken there, dropping kisses every few centimeters straight down her chest, enjoying every time she leaned into him when he brushed his 5:00 a.m. shadow against the sides of her breasts.

He swirled his tongue around her navel and dipped inside, smiling at the tremor that rushed through her as she clamped her legs around his.

"Kal…"

"Right here, Sam."

He certainly was. With plans to go lower.

Her fingers played in his hair, and Kal couldn't wait until she could only hang on in ecstasy. He nuzzled her hip bone, gently running his teeth along it, his tongue circling the sexy beauty mark there.

She moaned and spread her legs.

Perfect.

Kal moved between them. She was perfect. He lifted his head enough so his breath would whisper over her swollen, slick folds. "Do you like this, Sam?"

She looked at him as if he was insane to even ask that question. Of course she liked it and he knew she did, but still, he wanted to hear it. Needed to.

One long "Yessss" did it for him. Then he did it for her.

"Kal, I…" She sighed when he stroked her with one finger.

"What, Sam? What do you?"

He loved playing with her. Loved watching her belly flutter with every stroke of his finger. Loved the restless movement of her legs when he kissed her just above where she wanted him to.

Loved the long *whoosh* of breath she let out when he finally, slowly, lingeringly stroked his tongue along her swollen flesh.

"Yes, Kal. God… yes."

The one-word permission was all he needed. Kal separated her folds, running his finger along the insides as his tongue flicked and stroked, his lips suckling that part of her that throbbed for him.

Her wetness slicked his fingers, and he used it to ease them inside her, entering her to the upward movement of his tongue, withdrawing on the down stroke, playing her like a one-woman orchestra. And, ah, the music to his ears when he pulled back a bit, gently blowing over the wet curls and aching center of her, and she begged him with a pleading, "Kal, please…"

She was pink and wet and throbbing for him, and Kal didn't know how much longer he could last.

"*Do* I please you?" He kissed her, his tongue making a quick foray into her sweet center.

"Yes. But I…" She writhed, lifting her hips to his mouth.

But? There was a but?

There certainly was. Hers. He slid his hands beneath her, cupping the butt that was every bit as perfect as the rest of her.

"Kal, please. I wish you'd make me come."

Now that was a wish he needed no magic to fulfill. Tasting her, running his tongue around the swollen nub, his fingers working their own magic, he felt every tremor wrack her. Felt every beat of her pulse and the rising waves of sensation fill her.

She arched into his mouth, her hands fisting in his hair, then the sheets, then back to his hair, holding him in place, then trying to move him away when the sensations got to be too much. But he wasn't going anywhere. After all, this was what she'd wished for.

His tongue delved into her passage, and then he drew it up under the tight bunch of nerves, drawing a long, shuddering breath from her. She wrapped her legs shoulders, her heels driving into his back as she offered herself for his pleasure. And hers. Most definitely hers.

Kal tongued her again, this time not withdrawing his fingers when he felt her muscles clench around them. He worked them in and out of her, drawing her release upon her.

She panted. She flung her head from side to side and tossed her arms over her head, grabbing the sheets and pulling them down, only to toss them off and grip his hair, one mass of feeling, panting, yearning, sensual woman, and gods, what her sounds—her need—did to him.

And then, with one last hitch to her breath, a moment suspended in time as she waited to exhale, Samantha came, pulsing against his mouth, his name on her lips a long, drawn-out, reverential litany. He stayed there, tonguing her, making her pleasure last as long as possible.

When she finally relaxed her legs enough that he could crawl up her body, Kal placed one last kiss on her curls, smiling as her body jerked in reaction, her nerve endings frayed enough that every little movement set them off.

So he kissed his way up her body, taking special care with her breasts, drawing the tightened mounds into his mouth—first one then the other then back again—as he positioned himself where he wanted to be, his aching cock brushing her moist entrance.

"Sam?" His voice hoarse with the strain of restraint, Kal had to make sure this was what she wanted. A genie—even one who was a lover—couldn't take such liberties without permission. "Is this what you wish?"

A satisfied smile curled her lips as her eyes opened slowly. Sexy. "Oh, yes, Kal. This—you—are most definitely what I wish. But—"

But? Dear gods, please don't have her ask him to stop. "What, Sam?"

"What about... you know. Protection?"

Kal smiled, thanking the cosmos, Karma, the High Master, and whoever else was responsible for genie magic being all the prevention they'd need.

Earning her smile with his explanation, Kal sank into the hot, wet center of her in one long, gods-given stroke, and this—Samantha—was more a paradise than the Garden of Eden.

She lifted her arms to his back, her nails lightly brushing his sweat-slicked skin, and she smiled a sated, lazy smile as she opened her eyes. "God, that feels so good."

"Like it, do you?"

"You have no idea."

His cock twitched inside her, earning a gasp. "Trust me, Sam. I do."

She nibbled his shoulder, earning a grunt from him. "I like that, too, Kal. Very much."

He kissed her nose. "And I like *you* very much."

Her smile grew and her eyes sparkled with starlight. "I like you, too."

"I certainly hope so, considering where I am at this moment." He jerked his cock in case she didn't notice.

Sam gasped, then smiled again. "I like where you are, too."

"Good, because I don't think I could move if you wished me to."

"Oh, yes, you could." She arched her back. "Move, Kal. You'll enjoy every minute of it. Trust me."

She arched again, and, damn, if she wasn't right. She was *too* right, actually.

The blood rushed through him, his come roiling in his balls, threatening to end this moment before they'd really even begun.

He pulled out.

"Kal—"

He kissed her. "Shhh," he said when he could catch his breath. "I'm not going anywhere. After all, I'm here to make all your wishes come true."

Something shifted in her gaze as she stared at him. Something… profound? He didn't know if that was the word for it, but beside the desire, there was something else. "Sam? Are you okay?"

"I will be, Kal. Just please… I wish you'd be inside me again."

He didn't want her to think this had anything to do with their genie/master status. Because it didn't. This was between a woman and a man, permission and desire implicit in every stroke of her hand on his skin. Every gasp and nuzzle and kiss she made. Every look she gave him.

He kissed her again and she rose up to meet him, sucking his tongue into her mouth and wrapping her arms around his neck, her legs around his waist, the hot, wet center of her calling to him. And then she shifted so the head of his cock was right there—

"Samanth... aaaha—"

He hissed out the rest of her name when she moved enough to take just the tip of him inside her. He cradled her head with both hands, his elbows taking his weight while his thumb traced her bottom lip, flicking inside as he surged into her.

She nipped at him, her teeth sliding along his skin, then she shifted beneath him, turning her head enough to take his thumb into her mouth, drawing on it every time her thighs tightened around him, and he wanted to grant her every wish—the sun, the moon, the stars, every part of himself if she'd only do that again.

Whoa. Kal had to put the mental brakes on. This was too much. He'd had good sex before—okay, *phenomenal* sex before—but wanting to give her the moon and stars? He was in serious danger of losing himself here.

And then she raised her head and nibbled on his neck. "Make love to me, Kal."

Kal stiffened. Love wasn't a word in his vocabulary—in any genie's vocabulary.

"I—" Samantha's gaze flew to his. "I didn't mean that the way it sounded. I mean—"

"I know what you meant, Samantha." And he did, but still... *Love*.

The word was his undoing, and he couldn't even tell

her why. Couldn't tell her that love was a luxury genies couldn't afford. Rarely were genies in The Service ever together long enough to form a bond and saying, "I love you," to a mortal was out of the question.

He'd seen other genies do it, though. Understood the loneliness that caused them to, but after fighting for his freedom for two thousand years, Kal couldn't give it up.

He could, however, give them both tonight.

He kissed her again, letting his tongue mimic the movements of his body, swirling it around hers when he gyrated his hips, and capturing her moan with his mouth. He brushed kisses along her throat and nuzzled the hollow of her neck, the lilac scent there heightening his own arousal.

Her skin slid against his, and her heels dug into his back.

She lifted herself and licked his chest, her nipples stroking him, and for the longest, sweetest moment, Kal forgot how to breathe. Then Samantha clenched him inside her body and his breath rushed out.

"That feels so good, Kal," she whispered, her fingers swirling low on his back, drawing the response from his balls, and Kal gritted his teeth. He couldn't hold out much longer. He thrust into her again. Then again.

Samantha gripped his backside, widening her legs, taking more of him in, deeper. Tighter. Hotter. Wetter.

She flexed her hips, and he slipped in deeper. Then she clenched him tightly, kissing him, thrusting her tongue into his mouth, and he felt her start to come again.

Her release fueled his own, and Kal let it rush through him. He pounded into her, again and again, striving for that pinnacle that was just out of reach. One more surge should do—

No. Another. And another.

Samantha cried out his name, and that was the key. She tightened around him as she came, drawing his own orgasm from deep inside him, a hot geyser of need and want rushing through him into her, a moment of closeness so intimate, so real, so honest it was divine, and Kal thought he truly glimpsed heaven.

Time stopped. The world stopped. He swore his heart stopped, too. And for that moment, that long, amazing moment, Kal felt as if he'd found his true purpose in life.

Then her legs fell from around him, and the world rushed back in with all its sights and sounds and scents. And its reality.

His purpose, everything he was working toward, was to repair his reputation and take his rightful place in the hierarchy. This thing with Sam, it was just that… a thing. A really great thing. A sexy, heady, incredible thing, but a thing nonetheless. Mortals and genies were not a match made in heaven.

Her shallow, quick breathing slowed, and Kal tried to lessen his weight on her, but truthfully, though he knew he should find it, he didn't have the strength to move.

And when she wrapped her arms around him, he didn't have to.

18

ALBERT SKULKED BENEATH A LOW-HANGING LINE of laundry in the dark alleyway, the lack of any street lighting and a low moon making skulking easy. But it also made it damn hard to figure out where that car had gone.

He flicked the crystal from one side of the street to the other, looking for traces of the genie, enjoying the unexpected, but wholly appreciated, bonus of having the crystal become a flashlight by capturing moonbeams, because his cell phone battery had died about an hour ago. He had to be careful to angle the light away from the windows since he'd inadvertently destroyed two, and only by the grace of God, or whatever passed for this world's deity, had no one come running to investigate.

They were probably all off gambling, and what he wouldn't do to get in on that action. But first things first. The genie, then world domination. Then he could gamble to his heart's and wallet's content.

But the crystal wasn't picking up anything. Not a single trace that the genie had been here. For all he knew, the genie could have flown that car somewhere else because it was hard to see the skyline when he was working hard not to be seen.

He'd even almost run head first into a unicorn. A unicorn! If only he'd had something to capture it with and a way to transport it home… But as of now, the only transporting he was doing was a worthless crystal and dozens of objects weighing down his pants pockets. And the coin that now had about as much magic as his big toe. Which ached from all this walking.

"*Téigh i dtigh diabhail*, O'Malley! Watch yerself! Do ye think I'm made o' gold?" The joyous sound of coins pinging on the pavement interrupted Albert's thoughts, and he peered around the corner to see a line of glowing walking sticks illuminating a six-pack of leprechauns who were carrying slot machines and roulette wheels out of a building.

"I don't get it, Festwick," said the leprechaun with a buckle missing from his shoe. Must have been in the street fight.

Albert made a mental note to head back there and see how much gold he could clean up. Hedge his bets, so to speak, since he wasn't having much luck with the genie.

He winced. Hedging hadn't worked so well for him with Henley. But his luck had to break at some point, right?

He fingered the coin in his pants pocket. Some would say it already had; he just needed to capitalize on it.

"Why are we taking this stuff out? Aren't we supposed t' be spendin' our time usin' them instead o' stealin' them?"

"We're not stealin', O'Malley. We're taking them to a more centrally located place. Where everra'one can use them."

"You mean, where no one but us can make them work."

"You takin' issue with that?"

"No, but let's call a spade a spade."

"I prefer hearts, meself."

"That's 'cause you're a softie. Give me a club any day."

Albert leaned against the building. Much as he'd like to step out of the shadows and get in on whatever action those guys had going, that wouldn't help the big picture. He'd be better served by hanging here and picking up whatever info they had on the genie.

"So what odds will ye give me on Bart gettin' visitation rights for those dragonlets of his?"

Albert's ears perked up. Visitation rights?

Dragonlets?

"Well, first we gotta talk odds on them bein' his in the first place, but six to one on visitation. Maille's a cold-hearted witch and he did her wrong. She'll no' be givin' in t' him any time soon, I'm thinkin'. Barricaded the door t' him—and in Dragon's Blood Pass, that's tough t' do. Got the neighborhood in an uproar."

The uproar a missing dragonlet would cause was what Albert was thinking about. Parents, no matter their species, were protective of their offspring, and *dragonlet* sounded small and manageable. Had to be, at least more than a unicorn was. If he could get one of them, the parents would do just about anything to get it back.

Including turning over the genie.

"Six to one? Yer on! That's workin' in my favor! Put me down for a peck o' gold."

"A peck? Funds a little low these days, eh, O'Malley?"

"Doona be worryin' aboot me funds, Festwick. You'll have yer money *if* I lose. Which I'm no' countin' on. Me money's on Maille everra'time."

"Yer *eye's* on Maille, O'Malley. Always has been. What was it ye said aboot callin' a spade a spade?"

"Doona start wi' me, Festwick."

"Jes pick up your machine, O'Malley, and let's be done with this."

Albert couldn't wait for them to be done. Then he'd cross the street and head to this Dragon's Blood Pass place, nab himself a baby dragon, and put it up for ransom.

Piece o' cake, as his little green friends would say.

19

Samantha was having the best dream. Definitely better than the earlier one where she'd kept making wishes but none had come true, where Albert had been laughing at her, and the Oracle repeating over and over that she was their savior, all while a funhouse mirror had swirled around the perimeter, making a mockery of her.

She caught her breath, forcing her mind back to *this* dream. This pleasant, magical dream where she and Kal existed in the softest bed imaginable, with the sensuous slide of silk against their skin and the ultimate pleasure of sharing their bodies—

Her eyes flew open.

It wasn't a dream. In the pale dawn sifting in through the open skylight, Kal's face was inches from hers, his eyes closed, his breath warm and soft on her hands that were curled between them. His tousled hair was dark against the pale-yellow pillow, and a hint of stubble covered his jaw. She smiled, remembering how that had felt against her breasts. Between her thighs...

She'd slept with Kal.

Maybe she should be freaked out about that, but she wasn't. It wasn't as if she normally jumped into bed with just anyone, but these were not normal circumstances. She'd been up for longer than a day, had gone through an emotional service for her father, had dealt with Albert and that mess, had been whisked out of her familiar surroundings and into this other world with a talking fox—and a walking one—and if Kal turned her bad dreams to smoke and made everything right in her world, even for a little while, she could sleep with him if she wanted to.

The man was gorgeous and he turned her on in a big way. They were two consenting adults, responding to the other's touch for the sheer pleasure of it, not to use the other for something or to get something from the other, but because they wanted each other. And God knew, the sex itself had been phenomenal, so sue her. Sure, she hadn't planned it, but when she'd felt those arms around her, heard his soothing words, and felt the comfort his arms had provided, well, she was human as the next person.

Though the person next to her wasn't exactly human. That had worked to their advantage. All of the good without any of the consequences.

And oh was it good.

A sheet covered the rest of him, but Samantha didn't need to remove it to remember every glorious inch of him. The strong line of his jaw, the just-right firmness of his sexy lips, the breadth of his shoulders, the power and strength in his muscles, that chest, those abs...

The only nonhuman thing about him was his magic, but after her nightgown had disappeared, the only magic that had been in existence during the night was what they'd made together.

Curling her fingers into her palm, she replayed his gentleness when he'd held himself above her, the intensity of the look in his eyes as he'd thrust inside her. That undeniable pull between them wasn't about his magic or what she could do for or give him. That, more than anything, got to her. Turned her on all over again. There was nothing so utterly freeing as being wanted by a man because of *who* she was.

Utterly freeing and utterly sexy.

Samantha sidled a little closer and propped herself up on her elbow. His lashes were as dark as his hair. Long for a guy. Funny, she wouldn't have thought long eyelashes could be sexy, but on him they were. Pretty much everything on Kal was sexy... and she wanted him again.

Samantha raised herself a little higher. Moved a little closer. Lifted her lips next to his. Kissed him.

Kal's eyes shot open, meeting hers, and his hand caught her arm, his fingers biting into her skin for a second—the second it took him to realize what she was doing. Who she was.

Samantha didn't move other than to curve her lips into a smile.

He returned it a heartbeat later, grasping some of her curls, tugging her closer, and whatever kiss she'd thought she was giving him was firmly and completely taken over by him.

She didn't care. All she wanted was to get as physically close to him as possible and give him the same kind of pleasure he'd given her. Reality and its demands would return soon enough. For now, she just wanted to enjoy *their* magic.

Samantha thrust her tongue between his lips in a manner so blatantly erotic that it threatened to take her strength away. Luckily, that didn't matter because she found herself on her back so quickly that she hadn't even seen it happen.

Not that she cared. God, he felt so good pressing her into the silk, as smooth and sensuous as the sleek muscles of his back that flexed and contracted with every movement he made over her. Muscles that shuddered when she ran her fingernails lightly over them as he held her hostage and ravished the interior of her mouth, his tongue thrusting in a way she wanted the rest of him to be doing.

His lips made love to her jawline; there was no other way to describe it. With each press of his lips, he claimed a little more of her. With each stroke of his tongue, each nip of his teeth, she fell more completely under his spell, every nerve ending shivering in anticipation, her reactions ratchetting up when his lips moved a few millimeters down her neck, the whole clenching, rising-up-to-meet-him, sighing-when-it-stopped thing happening all over again.

She was restless beneath him, aching for closeness. For sheer abandonment. Something. He was too restrained, and her body ached for more. It ached to be above him. On him, around him. Doing to him what he did to her.

She turned her head to the side. "Kal, please. I wish—"

He blew against her throat.

God, that felt good. Maybe she'd let him do it a little longer. Then he reached the hollow beneath her ear and coherent speech failed her. Not that she'd been so successful at it moments ago…

"More," she finally panted and felt his lips curve against her skin.

"As you wish, Sam."

And there was more. So much more she couldn't process it. All she could do was feel.

Propped half on her, half on his elbow, he slid his other hand down the front of her, his palm circling on the tight bud of her nipple, and she felt wetness flood her.

"Kal—kiss me." She didn't care that she begged. She ached and she wanted and she needed. Reality could come crashing down later.

"As you wish," he breathed against her collarbone. His lips slid away from hers. That wasn't what she wanted. She wanted him to kiss her—

Ah. There. He kissed her nipple, the warmth of his mouth enveloping it, the gentle suction playing havoc with her nerve endings, and Samantha tried to draw breath into her lungs.

This wasn't going as she'd planned.

Then his erection throbbed against her thigh and Samantha didn't care what the plan was. She wanted him inside her. Wanted to take the full length of him in, clench him to her, hear his panted breaths, feel the shudders wrack his body.

She wiggled her hips, earning her a growl from Kal as he switched his attention to her other breast, his dark eyes searing her with their intensity as he looked up at her, almost daring her to object.

No way.

Decadence was watching his tongue lave her, watching his lips surround her nipple with the tiniest amount of suction to draw it up into his mouth, sending pleasure spiking through her like a laser beam, and she knew that if Kal didn't fill her right this minute, life would have no meaning.

"Kal—" She gasped as his tongue continued to work its magic on one breast, his fingers doing the same to the other. "Could you—" Oh, God, what *was* that move he just did?

She rolled her pelvis, lifted it, trying to show him what she wanted because the words... they just wouldn't come.

But she could. And she was so close. If only he'd—

"Oh God, Kal. I wish you'd be inside me already."

Not the most romantic way—or even a sexy one—to say it, but she felt the curve of his smile.

"As you wish." He shifted and there—finally!—was what she wanted. Pressure. Hard, hot, throbbing pressure against the part of her that was swollen and needy. That part that was drenched and aching with wanting him.

But he held himself up, his chest leaving her breasts to ache for his weight.

"Say it again, Sam."

Even the way he said her name could make her come.

"I wish you'd make l—I wish you were inside me."

She saw his smile for only a second before he covered her lips with his. Before he covered her body with his. Before he entered her.

And, oh God, it was better than before, and she had no idea how that was possible. Spirals of sensation unwound from her core, spreading to every limb, giving pleasure a whole new meaning. So much more than mere pleasure.

Frenetic, energetic, invigorating. A wild ride more intense than any carpet ride. It was soaring into the heavens and crashing to earth, only to avoid a collision at the last minute. This was flying at light speed, taking curves too fast and hanging on for dear life. The most exhilarating feeling in the world.

Kal stroked in and out of her in a rhythm so perfect it was as if he knew her own special secret. He cradled her butt with one of his hands, pressing her into him, sliding his finger—oh God, *there*—but it felt so right.

He held himself above her, enough that she could breathe—well, not really because catching her breath was *not* happening—but his chest brushed her nipples again, creating a whole new sensation.

It was too much; it wasn't enough. She arched into him, wanting... something. She didn't know what. All she knew was he had to go deeper. Harder. Faster. Pound into her. Make her scream.

She wrapped her legs around that gorgeous backside, locking her ankles, meeting his thrusts, crying out when he hit that one spot—

"Oh God, Kal. I've never... It's never..." She couldn't find the words. Hell, she could barely find herself.

"Come for me, Sam. Let me watch it take you."

Oh she was being taken all right. On a one-way ticket to perfection. On a trip to paradise. She gripped his sides with her legs as the wave built inside of her and she arched into him again, her breasts begging for him to taste them.

Oh sweet Jesus he did. Over and over, he licked her nipples, each successive stroke drawing a wave of pleasure low inside her, each tongue flick a spike in the pleasure. So intense it almost hurt but didn't.

Then he suckled her and she flew over the edge, coming so intensely, so soul-shatteringly intensely, that every part of her lay exposed to this one moment in time, every part of who she was poised on the brink of something as her body—and his—took her to new heights. New realms. New possibilities.

Then Kal thrust again, his breath a sharp hiss before he exhaled a long, low growl. His movements quickened, his thrusts deeper, the nip of his teeth sharp against her shoulder, and it started all over again. The rush, the wave, the sense of infinity. No boundaries. Elements and immortality... all things were possible in that one moment of suspended time when reality ceased to exist as they both came together and she wished... She wished...

Samantha felt the fire leave her in one quick *whoosh*, like the dragon's flame devouring that gnome's hat, as the reality of what they were doing crashed over her. The reality of what *she* was doing. What she'd wished.

Samantha rolled out from under him and dragged the silk cover with her, trying to catch her breath. She sat on the edge of the bed with her back to him, wrapping it around her like a shield. Or a tent she could hide inside of.

Dear God... She'd *wished*.

He ran a finger down her spine and she shuddered.

"What's wrong, Sam?" he asked, his voice low and husky. Sexy. Which only made things worse. "Talk to me, sweetheart."

Talk to him. That was the joke, wasn't it? Talking had created this mess. No. One little word had created this mess. *Wish*.

She'd *wished* him to kiss her. *Wished* him to make love to her. She'd used him.

Bad enough Albert had only wanted her for her

money and connections; Kal only wanted her because she'd *wished* him to.

Her life truly was governed by semantics, and, oh, what a rotten job they'd done. No—what *she'd* done.

"Samantha? What are you thinking?"

That was the problem; she hadn't been thinking. She'd been feeling. Riding the high of what they'd been doing, and the reality hadn't mattered until she'd remembered that word.

"Sam? You're worrying me."

She'd wished him into making love to her—wasn't that the biggest irony of all in having a genie? A being who made all your wishes come true?

She scooched sideways to face him. God, he looked so good. Sexy as hell. Beautiful. And utterly perplexed.

It was her fault. Everything was her fault. It'd started with that first wish and had ended here. Like this.

The funny thing was, most people thought it'd be great to have a genie. Someone to do your bidding. Make your life easy. Grant every wish.

Except that every wish came with complications and Samantha had enough life experience to know that anything handed to you on a silver platter usually tarnished like that silver over time.

"Sam?"

Samantha clutched the covers tighter to her chest and tucked some curls behind her ear. Curls he'd held on to... tugged on—

It didn't matter that he'd come on to her earlier. Didn't matter that he wasn't complaining. She'd taken away his choice. She, by virtue of being his master, had given him no choice, and she felt lower than that belly-crawling lizard of an ex-boyfriend of hers.

"Oh, God, Kal. I wish there was some way to keep from saying 'I wish' around you."

Kal sat up. "What? You can't mean that."

"I do. I wish I could stop saying 'I wish' around you."

Kal stared at her a moment longer and swallowed. Then he brushed some hair off her forehead. "If you're sure, I can make that happen, Sam."

"I'm sure. I don't ever want to say that word again."

He ran his fingers down the side of her face and along her jaw, his eyes following them all the way until they rested on her lips and Samantha wanted to groan with the travesty of it all. He was only doing it because of her wish.

"What word, Sam?"

She took a deep breath, not wanting to say it, but she had to own up to what she'd done to him. And then apologize like hell. "The word, 'wis—'"

He kissed her.

Somewhere in the back of her brain, the fact that she hadn't wished him to kiss her registered, but it was eclipsed by the sheer beauty of the kiss itself. The desire behind it and the fact that she'd like to wish it would never end but couldn't because his tongue was doing toe-curling things to her lips—which explained the slippers.

When he finally stopped, she needed a few seconds to find her breath. "What was that for?"

"Your wish, Sam. I granted it."

"What wi—"

He kissed her again.

She could get used to this because, oh, God, it felt so good. *He* felt so good.

But no—this was exactly what she couldn't get used to because she wasn't going to wish it ever again.

Out loud, at least.

Then again, she didn't have to. Kal caught her head in his hands and tilted it back, raining kisses along her lips, deepening them whenever she tried to speak, until finally, she just gave up. This would probably be the last time he'd kiss her after she apologized for making him do this.

His tongue traced the seam of her lips, and when it slipped inside, one of them moaned. She didn't think it was her. Then her breasts brushed his chest and she did moan. But so did he. Again.

Maybe she was wrong. Maybe she didn't have anything to apologize for… She put her hand on his chest—fighting with her fingers the entire time not to trace over his pecs, and it was such a fight. But she finally succeeded, wrenching her mouth from his. "Kal, about that wi—um, the thing I said."

"What about it, Sam?"

She exhaled. "I want to—no, I need to apol—" Her apology got cut short when not one, but two, fennecs dropped out of the sky—through the skylight—and landed on Kal's shoulders, scrambling all over him, little fox claws leaving tiny white streaks as they leapt onto the furniture.

Dirham—presumably, since he was the one bouncing—skittered off the side table, managed a quick bounce off the floor, and landed on the dresser with a double two-step, as if a dragon had given him a hotfoot, but it was the sentence he kept repeating that upstaged her apology like nothing else could.

"Izaaz, we have a problem!"

20

GODDAMNED LIZARD HAD SOME NASTY CLAWS ON him, and those baby teeth were like razor blades. Obviously, dragons didn't nurse their young. Didn't watch them all that closely, either.

Albert jostled the treacherous little thing in his coat, the lining of which was now in shreds. So were the pockets, and the trinkets had dribbled out like bread crumbs all the way from the dragons' house. He'd had to spend far too much time trying to hunt them down when they'd rolled away, until, ultimately, he'd just made sure no one could track him back to his hideout. It'd killed him to lose the treasures, but if he got the genie out of this, it'd all be worth it.

He *would* get the genie out of this. And damned soon, hopefully. The dragon might be a baby, but it was a handful.

He set the thing in the circle of bricks he'd hastily built when he'd arrived back at his hideout after snatching it. In a city full of magical beings, many of which were birds, there hadn't been one birdcage anywhere around, so he's had to make do with what he found.

Hopefully, he'd find the genie soon and could give this little Ginsu knife back to its parents.

The thing started chirping. Great. Just what he needed.

Albert tossed what was left of his jacket over the

top of the pen he'd made. Birds quieted down when covered; hopefully the same principle would apply to dragons. Thankfully, it worked.

Albert leaned against the wall, shifting when his spine bumped the edge of a brick where he'd pried another one loose. He checked his pants for the thousandth time, making sure he hadn't lost the coin or the crystal he'd put in those pockets when the dragon had made mincemeat of his jacket. They were the two treasures he couldn't afford to lose.

Except... The obelisk was gone.

Albert yanked the coin out and shoved his hand back into the pocket so hard he ripped the fabric. He stood up, jumping in case the crystal was stuck in his pant leg.

No.

He felt around in the other pocket. Nothing.

Son of a bitch! How was he supposed to find the genie if he didn't have the damn crystal?

Albert dropped to the ground, running his hands through the rubble and mortar he'd created when building the makeshift pen. Maybe he'd dropped it here and not along any of the hundreds of streets he'd traversed to cover his tracks all fucking night long.

Ten minutes later, all he had to show for his trouble was a pair of bloody hands, an aching back, destroyed knees, and a whiny dragon.

Albert slumped against the wall, one leg stretched out in front of him, the other bent. He rested his elbow on the bent knee, running the gold coin through his fingers. Worthless. It was worthless to him now. That damn thing didn't work to get him where he needed to go and it couldn't locate the genie like the crystal. What good was it?

He contemplated chucking it across the room, but besides the noise it would make, it was still gold. At the very least, he could trade it to the leprechauns for something. Like dragon food. The thing hadn't shut up for the last ten minutes of the walk home and was starting again with the noises.

What did dragons eat? There hadn't been anything by the nest when he'd lifted this one out. He'd been tempted to go for all fifteen, but the minute he'd picked this one up, he'd seen the inadvisability of that idea. One was a handful, and he didn't want to jeopardize his whole plan for greed. That could come later.

But he needed to make sure this one lived. His bargaining power lay in that.

He peeked beneath the jacket. It saw him and sneezed. Or maybe it was trying to blow fire because that looked like smoke rising from its nostrils.

God, he was tired and this was turning into a nightmare.

Albert sighed and tucked the coin into the breast pocket of his shirt, patting it to make sure it stayed put. He wished he could catch a power nap. Preferably in his own bed.

As the gold smoke started billowing around him again, the dragon leapt up, bit his finger, and held on.

21

"BREATHE, DIR, BREATHE!"

Kal finally caught the fox and sat him on the bed—as near to sitting as Dirham got. Samantha carried water in her cupped hands from the bathroom, the sheet wrapped around her in a sorry imitation of a sari to keep the evidence of what they'd been doing from Dirham and his friend, but the fox had such a wild look in his eyes that Kal had a feeling their state of undress was the last thing the fennec was registering.

Dirham started to hyperventilate so Kal yanked the pillowcase from a pillow and wrapped it around the fennec's snout. "Take deep breaths, Dir. You need to calm down."

"But… problem…" Dirham mumbled inside the pillowcase, his gasps segueing into choking when Kal sat on the corner of the bed.

It took two whacks between the shoulder blades for Dirham's breathing to get in sync, but his eyes were still the size of his ears and his tail was ramrod straight, every strand of fur sticking out as if he'd shoved all four paws into electrical sockets.

And it wasn't because he was looking at a naked djinni. The fennec had seen Kal naked many times and was too innocent in the carnal ways of the world for that to cause this reaction. No, while Dirham was inclined to get overly happy about a lot of things, he tended to keep his composure when things went bad, so the gasping, choking, "we have a problem" worried Kal. A lot.

"It's big. Really big. Huge." Dirham gulped, then leaned toward Samantha to lap up the water. He shook himself when he was finished, his haunches half-raised off the bed. "Right after Berosus made his big speech about changing destiny, I realized that, to change yours, we needed to report in about your change of master and hadn't. I figured I'd get the crystal while you guys were sleeping. You know, to help out and all."

Because that's what Dirham did. "And?"

Dirham's breathing kicked up, and Kal was afraid the fox was going to start hyperventilating again.

He put a hand on Dirham's back and the fox calmed down—becoming so calm that his words and tone went flat. "It's gone, Kal. The crystal's gone. And so is the amulet."

Kal didn't get hyper about bad things either, and this time was no different. Well, it was no different in that he didn't get hyper, but it definitely was different in being bad. Losing the crystal *and* the amulet put this situation so far beyond *bad* that, if he did get hyper, no one in the cosmos would condemn him for it.

He took a shaky breath and tried to keep his composure. If he lost it, Dir would, too. "Did you look around, Dir? Under the furniture? Behind it?"

Dirham stood on all fours and nodded, bits of fur flying off. "Yes. Everywhere. I looked and I looked and I searched and I sniffed. I even came back and asked Lexy to help me. She's the smartest fox I know, and even she couldn't find them. The leather bags were there, but the rest? Gone."

"Leather bags?" Samantha gripped Kal's shoulder which, under any other circumstances, would be welcome, but right now, he needed to focus on figuring out what had happened to the missing items. "You mean the ones that were in the safe?"

He and Dir blew out breaths together. "Did you do something with them, Sam?" If he could grant his own wishes, this would be the granddaddy of them all.

Unfortunately, the shake of her head shot that theory to *Al-Jaheem*. "They were in the back of the safe behind the lantern. I didn't have time to do anything with them before you whisked me out of there. What's the problem?"

"What's the *problem*?" Dirham cursed—in Mycenaean, his voice going positively basso profundo. Kal hadn't known the fennec knew that language, and he certainly hadn't known the fox knew *that* word. It was a good thing Samantha didn't understand Mycenaean. From the look on Lexy's face, she obviously did—and the fact that Dirham had overcome his shyness enough to ask the vixen for help only emphasized how dire this was. "The problem could be cataclysmic if they fall into the wrong hands."

Kal patted him on the head in hopes of calming him down again, but he came away with a handful of fur. "Don't panic, Dirham. We don't know whose hands they're in. For all we know, you just didn't see them."

"I didn't see them because they're not there!" The fox obviously didn't know the meaning of the words, *don't panic*. "They're gone. Someone took them. And I know the carnelian obelisk only affects you, but the Cleopatra amulet… Can you imagine what'll happen to that? Oh gods, oh gods, oh gods. This is awful. What do we do? What do we do? Who could have taken them?"

Samantha got stuck on the Cleopatra part. Her father had had an Egyptian treasure in the safe, too? No wonder Albert had been so insistent on opening the safe.

Albert.

"Is the amulet gold?" She knew the answer even before Kal nodded.

"Shiny, too," Dirham added.

And that explained where it was. After hearing the desperation in Albert's voice during that phone call, she knew he wouldn't have been able to resist the open safe, nor anything gold he found inside. And if he didn't know how to use it to do whatever it did for Kal and Dirham, she'd bet he'd know how to use it to earn himself a hefty paycheck—by auctioning it off to the highest bidder.

"How important are these pieces? What can they do in the wrong hands?"

Dirham's eyes widened and he shivered. "They're priceless. Beyond priceless. Too many people would kill to get their hands, paws, talons, hooves, whatever on them." He buried his snout in his paws and the other fox patted his shoulder.

"Who has them, Samantha?" Kal's voice was controlled. Even. The intensity of his gaze, however, was anything but. And that, more than Dirham's tone, worried her because she knew the passion behind that intensity.

"Albert."

"Albert?" Dirham squeaked, looking up.

"Not Albert Viehl?" Kal said something low and

biting in some language. Samantha would almost feel sorry for Albert if Kal got his hands on him.

Almost.

She nodded.

"You're still with him?" Kal's eyebrow arched. "Monty never thought it would last."

"I am not with him anymore. *Obviously*." She glanced at the bed. He couldn't really think she'd sleep with him if she was seeing someone else. Not if Dad had really talked to him about her. Which she found more than a little disconcerting, especially since he'd kept her in the dark about Kal.

Samantha shook her head. That wasn't important right now. Not with the two fennecs here and the missing items. But they'd talk later. About a couple of things. "So, what do these things do? What can Albert do with them—other than make himself a fortune if he sells them?"

"Sells them?" Dirham rolled off the bed and splatted onto the floor.

"Oh, Dirham!" The other fox leapt down after him and helped him to his feet.

Kal stood up, pulling the sheet off the bed and wrapping it around himself. "If Albert sells them, he's as big a fool for that as he is for letting you get away."

Okay, maybe there was no need for that talk.

But Albert was no fool. Foolish, perhaps, but definitely not a fool. And as for letting her go, her father had been right; she should have dumped him months ago.

Unfortunately—and contrary to the Oracle's proclamation—the past couldn't be changed, so they had to deal with the fallout. "So what do these things do?"

Kal swiped his hair off his forehead and kneaded the back of his neck. Dirham did the same thing with his paw, and the other fox sighed, none of which reassured her.

"The amulet will transport him wherever he wants to go in the world—yours and mine," explained Kal. "And as soon as he figures out how the crystal works, he'll show up wherever I am."

"Works? What does it do?"

"The crystal acts like mortals' GPS," piped up the other fox. She leapt onto the bed and daintily curled her tail around her front paws when she sat. "It's even called that, but in the magical realm, the acronym stands for Genie Placement System. The principle's the same, although Albert would have to know about you *and* what he has before he can come after you, Kal."

And Albert would come after Kal. Samantha knew that as sure as she was standing here. In a bedspread. From the bed.

She glanced at the aforementioned piece of furniture. The lantern was there, leaning against the side table. When Kal had dragged the sheet away, he'd pulled the lantern from where it'd been wedged after they'd—

No. She couldn't think about that now. She couldn't deal with the knot of jumbling emotions that were trying to beat out each other for control of her churning stomach.

Mortification and Guilt were neck and neck for the lead.

"Did Albert know about the safe, Samantha?" asked Kal.

Oh, yeah. Albert knew. He was shrewd. He paid

attention and was an opportunist—and she'd provided the biggest opportunity of all.

She explained about Albert's determination to open her father's safe, and they all arrived at the same conclusion: Albert not only knew about the safe and its contents, but he had to have a good idea of what the items were. Which meant he could know about Kal. And that upped the stakes.

Albert was going for the big prize. That's what he'd had his eye on all along. Her money was nothing compared to what a genie could give him. And she'd thought she couldn't feel any worse than when she'd overheard him on the phone? Boy, today was just full of surprises—and it'd barely begun.

She grabbed the lantern. "But you can't be his genie without the lantern, right?"

"Exactly." Kal tied a knot in the sheet he'd wrapped around his waist. "Which means that if he knows what he's got, he'll come after it and me. And you, too, Samantha."

"So what do we do? Should I wish—"

Kal leaned over and kissed her. Short and sweet—and definitely to the point. There would be no more wishing.

Semantics. Right.

Somehow she had to figure out another way to get Kal to grant her wishes so she could stop Albert. If only she hadn't wished to stop saying "I wish" in the first place.

She braced herself for another kiss, but, apparently, he really couldn't read her mind. Pity. Right now that would be a welcome trait. Maybe if she phrased it a different way… "Kal, I want you—"

"I want you, too, Sam."

"Yes, but I desire you—"

"I desire you, too."

She puffed out a breath. "Kal. I'm trying to get you to bring Albert here."

"You need to wish it, Sam."

"I was trying to."

"Oh." He touched her cheek, his gaze intense but inscrutable, and Mortification and Guilt started being eclipsed by the always capricious, never logical Lust.

Well, the Oracle did say the mistakes of the past were destined to be repeated unless one learned from them. Samantha might have been slow on the uptake when it came to Albert, but those days were behind her—and so was last night.

She took a step back.

Kal looked at her a moment longer, then tugged on the knot he'd tied in the sheet and tossed the excess over his shoulder like a kilt. "Actually, we don't want you wishing him here. If he has the amulet, he'll bring it with him and it has properties above and beyond genie magic."

"Yeah, I heard of a guy once who wanted to go to the moon," said Dirham, taking a seat next to Lexy on the bed. "Unfortunately, he didn't specify which moon, and let me tell you, he did *not* end up on a rock in outer space." Both foxes shuddered. "It wasn't pretty, and that's all I'm going to say about that."

"Yes, that was a lesson to all regarding the use of a goddess's power," said Lexy.

But to Samantha, the idea of Albert with his face pressed against someone's *moon* was extremely satisfying. "So what do we do? Should I wish—"

Kal kissed her again. Half as short, and still as sweet. But not productive.

"Kal, I think you might want to hold off on all the kissing. We have more important things to do now," said Dirham. "No offense, Samantha. I mean, you're pretty and all, but this is Kal's future we're talking about. His career. His reputation. He's worked too hard to re—"

"Dirham." Kal tapped the fox in the snout. "Let's keep the focus on what's important right now. We have to figure out some way to get the amulet from Albert."

"We could always take it from him," said Samantha. Nothing would give her greater pleasure. "After all, it is rightfully mine."

"That's true." Lexy said, tapping the side of her mouth. "The Djinn Code states that whatever the djinni owns is yours as well, so that includes his crystal. I'm not certain about the amulet because, technically, it belongs to the goddess Mayat, but since it was among your father's possessions, I believe you do have the right to use it. But Kal cannot steal anything. Genies and their magical-assistance assistants don't steal."

Mortals, however, did. Samantha straightened. Albert had taken enough from her.

"I'll get the amulet back, Kal." It was the least she could do.

"And the crystal," Dirham added. "You can't forget the crystal, right, Kal? We need that, or you won't be able to let the High Master know that—"

"That Samantha's my new master. Yes, Dir, I'm aware of that." Kal scratched his chest and Samantha fought to keep from staring. "*Kharah*. This is not what we need."

No, what Samantha needed was to take back control from Albert. Take back her pride. Her ego. Her autonomy.

Yet she'd taken Kal's from him.

The apology was on her lips, but she didn't want to slash his dignity by apologizing in front of everyone for something so personal. But when they were alone again... "So what should we do?"

Kal swiped a hand over his jaw. "If Albert knows what was in that safe, he's going to make the connection between magic and the amulet. He'll be here eventually because, for all the amulet's mystical powers, the travel charm is easy to figure out. All he has to do is place it next to his heart and wish to go somewhere—and he doesn't need specifics. Wishing to find us is about all it will take to get him in the general vicinity. We need to stay on our toes."

"Oh, I'm always on my toes," said Dirham. "It's how I roll."

Samantha finally found something to smile at. Dirham was the perfect comic relief in a situation that was by no means funny.

"All right, then. Let's get dressed and be on our way." Kal held up his hand, fingers ready to wave. "I know you can't make a wish, Samantha, but since I'm responsible for your comfort, I can conjure clothing for you. Is there anything specific you would like to wish for?"

Her first response had nothing to do with clothing, but *turn Albert into the lizard he is* didn't fall under the Seeing To Her Comfort category. Plus, she'd like to think she was a better person than that.

Still, she could enjoy that mental image. "No, whatever works for you."

Kal waved his fingers. Apparently he was quite fond of the harem outfit. For both of them. His included another vest that didn't close across his washboard abs, and hers, well, at least the sari-type top was comfortable. And it was teal, which was a good color with her hair.

"On, and don't forget this." Kal picked up the necklace the Oracle had given her and held it out.

Actually, she wouldn't mind forgetting it and everything it represented. "How about you hang on to that for me?"

"You're sure?"

"Definitely." She'd rather not have another anchor around her neck; Guilt was enough of one.

First chance she got, she was going to apologize. Then someone pounded on the door, guaranteeing that wouldn't happen anytime soon.

"I know you're in there, Kal," came an angry growl that Samantha didn't recognize. "Open up, or I'll blow the damn door down!"

22

KAL YANKED THE DOOR OPEN, HAND AT THE READY to either wave it for magic or punch someone in the face. No one threatened his master and got away with it.

Maille and Bart stood there: Bart, ready to smash the door with his puny fists, and Maille with her arms crossed and tapping one toe.

"Good gods, Bart, you were full of hot air even before you took the wyvern form," she said, her eyes blazing at her mate. "How in *Al-Jaheem* do you think you're going to blow anything down with how you are now? Planning to huff and puff?"

Bart got in her face. Too bad he was two inches shorter. "Don't start with me, woman. It's your fault we're here."

Dirham leapt off the bed and stood on the threshold. "Uh, guys? Is there something you need? We're kinda in a hurry."

Two sets of seething black eyes turned his way, and the little fox backed up behind Kal's legs.

"A *hurry*?" Maille screeched, advancing into the room. "You're not going anywhere. Not until you help us."

Kal stepped forward, blocking her. She might not have the capability of breathing fire in her human form, but those talons were still lethal and she already held one grudge against Samantha. "What's the problem, Maille?"

"Maille's the problem, Kal." Bart threw up his hands in disgust. Hadn't taken him long to remember how to use them.

"Stuff it, wyrm," Maille snarled at Bart, then looked at Sam. "The problem is that we need *her* wishes." Some of the fire went out of her bluster. "Someone took one of our hatchlings."

Bart uncrossed his arms and massaged the back of his neck with one hand. "Laszlo. The youngest."

For a moment, silence reigned. Then a collective gasp filled the room. Samantha plopped onto the bed next to Lexy, Dirham sat on the floor, and Kal let Maille into the room. He hadn't known Bart and Maille had a clutch together.

He quickly did the math while pulling out a chair at the table. Dragon gestation was a little over fifteen hundred years, one of the reasons they were an endangered race. They couldn't afford to lose even one hatchling. "Sit down, Maille. Tell us what happened."

The dragon sat and her bravado crumbled. Bart, too, looked shaken as he leaned against the door frame, an emotion from the wyvern that was as surprising as the fact that he'd reproduced.

"I woke up this morning to their chirruping. All fifteen—fourteen of them. Laszlo was missing."

"He didn't fly away?"

"He can't fly. He's newly hatched. Give him a few days to catch up."

"Just a little surprise my dear ol' mate waited fifteen hundred years to spring on me." Disgust laced Bart's voice, and Kal couldn't say he blamed the wyvern. To have children and not know it, then to find out when one was missing and possibly kidnapped...

"Give it a rest, will you, Bart?" Maille glared at him. "You're not the injured party here. Laszlo is. We have to find him."

"That's not what you said when you showed up at my place looking for him bright and early this morning, was it?"

Maille rolled her eyes. "Okay, I admit it. I thought, at first, that you might have, you know—"

"You thought it was me. Go on, tell them. Tell them that you'd thought I'd purposely take one of the hatchlings to punish you. Great opinion you have of me, by the way." Bart snorted and there looked to be a puff of smoke accompanying it. "As if I'd do that."

"I said I was sorry."

"After wasting fifteen minutes flaying me with that forked tongue of yours."

"Can we just focus on what's important right now, Bart? The kids. They're what's important."

"You think I don't know that? Who suggested we come here? Who talked you into eating the crow you served up nice and steaming hot to Samantha yesterday, eh?"

These two were enough to drive the gods to drink— which was how dragons had been created in the first place. One of the nastier side effects of *arak*.

"Maybe Laszlo's hiding." Kal had to get the focus off their marital troubles and onto what was important. He remembered what it'd been like losing each member of his family—and that'd been to old age. He couldn't imagine what the dragons were going through, though the purple stripe in Maille's hair that had turned gray told its own story.

Maille shook her head. "He's not. I turned the nest upside down. There's no place he could hide."

Kal grabbed the other chair, spun it around, then straddled it. "Any signs of a break-in?"

She shook her head. "None. But the rest of the clutch was huddled together as if they'd seen a ghost. And since it's been eons since any ghosts left Spooks' Nook, I doubt it. Besides, a ghost couldn't pick him up even if it did come to visit, and anyway, ghosts aren't known to snatch dragonlets."

"What about a fall?" asked Samantha.

"We would have found him there."

Maille was right; dragon nest accidents used to be the third biggest killer of baby dragons, after overeager knights in shining armor with Sleeping Beauty complexes who slayed any dragons they could find—even hatchlings—and gnome-weevils that bored into the unhatched eggs. The mutant creatures were one of the reasons the position of High Master had been created: to control genie magic. Run-amok djinn weren't pretty and neither were their creations. As the shining armor hysteria had phased out and the gnome-weevils had reached the end of their life expectancy, nest falls had risen to the number one killer spot.

Which meant that if Laszlo hadn't been below the nest and he couldn't fly away or hide, the only logical conclusion was that someone had taken him. And with the very real possibility of Albert having the amulet, Kal was betting he knew who.

He looked at Samantha. "I'm not a big believer in

coincidences." That was because most coincidences, like déjà vu, could be attributed to genie magic. Or magic amulets.

Samantha sat in horrified silence. Albert wouldn't resort to kidnapping, would he?

Kal seemed to think so. And if she were honest with herself, she could see it. Albert was desperate. The question was, what was he going to do with a baby dragon?

A bigger one was, what could she do about it? Of all the times to not be able to make wishes. She'd lost her own mother at such a young age; to be however indirectly responsible for Laszlo being taken from his... She could barely breathe, let alone think.

"So if you could just wish for Laszlo's return, we'd be in your debt." Maille lost the blistering, nasty look of a dragon for the mien of a heartsick, desperate mother, and Samantha would have liked nothing more than to be able to grant that wish.

"I'm so sorry, Maille. I'd love to, but I can't." The ramifications of her one careless, emotion-driven wish were washing over her like angry waves on the shoreline. She couldn't wish Albert here, she couldn't wish the baby dragon here, and she couldn't wish herself anywhere *but* here.

She *was* useless. And the baby dragon was going to pay for her ineptitude.

"Of course you can. Kal, tell her." Maille put a hand on Kal's knee. "Tell her all she has to do is say, 'I wish Laszlo was back home,' and everything will be all right. I don't even need to know who took him. I just want my baby home safe."

"Well, *I* want to know. I'd like to tear him apart. So

if you could undo this"—Bart waved a hand over his body—"and deliver the bastard to my front door, I'll take care of the rest."

"No, really. I'm sorry, but I can't," said Samantha, the knife twisting in her gut a little more. "I can't make wishes."

"Of course you can." Dragon tears filled Maille's eyes, and the knife twisted a full three-sixty. "You can't have gone through them all already."

"What she means, Maille," Kal's voice was low, "is that the last wish she made was that she wouldn't say the word *wish* anymore, so she actually *can't* make a wish."

There was a lull in the room—in speech, in breathing, probably brain waves, too, as they all tried to process the sheer inexplicability of that sentence, because who in their right mind would wish to *not* wish with their own personal genie around?

That would be her.

"Are you out of your smoke-laden mind?" Bart stalked across the room. "What kind of being makes that stupid wish? I've heard of wishing for more wishes, but *not* wishing? Are you insane? Mortals! I'll never understand them."

"Now wait a minute—" Dirham leapt onto her lap, his tail swishing angrily.

Maille put a hand on Bart's arm, those talons of hers encircling it. "You can't fry her, Bart, so don't even try. If you'd kept your big beak shut, we wouldn't be in this form in the first place and *we'd* be able to find Laszlo *and* fry the person who took him. But, no, you had to come out with guns blazing, acting all tough and mighty, as if you owned the joint. Now look where that bravado's gotten us. So like you to not consider the consequences. Always shooting your mouth off— well, now you're shooting blanks. How's that feel? You enjoying that?"

Kal shook his head and held up a hand. "Yo, guys. Focus. This isn't solving anything. There has to be a clue or something. Baby dragons don't just disappear."

Lexy stood on her hind legs and rested her front paws on the table. "Unless they have an amulet. Then they can."

Samantha's blood ran cold at the vixen's statement. If Albert had the amulet *and* the dragon, he could do whatever he wanted and there was nothing they could do about it. He had more magic than she did at the moment even though she was the one with the genie.

"There has to be a clue somewhere. Something." She was grasping at straws, but she felt responsible for this. If only she hadn't brought Albert into her life; if she'd seen him for what he was, greedy and sneaky and utterly heartless. If she'd figured it out earlier... Had kicked him out. Or closed the safe...

If she hadn't wished away her wishes.

"Of course I looked for clues," said Maille, "but I didn't find any."

"Was that before or after you turned the nest inside out?" sneered Bart.

Maille flicked her tongue at him, and it really was forked. Samantha thought Bart had been speaking figuratively.

"I was panicked. Plus, I thought *she* could fix this."

Samantha *wanted* to fix it. How could Albert have done this? He *knew* what not having a mother meant to her. How that was the one thing she'd ever really wanted in her life, but even Kal's magic obviously hadn't been able to make that happen. And now he'd purposely taken Laszlo from his mother. "We should look again. You might have missed something in your worry."

"*You're* going to find something?" said Maille, anger quickly replacing the forlorn look—and Samantha couldn't blame her. "Weren't you the one who screwed up having a genie? Pardon me if I'm not all agog with excitement over your offer."

Samantha tamped down a retort because Maille had a point. Still… "Look, if it was Albert, I know him better than anyone." Well, anyone here. But she obviously didn't know the Albert who would have done this. Still, they had to start somewhere.

"Who's Albert?"

"Her boyfriend," said the ever-helpful Dirham.

"Ex-boyfriend," Samantha and Kal said together.

Samantha kept her gaze firmly on Maille, but she could feel her cheeks flaming. Semantics came into play in all sorts of situations, didn't they?

"Your *boyfriend*?" Maille screeched. "Great balls of fire, you do know how to pick them, don't you? And I thought my taste in men was bad."

Samantha didn't need the reminder. "How about I give you Kal's lantern, Maille? Then he'll be your genie and you can wish Laszlo home." The idea just slipped out, but the minute she said it, Samantha knew it was the right thing to do.

Except that Maille started laughing. "Oh, now that's priceless! She's going to give me the lantern. Wouldn't *that* be a kick!"

Bart joined in. "And I said Kal had gotten himself a smart one? What was I thinking?"

Still, he gave her the once-over. Twice.

Samantha shuddered. Maille had a legitimate complaint.

The dragon flicked Bart's arm. "Yeah, as if you'd know smart, worm-brain."

Then again, Bart did, too.

At least Samantha had gotten the two of them on the same page—even if it was at her expense.

Kal took her hand. "That's very generous of you, Sam, but dragons, as the second most magical beings, can't command a genie. It's the system of checks and balances—no one magical being can have too much power."

"Except the High Master," said Dirham. "He has all the power."

"But he still answers to Nature and Time," said Lexy, which caused Dirham's ears to droop.

Samantha knew the feeling. "Well, what about Dirham? Can he be your master?"

Dirham splatted onto the floor again. "Me?"

Lexy shook her head and hopped down next to the Dirham. "Magical-assistance assistants can't be masters. It would upset the natural order."

"Speaking of which, we need to get going if we're going to find Laszlo." Kal waved his hand and the flying Mercedes showed up, hovering a few inches off the ground outside her door, with a second set of gull wings for the additional passengers since they could no longer fly under their own power. "Ready when you are."

Maille leapt a few inches out of her chair. "I thought you couldn't do magic."

"Only for Samantha's comfort. Getting you where

you need to go quickly is a fortunate by-product." He opened the door and looked at all of them. "Coming?"

Bart scowled. "Do I have a choice?"

"Sure," said Maille. "You can choose to jump off a cliff in your present form."

"Love you, too, Maille." Bart swept his hand for her to precede him out the door. "After you, my sweet."

The dragon stalked out. "My sweet ass, you mean."

"Don't flatter yourself, babe."

23

WHEN THE GOLD SMOKE CLEARED, ALBERT LET
out a *whoop!* Home sweet home.

With a dragon dangling off his bloody finger.

He didn't give a damn. He was just glad to be back
in his bedroom in his apartment, and, more importantly,
glad that he'd figured out how the coin worked.

He patted it again. "I wish I was in my kitchen."

More gold smoke blew around him and there he
was—in his kitchen. With his little nipper of an append-
age still attached.

He tried prying the dragon loose, but it wouldn't
let go, so he set it in the sink and turned on the water.
Yep, cold water had the same effect on dragons as it
did on dogs. It let go and leapt out of the cold stream,
its scrawny legs backpedaling to keep it from heading
down the drain.

Albert cleaned his finger and wrapped it with a paper
towel. He didn't want to risk losing the dragon by leaving it for the time he'd need to run to his bathroom for
a bandage.

Ah, but he didn't have to be gone all that long…

"I wish to be in my bathroom."

Before this round of smoke cleared, Albert had
grabbed the bandages and wished himself back into the
kitchen where the dragon was still fighting the stainless

steel slope in the sink, its claws clattering up a storm without it budging an inch.

Perfect. Just what he needed.

Albert quickly replaced the paper towel with a bandage, placed the broiling pan on top of the sink to make sure the dragon would be there when he got back, and said, "I wish to be in a vacant aisle in the pet store at the mall."

Six and a half minutes later—the coin couldn't make store clerks move any faster—Albert was standing back in his kitchen with the bird cage and lizard food he'd swiped out from under the teenaged salesclerks' noses, figuring they'd put his disappearing act down to whatever they were smoking these days.

Back in his kitchen, the dragon was still in the sink, its claws making a god-awful noise on the steel. Not that Albert cared; that noise was music to his ears. If he didn't have other plans for the dragon, he could make a killing with it—and avoid that same fate.

Ah, well, Henley would have his money soon enough.

Albert grabbed a spoon, positioned the open cage at just the right height, moved the broiler pan out of the way, and scooped the little *jackpot* inside.

Two seconds after he'd locked the door, ol' Jack started chirping and banging its head against the bars. Shit! Couldn't have that. Didn't need anyone coming to investigate the noise, and he certainly didn't want his meal ticket to kill itself.

Grabbing the packet of bird accessories he'd pulled from the cage, Albert found a mirror and fastened it to the side.

Jack took one look and fell in love.

Albert filled the water container, set out some of the worm-like things the pet store worker said lizards loved to eat, draped a few dish towels over the cage, then carried the contraption into the living room and set it on the coffee table. Then he put his feet up in the massager/recliner he'd recently splurged on for himself and lay back.

And not a moment too soon. With all the adrenaline that'd been coursing through him now crashing, Albert was exhausted. He and Jack would catch a few hours of sleep, then back to the genie's hideout he'd go—*after* he packed up a few necessities and crafted the perfect ransom note.

24

SAMANTHA HAD NO IDEA WHAT SHE'D EXPECTED A dragon's lair to look like, but it definitely wasn't this Tim Burton version of *Martha Stewart Living*.

The Hershey Kiss–shaped building was covered in silver plating that could have used Martha's special brand of polish, and faded, brick-red shutters hung lopsidedly from some of the windows. Others had no shutters at all. A shredded flag hung off the top of the pole in the conical roof, and dead purple flowers flanked the cracked mosaic tile path leading to the front door like shag carpeting from the '70s—and was in as bad a shape as if it'd been there since the '70s.

Samantha's first impression of the central room was chaos. She could see the possibilities with its minimalist Middle Eastern decor, but everything was covered in layers of newspaper.

And then she saw why.

More than a dozen winged creatures flew around the inside of the cone like a living, breathing kaleidoscope. Each about the size of her palm, they dipped and soared, climbed and dived like the sea monkeys she'd had as pets as a child. The papers were there to catch their, er, well, what needed to be caught.

"Curt!" Maille ran into the room, waving her hands. That only made the babies fly higher. "Leave Lisa alone!

And Gretchen, off the corbel, please. I know what you're doing up there, and that's not where we do it. You know better than that. Hank, don't pull on Martha's wings. Remember the tear you made in Bridget's yesterday and now she can't fly? What did I say would happen to you if you did that again?"

A navy-blue dragon spiraled out of the sky. Bart shot out his hand and caught him before he hit the floor.

Maille shook a finger at the red dragon who'd followed the blue one down and was grinning a few feet above their heads—just out of reach. "Hank, I told you no fire! It's not fair to scorch your brothers and sisters until they can do it back. Look what you've done to poor Freddy." She took the injured one from Bart and held him against her cheek.

Within seconds, the little guy was off and flying, not a mark on him.

"Dragon tears are a great cure-all," Kal whispered to Samantha before she asked the question.

"Tell me you didn't leave the children here by themselves this morning," Bart said.

"Of course not. Maisey's here. Probably preparing lunch."

Bart cursed. "Or sleeping off a hangover. Leaving them with that dodo is worse than leaving them unattended."

"Don't stand there and tell me how to parent, brat. If you'd been here instead of gallivanting all over the place, you'd see what I went through. But, no, you had to have your fun. You don't get to come in now and tell me what to do with them. Maisey's good in a pinch, she's sober, and I was planning to be right back. *With*

Laszlo. I didn't think I'd run into an issue with Kal and his master."

Samantha bit her lip. It wasn't as if she'd known Albert would stoop to these levels; he'd never given any indication when they were together. Of course, now she realized he'd just been playacting. He'd seen dollar signs every time he'd looked at her. Or gold coins, rather. Copper lanterns, flying carpets, whatever he wanted.

Which wasn't her.

All along, she'd wanted to believe in a fairy tale that hadn't existed, while he'd been after a real one right under her nose—or rather, behind the combination to the safe.

Well, she wasn't going to sit around and wait for Prince Charming to ride in on his white horse and fix this, because there was no such thing. With Kal's magic basically useless to her, she was going to have to figure out a way to save not only herself, but the baby dragon, too.

She wanted a chance to be more than window dressing? This was it. She knew Albert better than anyone here. If he was, indeed, the one who'd taken Laszlo, it was time to put that knowledge to use.

She looked at the eagle Kal wore around his neck. Maybe this was what the Oracle had meant about her destiny. "I'd like to take a look at the nest, Maille. See if Albert left anything behind that I might recognize."

"I'm not so sure that your ex *was* here, Samantha." Lexy stepped out from behind Kal's legs. "I've done a preliminary scan of the doorway and am unable to detect any mortal presence other than yours."

"But if he used the magic amulet, wouldn't that cover his tracks?"

Lexy tapped the floor with a claw. "The amulet wouldn't, per se, but its Glimmer might have." She looked at Dirham. "Dirham, perhaps you could start on the opposite side of the room and work your way in toward the middle to double check my results."

"Me?" Dirham squeaked. "Double check? Sure, I can do that." He looked over his shoulder to the lavender dragon hanging on to his back like a possum. "Uh, kid? You want to let go?"

The dragon wrapped her claws more firmly into his fur and snuggled in. Dirham shrugged and disappeared beneath the furniture.

Samantha investigated the nest, a mass of intertwined branches and bits of leather, but found nothing, not even a dragon's eggshell. Those were on the floor, presumably because of Maille pawing through the nest first. Whatever Albert might have left behind was gone.

Kal and Bart made a higher level reconnaissance of the room, while Maille shooed all the babies into the nursery next door—except for Dirham's hitchhiker and the one on the corbel. That one wasn't cooperating.

"Gretchen, I said to come here now," said her mother.

The little dragon shook her head and walked closer to the wall where they couldn't see her.

"I mean it, Gretchen. You come down or you're grounded until you're five hundred."

"There's a threat," Bart muttered.

Maille gave him the Evil Eye. "Gretchen, come here this instant."

The little dragon peered over the edge with her pointed beak. She looked like she was enjoying thwarting her mother.

"Are you going to come down?"

Gretchen shook her head. "Pretty!"

The scowl on Maille's face transformed itself into an awestruck smile. "She spoke! My baby spoke her first word."

"Figures she'd go for something as shallow and vacuous as 'pretty,'" Bart said. "She's her mother's daughter."

"Can you just let me enjoy the moment, already? Why do you have to ruin everything?"

"Why should you have all the fun?"

Samantha dragged one of the mushroom-shaped stools beneath the corbel. "Maille, how about you try to get her to come to you now?"

With one more black look at her mate, Maille climbed atop the stool and held up her hand. "Come to Mommy, Gretchen. I'll give you lots of pretty shiny things if you do."

"Sure. Bribery. Why not?" Bart said, sarcastically.

"Hey, if you have any ideas, I'm listening, but so far all I've gotten from you is sarcasm. It'd be different if I could fly up there, but *someone* had to go and open her big mouth."

"I said I was sorry. I can't change the past." Samantha was getting sick of having to apologize. "If I could, I would. Trust me. There's nothing I'd like more than to go back and pretend this never happened."

"Me, too," Maille grumbled.

Kal aimed his fingers at her. For a second, Samantha thought he was going to unleash some magic.

Maille did, too. She took a step back and almost teetered off the stool.

But Kal unleashed anger instead. "Let's get one thing straight, Maille. We're here out of the goodness of Samantha's heart, not because she owes you anything. She's not responsible for Albert's actions, nor the fact that she has my lantern. None of this is Samantha's fault, so don't go throwing her help back in her face. Got it?"

Even Bart took a step back at the vehemence in Kal's voice.

"Pretty!"

"Not now, Gretchen." Maille waved her hand, dismissively.

So Gretchen dropped something onto her head. Something rectangular, orange, and hard enough to elicit a blast of steam from her mother.

A crystal.

It bounced off Maille's head and landed at Samantha's feet.

"Kal! She found it!" Dirham started bouncing faster than Samantha had seen him do so far. Good thing the lavender dragon had such a tight hold. "Gretchen found your crystal!"

Samantha picked it up. Shaped like an obelisk and about six inches long, the crystal didn't look like anything special.

"What does it do?" she asked.

"Wave it," said Kal.

When she did, orange glitter formed Kal's outline in front of him.

"Now sweep it around the room where I walked."

Orange glitter shimmered all over the place.

"It's a bio-transmitter," said Lexy. "A mechanism for the High Master's vizier to use to track djinn. Or rather, that's what they were used for until a certain rogue genie—"

"She wasn't rogue," said Dirham, handing the lavender dragon off to her mother.

"I beg to differ, Dirham." Lexy sat and curled her tail around her front paws, her nose raised a degree or two more than perpendicular. "Eden's actions qualified her to be considered rogue, but that's neither here nor there. She was responsible for returning the crystals to every djinni in The Service, which was how this came to be in Kal's possession. She was a hero, if you will."

Samantha "willed;" *hero* beat *window dressing* hands down. She handed the crystal to Kal. "So this is how he expects to find you?"

Kal took it and glitter scattered all over the place. "Not only that, but it proves he was here and has the amulet. And since we aren't able to detect his scent or the amulet's Glimmer, that means he was here long enough ago that all traces have disappeared. That worries me. Albert's a newcomer to Izaaz. Where's he been hiding all these hours? And with a baby dragon, no less. We all know they aren't exactly the easiest creatures to control."

Four pairs of human eyes, and two vulpine, looked up at the corbel.

Gretchen smiled down at them and chirruped.

"So now what?" huffed Bart. "We found the damned crystal, but the prick still has my kid."

"*Now* you decide to care," sneered Maille.

A raised eyebrow was Bart's only reaction. "Can we get a reverse lookup on that thing?" He nodded to the crystal. "Since he's touched it, it has to have captured some of his essence, right? We should be able to trace that back to him and find Laszlo."

Kal shook his head. "Crystals are imprinted on only one person. In this case, me. The good news is that without this, Albert can't pinpoint where I am. The amulet does an approximation unless you specify the exact location." He tucked it into the side pocket of his pants. "But the bad news is that we still have to figure out where he is without him knowing we're on to him. With him having the amulet, that's going to be tougher than I'd like."

"Unless…" Maille climbed off the stool and tossed her hair over her shoulder. Part of the gray stripe lingered. "There's someone who knows how to find people without being found."

"Oh no. No way," Bart growled. "Don't even say his name, Maille."

"Harv."

No one said a word.

Except Gretchen.

"Pretty!"

Then Kal spoke—another curse in another language that needed no translation.

Bart, on the other hand, cursed in perfectly good English. "You'd love that, wouldn't you, Maille? Let your old boyfriend save the day."

"You seriously need to get over that, Bart. It was eons ago."

Samantha didn't want to know how many. "Can you two knock off the bickering? We have more important things to worry about." She looked at Kal. "Who's Harv?"

Troll? Ogre? Abominable snowman? Grim reaper? Anything was possible.

"Harv is delusional," Bart said.

Maille threw up her hands. "You're just jealous because he's got the *huevos* to back up his bad-ass reputation that you don't."

"I am not jealous of Harv. You'd really get off on it if I were, wouldn't you?"

Kal answered Samantha. "Harv's sort of the unofficial gatekeeper for Izaaz. Has his finger on the pulse of the town and knows the minute anyone shows up who's not supposed to be here."

"That's 'cause he wants them for lunch," said Dirham. "Usually as the main course. Your boyfriend's going to be in big trouble."

Samantha didn't bother correcting him. Semantics were the least of her worries, though it seemed like this Harv guy would be Albert's biggest.

"Don't tell me you're actually considering this." Bart leaned against the armoire. "Oh for gods' sakes, you're all just as delusional as Harv. You're leaving the fate of my hatchling in his hands, Maille, and you call me an unfit parent?"

"Harv has nothing to do with why you're unfit," Maille spat back.

"Actually, Maille has a point. Well, about Harv," said Kal. "And we really don't have a choice. With my hands tied, magically speaking, Harv's the best chance we have for finding Albert. And maybe even doing something about it. There's nothing worse for a thief than coming face to face with the mother of them all."

Dirham cocked his head. "Don't you mean father? Harv's a boy."

"Good point, Dir. Thanks."

"No problem. Anything to be helpful."

Because that's what Dirham did.

Now if only the fox could help her figure out some way to get the magic back. Then she could fix this, shed her window-dressing image, and save Laszlo.

25

SAMANTHA TUCKED THE LANTERN MORE SNUGGLY beneath her arm and followed Kal through the rusted, corrugated drainage pipe he said was the way to Harv's lair. She had serious doubts about that because the ancient sewer tunnel was so strewn with debris that no one should live there.

Bart had the same opinion and made no bones about it. Kicked a few, too, and hadn't stopped cursing from the minute they'd stepped out of the car.

"Are we there yet?" Dirham asked for the fifteenth time.

Samantha knew it was fifteen because she'd been counting.

"No, Dir, not yet." Kal responded for the same number of times before consulting the map she'd first seen yesterday on the flying carpet.

"Do you think he'll help us?" This was only the third time Dirham had asked that question.

"I hope so." And the third time he'd gotten the same answer.

"Hope?" Maille screeched again. She'd been doing that ever since they'd left her house, which explained why this was the first time she was hearing the answer. "*That's* the plan? Good gods! Hope's about as useful as Bart's foreplay."

"Don't start with me, woman," her ex growled from the shadows behind them.

"Trust me, Bart, I have no intention of starting anything with you. I wish I hadn't gotten you involved in the first place, and if chicky here had kept her big mouth shut, I wouldn't have needed to."

"I said I didn't do it on purpose, Maille," said Samantha.

"Even worse."

Kal started to say something, but Samantha put her hand on his arm and shook her head. Maille was right, but more than that, the woman was hurting. Dragon or human, she was worried about her baby, and Samantha was willing to cut her a lot of slack because of it.

Bart, however, wasn't. "So tell me again why the kids were unattended and this Albert person had the chance to snatch them, oh Great Parent? What were you doing that you couldn't watch them?"

"I don't watch them while they sleep, smoke-breath."

"I'll thank you to refrain from the insults, sweets."

"I'll thank you to refrain from breathing."

"Right after you, babe."

"Guys!" Kal turned around and everyone stopped within the firelight's glow. "Save it for later. Harv doesn't encourage visitors, so we need to keep our eyes and ears open."

"Oh I'm good at that. Especially the ears part," said Dirham, waggling the appendages in question. "So, are we here now?" A variation on the theme, but still, Number Sixteen.

"Does it look like we're here, muppet?" Bart growled. "This is a really bad idea. We should go back to the house and question the kids some more. Or better yet, the neighbors. At the very least, grab a few more torches since, according to Kal's skewed logic, Samantha only needs one, leaving the rest of us to fly blind."

"You do that?" asked Dirham. "It doesn't sound very safe."

Lexy whispered in Dirham's ear and the little fox turned pink—an interesting ability given that he was orange. "Oh."

Maille shook her head. "Quit bitching. A wyvern is supposed to be used to dark, creepy places."

"You so do *not* want me to go there, babe."

Maille bared her teeth. "Go here then. I already questioned the older hatchlings, but they were so frightened that I couldn't get much out of them, including the info about the crystal. They have no idea where Gretchen came up with it. I'm not incompetent, you know."

"So says you."

"Can it, *brat*." Maille huffed.

"No, I'm not going to can it." He looked at Kal. "This is a waste of time. We should go back and question the neighbors. This prick couldn't have just waltzed in and out without anyone seeing anything."

"Yeah, 'cause Dragon's Blood Pass isn't for the faint of heart." Dirham shivered.

"True, but those faint hearts do taste delicious." Bart swiped his tongue over his lips, and now it was Samantha's turn to shiver.

"You're thinking about food when our child is missing?" Maille spun around and her hair whipped him across the face. "What kind of father are you?"

He spit out the strands. "Who says I *am* the father?"

Samantha and Kal didn't even have to take a step

back to get out of the fray; Maille shoved Bart so hard he went backpedaling across the tunnel, windmilling his arms to stay upright while Maille kept going, laying into him with her forked tongue—literally and figuratively—until they disappeared down another tunnel.

"Do you think we should follow them?"

"Ooh! I will! I will!" Dirham disappeared into the darkness with a sighing Lexy right after him.

"Kal?" Samantha nodded toward the torch.

Kal raked a hand through his hair. "We probably should." But he didn't move.

Samantha didn't either. If she hadn't felt so guilty, she'd have washed her hands of those two; *she* seemed to care more about the situation with their child than they did.

Or felt guiltier about it.

She wrapped her arms around her middle and rubbed her hands up and down.

"Are you cold?" Kal put a hand on her shoulder. "I could conjure a blanket for you."

She shook her head. The last thing they needed was a blanket anywhere near them. "No, thank you. I'm worried. And annoyed. Don't they get it? What's with all the bickering?"

"Maille and Bart have always bickered. It's part of dragon nature."

"Be that as it may, it's not productive. I just wish—"

He kissed her. That wasn't quite what she wished, but, God, he felt so good. And right now, she could use his kind of feel-good.

She leaned into him and slipped her arms around his waist, thankful for the short vest he wore so she could feel the heat of his skin against her palms. Feel the catch of his breath when she answered his silent request to open her mouth so his tongue could make quick strokes along hers, sending her right back to this morning and last night and, God, she was on fire. One simple kiss and she turned to lava in his arms.

She pressed herself against him, reveled in the feel of his arm as it slid over her shoulder and down her spine, pressing against the small of her back so she was as close as could be, heat suffusing her, surrounding her, and she groaned. His touch was magical; every millimeter of skin he stroked sparked to life. She could almost smell the smoke—

Samantha's eyes shot open.

There *was* smoke. And it was coming from Kal's back.

Never mind having wished—*again*—for him to kiss her, now she was burning him to a crisp.

"Oh, my God, Kal! You're on fire!" She tried to tear herself away, but he merely smiled and wouldn't let her go.

"I know. So are you."

She swatted at his waist. "No, you idiot, you're on *fire*. Drop and roll, drop and roll!"

Kal hadn't heard of this type of kink, but, hey, if she was into it…

He knelt down and dropped the torch. It rolled out of the way, providing such perfect atmosphere that it was as if he'd conjured it for this moment. He leaned back, tugging her with him. They'd have to make this quick before anyone returned—not that the quick part would be a problem since last night had only whetted his appetite and this morning had fueled it even more. Not to mention those hundred-plus years of celibacy…

"Hurry up!" She was of the same mind, pounding a fist against his chest, and Kal didn't think he'd ever have enough of Samantha.

"Come on, Kal! We have to put the fire out!"

Kal was focusing on her fingers against his skin, but as his back reached the ground, the words finally registered. So did the heat. And the smell of burning fabric.

Fire. On his back.

Son of a Sumerian—the torch!

Kal rolled back and forth, extinguishing the fire and cradling Samantha—if he was going to have to lose the vest off his back and hear about this from Bart ad nauseam, he might as well get something from it.

And, yes, it was totally and completely wrong of him to hold her like this, to use this opportunity for his own selfish purposes, but, frankly, he couldn't summon the wherewithal to care. Not with Samantha nestled against him, her legs cradled between his, her head tucked beneath his chin, her fingers splayed against his chest. If Bart and Maille didn't feel a sense of urgency, if they didn't care, why should he?

Because… he did.

He stopped rolling, but he stayed where he was just a moment longer. Maybe two.

"Kal?" Samantha whispered. "Are you okay?"

He was just fine. His dick was turning to wood and he had a beautiful woman plastered against him on the floor of a messy old tunnel with two dragons and two fennecs who-knew-how-far-away, the ever-present promise of Harv showing up, a missing dragonlet, and a possible threat to everything he'd worked toward for all these years, but yeah, he was fine.

"I will be, Sam."

She lifted her head, her curls brushing his chin, and looked at him. "How's your back?"

His back was the least of his worries—especially if she couldn't feel that hard length of him pressing against her. "It's fine, but the vest isn't."

She rested her chin on his breastbone. "I'm really sorry, Kal."

"Sorry? For what? You didn't catch my vest on fire."

"Not that." She glanced away and her tongue flicked over her lips again before she met his gaze. "For making you sleep with me last night."

If there was one thing he never would have expected to come out of her mouth, it was that. She thought she'd wished him into sleeping with her? Gods, his technique must be really off if she thought he'd been under duress.

He'd have to rectify that. "Trust me, Samantha, you didn't make me do anything."

"But I did, Kal. I wish—"

Kal grabbed a quick kiss. She felt so good atop him. Beneath him, too, so what she was saying made absolutely no sense. "Sam, you have absolutely nothing to apologize for."

He, however, was going to have to make a shitload of apologies when four hooves clattered next to them and a glowing green light revealed the guy standing above them.

"You're kidding me, right? Here?" The language was a dead one, but the sarcasm all too alive—and familiar. "You need some serious lessons in seducing a woman, Kal, if this is how you go about it. Move over and I'll show you how it's done."

Kal sighed and helped Samantha sit up.

"Samantha Blaine, allow me to introduce you to Harv. Short for Harvard, who went to Princeton, and is a Yale. In other words, a blue-blooded, Ivy League… thief."

26

JUST WHEN SAMANTHA THOUGHT SHE WAS GETTING used to all the strange things in Izaaz, life took a sharp turn sideways.

Kind of like Harv's horns were doing. One was going left and the other… southeast?

"I find the term 'thief' extremely offensive, Kal. Besides, isn't that a pot/kettle thing?"

Harv, a bundle of muscle covered in thick black fur, was similar to, and as big as, an elk, but with the tusks of a boar and two antelope horns that looked strong enough to skewer a bull. Horns that rotated. And twisted. And turned. Could probably do the hula, too.

Samantha grabbed the lantern from where it'd fallen to the floor beside Kal—he'd warned her to keep a tight hold on it in the event they found Harv—and scrambled to her feet, checking to make sure everything that should be covered was. "Um, hi?"

She wasn't sure what the protocol was for greeting someone with that sort of introduction—and hooves. Should she offer to shake? Bow? Curtsy? Put her hands in the air à la "stick-'em-up," or snort and paw the ground?

One of the horns answered that question for her. Not that it actually talked, though frankly, she wouldn't have been surprised after watching it turn toward her and angle down to slide beneath her palm, which it then raised, bringing her hand to Harv's lips so he could gallantly kiss the back of it.

"*Enchanté, ma belle.*"

The man, er, elk, er, *Yale* was good. Smooth. Charming. Suave. All he needed was the tweed jacket with leather elbow patches and a pipe to complete the Ivy League image.

And bipedal appendages, of course.

Odd to be saying this, and even odder to be feeling it, but if she disregarded what he looked like—and what he was—and focused on his deep baritone voice and the bedroom eyes he turned on her, she'd say that Harv knew how to make a woman feel like a woman.

Or maybe that was because she was still swimming in the hormonal maelstrom Kal and his kisses had conjured, and the contact of Kal's hand on the small of her back that was doing crazy things to her nerve endings.

Always a possibility.

"Pleased to meet you." She glanced at Kal. She was pleased to meet him, right?

Kal, with the mind-reading ability he claimed he didn't have, nodded.

"Hey, guys!" Dirham's voice echoed through the metal tunnels. "Where are you? We can go look for Harv now. Maille and Bart promised they'll be good. No more fights."

"I'll believe that when I see it," Kal muttered.

"I can't believe you're still shackled to Dirham," said Harv, chuckling. "You must've pissed off ol' Faruq something good."

"Don't underestimate Dirham, Harv. There's a reason he's a magical-assistance assistant."

"Yeah, because the dust mop position was already filled."

Kal glared at him. Harv smiled back. Samantha rolled her eyes and crossed her arms.

"Kal? Samantha? Where are you?"

"Over here, Dirham," she shouted because these two were too invested in their pissing match to do so.

"Been a while, Kal."

"I've been busy."

"Not so much, I've heard."

"You heard wrong."

The posturing was ridiculous. There was no time for this, and they were flinging enough testosterone around to impregnate the entire town. Samantha wanted to throttle both of them.

She opted for stepping between them and putting a hand on each one's chest. "Can we stop, please? We've got more important things to do."

Harv instantly turned on the charm again. An antler trapped her hand over his heart, and he turned his head to give her the full effect of those eyes.

If he weren't a four-legged animal covered in fur, it might have worked.

"I hear you're looking for me, little lady."

Before she could answer, Samantha found herself levitating a few inches off the ground, then landing a good two feet behind Kal.

"Nice try, Harv, but give it up. The lady's not interested."

Kal then made a big production of shrugging out of the two halves of his burned vest and tossing them against the wall, and Samantha became very interested. But definitely not in Harv.

She had a feeling that's exactly why Kal had made such a big deal about it. Guys were the same no matter what the species.

Still, part of her was thrilled he cared enough to be jealous. That had to be it, because he wasn't going all macho just because she was his master; there'd be no need. No, he was staking his claim, and for as Neanderthal as that sounded, Samantha didn't mind. There was a lot about Kal that she didn't mind. A lot that she really liked.

Harv glanced into the shadows where Kal had tossed the clothing and raised an eyebrow. "Not interested? Then why was she looking for me?"

"Bad news travels fast in Izaaz."

"Bad news and intruders. Both of which I'm guessing have something to do with why you're here, Kal."

"Know anything?"

"I might. Then again, I might not." One of the antlers scratched his shoulder blade.

This was getting them nowhere. Samantha picked up the torch and stuck herself between the two of them again. "Have you heard of a guy named Albert Viehl—and do you know where he is?"

She wished she'd taken Kal up on that blanket offer when Harv ran his gaze over her, lingering on places she'd rather he wouldn't.

"*Albert?*" Harv leaned around her to smirk at Kal. "Losing your touch, buddy?"

Kal put his hands on her waist and Samantha had the distinct impression he'd been about to physically lift her out of the way, but Dirham re-entered the tunnel just then, injecting his special brand of bounciness into the atmosphere, and Kal slid his arms around her waist to pull her back against him instead.

"Kal!" The fox screeched to a stop so abruptly that little puffs of dirt billowed out around all four paws. Four more when Lexy stopped just as quickly behind him. "So this is where you are. And you found Harv!" He bounced twice.

Samantha wasn't about to correct him, since , technically, Harv had found them. In a rather compromising position, no less.

"Yes, Dir, we found him."

"Awesome! I knew you would!" Dirham added a back flip to his repertoire.

Harv turned around, his hooves making almost as much noise as the antlers that were clacking together in a bone-on-bone way that grated on Samantha's nerves. "Give me a break, fox. If I didn't want to be found, I wouldn't have been. Don't go giving Kal any laurels he hasn't earned. Which, I've heard, are very few these days."

Samantha didn't understand the undertones between the guys. They were like rutting animals—which could work for Harv, but what was Kal's excuse? After last night, he couldn't possibly think she'd have any interest whatsoever in Harv.

Actually, she couldn't believe he'd *ever* think that. She wasn't sure what she thought of the social mores here in Izaaz, but to her way of thinking, that would just be wrong.

She stepped out of Kal's embrace. "Look, everyone, I don't know what's going on here, and, frankly, I don't care, but if we could get to the part about Albert, I'd really appreciate it."

Harv's head whipped around—the antlers stayed where they were—and he looked at her with new respect. "Whoa. The lady's got a backbone. Not your typical kind, Kal."

"She's my master, Harv. Leave it alone."

"*It?* Are you sure that's the pronoun you mean?"

Kal said something in that other language of his, and Harv responded, his chest puffing up like a peacock.

"Speak English, please," said Samantha. "And can you answer the question, Harv? Do you or do you not know where Albert is?"

"I might."

"That doesn't help."

"What will you give me to find out?" He undressed her with his eyes.

Yeah, she wouldn't mind that blanket now. Too bad she couldn't wish for one. But then, she wouldn't be in this situation if she *could* wish so the point was moot. "Look, we don't have time to play these games. Albert kidnapped a baby dragon. You're not going to let someone just waltz in here and kidnap a baby, are you?"

Harv flicked an antler beneath her chin. "First off, gorgeous, it's not my kid, so I don't care. Second, I challenge anyone to waltz in here and help themselves to something I *do* care about, and, third, does this guy really waltz? Didn't that go out in like the last century? Got yourself a real Renaissance man, have you?"

"Can you help us or not?" She crossed her arms, determined to win her own pissing contest with the Yale.

Harv studied her—all of her. She held both her tongue and her breath; Laszlo's safety was worth a couple of leers.

Finally, Harv nodded. "We'll talk. Let's see what my scouts have to say. I haven't gotten a report yet today, but as of this time yesterday, he wasn't here."

"Is it possible he could have shown up and you wouldn't know?"

His antlers pointed forward like a pair of lances. "If you weren't a newcomer here—and hot—I'd skewer you for that."

Kal moved the antlers with a finger on each. "We know he's been here, Harv."

"Not possible. My minions, er, network would know."

Kal pulled the crystal from his pants pocket. "He dropped this at the scene of the crime."

Harv's antler swished down to touch the crystal, but Kal pulled it out of reach and stuck it back in his pocket. "I wasn't born yesterday, Harv. No way you're getting your antlers on that."

"So how did your guy? I'm having a really hard time believing you, Kal. You're not usually so careless… Unless *she's* got something to do with it?"

"Geez, give it a rest will you?" Samantha exhaled.

"Sure thing, gorgeous. I'll take a rest with you. Or, better yet, we could do something to get ar*rest*ed. How's that sound?" Harv waggled his eyebrows, and Samantha was at a loss for words. Even in Izaaz, this guy was a real character.

"Albert has one of Mayat's amulets," said Kal. "*That's* how he's avoided detection."

The antlers fell back against Harv's neck and he stopped leering. "Then you're fucked. That screws the whole equation. No one can track those amulets. Their Glimmer doesn't last as long as a djinni's."

"So there's no way to find him?" Samantha asked.

"I didn't say that, gorgeous."

"Then there is?"

"There might be."

"You're infuriating, you know that?"

"I've been told."

"So what do we need to do to find Albert?"

Kal touched her arm. "Sam—"

An antler waved in the air, cutting him off. "Now, now, Kal. The lady did ask me. Isn't there something in your Code about usurping powers or some shit like that?"

Kal muttered in that foreign language again. She was going to have to have him teach it to her when this was all said and done.

"So… Let's see… What can you do?" Harv sidled closer. Samantha's skin crawled, but she wasn't going to let him see her sweat. "For starters, you can hand over that lantern."

"Kal's?" Samantha held it up.

"Unless you're double-dipping on the genie front."

She snatched it away before Harv's snake-like antler could grab hold of it. "But I thought it wasn't of any use to you."

Behind her, Kal groaned.

"No use? Hmm… I didn't think djinn could lie to their masters. Kal? You want to clarify please?"

Kal was pinching the bridge of his nose when she looked at him. "Dragons can't have lanterns, Sam. Yales, on the other hand—"

"I prefer hoof, if you don't mind."

Kal glared at him "Hoof, then. Anyhow, Yales can

command genies because they don't have any magic other than the obvious." He waved toward Harv's antlers.

"So, Harv, you want me to give you Kal's lantern—Kal essentially—for a *maybe*?" She shook her head. "I don't think so. How about we hear what you know and then decide?"

Harv scoffed. "No dice, gorgeous. You want what I got, you gotta play by my rules."

"Don't do it, Samantha." Dirham jumped as high as her chin.

Kal caught him before he hit the ground. "Dir—"

"No, Kal, I have to say this. It's not against any of the rules, but Samantha, you can't give him the lantern. If he ends up with it, this place will never be the same."

Harv snorted. "Have you seen this place, dirtbag? That would be a good thing."

"Don't call him that," said Lexy, her fur bristling.

Harv's antlers went straight up. "Sorry, little lady. Didn't mean to ruffle anyone's feathers. Or fur, as it were." He cocked an eyebrow when he looked at Samantha, and his antler stroked an imaginary curly mustache. "So, do we have an agreement?"

Samantha tapped her lips. Dirham chewed on his. Lexy's tail was flicking nervously. Kal looked like he wanted to punch something—some*one*—and Harv was rubbing his antlers together as if he'd won the lottery.

She looked at the lantern. It was one thing to give Kal up to a mother trying to find a missing child; quite another to give him up to an animal—in both the true sense of the word and the vernacular.

And she didn't want to give him up at all.

She jumped when Kal's cheek touched hers.

"Samantha, it's okay," he said for her ears only. "Our one other option is to put out an APB on Albert, but if we do that, he'll transport himself anywhere in the world he wants the minute he finds out. We need to keep him in town so we can find him before he does something to Laszlo that we may not be able to undo. A growing dragon is only a handful for so long before he becomes a liability for Albert. We don't want to risk that. Go ahead and agree, but be sure you tell Harv to deliver Albert and then you'll deliver the lantern—in those exact words. Everything will be fine if you do that."

Semantics as usual.

"Any day now, gorgeous. Clock's ticking."

Samantha didn't like this, but what choice did she have? "Are you sure there isn't another way?"

Kal's eyes were soft. Melty. And it could be the last time she saw them like that. "If I could come up with one, I'd take it. But I can't. He's Laszlo's best bet, as wrong as that sounds."

"If only I hadn't—"

Kal put a finger to her lips. "What's done is done. All we can do is move forward, so don't beat yourself up over it, Samantha. You certainly didn't plan for this to happen. Just make sure you tell him to *deliver* Albert."

She hadn't planned for any of this to happen. Not the least of which was caring for a genie.

But she knew what it was like to grow up without a mother, and she couldn't sentence poor Laszlo to that. Not when it was her fault that she'd had what Albert wanted and also now had the ability to fix the situation. She certainly hoped Kal knew what he was doing. She'd wish it, but wishing wasn't exactly her forte these days.

Gritting her teeth, she tucked the lantern under her arm and turned to face Harv. "Okay, here's the deal. You deliver Albert and I'll deliver the lantern. That's the best you'll get. Take it or leave it."

"You're sure I can't take you instead?"

Samantha shuddered. One depraved animal in her life was enough and Albert filled that role too perfectly.

"*I'm* sure," Kal answered.

Harv smirked. "Just checking."

She so wanted to wipe that smirk off his face. To the point that she almost hoped he didn't have any information, but that wouldn't help Laszlo.

Frustrated—at Harv's greed, Kal's altruism, and her lack of wishes—Samantha plucked the torch from Kal. "Fine, Harv. You've got a deal. And now we have a dragon to find." She strode toward the intersection of the tunnels, raised the torch, and looked back at Harv and Kal. "Coming, gentlemen?"

—⁓—

She looked like a goddess herself, standing there with the torchlight casting a halo around her head, the fire in her eyes at Harv's ridiculous proposal, and her determination and compassion to get Laszlo back.

Kal loved that about her. Every single bit. Especially the fact that Harv had never been bested by a woman, and whether the Yale knew it or not, he just had been. Sam probably didn't even realize it, but Dirham had caught the stipulation he'd purposely made her say and they'd shared a quiet chuckle at Harv's expense.

But he didn't refrain from grinning while he swept

a hand in front of the Yale. "You heard the lady. Let's get moving."

Harv raised an eyebrow. "I would've expected more of a fight about her giving up the lantern."

"You have to find Albert first."

"You doubt me?"

Kal shrugged. "You never know what life's going to throw at you. Karma gets pissy if you try to direct her, so I just go with the flow. Works better for everyone."

Harv didn't say anything for a few seconds. Probably trying to figure out Kal's angle. Good, let him. The Yale didn't live by the same set of rules as Kal; he'd never even think to see the loophole, which was the reason Kal had suggested it in the first place.

"You know what keeps me amused, Kal?" Harv asked as he started off.

"I don't particularly care."

"How you can stand taking orders from the likes of her and her kind. I'd go out of my freaking mind."

Kal gave him the answer every djinni learned in the first year of training. "Eye on the prize, Harv. Eye on the prize."

"She's definitely a prize. Have you hit that yet?" said Harv, crass despite the Ivy League pedigree.

Kal had to repeat the *prize* mantra to himself— twice—before he could respond. His relationship with Harv had never been what you'd call friendly, more of a mutual you-live-your-life, I'll-live-mine sort of thing. He never knew when he'd need someone with a skill set different than his—Harv had more skill sets than were legal on six of the seven continents—so it worked between them. But that comment about Sam negated the last thirty-seven hundred years of tolerance.

"You don't really expect me to dignify that with an answer, do you?"

Harv grinned. "You never were easy."

"And neither is she, so get your mind out of your own personal gutter."

"Damn, man, I've missed sparring with you. How long 'til you get out?"

Kal nodded at Sam as she turned the corner to go down another tunnel, Dirham bouncing beside her. "One more."

Harv whistled. "Her? All you have to do is finish up with her and then you're free? So when I get the lantern, you'll be back to being full-fledged? All powers fully restored?" His antlers rubbed together, generating the fluorescent green light that made the darkness bearable.

More than Harv was anyway. "You have to get the lantern first."

The antlers stopped. "Why do I not like how you said that?"

Damn. Overplayed his hand.

Kal shrugged, opting to let Harv think it was bravado. He didn't need to give anything up before they got what they needed. "Because I don't want you to?"

"Too bad your wishes don't count for anything. Unless, of course, you wanted me to do something about her." One of the antlers thumbed in the direction Samantha had gone. "I could take her out right now if you want. Get you those powers back right away."

In Harv's world, he'd just complimented Kal, but all Kal could picture was Sam lying in a pool of blood. The thought was more repugnant than losing out on the vizier job. "Don't touch her, Harv. Not a hair on her head."

"What about elsewhere?"

Kal punched him. He didn't think about it, hadn't seen it coming, and didn't register it until his hand started to hurt like shit.

"What the fuck was that for?" Harv cursed as he got off the ground.

Kal shook his hand. Damn, that hurt. "Don't talk about her like that. Don't even think about her like that. Keep your grubby hooves off of her. She's so out of your league you shouldn't even be breathing the same air."

"Whoa." Harv's antlers went straight up. "Chill out, man. Fine. I'm backing off. And you can get your info from someone else."

The Yale turned to leave, but Kal waved his hand, trapping Harv in an invisible box. If anyone asked, he'd remind them of the danger Sam would be in if they didn't get answers from Harv. It was weak, but he could argue it.

The gods and High Master willing, he wouldn't have to.

"You did not just do that." Harv snorted and pawed the ground, going feral.

"We need what you know."

"You've got a crazy way of showing it."

"You've got a crazy way of coming on to my master."

They glared at each other until Harv finally started laughing. "Man, Kal, talk about *Karma* being pissy. Looked in a mirror lately?" His antlers circled around his ears and settled on his head like a crown. It was a look he wore often for just that reason. "Fine, Kal. Take down your force field. I made the deal, so I'll give you what you want. Question is, will she?"

"Back. Off. Harv." Kal raised his fingers, pausing only to try to come up with a sustainable argument for sending a bolt of lightning through the spectrasphere and into the Yale because, technically, talking smack about someone's master wasn't considered magic-worthy.

Kal so wanted to have the chance to shoot off a few rounds, but Harv, damn him, raised his antlers in surrender, negating the necessity and the excuse.

"Fine. She's off limits. I get it, Kal. But do *you* get that even when the High Master frees you from that prison, she's going to have you tied up in another? She's already got you wearing a gemstone tracker. Is she afraid you're going to run out on her? And, man, it's too bad you can't explain any of this to her."

Kal refused to let Harv get a rise out of him. His relationship with Sam was none of the Yale's business.

He removed the force field from Harv just as Samantha poked her head out from the corner she'd gone around.

"Are you two coming?"

Harv snorted. "Yeah. Kal, are you?"

Kal flipped him the bird, a universal symbol no matter what shape you came in. "Be right there. Sam."

"Ah, crud, man. You got it bad."

"Don't make me hurt you again, Harv."

The Yale chuckled. "Oh, Kal, it's you who's gonna be hurt."

27

ALBERT CHECKED THE SUPPLIES IN THE TRUNK ONE more time. He had the slickest bowie knife he could find to threaten the dragon with, and enough firepower to level the entire magical town to threaten *them* with if it came to that. Harming the little four-legged matchstick would almost be an afterthought.

He fingered the gold coin. This thing came in handy. He had hit up a few weapons shops, dropped into a pair of bank vaults, and topped the day off with a visit to a Ferrari dealership followed by a little "hop" to Monte Carlo. All without so much as an alarm going off, TSA pat-downs, or payment exchanging hands.

He patted the duffel bag on the floor in front of the passenger seat. Well, money had exchanged hands—it'd gone from his left hand to his right as he'd cleared out the cash drawers, then right into the casinos for chips. He almost wished he could watch the U.S. news reports to see what spin the police put on the lack of clues, but he had more important fish to fry.

Make that, dragons to barter.

He picked up the little fire-breather's cage from the fireproof box he'd swiped at a hunting store. The lizard had tried to prove the old "where there's smoke, there's fire" adage, and Albert wasn't a big proponent of melting the Ferrari's leather.

"Knock it off, Jack," he said as the thing, once again, singed the dish towel. He should have used aluminum foil instead. Or a grill cover.

He was going to have to leave Jack in the car, check into the hotel, and then pop back out to retrieve him. Ah, well, this part of the plan he could improvise.

He made sure the ransom note was in the breast pocket of the designer tux he'd swiped. Two notes, actually, in case something happened to one of them. This was no time for mistakes. Come tomorrow, he had one shot at this.

And then the genie would be his.

Harv and Kal had emerged from the tunnel, laughing and scowling respectively, and Samantha wished it were the other way around. It also hadn't helped matters that, after a terse acknowledgment—barely—of the other's right to live, Bart began muttering beneath his breath every time Harv took a step.

Maille seemed to be heartily enjoying Bart's jealousy, which made no sense, but then, what in Izaaz did?

Dirham's chatter with the Yale certainly didn't. He kept asking Harv why he lived in a tunnel and what the conditions were like, his high-pitched voice reverberating through this larger tunnel until Bart had had enough and snapped.

"First bolt of fire I get, so help me, fox, I'm singeing your fur."

"Oh no you're not," said Lexy, her fur bristling. "You're not touching him. Dirham's done nothing to you."

"He annoys me. That's reason enough for shish kebab."

Dirham grabbed her by the tail when she went into a crouch. "It'th okay, Lexthy. He won't acthually do it."

"Try me," Bart shot back.

Dirham shook his head. "No thank you," he muttered with her tail still in his mouth.

"Nice, Barty," mocked Harv. "Scaring the little vixen. Make you feel like a big man?"

Bart stomped two steps toward Harv before Maille caught his arm. "Let it go, Bart. You can't take him. Not in this form."

"Say that to my face when I've got my scales back, Yale," Bart snarled. "Then we'll see who's feeling big."

Harv flicked an antler. "Let's not forget that *you* came to *me*."

"This was not my idea."

"Yet you're here. I swear the three of you have lost your *cojones* the way you're following these women around. And, yes, I'm including you in that, dirtbag."

Lexy, out of nowhere, bit Harv on the hind leg.

Who knew the vixen had it in her?

Harv bolted and howled, back-kicking the fox into Maille, who fell against Bart, who shoved her out of the way right into Samantha, who then fell down and dropped the lantern which went skittering off into the darkness. The tunnel was wide enough that she didn't hear it hit the wall.

Kal ran to her side so fast that the torch brought a trail of flames with it like a comet. "Are you all right, Samantha?" He set the torch down beside her and the flame flickered off the metal walls like something from a horror movie. Considering what she was about to tell him, it *was* a horror movie.

"I will be, but the lantern's missing," she whispered.

Four hooves went cantering by in the darkness.

Kal threw the torch after the Yale. "Get away from it, Harv!"

"Yeah, right! Be prepared to serve me, djinni!"

"The lantern? Oh, no!" Dirham leapt over Samantha and followed the torch after Harv.

"Dirham, wait for me!" Lexy went after him.

Bart was next. Maille, however, didn't budge.

Samantha turned around and saw the foxes scramble between Harv's legs, tripping him up. Bart brought him down with a *thud*, a grunt, and a couple of curses, the Yale's hooves flailing in the flickering light.

"Give me that lantern!" Harv said with another round of foreign curses and a *clunk* or two.

There was a yelp, then Dirham limped out of the shadows on her left, dragging one of his back legs and the lantern with him, with Lexy running interference, worry etched into her little face.

"Don't hyperextend your leg that way, Dirham. Luckily, Harv's hoof only clipped it, but you could still damage the tendon. Leverage the lantern instead of lifting it." Lexy stuck her muzzle beneath the spout, balancing it on her nose. "Let me help you."

The two of them dropped the lantern in Samantha's lap. "Here you go, Samantha. You need to be more careful with it. Remember what I said about it. That was too close." Dirham looked over his shoulder at Kal. "You might want to do something about that, Kal."

Samantha clutched the lantern to her chest. Close? It was almost a disaster. On more than just the losing-their-bargaining-chip-with-Harv front.

"I have to have a reason, Dir, since she can't wish it."

"Keeping it away from that clown until he tells us what he knows is a good reason," said Bart, brushing his hands together and swiping at a bloody gash across his cheek. "And since *she* obviously can't be trusted with it, I'll take it." He lunged toward Samantha as if he still had wings and almost ripped the lantern from her grasp.

Samantha held on tight, and Kal slashed his hand in front of his face. The lantern disappeared at the same time that Bart hit the ground with a *thud*.

Something hit Samantha's chest with a *thud*. A lantern-shaped pendant.

She picked it up to get a closer look, but Harv climbed to his feet at that moment, so she tucked it beneath her shirt. No sense tempting the Yale, though she had a feeling that where it now was would tempt him more.

"Gods-damned gnomes! I almost had it." Harv kicked something out of his way and a *clang!* reverberated along the corrugated length of metal. "They leave their shit everywhere."

"They do? Ew!" Dirham sniffed the air. "I don't smell anything."

"Oh, for Achaemenes's sake. You are really going to make me work for that lantern, aren't you?" Harv cantered off into the darkness, his glowing antlers leading the way. "Come on. Let's get this over with."

Samantha hung back with Kal while everyone else traipsed off after Harv.

There had to be some way to fix this. All of it. The dragon, Kal, Albert—she *really* wanted to fix Albert. "Are you sure about this, Kal?"

"I am, Sam. Trust me. He's not going to get the lantern." Kal picked up the torch. "Don't worry."

Worry was her middle name nowadays. As for trust, well, she actually did trust Kal. He was telling the truth; his Code demanded it. But more than just adhering to The Code's standards, Kal was that kind of guy. "You seem pretty sure of that."

"I am." He smiled that sexy, half smile that turned her knees to mush.

"Why?"

Kal tapped the end of her nose with a finger. "Semantics."

Samantha blew out a breath. Why wasn't she surprised? "But if Harv isn't going to get the lantern, why are we following him? He'll never give us the information if he knows he's not going to end up with control of you."

He held out his hand and helped her climb over a rusting pipe that bisected the tunnel's floor. "That's the best part. He *doesn't* know. He actually thinks he's going to outsmart me. Trust me, Sam, I am so going to enjoy telling him, but not until *after* we find out what his network of spies has to say."

"I don't understand."

"I know, and it's best if you don't. That way you can't give anything away. Just remember: semantics."

She was trying to *forget* semantics. Word choice and double meanings were what had gotten her into this predicament in the first place.

Well, no, actually *Albert* was the one who'd gotten her into this predicament, and like Kal with Harv, she'd revel in the poetic justice of besting Albert.

She just had to figure out how.

28

AFTER TEN MINUTES OF SILENCE—UNLESS SAMANTHA counted Bart's grumblings and Maille's hissed "quiet!"s—they finally arrived at a large metal gate in the tunnel wall. Harv rapped on the upper right corner with both antlers like a drum riff, and it swung open on squeaky hinges.

"Hurry inside," he growled, which, coming from a talking heraldry symbol, was just wrong. But then, all of Harv was wrong. "I don't need any of my neighbors knowing I actually talk to fennecs. It's not good for the image."

Dirham, who'd rejected Samantha's offer to carry him, teetered to a halt on his three uninjured legs, his tail shooting vertical. "Hey, I resent that."

"And you resemble it, too, so get over it." Harv held the door open and nudged—shoved—the fox through with a hoof.

Lexy snapped at him, missing when Harv leapt out of snapping range. Then she trotted inside with a hum of "oh, you poor thing"s to Dirham and bared-teeth snarls to the Yale.

Making sure Kal's lantern necklace was tucked safely between her breasts, Samantha scooted past Harv as quickly as possible, but that didn't stop him from leering.

Kal elbowed him in the neck.

The torch lit the small room they walked into. As rooms went, it was straight out of a classic B-movie bad-guy hideout. So much so that the black Stetson on the scarred wooden trestle table surprised Samantha only because it wasn't dusty and worn like a cowboy's would be. But the requisite knives and gas lamps were there, albeit Persian curved blades and iron scrollwork. A Jim Beam "genie" decanter played the part of a whiskey jug, though the whiff she got from the open stopper was more along the lines of absinthe.

"Sit." Harv locked the metal door behind them and scraped an antler along the tabletop, creating a spark on the tip that he used to light several oil lamps. The other antler struck a big metal pipe in the corner that ran up through the ceiling, the sound reverberating through the small room.

Maille swung one leg over the bench and sat down, her fingers strumming the tabletop. Her nails had been bitten to the quick. "So where's this crystal ball, Harv?"

Harv leered. "Come on, Maille. You of all people know they aren't crystal."

Bart huffed, then did it again when no smoke came out.

"Enough with the innuendo," said Maille, staring Harv down. After five thousand years of being a dragon, feared and revered by every culture on the planet, Maille had to be used to getting her way. "We're desperate here."

She won the battle of wills with Harv, too. He dropped eye contact and sighed. "Fine. Dieter will report in and we can find out about this clown, Albert. Then you can give me the lantern and get the hell out of my lair."

"Albert's not a clown," said Dirham, pulling himself

onto the bench next to Lexy with a grunt. "He's a businessman. Always making calls to some guy named Henley and another one named Bookie and lots of bankers. Or maybe that's backers. I never could tell 'cause I was trying to stay away from him. But he liked to skulk around the house so I'd occasionally have to duck out of the way to avoid him."

"He did what?" Samantha was surprised. With Albert's delusions of grandeur and self-entitlement, she wouldn't think he'd skulk—unless he was doing something he shouldn't.

Like trying to steal a genie. He'd been after Kal and the lantern for a long time.

And *bookies* didn't sound good. That kind of desperation put a whole new spin on his reasons for coming after Kal and kidnapping the dragon.

"Oh, yeah," said Dirham, nodding. "He liked to hide behind those long curtains in the hallway outside Monty's office. That was always the riskiest part for me, coming and going. I never knew when I'd run into him."

Eavesdropping. She shouldn't be surprised—though she completely enjoyed the cosmic retribution of Karma allowing her to find out about him in the same way. Now she just had to beat him at his own game.

And she would; Albert didn't have any clue what she was capable of. Not that she did either, but sheer determination had to count for something. She could be a hero, too.

A sudden clattering in the pipe that sounded like a horde of tap-dancing cats pulled her focus back to the scene at hand, and Samantha braced herself for any eventuality. Harv hadn't specified what a Dieter was, so it was somewhat of a dénouement when only a gnome with wooden little-Dutch-boy shoes backed out of the pipe, landing atop the worn chest of drawers beneath it.

The gnome spun around, swiped the pointed cap off his head, clacked his heels together, and saluted. "Dieter reporting in, sir!"

Harv returned the salute—Albert wasn't the only one with delusions of grandeur. "Have there been any intruders, Dieter? Aside from Kal and his friend, that is." He smirked at Kal as if to say that Kal didn't know what he was talking about. Or maybe Harv was counting the minutes until the lantern was his. If only she could wish for a way out of this.

If only she could wish.

The grim line of Dieter's mouth got grimmer. His miniature look-alike companion poked his head out of Dieter's hat, shook his head, and said, "We aren't certain, sir."

Harv's smirk disappeared. "What do you mean you're not certain?"

Dieter glared at the littler gnome, then gave the hat a hard shake. His partner in crime disappeared into the bottom, while Dieter straightened his shoulders and clacked his Dutch-boy shoes together again. He plopped the hat on top of his head. "Last evening, there was a disturbance in the spectrasphere surrounding Valerie Ann's Sundries Shop. But the fight was going on in the street out front, too, so the ripple could've been caused by that magic being hurled about. The leprechauns alone generated more wattage in that short period of time than they had over the entire previous month."

"That's true," said Lexy, standing on her hind legs on the bench, and resting her front paws on the tabletop. "With so many magical beings around, the cumulative effect of the magical matrix could have ignited a magikinetic infusion and, depending on the magnitude and velocity of the directives, it could indeed have created a string-theory type reactive, thereby disrupting the stability of the spectrasphere. I've been studying just such phenomena for my thesis." She looked at Dirham. "If you wouldn't mind, Dirham, I'd like to collect a few samplings from the charge-pulse remnants inside that store when we've finished locating this Albert person."

No one said a word for a full thirty seconds after Lexy finished her dissertation. Then Dirham nodded—slowly—and Dieter's little friend peeked his own pointed hat out from under Dieter's and asked, "Did we get sucked into a black hole or something?"

"That isn't possible in Izaaz," said Lexy. "The gravitational anomaly that allows the sand walls to support the glass ceiling, as well as the environmental irregularities that have to be sustained, point to the curvative theory of sand/wind generation, which was proven by Seleucus to retain its solidity in the face of possible vacuum vortex conditions. An article about it will be in next month's issue of *Magical Mental Musings*." Lexy sat back on her haunches and slicked a hand over her snout, pausing after a few seconds of silence to look at them.

Dieter's doppelgänger's jaw was at his knees, Dirham's pride was written all over his face and his chest was puffed up like a strutting rooster, Bart scowled, Kal tried to hide his smile, and Maille managed to look impressively unimpressed.

"What?" said Lexy. "The editor's a friend of mine. It's no big deal."

Harv clapped his antlers. "Well bully for you, foxy loxy."

"It's Lexy." Dirham said. The accompanying snarl was the first one Samantha had heard from him. "*Doctor* Lexy."

The antlers made circles in the air. "Yeah, yeah, whatever. Kumbayah and all that camelshit." Harv sauntered over to his wall of swords, removed a katara, and slapped it on the table with a *thwack!* "So Dieter, was there anything in our resident genius's lesson you can use to locate the cause of the disturbance?"

"I don't know. What'd she say?" Dieter looked as if one of those vacuum vortices had sucked the words from his mouth.

Dirham stood up next to the vixen. "She said that while the amulet could explain the ripple, so can all the magic, therefore, we don't know any more now than when we got here. Is that right, Lexy?"

The vixen beamed at him as if *he* were Mensa material instead of her.

"Oh. Well, in that case, she's right," said Dieter. "But it doesn't explain the other ripple."

"There was another one?" Maille shot to her feet, smoke coming out of her ears. Literally. "When were you planning to mention that?"

"He just did," said the Mini-Me gnome, peeking out from Dieter's hat.

Dieter shoved him back inside. "I was getting to it, but Miss Smarty Pants didn't give me a chance."

"Lexy doesn't wear pants," said Dirham, ever so literally.

Lexy nudged his shoulder, then rubbed her cheek against to his.

"So there you have it." Harv's one antler unfurled toward Kal, the tip making a "come on" motion like the flexible end of an elephant's trunk. "Hand over the lantern. I did my part of the bargain."

Kal held up a hand, and the antler tip poked his palm. "Not so fast, Harv. The deal was for you to *deliver* Albert. You haven't, so no go."

"What? No fucking way you're weaseling out of this one! That lantern is mine, fair and square. *You're* mine."

"Technically, he's his own person," said Dirham.

"Not exactly, *dirtbag*. Whoever owns the lantern, owns the genie, so he will be mine."

"*Own?*" said Samantha, shooting to her feet, the idea so repugnant that all she could think of was getting the lantern off her neck and into Kal's hands.

She whipped the chain over her head. "Here. People shouldn't own other people, genies or not. Wars have been fought for that very reason. Here, Kal. Take this and be fr—"

Harv lunged toward her. "Oh no you don't! Kal's mine!" His antlers glanced off her fingers as Kal yanked her out of the way.

"Gods-dammit! I almost had it *again*!" Harv back-kicked the dresser and the gnome teetered over the edge of it, arms windmilling. The little guy in the hat did the same thing.

Kal took the necklace, hefted it for a second or two, then draped the chain over Samantha's head again. "Thank you, Sam. That's a very generous offer, but it doesn't work like that."

"That's true. You'd have to—" Dirham yelped when Lexy stepped on his paw.

Kal shot a pointed look at the fox. "As I was saying, I really appreciate the offer, but being a genie is an honor. It's more than my job; it's who I am."

As someone who knew what it was like to be used for personal gain, who knew how dehumanizing it was, how it stripped away all sense of self-worth, Samantha didn't agree with him. Being used was being used. But she had to respect his interpretation, though it didn't make being on this side of the equation any easier.

"Bunch of mumbo-jumbo if you ask me," said Harv, rubbing his back hoof with an antler. "All the powers of the universe at your fingertips, and you voluntarily restrict yourself to a master's wishes. I'll never get it."

"You don't have to, Harv," said Kal. "It's the way of the Djinn and what we were born to do." *Kharah!* It'd all but killed him to give the lantern back to Samantha, but rules were rules. Better to finish out his sentence with her than grant even one wish for Harv. And forget about trying to find the opportunity to finagle an appointment with the High Master if he got a new master; that's why he was so desperate to complete his sentence with Sam; there would be no other master after her.

Damn Harv. If she'd only finished that sentence this would all be over and done with. He'd be free of his sentence. Free to pursue the life and career that should be his.

Free of her...

"Yeah, well," said Harv, combing an antler through the tuft of hair behind his ears. "I was born to roam the plains and eat grass. Not quite the way I envisioned my life, if ya catch my meaning. Izaaz's a damn sight better than being target practice for griffins."

"Griffins don't eat Yales," said Dirham.

"That's 'cause there aren't many of us left, thanks *to* the griffins. See how that works, dirtbag?"

Lexy leapt onto the table and growled. "*Don't* call him that!"

Harv speared the Stetson with an antler and threw it at her, but Lexy leapt back onto the bench beside Dirham and the hat sailed over both of their heads, landing on the floor at Bart's feet. Who took great joy in crushing it. Typical Bart.

Harv grabbed the katara and jerked it toward Kal. "Enough. Hand it over. I won."

Kal shook his head. "No, you didn't. We still don't know where Albert is. If he's even here. For all we know, he could be sitting in Samantha's living room right now."

"Probably not." Dirham climbed out from under the table. "Albert never sits. He paces."

Kal arched an eyebrow. "Just how often did you almost run into him, Dirham?"

Dirham looked sheepish—an affectation Kal had learned to see through centuries ago—and the fox suddenly found a wormhole extremely interesting. "Well, I…"

Maille stood and slammed her palm onto the table. "Who cares what this Albert does? He has my baby. Or are you trying to tell me that this is all one big coincidence? The disturbance… this mortal… Laszlo? That they all just happened at the same time but aren't related?"

Kal raked his hands through his hair. "There are no coincidences, Maille."

"Burroughs," said Lexy, nodding.

Dirham cocked his head. "What do donkeys have to do with anything?"

"Not *burros*, Dirham," said Lexy, patting Dirham's paw. "*Burroughs*."

"I don't see the difference."

"William S. Burroughs. It's his name."

"Whose name?"

"Burroughs's!" Kal loved Dirham, but the guy could be a test. "The guy who coined the phrase."

"About donkeys?" Dirham tapped his other paw to the side of his head. "I'm sorry, but I still don't see what burros have to do with coincidences."

"Oh for gods' sakes! Just drop it, will ya? Maybe a donkey will show up in Kal's lantern." Harv made no attempt to hide the sarcasm. "Given what an ass he can be, that'd be a hell of a coincidence."

"Actually it'd probably be a miracle," said Dirham. "We had the place sealed against magically appearing animals ever since an unfortunate camel incident."

Kal remembered that occasion vividly. He'd mentioned he was hungry enough to eat a camel and Dirham had, in his infinite helpfulness, delivered one to the lantern. The animal had left enough "presents" that it'd taken half a century to air the place out.

Maille wrested the katara from the antler. "Enough!" She *thwacked* the blade on the table. "This isn't about winning a bet or playing word games. This is about Laszlo and how we're going to find him. Remember?"

With the grace of a champion fencer, she flicked the

blade toward Dieter. "I want to know more about those disturbances. The velocity, magnitude, composition, and exact time and sites they occurred." She arced the sword toward Bart. "And if I hear one more breath about you not being their father, I will personally see to it that you'll never be *anyone's* father."

"Too late," Harv taunted the wyvern.

Maille swung the sword at him. "Keep it up, Harv, and you're next." She slid the katara through the sash tied around her hips and glared at Samantha. "And as for you, I ought to torch you right where you stand."

"But you can't torch anything," said the ever-helpful Dirham.

Maille glared at the fennec.

"Torching won't be necessary." One antler stroked Harv's chin. "I'll take her."

Over Kal's dead body. He cracked his knuckles.

"Hello? I'm standing right here." Samantha took a step behind Kal. "With a genie?"

"For now." Maille spat an ember. "I don't care who does what with the mortal. All I know is that my kid's with this piece of trash, so we'll head out and look for him. First one to find the mortal and my kid gets to trade them for a pet genie. Let's get moving."

Kal grabbed Dirham by the scruff when the fennec went to defend him yet again. "Pet" was an insult in the Djinn world, but that didn't matter now. What mattered was getting Laszlo back.

"Let's split up to cover more ground quickly. Albert wants me, not a dragon who's going to be unmanageable soon, so he won't go far, even with the amulet. Let's put out some feelers. Someone has to have seen something."

"Don't count on getting any takers," said Bart with a sneer. "My ex hasn't exactly been spreading goodwill with her fire-breath."

Maille whipped the katara out of her sash and sliced the back of his vest so fast that the momentum slid the separate pieces down his arm. "Don't piss me off, Bart."

"This is you *not* pissed? And you wonder why I left?"

Kal grabbed the sword before Maille could shove it through the wyvern's heart. "This bickering is slowing us down. You two head back to your home and canvass the neighbors. Harv, you do your thing with the underground inhabitants. Dir and Lexy, you check out aboveground, and Samantha and I will check out the sites of the disturbances."

"No way." Maille shook her head, purple slithering along the gray streak like a spark trying to ignite. "*I'll* check them out. I don't trust you."

Bart grabbed her by the arm and shoved her toward the door. "That's your problem, Maille. You don't trust *any*one. No one can do as good a job as you. At anything. Well, guess what, sweetheart? Even Maisey managed to keep the kids from getting kidnapped, something you couldn't."

Kal winced right along with Maille. That was harsh.

"So, Kal," said Bart, rattling the door to the tunnel, "mind lending us the Benz since it's because of you that we can't fly there?"

"Actually," said Maille as she yanked her arm from Bart's grasp, "it's thanks to Samantha that we can't."

"That's enough, Maille," said Kal.

"Enough? I don't think so. But I'm willing to let it go. For now. You just better hope we find Laszlo in one piece, Kal," she said, turning a feral smile on Samantha, "or *she* won't be."

"You'll have to go through me to get to her, Maille."

Because that, even more than Harv having Samantha, would be over his dead body.

29

ALBERT CLIMBED OUT OF THE FERRARI INTO THE dimly lit building. He probably shouldn't have brought the car, but he wasn't ready to part with it yet. The thing drove like a dream.

He wondered what a flying carpet drove like. He rubbed his hands together. He'd find out soon enough.

Too bad Samantha wouldn't. And couldn't. He was still shaking his head over what he'd overheard from another group of leprechauns. She'd wished away her wishes, and the leprechauns had been taking bets on how long the genie would remain with her. Albert shook his head. Only someone as spoiled as Samantha would do something that stupid.

Only someone as clueless as Samantha *could* do something that stupid.

She'd see. She'd find out what it was like to *not* have everything handed to her on a silver platter. To have to do without. He was so going to enjoy taking the genie from her, an additional bonus he hadn't considered when he'd thought about what the genie could give him.

The dragon whined. Again. Christ, he couldn't get rid of this thing soon enough. Needy little lizard.

He grabbed the cage off the passenger seat, clicked the fob to lock the car, then brushed his hands over the sweet tail end. Monty hadn't wanted to give "Samantha's boyfriend" a company car. Said only family members got one.

Well Monty could eat his heart out; Albert didn't need the old man's condescending handouts anymore, and this car was only the beginning of what Albert would have.

Checking to make sure the coin was in his pocket where it should be, Albert took one last look around the spacious interior of the old domed building. This was the last time he'd stay in something this dumpy. From now on, it'd be first class all the way. Life of luxury. Cream of the crop and top shelf.

All his.

The dragon nailed him in the leg with one of its claws and Albert cursed. Damn thing's aim was getting better. He'd better keep his mind on the task at hand and save the daydreaming for later. Didn't want to die of rabies before he got to enjoy the fruits of his labor.

Speaking of which, he had to deliver the note. The helicopter he'd commandeered—a more P.C. word than *hijacked*—had managed a quick survey above the glass ceiling to find the perfect spot for this exchange to go down. The genie would never suspect it on his home turf, and that'd be his mistake. Too many had underestimated Albert, Henley and the helicopter pilot included. They'd learn.

The pilot had. A little too late, though. Ah well…

The dragon coughed and a tiny flame shot out. Hit Albert in the pants and torched a hole through one of the legs before he could put it out. Seared a patch of hair off, too.

This couldn't be over with quickly enough.

Albert felt for the coin. The minute he got his hands on that lantern, he was out of here. But where would he go?

He snorted. That was easy. An uninhabited island in the South Pacific where he'd have the genie zap in a harem of Playmates, a personal chef, and every creature comfort he could think of. Maybe he'd get tired of it after a month or two. Or six.

Or not.

The dragon growled. Albert dropped the cage, the *thud* as it hit the floor enough to silence the whiny thing. But then the cage tipped over and one leathery wing stuck out awkwardly between the rungs.

Oh, hell. Had he damaged the dragon? Killed it?

Albert grabbed the cage, yanked the dish towel away—and got blasted in the face with a thick cloud of smoke that had a grinning dragon behind it.

Evil. Dragons were pure evil.

Albert cursed and dropped the cloth back into place. The dragon incinerated it with two breaths.

Yeah, the exchange would definitely go down on that island in the river. That way he could threaten to drop the little pyromaniac into the water if they didn't do what he said. He'd heard enough chatter on the street to know that once the genie was his, he'd be calling all the shots. If he wanted the dragon to take a dive—and never come up—there was nothing the genie could do about it.

He tapped the top of the little flame-thrower's prison. "Keep it up, Jack. Just keep it up. Once I've got that lantern, whatever bargain I've made won't matter. I'll be the most powerful man on earth, and there won't be anything anyone can do to stop me."

Especially Samantha. That idiot had gotten rid of her wishes. Albert would find that funny if he hadn't almost chosen her to be the mother of his children. Although, since she no longer would be, he actually *did* find it amusing. The pampered princess would now have nothing to make all her wishes come true, not even the inheritance her father had left her.

That would belong to him.

30

AFTER GRABBING A COUPLE OF POMEGRANATES from the trees she'd wished into being in the center of Palm Street earlier, Samantha and Kal made a thorough exploration of both disturbance sights. The only thing they found unusual at the abandoned pawnshop was that some gold- and jewel-encrusted items were still lying around. After the conversation she'd overheard, Samantha would have expected Albert to fill every pocket with the loot. The fact that he hadn't meant either he didn't see the need—a tough thing for her to believe—*or* he wasn't their villain, which was even harder to fathom.

Then they arrived at the second location and found the Ferrari. Nothing indicated that it was Albert's, but besides the fact that this was too much of a coincidence—he'd coveted the cars her father's company designed and built—it'd be just like Albert to buy from a competitor to rub it in her face.

The scorched jacket they found, however, confirmed that not only was Albert the guilty party—she'd given him that jacket for his birthday—but also that they were running out of time. With Laszlo now having fire, the clock had started ticking faster. Albert wouldn't want a dangerous hostage; he'd either make his demands or do something with the dragon no one wanted to think about.

They climbed the minaret's circular stairs to look for

other clues Albert might have left behind and had just reached the top when Dirham's cry of "Kaaaaal!" rose above the beat of wings and the scrape of talons along the outer wall as Kismet reached the top of the minaret.

Exhausted, the Simurgh clawed the ledge and tossed her long neck and wings over so Dirham, Lexy, and Maille could disembark.

"He sent a ransom note!" Dirham slid down Kismet's neck waving a piece of paper. "He wants Samantha!"

Samantha read it by Kal's side.

Samantha, it read:

> *I'm assuming you've figured out by now that I have the dragon. I don't want him; I want the genie. Bring him, locked up nice and tight in the lantern, to the island in the middle of the river beyond the gates at sunset. Come alone. No dragons, no unicorns, no centaurs, nothing. Not even that annoying little fox. Do as I say or the baby dragon gets it. Don't try to outsmart me, Samantha; you can't.*

The note wasn't signed. It didn't have to be.

Samantha felt sick. The Albert Viehl she'd thought she'd known had never existed if this was what he was capable of.

"You aren't going without me," growled Maille, ripping the note from their hands and crumpling it. "I'm going to make that son of a wyrm pay."

"No you're not," said Kal. "You're staying here."

"Like hell I am. That's my kid we're talking about."

But it was *her* ex-boyfriend and Samantha was afraid

Albert would do what he said he would. "You should listen to Kal, Maille. Albert's desperate. There's no telling what he'll do."

"Oh and you'd know? Weren't you the one going to shackle yourself to him in the first place?"

"And I've learned my lesson. Don't make the same mistake I did by underestimating him." Hmmm, maybe the Oracle *did* know what he was talking about.

"I'm not placing much stake in anything you have to say, mortal. You can't even manage a genie correctly and how hard is that?"

"That's enough, Maille," said Kal, quietly but menacingly.

"No it's not enough. Why does she get to call all the shots? Why do you? This is my child."

Kal exhaled. "Because it's me he wants."

That shut Maille up for a couple of seconds. It cut off Samantha's breath for twice that long.

"What are you going to do, Kal?" asked Dirham.

Kal raked a hand through his hair, then kneaded the back of his neck. "Samantha's going to give him the lantern."

His words sliced through her, and Samantha lost her breath all over again.

"What?" Dirham's legs splatted out from under him. "You can't be serious!"

Oh he was. And with good reason. Samantha ran through a few scenarios, and with each one she came to the same conclusion Kal had. They had no bargaining power—and what was worse, no magical power.

"You're not gonna do it, are you, Samantha?" Dirham whispered from his spot on the platform floor.

"I—" She didn't know what she was going to do. Saying she'd give him up was one thing; doing so was quite another. But what choice did she have? What choice did any of them have?

Kal helped the fox back to his feet. "Yes, she is, Dir. It's what we have to do. The only thing we *can* do because, without magic, I can't save Laszlo. This is no different than the agreement with Harv."

"Oh yes it is. You were tricking Harv. How are you going to trick Albert?" The fox was bouncing again but in short, little bursts as if he were a piece of popcorn in hot oil. It felt like they were all in that pan with him.

How could Albert do this? How could she?

Kal reached for Samantha's hand. "Do what you need to, Sam. I'll be fine."

Samantha dragged in a breath. She couldn't live with herself if something happened to Laszlo. Kal had been a genie for four thousand years, another forty or so with Albert would be the blink of an eye for him. For her, on the other hand…

It was amazing how much he'd come to mean to her in such a short time. By rights, this shouldn't have happened, but then, *none* of this should have happened: Izaaz, flying carpets, magic, none of it.

Especially falling for a genie. And so quickly.

But Dad had fallen for her mom quickly, too. It'd been a story he'd loved to tell, how he'd seen her at a disco beneath the sparkling ball, and he'd been captivated. They'd danced for hours, and by the time he'd driven her home, he'd known he was going to marry her. Six months later, he did, and the rest was history.

Samantha smiled and touched the necklace at Kal's throat. She'd have to tell Berosus that sometimes, you *could* learn things from history that weren't mistakes.

"How long until sunset?" she asked.

"Half hour tops," said Maille. "Long enough for Kal to get us hidden on that island before lover boy shows up."

Samantha's skin crawled at the description. To think she'd thought to spend the rest of her life with Albert.

"You're not going, Maille," said Kal, his voice firm.

"Try to stop me."

"I don't have to. I just won't take you. Kismet's in no shape to transport anyone now, and by the time you walk to the river, let alone get someone to ferry you to the island, it will all be over."

Maille scraped the floor with her foot like a charging bull and hissed, but nothing came out except enough foul language to put a fleet of merchant marines to shame.

Kal still didn't give in. "We're trying to save Laszlo, Maille. If you show up, Albert might disappear faster than you could get to him. It's not worth the risk. Without you, there won't be any risk. Samantha will hand over the lantern and Albert will hand over Laszlo; after all, Albert's not after a dragon."

"Try and talk him into one, will ya?" said Maille. "Then you can summon me and I'll fry his brains and eat them like toasted marshmallows. Deal?"

A bit bloodthirsty, but it worked for Samantha.

"Isn't there some other way?" Dirham's bounces had diminished to mere hiccups.

Lexy shook her head and dashed a tear from her eye with a paw. "It makes sense, Dirham. One more master won't make a difference to Kal, but it'll make all the difference to Laszlo."

"That's not true, Lex." Dirham sat back and crossed

his front paws over his chest. "One more master *will* make a difference to Kal. He'll be able to—"

"Dirham." Kal tapped the fennec on the snout. "I'm not out of the woods yet. Let's focus on this problem and then we'll worry about the rest."

"Rest?" Samantha asked. "What else is there?"

Dirham snapped his snout shut, his eyes as big as his ears. "Um, that is… I mean, um… how we'll get you home." He turned those big eyes to Kal. "Yes, how's she going to get home? By giving up all her wishes, she's going to be stuck here and I don't think that's advisable."

It wasn't the wishes she'd be giving up—if she could even wish them—that would hurt; it'd be losing Kal that would.

"No need to worry about Samantha," said Kismet. "I'll take her home. After all, no good deed should go unrewarded."

"That's not how the saying goes." Samantha tried to muster a smile at the botched cliché but couldn't. Rewarded? By losing Kal? Forget about losing the magic and her wishes. Forget about giving Albert confirmation that she wasn't smart enough to outwit him; losing Kal put everything else in perspective.

She couldn't lose him. Not when she'd just found him. But what choice did she have? He was bound and determined to do this. She'd have to take solace in Laszlo's safe return. That'd be all that was left to her from this debacle.

And Albert would end up with everything, his plan from the beginning. The man had no heart. No soul. And she'd played right into his hands, the slimy lizard. She so wished she'd turned him into one.

Dirham rubbed a paw under his nose. "I still don't see why you're going to go along with what he wants, Kal. You don't deserve to have this happen, Samantha doesn't, and Maille *definitely* doesn't deserve our help."

"Watch it, furball," said the dragon lady, her bark just as dangerous as her bite now. "I might not be able to incinerate you, but I'm very handy with knives, and I could put a fox coat to good use."

Dirham shivered. "I don't have enough fur to cover you."

"A hat then. Point is, don't tempt me."

Kal was tempted to whisk Samantha out of there to someplace where he could take her mind off all they were facing and tell her the truth: that he had no intention of going blindly to Albert if there were any other chance to get Laszlo away safely.

But neither of them would be able to live with themselves if something happened to Laszlo, and if Kal did end up kowtowing to Albert, it'd only be until he was granted an audience with the High Master. This was actually a better scenario for him. He'd be free of his sentence and, once he became vizier, free of masters.

Free of Samantha.

Actually, maybe that wasn't a better scenario after all.

The sun sank lower on the horizon. The time for planning was up; they needed to go. Whatever happened, happened. As long as Laszlo ended up safe in the arms of his mother, everything else would work out. That's what Kal had to keep telling himself—even while he prayed to a higher power that he'd be able to come up with some way to make it work to their favor.

Kal waved his hand and conjured another carpet. This one, woven of golden Muga silk with a touch of genie magic, was traditionally used only for royal processions, but for this trip, the last he and Samantha might take together, he wanted the carpet to be special. He wanted to be that Prince Charming she'd called him.

"Come on, Sam. It's time." He held out his hand and crooked his knee for her to step on. "Your chariot awaits."

He got a smile out of her, one that touched his heart. His *heart*.

Kal closed his eyes for the briefest of seconds, but it was long enough to see the future. One without Samantha. And it wasn't a pretty sight at all.

Somehow, she'd slipped past his ambition, wended along his dormant emotions, tiptoed among his memories, and wedged herself in the one place he'd thought would be the last place anyone would touch him again.

But she had.

He'd fallen in love with her. Fully, wholeheartedly in love with her.

And now he could lose her—and the bitch of it all was that he couldn't tell her because to do so would not only cost him his magic, immortality, and the chance to clear his name, but it would also cost Laszlo his life.

So here he was, with the utterly shitty irony that he, who had a shot at the highest title in his world and unlimited powers, not only couldn't grant his master's wishes but couldn't make any of his own come true, either.

31

THE DELTA THEY FLEW OVER ON THE ROLLS ROYCE
of flying carpets was as lush as the rest of Izaaz was barren, the change so stark that Samantha couldn't help but
equate it with the turn her life was about to take.

Not only would she never see Kal again, but Albert
had played to her deepest anguish, the bond between parent and child. She barely remembered her own mother;
the thought of Laszlo, scared and alone, not knowing if
he'd see his mother again, tore her apart.

And Kal throwing in the towel was even more dis-
heartening. Samantha was racking her brain, trying
to come up with some other plan, a way to outsmart
Albert—and show him that she could—but Kal was
already consigning the ransom drop to done-deal status.

She'd offered a couple of alternate scenarios where
they wouldn't have to hand over the lantern, but Kal had
shot down each one. The amulet was Albert's ace in the
hole and there was no way to beat it without Kal's magic
being hers to command.

Samantha wanted to cry. She *couldn't* lose to Albert.
Not in this. Hadn't he taken enough from her already?
Her future, her fundamental belief in her own judg-
ment, her faith in him? He *couldn't* win. There had to
be some other way to save Laszlo and still be able to
keep Kal.

The bad guy couldn't win. Karma wasn't that capricious... Was she?

Samantha looked at Kal from beneath her lashes. He was seated beside her, legs stretched out in front of him touching hers, his index finger strumming softly over the back of her hand.

He hadn't even questioned giving in to Albert's demands; he'd just made the decision as if he'd known she'd go along with it. It burnt her up that, by virtue of his utter lack of conscience, Albert was calling the shots. Regardless of their personal wants and desires, this was what they had to do.

But oh, did she want. Did she desire.

Damn, Albert. This shouldn't be happening. She shouldn't have to choose. Shouldn't have to give Kal up. He was supposed to be hers.

She shifted her weight and turned her hand over so that Kal was stroking her palm. Shivers raced up her arm.

Kal traced a path down to the tips of her fingers, intertwined them with his, brought them to his lips, and kissed each one.

Shivers raced elsewhere.

"It'll be okay, Sam."

She didn't want *okay*. She wanted the whole thing: Albert mourning all that he'd lost, Laszlo home with his parents, and she and Kal together.

Yeah, and *that* was more of a fairy tale than the life she'd been leading back in L.A.

The carpet dipped to just above the line of palm trees flanking a rush of water that cascaded down the wall of sand and formed a river at least three city blocks wide. At the mouth sat a set of gates so beautifully and intricately carved that they could have doubled for heaven's pearly ones—if not for the viper she and Kal were about to encounter.

A breeze buffeted the carpet and ruffled the trees as they descended, the fronds swaying in perfect synchronicity, swirling the scents of the flowers that dotted the river bank: hyacinth, hibiscus, jasmine, gardenia, and more she couldn't name. She wouldn't have been surprised to see mermaids beneath the frothy surface.

"No mermaids, Sam. Mortals haven't yet found Atlantis so the Mer are safe there, though it's probably only a matter of time."

Everything was only a matter of time—and that was running out.

The carpet came to a gentle stop, hovering in front of the gleaming white gates that sparkled with iridescent rainbows caused by the mist covering them. The gates soared straight up for at least three stories, then curved back and ran all the way into the waterfall, locking the island away from the outside world.

"So how does this work?" Samantha asked. "Open sesame?"

The gates swung inward.

"You have *got* to be kidding."

"Where do you think mortals got it from?" Kal waved his hand and the carpet floated inside, then circled around the perimeter as crisp, cold spray from the falls misted on her eyelashes. She had to blink it away.

At least, that's what she told herself it was, but Kal didn't fall for it.

He cupped her cheek and brushed a trickle from her nose. "Don't cry, Sam. I never wanted to make you cry."

Never was an awfully long time when she wouldn't see him again.

Not wanting him to see what he didn't want to see, she kept her gaze trained on the column of his throat where the eagle necklace rested. A bead of water trickled along the top of it, then curved over the beak and dripped onto his chest. She followed its path with her fingertips, the stone warm from his body heat. "So much for having knowledge at my fingertips."

"In your heart, Sam, not your fingertips."

"What?"

Kal lifted the eagle. "This. The Oracle said this would remind you that the knowledge you need is always in your heart."

She looked up at him. "But this isn't in near my heart. It's near yours." She took the stone from him. "You don't think…"

Kal slipped the chain over his head. "Worth a try. I know Berosus was a bit obscure—"

"You think?" she scoffed.

He placed the chain around her neck. "But there's something to Oracles, Sam. If he says you'll know what you need when you need it, now must not be the right time."

She wanted to know when *would* be the right time. Albert wasn't even worried. *Don't try to outsmart me, Samantha; you can't.*

How was she supposed to save a baby dragon *and* a genie?

"There's got to be some other way, Kal. Some way that doesn't involve handing you over."

He lifted her other necklace, the one that held his

lantern, and ran it through his fingers until the lantern rested on his palm. "We've been through this, Sam. Unless Albert does something foolish with the amulet and we can get hold of it, our only chance is if he does something directly to you while I'm still yours. Then all bets are off."

Still yours.

Kal *was* hers. And neither of them was talking about the genie part.

Though there was something in what he'd said... But she couldn't put her finger on it. A niggling thought in her brain.

But what good were niggling thoughts when she stood to lose Kal? She cupped his cheek. Traced his bottom lip with her thumb. Met his gaze with an intensity she hoped was as deep and true as his.

"Kal, I..." She caught her breath; she'd almost wished that he was hers.

If only she could.

Actually... she *could* wish it. Didn't mean she'd get the rest of the words out, but at least she'd have that.

She smiled. "Kal, I wish—"

The kiss was soft. Gentle. Sweet for its chasteness. Painful for the longing it summoned.

She speared her hands through his hair and held him closer. Slipped her tongue into his mouth and leaned in to him, needing more.

Kal swept a hand across her cheek and stroked beneath her chin, a light, feathery touch that called forth more shivers.

Samantha leaned forward, curling her legs beneath her to kneel into him but Kal gripped her upper arms and tugged her back.

"Don't, Sam. Don't make this harder than it has to be."

She didn't think it was possible to make it any more difficult. But she sat back down, dashed the "mist" from her lashes, and nodded. "I guess we should get it over with."

"Yeah. It's almost sunset." His voice was husky as he waved his hand again and the carpet sailed over the crests of the small waves toward the island.

The pink sand beach gave way to grass so green it almost hurt to look at it, springy and soft, like a perfectly manicured golf course. A paradise. That was about to be polluted by Albert's greed.

Kal stopped the carpet at a low wall made of seashells and held out his hand when he climbed off. "We'll walk in from here. Once it's done, take the carpet and go back to Maille's home. Deliver Laszlo and then find Kismet. I want you out of here before he gets any other ideas, okay?"

"I wish—"

He kissed her again, and this time, she wouldn't let him end it quickly. This time, she needed to feel his arms around her. Needed to know that he'd miss her as much as she'd miss him. Needed to know that he cared.

She almost said the words but stopped herself. What good would it do? He'd be gone, and she'd, well, she'd be gone for good eventually. One mortal lifespan was nothing when compared to four thousand years.

She'd like to think *her* lifespan would mean something to him, but she was done deluding herself. Albert had opened her eyes to the truth, and the truth was that even if Kal did care for her, there was nothing they could do about it. Acknowledging it would only make the situation harder.

One last lingering taste of his lips and Samantha pulled away. Her fingers slid from his hair, caressed his cheek, touched his lips.

He kissed them once. Twice.

She placed them on her heart just as the sun slipped below the horizon.

"It's time."

32

THEY ENTERED A FOREST OF TALL REEDS WITH trunks as thick as marble pillars and stacked so tightly in circular rows around a clearing that not a bit of outside world peeked through. Luckily, the fireflies flickering among the reeds provided enough light until a blanket of stars spread across the sky.

And, now, a half hour later, there was still no sign of Albert.

Kal conjured a pair of ottomans for them to sit on—*poufs*, he'd called them—and sparked a fire in a stone ring by the entrance to the glade. He waved his hand and a table with bowls of delicious-smelling stew appeared in front of them.

"What's this?" Samantha asked. Not that she cared; she was famished. It'd been too long since she'd eaten anything that constituted a real meal.

"*Fesenjan.*" Kal handed her a spoon. "It's one of my favorites. Your father liked it, too. I whipped it up for him occasionally."

"Oh, that's right. I recognize it now. It was on the menu for his life celebration." Which seemed so long ago. Funny how a lifetime could happen in days.

Well, not so funny, given what was about to happen in a few minutes.

"Do you think he's going to show?" She took a

bite of tart chicken in pomegranate broth. "What if he doesn't?"

"He will. He won't let this chance get away."

"Good to know you're a smart genie."

Samantha dropped the spoon and the stew splattered all over her. But that was the least of her worries since Albert had materialized in the middle of the clearing.

Kal went right on eating.

"Problem with your manners, genie?" Albert set the cage he carried down behind his legs.

Samantha squinted, trying to see if Laszlo was inside, but Albert had draped something over the cage. Looked like tinfoil.

Kal took another spoonful of stew and cleaned up her outfit. Then he patted his mouth with one of the cloth napkins he'd conjured and took a sip of the mint tea that followed two seconds later. "Me? Problem with my manners? Not unless you consider civility a problem. Oh, but then, I guess you do."

"You think you're so smart." Albert tapped his shirt pocket, and the next thing Samantha knew, he was standing in front of the table. "Let's not forget who holds the power here."

Kal waved his hand and Samantha found herself in the most comfortable chair she'd ever seen. Down-filled and silk-covered, it floated two feet off the ground and cradled her back as if it'd been made for her—or conjured for her.

"Yes, let's not forget," said Kal, wiping the corner of his mouth again, and the chair descended until her feet touched the grass.

Albert got a look on his face like the time he'd eaten

bad clams on the Sheridans' yacht. She wished he'd suffer through the same sort of torture he had then. If only she could wish.

"We all know why you're here, genie, so this posturing is doing you no good." Albert faced Samantha and leaned on the table in front of her. "Hand over the lantern."

She drummed her fingers on the armrests. "Hand over the dragon."

Albert scowled. "You really aren't that bright, are you? I mean, I always thought you were a little dense—which worked to my advantage—but you really don't get it, do you? You don't have any bargaining power, Samantha. If you want the dragon, you'll do what I say or you won't get him back. And I say hand over the lantern."

"How do I know you have him? And what's to prevent me from having Kal take him from you?"

Albert smiled then and the look slithered through Samantha's system in the same way the clams must have done to him.

"If you could, you would've already done it. I *know*, Samantha. I know all about your stupid wish. Only you could do something that idiotic and play right into my hands."

The reality of his contempt stung. "You really don't like me, do you? How could you ever think to marry me if you hate me so much?"

"I don't hate you. In order to do that, I'd have to feel something for you. I don't. Your biggest attraction for me was your bank account and the company. Then I overheard your father talking about the genie, and, well, the company's chump change now. I want more, and thanks to your boneheaded move, I'll get it. So hand over the genie or the dragon dies. And there are a lot more where he came from. Don't think I can't get them."

Kal was seething. And there wasn't a damn thing he could do about it. Albert hadn't threatened Samantha. The words he'd used hurt, Kal could see that, but she wasn't in any physical danger. What he wouldn't give to tear this guy apart.

What about your reputation? The title? The position? Would you give those?

For half a second he considered it, but the only way to give all of it up at this moment was by renouncing his powers which would be pointless since he needed them to hurt the prick—and make sure the prick didn't hurt Sam.

Catch twenty-two was a worse number than the one thousand and one he'd been cursing for the past two thousand years. Kal really hated having his hands tied.

He looked at his hands, at the silver cuffs that defined him and held him captive. If they were the gold cuffs of a full-fledged genie, he'd have a lot more options, but these restricted his magic. Only if Albert attacked Sam could Kal act, and the shitty catch twenty-two now was that he couldn't manifest a situation where Albert would go after her because genies couldn't knowingly put their masters in danger. The cuffs might as well be manacles for all the power he could summon.

If only she'd given him his lantern. If only Harv had allowed her to finish that sentence.

All the "if only"s wouldn't change reality. He had to find some way to get that amulet, either before or after Albert became his master. Preferably before.

Albert tapped his shirt pocket again. He reappeared in the middle of the clearing and lifted the tinfoil-covered cage.

Kal hid his chuckle. That explained the burn mark on Albert's pants leg. "Way to go, Laszlo," he said beneath his breath.

Laszlo must have heard him because the little guy raised his head and hopped to his feet—all four of them. A dragon, not a wyvern, but his face was all Bart. There was no doubt who Laszlo's father was.

"Here he is, just like I said." Albert held the cage out in one hand; in his other, he held a knife. And it was close enough to Laszlo to do major damage. "Now hand over the genie, Samantha."

Sam looked at Kal, stricken, and he plastered what he hoped was an encouraging smile on his face, but inside he was seething. And aching. He didn't want it to end this way, but unless he could get that amulet, they didn't have any other choice—and neither did Laszlo.

Kal sighed and nodded at her. Samantha slipped the chain over her head. The copper sparkled in the star-light as his home, his future, his whole life, rested on her palm.

In all his four thousand years, Kal had never felt less in control than he did at this minute. Even at his sentencing, he'd known the consequences of removing his cuffs. Had known them before he'd removed them. He'd been willing to take the risk once Faruq had stolen his job so he could leave The Service that no longer held anything for him but endless loneliness, but this... He wanted nothing to do with this. But he was bound by The Code he'd sworn to adhere to.

"Hurry up. I haven't got all night."

"Actually, you do, Albert," said Kal, trying to buy some time for a miracle. And on this island, miracles were always possibilities. Hufaidh was a magical paradise and had been known to be witness to a few miracles throughout history. But as with Oracles, you couldn't count on miracles happening when you needed them to. "I can take you on a trip around the world and stay one step ahead of the moon. Or we could visit one of the poles for the midnight sun phenomena. Or even visit other planets to alter your biorhythms. Venus has a few spots that are nice to visit."

"Are you trying to get rid of me, genie?"

Kal almost asked him to define *get rid of*. He'd love to get rid of Albert permanently, and if that meant leaving him in a colony on Venus, so be it. Those Venusians were an accommodating race; the guy could die a happy man. And due to that planet's proximity to the sun, his death would be sooner rather than later, a bonus as far as Kal was concerned, but he wouldn't exactly want to explain it to Albert.

"Of course not. But a genie is supposed to grant his master's every wish. I'm trying to ascertain what those are. Do you wish to visit a palace? What about a Mediterranean island? The South Pacific? I know where there are elephant burial grounds. All the ivory you could want. Or pearls. I know the best sea beds. The best diamond mines, the best emeralds. Oil deposits, if you're into that. Whatever you want, all you have to do is ask. We could go there now. What about the top of the Eiffel Tower? The bottom of the Grand Canyon? Angel Falls? St. Peter's Square? Disneyland?"

Albert held up his hand. "Enough. I don't need you to visit those places. I already have the means to do so. And now…"

Albert tapped his shirt pocket, appeared in front of the table, yanked the lantern chain from Samantha's hand, slammed the cage down, and was back at the center of the clearing in less than three seconds.

Maille could move fast, but not even a dragon could outdo the amulet. Only genie magic could come close.

"And now I have the means to get whatever I want." He dangled the lantern in front of him. "And what I want from you is wealth. Power."

Kal had heard all of this before, and, gods forgive him, he had to grant it—though, come to think of it, it *was* the gods' fault.

Another agenda item for the meeting with the High Master. But first things first. There was The Code to adhere to or he could kiss any hope of a pardon good-bye.

Hope—he'd have to remove that trunk from Stavros's office once he became vizier. And finally open it.

"Money? Power? Isn't that a little unoriginal?" Samantha asked sarcastically.

Kal shot her a look. He wanted Albert to forget she was there.

"Figures you'd sneer, Samantha. You never knew what it was like to want for anything in your life." Albert rubbed his hands, just warming up. "Everything you ever wanted, *poof!* handed to you on a silver platter. You don't know what it's like to work like a dog to make it. To have to make sacrifices. Suck up to people who are so far below your intellect and pretend to like it."

"Well then, why don't you make yourself king? Rule over the peons who slighted you. That ought to make you feel better."

What was she doing? Kal half hoped Albert would wish she'd shut up so Kal could make her stop talking. The *last* thing Albert needed was a bunch of suggestions on how to use Kal's power.

"King, huh?" Albert rubbed his chin. "You know, you actually have a good idea. Who would have thought it?" He looked at Kal. "Can you do that? Can you make me king?"

"Of course." Any djinni could, which explained the state of the mortal world these days.

Kal shook his head, stood, placed his feet shoulder-width apart, put his hands on his hips, gritted his teeth, and said, "*Salam wa aleikum.* I am Khaled, the genie of the lantern," all but gagging over the traditional words of Servitude. "What country would you wish to be king of, master?"

That last word made him definitely made him gag.

"The whole world."

That drew some bile to the back of his throat. "Unfortunately, that's not possible. There has to be a series of checks and balances in Nature, and She doesn't allow for an absolute ruler."

"If I wish it, it has to happen!" Albert came *this* close to stomping his foot.

Kal tried to keep the irritation out of his voice. "I must adhere to The Djinn Code which states that we can't create an aberration of nature." Although, apparently *Nature* could; Albert was proof of that. "A supreme ruler would be an aberration."

"Hey, you could always pick this place to rule over," said Samantha.

Kal shot her a look. Here? With all its magic? Did she *want* Albert to have that kind of power at his fingertips?

"Seriously, Albert. Think what having magical beings as your minions would be like. All that power."

Apparently she did. What in the cosmos was she doing? Kal *really* wanted Albert to wish for her to be quiet. But then he saw a flicker of a smile on her lips.

Samantha was up to something.

"Minions." Albert stroked his chin. All he needed was a pointed goatee and he'd look like Faruq. Matter of fact, if Kal didn't know Faruq was locked up in his own lantern in the High Master's study, he might wonder about the resemblance. "I like that word, minion."

No surprise there.

"And I like your idea, Samantha. Yes, having all the beings at my beck and call would be a coup no other ruler on Earth could beat. I'd be more powerful than all of them." Albert pocketed the lantern next to the amulet. So freaking close, yet it might as well have been in the next solar system since genies couldn't steal from their masters.

"Everyone here can be my minions. Nothing like having a world of magical beasts bow to my every whim."

Genies also couldn't talk their masters out of their delusions of grandeur.

Kal couldn't figure out Sam's angle. Albert's was easy to see, though most people usually chose to go back to where they grew up, wanting to lord their successes over the people they perceived as having done them wrong. High school was always a big revenge scenario with new masters.

"Yes, that's it." Albert snapped his fingers. "Here. I want to rule here."

Samantha crossed her arms, covered her mouth with her hand, and pretended to cough—but Kal saw the smile.

"You do that, Albert, and I'll go return the dragon to his parents."

Albert waved his hand. "Yeah, yeah. Whatever. Why are you even still here? I would have thought you would've taken your lizard and beat it by now."

Kal didn't like the tone, but he'd overlook it to get Samantha out of harm's way.

"Fine by me. Happy ruling." She hopped out of the chair and swept up Laszlo's cage. "Don't forget the gnomes, Kal. They'd make the perfect minions. Oh, and the leprechauns."

With a quick, meaningful glance at him that Kal wasn't sure how to interpret, Samantha spun around and strode from the clearing.

Gnomes and leprechauns? Together? He hoped she knew what she was doing—and what *he* was doing because he wasn't so sure giving Albert this wish was a good idea.

33

"I'M TELLING YOU, WE NEED TO GO THERE AND HELP out." Dirham bounced into Stavros's office and onto the desk so frenetically that Stavros was worried the little fox was on something. "We'll round everyone up and get to the island without Albert knowing. Or Kal, either 'cause if Samantha *did* give Albert the lantern, Kal has to protect him at all costs."

The fox's back legs narrowly missed the picture of Colette on the next bounce. "We'll have to convince the trolls to open the marina because Kismet's out of commission. And the griffins are too big and oxen-like to go in undetected. There have to be a few seaworthy boats to get to the island, but we'll need to go in quietly."

Lexy leapt onto the crate by the door. "Maybe the phoenixes can transport a few baskets of gnomes over. We'll have to discuss the importance of not spontaneously combusting over the water with them first, however."

"Good point." Dirham started pacing atop the desk. "Or the *peris* could pair up to carry a few gremlins over."

"Gremlins?" Stavros shivered. Gremlins were just as bad as villainous mortals. "What for? There's nothing mechanical on the island for them to destroy."

"Have you ever seen a bored gremlin, Stavros? They're worth more than a passel of brownies any day."

Dirham tapped his snout. "But we should get the gnomes and ogres over first. They're the most knowledgeable about land; they can give us the best insight."

"Hold up, guys—I mean, guy and vixen." Stavros stood on his chair. "I hate to put a damper on your community service project, but we can't do anything for Kal. His magic beats any we have, paws down. If he can't defeat Albert, there's no way we can. Besides, his Code doesn't allow for outside interference."

"Technically, that's true, Stavros," said Lexy, "but, while we may not be able to do anything to Albert or for Kal, there's nothing to stop us from doing things to where they are. The gnomes would come in handy in that clearing. Gnome holes can be very damaging to mortals' ankles. Even cause broken legs."

Dirham's head bobbed as if he were bouncing, but for the first time that Stavros could remember, the fennec was calm. Almost preternaturally. And focused. And serious. "That could work."

Stavros scratched the ring of hair around his crown. "But what would that buy us? Ten seconds? I'm sorry, Dirham, Lexy, but we don't know if they're still on the island or if they'd even stay long enough for us to get there. Not to mention, *can* the gnomes wreak havoc on Hufaidh? The island's a law unto itself. We could be setting ourselves up for not only a big fail, but something dangerous. I'm sorry, but I can't risk the citizens of Izaaz."

"How can you say that?" Dirham leapt so high he hit the ceiling fan and grabbed the pull chain on his way down, sending a slew of papers flying around the room.

So much for calm.

"Kal and Sam helped you out, Stavros. They helped everyone in town out. Are we going to leave them to fight their battles alone? They're even saving one of us now when they don't have to. Doesn't any of this convince you?"

Stavros rubbed his jaw. It'd been too long since Izaaz had looked as good as it did now, and that was a direct result of Kal and Samantha's generosity. If not for them, this place would still be two hoofprints away from anarchy. The kits had a point.

Still, it was too dangerous. Survival of the fittest didn't apply to just mortals. "There has to be something else. Some other way we can help without sending in the troops."

Dirham let go of the pull cord and landed in a somersault on the desk. Then he brushed off some dust and shook his head. Back in control. "No. There's no other way. We have to go. They need us."

"Actually…" Lexy brushed some of the papers off the crate she was sitting on. "There might be another way."

Stavros and Dirham swung their heads her way in unison.

"We might want to open this."

"A box?" asked Dirham. "What could possibly be in the box that would help them, Lexy?"

Stavros said the answer along with the vixen as he lifted the lid.

"Hope."

———

Samantha hurried from the clearing, Laszlo's cage clutched tightly to her chest. Luckily, the dragon seemed to know she was here to help him and didn't scorch her. She'd be sure to tell Maille to praise him for being resourceful enough to torch Albert. Pity he hadn't had enough fire power to damage anything but clothing while at Albert's mercy.

Where Kal was. And, unfortunately, *he* couldn't use all the firepower he had.

She hoped her idea worked.

She hoped Kal figured out what she was trying to do. She hoped Albert didn't until it was too late.

Well, if she couldn't wish, at least she could hope.

But aside from hoping, she also needed to do. She wasn't as useless as Albert thought, and if this worked, she was going to love telling him so. But first she had to get back there to watch it play out. Help it along.

She plopped Laszlo's cage onto the middle of the carpet, then tugged on the carpet's fringe to get its attention. "I wish for you to take Laszlo home." Hmmm, apparently she *could* wish, but, sadly, it couldn't do her any good now because there was no one around to make wishes to.

The carpet wriggled, then rose off the ground, hovering there with the fringe rippling like a centipede. Laszlo squeaked through the bars of his prison at her.

She patted his beak. "You sit still. I don't want you to go rolling off into the water. The carpet will take you home to your mom and dad where you'll be safe. I'm going back in there to see what I can do to help Kal."

Laszlo settled onto the floor of his cage and chirruped again, but he didn't look happy about it. Truthfully, she wasn't, either, but she couldn't leave Kal in there with Albert.

Before she could change her mind, she slapped the end of the carpet and it took off like a galloping horse, fringe flowing behind it like a tail, leaving her alone to face Albert and Kal's magic.

34

"You're sure you want me to bring the entire population of Izaaz here? To this island?" Kal looked at Albert with what he figured Albert would see as awe, but which Kal meant solely as disbelief. He'd dealt with narcissists before, but Albert might actually be Narcissus reincarnated.

"I'm not speaking Greek, genie. Though I presume you could understand if I did?" Albert held his mouth open for a nymph to drop another grape into it. He'd wished for nymphs the minute Sam had left. The request for a gold throne atop a marble dais had come shortly thereafter.

Kal turned away, the sight threatening to make him erupt into either maniacal laughter or fits of revulsion. Just once, he'd love for someone to come up with something entirely new. Samantha had; he'd never had anyone not want to make wishes.

Kal shook his head. He didn't know what she had up her sleeve, but no matter what happened, Samantha was in the past. She had to be.

"Well, are you going to get working on it?" Albert demanded.

Kal composed himself and turned around. "We need to cover a few of the ground rules, Al—er, master." Gods, that stuck in his craw. "First, you need to—"

"I don't need to do a damn thing. I make a wish and you grant it. Got it? And I wish for everyone to show up and bow to their new sovereign."

Kal took a deep breath, shook out his fingers, and metaphorically shrugged his shoulders. Some people had to learn the hard way.

With a wave of his hand—with the newly minted gold cuff on it, a sign of full-genie status that he couldn't enjoy—the gates opened and people started dropping out of the sky.

"Kal! We were planning to rescue you!" Dirham was first. After all, Albert didn't specify *who* he should bring. That's why Harv was second. Bart third, and Maille right on his heels.

Kal left Maisey back in town; someone needed to watch over the dragonlets.

"You lousy son of a wyrm!" Maille was halfway up the dais before Albert swallowed the grapes.

He started choking.

"I'm going to rip you limb from limb!"

Kal sighed, not even waiting for Albert's screeched, "Genie!" to turn Maille into a statue.

If only she hadn't gone on the attack. Subtlety; that's what was needed here. Subtlety… and strategy. He finally understood what Samantha had been trying to tell him, and it was all he could do not to laugh. Bart, on the other hand, had no such problem. With one look at Maille, the wyvern gave him a double thumbs-up.

"Where are the rest of the beings who live in that dust bowl?" said Albert, waving another nymph forward, this one with the ewer of ambrosia he'd demanded.

Too bad for him that he hadn't qualified that

demand. Sour ambrosia was still ambrosia as far as Kal was concerned.

"They're coming." Kal swallowed the *master* he normally would have used. For the first time in his four thousand years, saying that word left a bad taste in his mouth. But not as bad as that ambrosia would leave in Albert's. Too bad it couldn't do more, but Kal was forbidden from inflicting injury on his master. And given what he was about to do, he had to at least give Albert a warning. "But if I bring everyone at once, it could sink the island. It was never designed to hold so many."

Albert flicked his fingernails and looked around. "Yeah, I guess I can see that. Not much to look at, is it?"

Only someone as self-absorbed as Albert would fail to see the beauty in the simplicity of Hufaidh. Hidden by the Djinn in Izaaz when mortals began advancing into parts of the world they shouldn't have, the island was a paradise very few got to see. Created by the gods as a vacation spot, it contained only basic necessities besides this gathering place: a grove of fruit trees, a pool of spring-fed water, simple but comfortable shelter, and all the privacy one could want.

But now, with Albert here, the place would have to be fumigated before any of the gods would set foot on it again. Kal would make that his second priority once he was vizier. The first would be to round up all of Mayat's amulets and keep them out of mortals' hands.

"More, genie. I want more minions."

Harv snorted but wisely kept his mouth shut. Harv knew how to work an opportunity. And so did Kal. Samantha's plan was brilliant, and if he played his cards—and his magic—right, he could tell her so.

The first wave of his hand brought the gnomes. The next, the leprechauns. All seven clans, including the ones that didn't get along.

And it didn't take long. Just as Samantha had planned. Festwick hurled the first insult, Seamus the first punch. After that, it was a free-for-all.

Dirham ducked behind Kal. "Aren't you going to stop them?" he asked as a row of reeds got trampled, a sacrilege to those who knew the island's history.

Kal shook his head. Not only couldn't he do anything to anyone without the express wish of his master, but he wanted the chaos because, with all of this going on, somehow he was going to get the amulet. At least, that was the plan.

Gods, did he love vanity and self-centeredness. Particularly in one person. Albert was going to ego himself out of an amulet, and hopefully, out of a genie.

O'Malley said something about Finnegan's mother, which made not only Finnegan go ballistic but the rest of his clan, too. Pots of gold went sailing through the glen, the resounding *thunk* on the cracked skulls adding to the din. Which meant Kal couldn't hear his new master's wishes.

He flew a herd of centaurs in next, with Wayne at the head. Wayne took one look at Kal, another at Albert, then at the melee, and got the picture immediately.

Two gnomes went flying into the pileup. That Wayne was a smart one; Kal could always count on him.

Harv trotted over to him. "How long are you going to let this go on?"

"Who says it has to stop?"

"True." Harv's antlers split one of the reeds, and he stuck an end in his mouth. "You want to bet on the outcome?"

Kal shook his head. For all the fun Harv was having, Kal was intensely invested in the continuation of the fight.

He brought in Lexy, Stavros, and the trolls next. Orkney and his crew refrained from stomping the ground—probably a good idea, given that the island floated—but they weren't averse to tripping anyone, centaurs being the most likely targets.

Albert was yelling something in the background.

"Uh, Kal?" Harv's antler flicked toward the dais behind them. "I think your master wants something."

"You do? That's nice." No way was he turning around.

"Ah." Harv stuck the reed back between his teeth. "It's like that, is it?"

"No clue what you're talking about."

"'Course not." He crossed his antlers. "You know, you might want to bring in the gremlins. They'd love to get in on this action."

"Hey, good idea. Thanks." Kal waved his hand and it started raining gremlins. The little furballs bounced when they hit the ground.

"No problemo," said Harv.

With gremlins added to the mix, the melee devolved into utter pandemonium. Dirham managed to trip up Bart, who was dropkicking gremlins into the fight whenever they got tossed out, Wayne and his cronies were playing their favorite whack-a-gnome pastime again, and the leprechauns were twirling their shillelaghs in the trolls' dreads and yanking. Nothing like a troll hitting the ground, writhing with the pain of an uprooted hunk of hair.

"What about the goblins?" asked Harv. "They're always up for a good battle."

"How right you are." Kal waved his other hand and goblins crawled out of the reeds like ants at a picnic, which set the gnomes off because they considered themselves the masters of those domains. The dwarves Kal brought in next took issue with both the gnomes *and* the goblins, and, pretty soon, chunks of earth were being lobbed all over the place.

"Bit of a sacrilege," said Harv, wiping a clod of dirt off a hoof.

Kal shrugged. "He wished for this."

Harv nodded. "How far are you going to let this go?"

They watched a rock sail over the top of the fight and land at the base of the dais. If the dwarves had hit the rock layer, that meant they'd brought their pickaxes. This could go downhill fast. Just what Kal had in mind.

And then he saw something that turned his blood to ice. Sneaking through the outer ring of reeds, showing a flash of color every so often where there was a break in the plants, was a figure in teal-colored fabric. With copper hair.

Sam.

Kal shot a look at Albert before taking a breath. Not one of relief because even though Albert's horrified gaze was riveted to the now boulder-sized rocks being lobbed his way, it would only take one wrong look to see Samantha circling around behind the dais.

And there wasn't a damn thing Kal could do about it.

So he did the only thing he could: he kept granting Albert's wish. He flew in the phoenixes for some blinding flashes to give Sam a better chance of not being seen, and the *peris* to add their good-natured confusion to the scene, flitting around with the trailing ribbons that they'd drop on anything they deemed in need of sprucing up. Given all the divots in the ground, they'd run out of ribbons before the leprechauns would run out of ornery.

"Uh, Kal?" Dirham peeked out from behind his right leg, Lexy from behind the left. "Don't you think you want to ease up a little? The island can only hold so much."

An extremely important point.

Right now Albert was safe on his dais. What if everyone else wanted to be safe, too? It'd get awfully crowded up there. Anything could happen.

Perfect.

Kal whisked in more ogres, every griffin in Izaaz, and the two reclusive hippogriffs as well. They weighed as much as six ogres.

Gaelic curses spewed above a barrage of Farsi. Akkadian fought with grunts, and Phoenician diatribes cut off Greek expletives, all of it drowning out the screech in English from behind him.

Kal wanted to turn around to see where Sam was, but then he'd have to listen to Albert. As long as he couldn't hear the man's specifics, he wasn't honor-bound to grant them.

Ah, semantics. How he loved them.

"Uh, Kal?" Dirham stood on his hind legs with his paws on Kal's knee. "I think I just felt the ground move."

"That's what she said," said Harv.

Kal couldn't help but laugh, both at the inappropriate comment from Harv that went right over Dir's head and at the fact that the island *had* moved.

He waved his hand and brought in a herd of karkadanns. Ever elusive and self-governing, the rhinoceros-like beings kept their distance for a reason:

they didn't like anyone—including each other—and every encounter usually erupted in knockout, drag-down fights.

Tonight was no different: two dozen of them charged at once, and the thundering hooves and scattering crowd did what Kal wanted: the island started sinking.

It took about twenty seconds for everyone to realize what was happening, another ten to get over the shock, and by the time they started looking for the highest ground around, the water was sloshing over the gnomes' knees.

And in one beautiful, almost choreographed movement, they all headed toward the dais.

───✧───

It was over almost too easily. Hundreds of beings converging on a tiny piece of marble where one man sat in supercilious self-importance was the perfect storm.

Kal allowed himself to get swept along with them and kept his eyes firmly downcast. Oh, he was still honor-bound to protect Albert, but the beauty of The Code was that the master's protection was at the sole discretion of the attendant genie. As long as Albert didn't die, Kal would be able to argue that whatever he'd done had been enough.

Unfortunately, that meant he had to keep the prick alive. Which was just one more reason to seek him out amid the masses and hoist him off the throne before it was toppled. And if his hand somehow managed to be in Albert's shirt pocket, well, that would surely be an accident.

Finding Albert's pocket empty, however, was a disaster of cataclysmic proportions.

35

"GET BACK! LEAVE ME ALONE! TOSS THEM IN CAGES! How dare they attack me! Genie, get me out of here!"

Kharah! The latter was the one thing Kal didn't want Albert to wish.

Although, technically, Albert *hadn't* wished it. Samantha could complain about semantics all she wanted, but in this instance, they were a godssend.

"Genie! Did you hear me? I said to get me out of here!"

With two centaurs between them, a gnome hanging on to one centaur's ears and cursing in Bavarian, and a clump of dirt landing on the other's forehead with a giant *thud* and splatter, Kal shook his head as if he *couldn't* hear, which was what Albert would think, but which, in reality, was his answer to the "get me out of here" part. He couldn't take Albert anywhere until the guy wished for it.

Should have listened to the rules.

The island shuddered and everyone scrambled on top of each other more. The gnomes were the best at it, forming pyramids on the centaurs' shoulders, the trolls' flat heads, and even Harv's antlers. The birds took off with no magical nudging from Kal, and the *peris* disappeared en masse with one gust of wind. But the rest were stuck on a sinking island.

Kal monitored the crowd. He only had to act if

Albert was in danger, and so far, the *ibn el-kalb* was only inconvenienced.

"You enjoying this?" Harv *oophed* when a gnome's foot landed in his eye.

"It has its moments." One being when O'Toole went to bop Seamus on the head with the shillelagh and conked Albert instead.

Kal would have to check The Code to see if that constituted danger. He'd look into it tomorrow.

"Son of a bitch!" Albert hollered.

This time O'Toole hit him on purpose. One didn't insult a leprechaun's mother without risking the consequences.

"Any plans to fix this anytime soon?" asked Harv.

"Fix what?"

"That's what I was afraid of." Harv flung his head and the gnome went flying.

Kal looked around, trying to see where Samantha had gone. The water was only shin high on the land surrounding the dais, so she should be able to get back to the carpet before there was any real danger.

But what was she doing here in the first place? He'd sent her away to keep her safe. He had enough on his plate, what with not knowing where the amulet and his lantern were; he didn't need to worry about her, too.

Not that he had a choice. Master or not, Sam was always going to be on his mind.

Samantha ducked behind the stupid gilded throne Albert had had to have. She had no doubt he'd wished it; he'd joked about getting a matching set for the dining room once they were married.

He hadn't been joking.

He could kiss those days good-bye—just like he could kiss the amulet good-bye. And Kal's lantern, too.

She tightened her fist around both. Thank God Kal had figured out her plan. Thank God Albert was so transparently greedy. Thank God the gnomes and leprechauns were so predictable.

She'd been counting on their propensity for creating chaos. The rest of the townspeople, too. The perfect cover to reach in and snatch back what was rightfully hers. Albert had been so caught up in the prospect of getting hurt that he hadn't noticed her circling around behind him. When the masses had climbed onto the platform, it had been easy enough to jostle him and steal both pieces.

She strung the necklace over her head and tucked it beneath her shirt. Torn and dirty in spots, her shirt was still the best hiding place she had. The amulet was a bit tougher to conceal, and in the end, Samantha decided to keep it in her hand, wishing all the while that she could somehow get it to Kal.

Wait a minute... She knew how to do that. Placing the amulet over her heart, she whispered, "I wish it would take me to Kal."

Unfortunately, Kal was standing right next to Albert when she transported there.

"You!" the slimy lizard-breath screeched the second he saw her. He lunged the next second, his aim going right for the amulet.

Samantha jerked out of the way and the necklaces swung free, practically hitting Kal in the face. She didn't think she'd ever seen him smile so big.

"Sam! You have my lantern! You're my master again!"

She hadn't made that connection yet, but the minute he said it, she did. And she knew just what to do.

"Kal, I wish you'd turn Albert into a lizard!"

After all, it was only fitting.

36

THE WATER DAMAGE WAS NEGLIGIBLE, AND THE ISLAND returned to its normal height in the river once Samantha wished the majority of townsfolk back to their homes.

She took a few minutes to give Bart and Maille a piece of her mind about the importance of parents being there for their children and putting their family back together before wishing them back to their winged and scaly state. Then she kissed Dirham on the head and shook Lexy's paw and wished them off to a well-deserved vacation in the Himalayas to visit with some distant relatives.

She just laughed at Harv when he put the moves on her yet again, and as for the lizard Albert had become, well, she let him see how much fun it *wasn't* being holed up in a cage. She gave the cage Kal conjured to Stavros, figuring it was as much a prison as any the satyr could keep him in.

That left just her and Kal. Alone on the island amid a dusting of orange glitter, with the amulet and the lantern and all the privacy they could want.

"We did it!" She threw herself into his arms. "You understood what I was trying to tell you!"

Kal hugged her. "And you got the amulet *and* the lantern! Have I ever told you how brilliant you are? That was sheer genius."

"Just call me Einstein." Albert could stick that in his craw and munch on it.

With his tiny little pointed lizard teeth.

"Not Einstein," said Kal, threading his fingers through her curls. "Your hair is prettier."

"Okay, then how about Plato?"

Kal shook his head, his gaze on a curl he was tugging on. "He had too much facial hair."

"Socrates?"

"Too old."

"Da Vinci?"

"Too bizarre. He talked to himself all the time. Probably because he was the only one who could hold an intelligent enough conversation with him, but still... His social skills weren't up to par."

Samantha looked at him. "Tell me you didn't know them personally."

"Is that a wish?"

She smacked his arm. "Seriously. Did you know them?"

Kal shrugged. "Sam, the past isn't important. It's the here and now that is. And I can honestly say that I'm very happy with where and when I am."

Not quite what Berosus had said, but she really didn't want to think about the Oracle and his word problems right now.

She tucked the amulet into Kal's pants pocket, linked her hands around his waist, and looked up at him. "I like where you are now, too."

And just like that, the moment changed. No teasing now, no word games. No double meanings. Just, raw, honest, *real* desire.

"Kal, I'd like you to kiss me." Couldn't be any more honest than that.

He tilted her chin up with a crooked finger. "That's

right, Sam. You don't have to make it a wish. I'll gladly do it without you wishing me to."

"Then do it."

He did.

Oh how he did.

Cradling her head in both of his hands, stepping closer until there wasn't room for air to wisp between them, Kal claimed her lips with the softest, sexiest, most compelling kiss yet. It spoke so much of want and need and admiration and desire and caring and longing that it took Samantha a few minutes to realize she no longer had her feet on the ground.

Kal had kissed them right out from under her.

They were flying again. On the gold carpet, hovering just above the ground, the movement so ethereal it was as if she were walking on air. Actually, with Kal kissing her like this, she could have been.

He tucked her against his chest, and she could hear the beating of his heart beneath her ear. Hers matched its rhythm, and she couldn't stop the words.

"Kal, I want you." No wish this time.

She felt him swallow. Heard the breath *whoosh* from his body. Felt his arms tighten around her. Felt him harden against her.

"I want you, too, Sam."

He kissed her again, and her stomach fluttered when his tongue slid between her lips.

Or maybe that was because the carpet went soaring over the tops of the reeds, then coasted down behind them as if they were surfing a wave, all the tummy-swirling turbulence mimicked in the feelings evoked by his kiss.

They flew over a starlit field of lavender, and still Kal kissed her. She had a momentary thought about flying blind, but then Kal changed the angle of his lips and the worry flew off with the wind rushing behind them.

She could finally come up for air (not that she was complaining) when the carpet landed on the far side of the island in front of a grove of fruit trees. Sweet-smelling honeysuckle and wisteria braided the trunks like garland, their teacup-sized flowers blossoming in controlled chaos like an artfully messy hairstyle, wisps here, tendrils there. Some kind of fluorescent vine draped through the banana trees, ringing the grove about two stories up, and provided a soft white glow like Christmas lights around a porch.

Mushrooms in various shapes and sizes dotted a clearing that had a stone circle filled with glowing orange rocks at its center. Off to the side, a round, thatched hut was nestled between the overhanging branches of a weeping cherry tree and a moss-covered hill. A thin ribbon of water cascaded from the hill and formed an intimate pool with pale blue light rippling up from the bottom. Neon moths fluttered along the banks, and a flock of fireflies formed figure eights over the center, then zipped up over the roof of the hut, playing tag with each other, their lighted tails like a comet of rainbows.

"Oh, Kal, what is this place? It's perfect. Paradise."

Kal waved his fingers, and the flying carpet rolled itself into a compact roll. He set it beside a cluster of rocks and picked a bouquet of white forget-me-nots that he handed to her. "*Now* it's paradise."

As if she'd forget him.

Kal captured her fingers with his when she reached

for the flowers whose fragrances were a mixture of tart apple and something she couldn't name. Exotic. Otherworldly. Like here. Except... this didn't feel otherworldly. It felt right.

It felt like home.

Funny how, now that she had the means to return home, all she could think was that home was where Kal was.

She was beautiful, standing there in the clearing, the soft blue light from the pool sending shimmers across the iridescent threads in her outfit, hinting at the shadows and hollows he'd explored—was it only last night? Gods, he felt as if he'd known Samantha forever. Yet, as with the scene in the clearing, when she'd come up with that perfect solution to the problem of Albert and the amulet, he felt as if there was still so much more about her to discover.

He didn't want to rush any of it. He wanted to peel back the layers to Samantha as if he were unwrapping a precious gift, because, really, that's what she was.

He tugged her fingers and she stepped closer. The heat of her body reached out to him, her scent wrapped around him, and it was all Kal could do not to take her then.

He needed to cool down. "Sam, how about a swim?"

"A swim?"

"Yeah, you know, float in water? Have it lap at our skin?" Their naked skin. "I promise you'll enjoy it."

He'd make sure of it. Gods knew, he would.

In one movement, Kal whipped the sash from his

hips and shucked his pants. Naked, he held out his hand. "Care to join me?"

He had to smile when she tried to speak but couldn't. He liked that she wanted him and wasn't afraid to say so, but she was no match for him; he had a over a hundred and sixty years of pent-up desire to unload on her—

No, make that over four *thousand* years because that's how long he'd been waiting for her to come into his life.

Dropping his hand to his side, Kal smiled wider when her gaze followed; he knew what she'd see. He wanted her to see—and to know—how she affected him. He couldn't tell her, but he could definitely show her.

He turned away, giving her another view. "If you don't want to join me," he said over his shoulder, enjoying the way she was staring at him, "I'll be back in a few minutes. After I cool down."

Like that'd happen.

He heard a splash when he surfaced in the middle of the pool and shook his head to clear the water from his eyes.

Two seconds later, Samantha surfaced in front of him. A second after that, she was in his arms. A half second later, she was in his heart for good.

The water was the perfect temperature—but on this island, that was to be expected. It was also the perfect buoyancy so he didn't have to work to keep them afloat and could put his hands to better use; the perfect taste when it slid down her cheeks into the sweet groove of her lips; the perfect silkiness when he slid his palms down her back. Around her waist. Up to cup perfect breasts, his lantern resting between them.

It was all perfect. *She* was perfect. For him.

And then Samantha wrapped her perfect legs around his waist, fitting herself above him perfectly. Fitting herself *on* him perfectly. Ah, gods… Talk about paradise.

She moved then, and it was all Kal could do not to let go. She took him so high in the space of one little gasp. The sound at the back of her throat when she settled herself down on him, the wiggle in her hips… it all but undid him.

He gripped her hips, holding her there. Needing to feel her all around him before she slid off. Needed to know what it felt like to be cocooned in her warmth, to have her around him, enveloping him, to have this memory to sustain him when she was eventually gone.

Sure, he might have fifty or sixty years with her, but the reality of facing eternity without her stung. Flipped him upside down and inside out. A life without Samantha…

"Sam, I 1—"

He kissed her.

He kissed her because he wanted to. Because he had to.

Because she was right there, looking so damn good—and because he'd almost done it. He'd almost given in and said the three words a genie should never say. The ones that'd take away his power, his life.

Kal closed his eyes, wrapped his arms around her, and inhaled, letting Samantha's lilac scent wrap itself around him. Around his heart. It was all he could do to not tell her everything he was feeling.

But he couldn't. The only way he'd ever be able to tell her how he felt was if he gave up who he was, and that wasn't what love was. Love wasn't subjugating yourself for someone else. Becoming less of a person to fit into someone else's life. Giving up who you were to be who they wanted you to be.

Love was about two people coming together. Joining who you were with who your partner was. Making a commitment. Except *he* couldn't make that commitment. He couldn't say those words.

And that was more of a prison sentence than the one the High Master imposed had ever been.

37

KAL SHIFTED BENEATH HER, AND IT WAS AS IF something shifted inside her. And she didn't mean him, though yeah, he did. And he thrust. And he moved. Bearing down on her hips with his fingertips, lifting her up, then burying himself inside her. Samantha didn't know how he was keeping them afloat since their hands were busy creating pleasure on each other's bodies, their legs grasping as tremors wracked them, and she didn't care.

His hands slid to her shoulders. "Sam… Trust me."

She did. That was the thing; she did trust him. She had no reason not to.

With a gentle nudge, Kal laid her in the water. "Open your eyes, sweetheart. Watch what I do to you."

Overhead, the soft white tree lights reflected off banana leaves blocking the starlit sky, but that was okay because, with the first stroke of his palm from her collarbone to her hip, Samantha saw her own stars. Flashes of light as if they were attached to every nerve ending she had.

He cupped her and his fingers played in her curls. "You are so beautiful, Sam."

He made her feel beautiful. Made her feel cherished and desired and wanted. His eyes were that warm, meltiness that was her undoing. She touched his cheek, drew his face to hers, and kissed him. Softly. Stroked the stubble on his cheek.

"I like this," she whispered when they came up for air—but not too far apart. Their breath mingled as their bodies soon would.

Kal smiled and kissed her shoulder. Then he moved across her skin to just above her breasts, the sexy scruffiness along his jaw firing even more responses from her nerve endings, and Samantha couldn't hold back a moan.

"That's it, Sam. Go with it. Let the sensation take you."

Oh she was.

His fingers delved inside her, his thumb stroking that sensitive part of her, and Samantha widened her legs, the feeling of the water lapping against her swollen flesh as erotic as what he was doing to her. She'd never made love like this. Never in water.

And she'd only ever *made love* with him.

"Kal, I…"

Kal's lips found her breast and she lost the ability to speak. All she could do was arch into him and trail her hand down his body to find him beneath the water. His cock jerked when she closed her hand around it.

He panted against her breast. "Careful, Sam. It's not going to take much."

She looked down at him, her nipple pebbled beneath his tongue, the chains of her necklaces encircling that one breast, a sight so erotic she almost came just from the sheer imagery. "Tell me about it."

And he did. He told her everything he was going to do to her. Told her when he was going to spread her wide. When he was going to feather soft, butterfly strokes over her. When he was going to press a little harder. Then a little softer. A little faster. A little slower. He told her when his fingers would go inside her. When they'd withdraw.

The anticipation was incredible, but his actual touch… Samantha was so on fire *she* could have lit up the clearing.

And then he floated her in front of him. How she remained above water, Samantha didn't know. Didn't care. All she cared about was where he was going to stop her.

He spread her legs and drew her toward him.

Tremors wracked her body.

"Cold?" His palms closed over her breasts.

Samantha shook her head, her wet curls clinging to her neck. "No," she managed to croak out between dry lips. It didn't make sense that she had absolutely no moisture in her mouth, but elsewhere… She was drenched.

Kal lowered his head, groaning when his lips made contact, and Samantha groaned, too.

Then she moaned when his teeth gently stroked the sensitive nub, his chin gently rasping across the rest of her swollen flesh.

She spread her legs wider.

His hands cupped her backside, his thumbs working more magic by spreading her even more for his tongue, and oh God, the sensations…

She arched, she twisted, she pressed toward him, trying to get closer. Trying to stem that rising tide or invite it, she didn't know which.

Kal stroked her fast, then slow, then almost not at all, and she thought she'd go crazy at the last. "Please, Kal."

"Please, what? Say it, Sam. I've got to hear you say it. Tell me what you wish."

She wanted; she didn't wish. A world of difference in meaning—there were those semantics again—but she could barely say, "Lick me, Kal. Make me come," let alone anything else.

And then she didn't have to.

He sucked her between his lips, his tongue working her, and Samantha could feel the sensation rise within her. Felt it coiling there, churning, waiting to rush over her.

She grabbed his head and pulled him into her, not having a clue how he was breathing and not worrying about it. He was a genie; he'd figure something out.

He brought her to the edge; she was panting his name. Chanting it, desire wringing it from the depths of her soul. Then he stopped, blowing gently over her instead, and Samantha raised her head. "Kal?"

He smiled a wicked, wicked smile. "Like that?"

Her "yes" was one long hiss, cut off at the end when he tongued her again. And this time he didn't stop.

No matter how much her body writhed or her legs wanted to close against the overpowering sensations, Kal didn't stop. He built the tide, working it, feeding it, until finally, with strokes so fast and strong and hard, she shattered against him, her cry rippling through the oasis.

And she didn't care.

Her body trembled as the waves rolled over her, her fists protesting when she gripped water that slipped away.

Kal slid his hands to hers, never releasing that one point of pleasure, but then he created more when he intertwined their fingers, and, palm to palm, he pulled her toward his mouth again, wringing every last sensation from her, every last pulse of pleasure.

Finally, Samantha's body went slack, floating on the water's ripples in the aftermath of what he'd done to her, those ripples perfectly in tune with the ones inside her.

———

The sand was soft beneath her back and didn't cling to her skin. That was Samantha's first coherent thought after Kal had taken her to paradise—he'd been right about that.

Her body hadn't been hers to command afterward, and, thankfully, it hadn't mattered. Kal floated her to the beach beside the pool and managed to get her onto it while all she felt was the touch of his skin against hers, the rise and fall of his chest, the scent of him and their lovemaking.

And she wanted him all over again.

Kal rested on his elbow beside her and ran his fingertips along her collarbone and down her breast, her nipple pebbling when he brushed over it lightly. Her stomach quivered when his fingers passed over it, her legs falling open when he circled on her hipbone.

When he went lower, she felt herself swell again. Felt the moisture form. "God, what you do to me," she whispered when his finger found her again.

"What do I do to you, Sam? Tell me."

His lips followed the same path his finger had taken, and all the while, that diligent finger kept up the teasing. The sweet and utterly divine torture.

"You drive me crazy," she whispered, feeling her breath catch again. "You make me want to do everything with you. To never stop doing this. To give myself to you again and again, and take everything you have to give, Kal."

"Go with that, Samantha. Your instincts are right on."

And then *he* was right on. And in.

And Samantha could only grip the muscles in his backside and hold on as he took on her on a ride better than any magic carpet could.

38

SAMANTHA WOKE TO THE SWEET SMELL OF MORNING glory, a perfect scent to wake up to on a perfect morning after a perfect night.

With the perfect man asleep beside her.

She stretched, smiling at the twinging muscles, the memories flooding her. She picked up the two pendants where they'd fallen beside her ear and brought them to her lips. Kal's lantern and his gemstone; he was hers now and no one was going to take him from her.

Sunlight winked through the large, overlapping banana tree fronds, catching the flicker of his lashes and the morning shadow of a beard.

She could get used to waking up next to him.

The thought crept in, soft and sweet and full of promise. He felt something for her; whether or not it was what she felt for him, she'd have to find out. But he did feel something; she wasn't just a one-night stand for him. Or two-night, as the case may be.

No, he was here with her for the long haul. And she was going to make the most of that opportunity. Not only was Kal sexy, but he wanted her. He respected her. He liked her.

And best of all, he was a genie with enough magic that he didn't need anything from her. She liked that.

As she lay there watching the hummingbirds flit by

with their jeweled feathers, Samantha let her imagination take flight with them. Of a future with Kal in it. He'd have to stay, right? He was, after all, her genie, bound by his Code to fulfill her every wish.

He'd fulfilled quite a lot of them last night.

Smiling, Samantha slid away from him and gathered her clothes and the amulet from his pants pocket. The future might look wonderful and full of possibilities, but the present was demanding food. Last night had worked up quite the appetite.

Several of them.

She took one last look at Kal sleeping there, blew him a kiss, then slapped the amulet to her chest and whisked herself off to Paris for croissants.

39

"SO DID YE GET THE LANTERN, LAD? FROM THE LOOKS o' this place, ye certainly had yer chance." O'Malley stood on the beach with another leprechaun Samantha had never seen before.

"Jesus J., O'Malley!" Kal shot up to a sitting position on the carpet that hovered a few inches off the ground—sort of an air mattress in the real sense of the word—and yanked the corner of the rug over his nudity. "O'Malley, what are you doing here? And where's Samantha?"

Samantha didn't know why the modesty; Kal should be naked for the entire world to enjoy. Which she certainly was.

Samantha ducked behind the hut she and Kal had decided not to use last night. Good thing she was up and dressed before these two decided to show up. *That* would have been embarrassing. But what were they doing here?

O'Malley thumped his shillelagh on the sand. "Me an' Paddy here, we're tryin' t' get some inside information. Seamus wants t' win back everra'thin' he took from us on the last bet, and we want to stick it up his big ol' porker of a nose. Thinks he knows everra'thin', he does. So, come on, Kal, give us a hint."

The other leprechaun, Paddy, piped up, "Ye know,

it's no' a good thin' t' be losin' yer masters, Kal. Kinda makes it hard t' keep to The Code and Serve them."

"Oh, he doesn't care about that. Isn't that right, Kal?"

Kal rolled over in all his naked glory—that she'd had her hands and lips and tongue all over last night—and stood. The cuffs at his wrist twinkled in the sunlight.

Gold. They'd changed to gold.

Something to ask him about. Did he get new cuffs with each new master? She hadn't paid any attention to them last night, nor had she noticed what metal they'd been during the short time Albert had been his master, but then, it'd been dark and she'd had other things on her mind.

She had other things on her mind now.

Sadly, Kal waved his hand and a new pair of pants showed up. Probably for the best; O'Malley and his buddy didn't show any signs of leaving.

She could always wish them gone…

Samantha fiddled with the lantern chain. He'd said he didn't want his freedom, that being a genie was an honor. But she should give it to him just in case he changed his mind.

Although she could lose him that way.

Samantha's heart stuttered for a few seconds. She'd only known him a short time, but it felt like forever. They fit together. Did she really want to risk him taking off?

Do you really want him to stay because he has no choice?

Love was a gamble, no matter if the guy was a genie or a prince or a regular Joe. Making him stay with her because of the lantern was no way to build a relationship.

Relationships were built on mutual respect and trust, with a big dose of passion thrown in. They had the passion, there was definitely respect, and she had no reason not to trust him.

She took the chain off her head. The one with the eagle, too. As soon as O'Malley and his friend left, she'd give Kal the necklaces. They were his to do with what he wanted and she'd just have to trust that he'd choose to stay with her.

"Yer gonna have to get it from her some time, ye know, if ye want that job ye've been hankerin' after for all these centuries," said Paddy. "Just come out with it an' tell her, for gods' sakes. That way me and O'Malley can stick it t' ol' Seamus an' ye can move on t' yer job. 'Twas only a means t' an end, anyhow, this Service thing, right?

"Once she gave ye up to that Albert guy, yer sentence was done, so ye should be able t' move on, right? I'd think yer Samantha would be pleased t' hear she could help ya in that. 'Course I'm guessin' ye might not want t' tell her, given what ye two have been up to. She might think ye've been usin' her."

"Well, of course he has, ye nitwit." O'Malley conked Paddy on the head with the end of his shillelagh. "She was the last master of his sentence. Albert was number one thousand and two. There's no reason fer Kal t' be hangin' around w' her now. He's no' stupid; he's no' gonna fall in love with her, for St. Pat's sake. Ye know genies canna love mortals or they'll lose their magic an' immortality. Me, I'd do just what he did. Enjoy the perks, but take the lantern an' run. Be free as a bird as soon as possible."

The words were hitting, but not computing. What did O'Malley mean about her being Kal's last master? About him needing the lantern? About him "enjoying the perks" while waiting for the lantern? About using her?

Samantha dropped the pastry box and ducked behind the hut a little more while her brain made the leaps it needed to to connect all the dots. Kal needed the lantern to be free so he could get the job he wanted.

She *had* the lantern.

Oh God. He'd used her. He'd wanted the lantern and had used whatever means he could to get it—and she'd gone right along with the plan. It wasn't as if *that* had never happened to her before.

Samantha tried to stem the oncoming hyperventilation.

Was that what all the seduction had been about? Was that all she was to him? All she meant? A means to an end?

Well, duh. What'd you think? The guy has been running around the planet for the last two thousand years unable to get his hands on that thing. You think you're a bigger prize? Wake up and smell the hookah, baby. You've been played by Kal every bit as much as you were by Albert.

The croissant she'd had in Paris lodged in her throat. God, was she that much of a patsy? That much of a door-mat? That gullible?

But he'd turned her down when she'd tried to give it to him. Had that been a halfhearted refusal? One he would have caved in and "reluctantly" accepted when she offered it to him again in a gracious, *if-you-insist* protestation designed to keep her suspicions at bay?

And here, she'd been planning to *give* him the lantern;

wouldn't that have been ironic? Just hand it over, free and clear. Then what? He'd fly out of her life on that magic carpet, leaving her high and dry?

Oh, the pun. The stupid, silly, ridiculous pun about being left high and dry in a desert. Duped, then dumped. All under the guise of caring for her and her own delusions of grandeur.

She'd been played. Again.

So much for learning a freaking lesson from past mistakes.

Samantha swiped at the corner of her eyes. She wasn't going to cry. Not here. Not now. Not in front of those leprechauns and sure as hell not in front of Kal.

"I say ye just grab it and run. What's she gonna do, follow ye?"

"She has the amulet, O'Malley." Kal's first words in his defense were the ones that condemned him. Where was the "I don't want the lantern. I want Samantha"? Where was the "I don't care about anything but her"?

She knew where it was: lodged in her stupid fairy-tale-believing mind right next to the one about Albert and happily ever after.

That Oracle hadn't had a *clue* what he was talking about. She was a fool. A damned fool. And she had no one to blame but herself.

Hot tears stung the backs of her eyes. Samantha blinked and looked away. She'd wanted it so badly. To be valued for who she was—just once—and not for what she could do or give or bring to the table.

She was fooling herself. A fool fooling herself. It was all a sham.

Clueless. A worse adjective than *useless.*

And the sucky thing was that Albert had been absolutely right. The lizard—literally and figuratively—had been right about her. And if *that* didn't make her feel worse...

How easily she'd given in to Kal. How easily she'd fallen for him. His words. His lies. And all along, he'd only wanted the lantern.

The damned lantern.

Samantha closed her fist around the pendants. If only she'd never found the damned thing, none of this would have happened. She would have celebrated Dad with his memorial service, broken up with Albert in due time, and then gone about finding someone to share her life with in the normal way.

Instead, she'd given her heart and her trust to someone who only wanted to use her. Again.

No one wanted her for herself. For who she was. Even Kal. He'd made love to her as if she'd meant something to him. As if she could give him something no other woman before her could—

But then, she could, couldn't she? That damned lantern.

Samantha looked at it. At the gemstone. These... these *things* that were the cause of all her troubles. Albert, Kal, the desert, the talking fox, the dragons, the leprechauns... all of it.

She was done with all of them.

Samantha marched across the clearing. It took Kal about two seconds to see her; the leprechauns about five times that long. But the birds in the reeds saw her first and understood immediately what she was feeling.

The clearing went quiet. So quiet that Samantha thought she could hear her stupid slipper shoes hitting the ground.

"I still say ye should just tell her what's what. Women. They need a firm hand—"

If Kal hadn't given Paddy a firm hand across his mouth, Samantha would have.

The smile Kal had on his face disappeared. "Samantha, what are you—"

She thrust the tangled necklaces—that *damned* lantern—into his chest. "You know what's really ironic, Kal? All you had to do was ask for them and I would have handed them over. Just like that." She snapped her fingers. "You did all this game-playing for nothing, and I, gullible fool that I am, would have just handed them over as if they were nothing."

Kal looked at her hands, then her eyes.

"I couldn't ask you for it, Samantha. It's against the rules."

She would not fall for the look she saw in his eyes. Not again. "Fine. Then don't ask. Here you go. They're yours. Enjoy your freedom."

"But Sam—"

When he didn't move, she thrust them harder. "Take them. I don't want them. I don't want *them*, I don't want *you*, and I just want to get the hell out of here."

Kal looked at her. Then he looked at the necklaces. Then he looked back at her.

It was there. That gleam in the eye that everyone got when they were getting exactly what they wanted from her. God knew, she'd seen it enough to recognize it. *Samantha capitulated*, it said. She couldn't bear it in *his* eyes.

Samantha dropped the necklaces, uncaring where they landed. The damned things could break for all she cared. She knew enough about breaking.

"I've got 'em!" O'Malley dove to the ground.

Paddy was right after him. "No, they're mine! Mine, I tell you! I need a genie."

They smacked heads and collapsed in a heap.

God, she couldn't even do this right.

Samantha bent down, yanked the chains out from under the leprechaun mound, separated them, and draped them over Kal's head. "There."

"Sam—"

No. She couldn't listen to him. Didn't want to hear the platitudes. The excuses. The half-truths.

The lies.

"Just leave me alone, Kal. You have what you want. What you were after. I don't need this." She didn't need *him*.

O'Malley cursed and Paddy grumbled as they stumbled back to their feet, casting malevolent glances her way.

Kal, however, just looked resigned. And maybe a little bit sad.

She wasn't falling for it. "I just wish I could go back to before we met and forget this ever happened."

Kal sighed and jerked his hand, with something that looked suspiciously like tears in his eyes. "As you wish, Sam. As you wish."

40

A few hours later
Well, in Al-Jannah time…

"Congratulations, Khaled," said the High Master when Kal entered the office he'd been summoned to on Cloud Thirteen.

The High Master waved a hand toward the microfiber seats beneath the ninety-six-inch, high-def TV, then tapped his iPad screen. A scene from Google Venus popped up. Probably a prototype; the High Master was a huge technology geek. "I hear you've fulfilled your sentence."

"Yes, Sir." Kal went with the shortest answer possible, because arguing that it was a sentence he never should have been given would get him nowhere at this point. Especially since it had already cost him Samantha.

He couldn't believe she jumped to that conclusion about him. Although, in all fairness to her, she hadn't been far off. He would have jumped higher than Dirham could at the chance to get his hands on his lantern if Harv hadn't cut her off, but that didn't mean he would have left her.

She'd changed him. She'd shifted something inside him, so that when he should have been rejoicing in the sweetness of restoring the honor to his name and his family, of having the job he'd wanted for so long within his grasp and gaining ultimate power, the taste on his tongue was anything but sweet.

Gods, how could she have run from him? She'd given him his freedom—didn't she know he'd choose to spend it with her?

"Now that you've fulfilled your debt to Djinn society, we can get down to business." The High Master motioned for Kal to take a seat on the sofa.

Kal did what was required as if on autopilot. He'd been like that a lot in the time Sam had been gone.

"Kal?" The High Master sat on the other end of the sofa and looked at him expectantly.

What the High Master had said finally registered. Didn't make any sense, but it registered.

"Business?" Kal asked. "What do you mean?"

"You want the vizier job, correct?"

He blinked. Was the High Master offering…

"Speechless." The High Master chuckled. "Yes, I can see where being given your life's dream would do that to a man."

"Being *given*? Aren't you going to read this?" He set his thesis down on the table. "Don't I have to jump through hoops or something?"

The High Master shook his head. "I already know what's in that." He nodded toward the bound doorstop Kal had spent years crafting. "Perks of the job, you know. And hoops are for show dogs and circus animals. Where do you think I found Dirham?"

Dirham. Kal was going to miss the little guy. Full-fledged genies had no need of a magical-assistance assistant. "So you're just going to hand it over? As if nothing's happened? As if I hadn't gotten rid of the bracelets?"

What was he doing? Did he *want* to get thrown back under lantern-arrest?

The High Master conjured a tray of food. It hovered an inch off the sofa between them. "Of course. You paid your debt to society, and the job has always been yours for the taking."

"What?" Kal leaned forward. He wasn't on autopilot now. He was on auto-pissed. "What do you mean it's always been mine? It was Faruq's."

The High Master shook his head and helped himself to some satay. "Faruq *thought* it was his. And I had to be sure that you understood the rules and the importance of living by them. Our personal wants and needs can't come before the greater good of our people, and the vizier and High Master must recognize that their leadership needs to be focused on what's best for Djinn society."

"So this was a test? You put me through two thousand years of hell as a test?"

"You can't say it was all hell. I know for a fact you had many more decent masters than jerks. I do have some pull with the cosmos and Karma, you know."

No, Kal didn't know, and frankly, he didn't care. Because, all of a sudden, this stunk.

"So you're saying that the job's mine? That all I have to do is agree, and I'm the vizier?"

The High Master nodded and took another skewer of goat meat. "Seems like there should be more to it, I know, but, nope. That's it in a pistachio shell."

Sam would have corrected the High Master's semantics.

Sam. He couldn't stop thinking about her. Wondering about her. Had she really forgotten everything?

The question was rhetorical because, as much as he'd like to believe otherwise, the truth was a bitter pill to swallow. Magic erased the memory if it was wished for.

And she'd wished.

The thought of her forgetting what they'd shared hurt more than any of the last two thousand years. He would've hoped the magic they'd created together would be stronger than just his.

Hope...

If only he'd opened that box, at least he'd have a prayer of having some hope.

But he had the power to make his own wishes come true now; he didn't need hope. And he didn't need magic. He just needed a little luck. And a lot of love.

"I don't want it." Until the words came out of his mouth, Kal hadn't realized what he was going to do.

Once he'd said them, however, it was as if the cap-stones of the pyramids at Giza had been lifted from his shoulders.

"What?" The High Master dropped his food.

"I don't want the job. I want Samantha."

"But you wrote the thesis. I'm all set to announce it next week. And she's a mortal."

"I know."

"Kal, you have to seriously think about what you're doing."

No he didn't. He knew what he was doing. And how to do it.

Kal conjured a diamond the size of a robin's egg, slid it along the width of his gold cuff, ready for it to fall off.

Only… it didn't.

Kal tried it on the other cuff. This was how he'd gotten free two thousand years ago, the action that had started all the trouble.

"It doesn't work like that anymore, Khaled," said the High Master.

"What?"

The High Master nodded at Kal's wrist. "Diamonds don't open the cuffs."

That was unacceptable. "Then what does?" Kal yanked at the cuff, a seamless piece of gold wrapped around his wrist and contoured to his forearm, trying to slide it off, or rip it apart. He wanted these gone. And this time, for good.

"I can't tell you that, Khaled."

"Take them off." Kal held out his hands, palms up.

The High Master studied him. Stroked his chin, his blue, blue eyes so concentrated it appeared as if the pupils were whirling.

"Are you certain this is what you want?"

Kal nodded. "Yes. Pl—" His voice broke, and he got the word out on a hoarse whisper. "Please."

The High Master studied him some more. Then he heaved a sigh and leaned forward, taking Kal's carnelian necklace from around his neck and holding it out to him. "You understand this doesn't absolve you from The Service? You can't just remove the cuffs and consider yourself out and expect it to be so. There's protocol, and you're still bound by The Code."

Kal took the gemstone and drew it along one of the cuffs.

It fell off.

Kal smiled and removed the other. "Not for much longer."

And with that, Kal *poofed* himself to the mortal realm.

41

Three Days Ago
Sort of…

IF THERE WAS ONE THING SAMANTHA BLAINE KNEW how to do, it was throw a party.

Or funeral, as the case may be.

"Leave it to you, Samantha, to turn a somber occasion into something fun." Dale, her father's golf buddy, took two pita wedges topped with dollops of lemon-garlic hummus from the waiter and offered her one. "Your father would be thrilled."

"Thanks, Dale." It was true. The party was exactly what Dad would have wanted—because he'd stated exactly what he wanted in his will. So now there were hundreds of people in costume milling around Casablanca-inspired tents with Middle Eastern–themed food and entertainment as specified. David, the owner of The Main Event, the company she'd hired for the props, had outdone himself.

Samantha brushed orange flecks from the sleeve of the long, blue *djellaba* she wore—the iron lanterns must be rusting. Dad had liked blue, which was why she wore it and had carried the theme throughout the tents. Various shades of blue silk panels covered the ceiling, and carried through in the sofas and thick, handmade rugs. A rainbow of *poufs*—authentic Moroccan ottomans—and pillows broke up the color scheme somewhat, as did those scrollwork lanterns hanging from tent posts and gracing the carved wooden tables, most of which were covered in plates and glasses, a sure sign of a successful party.

"Great as usual, Samantha," said Todd, an IT guy from Dad's company—*her* company now if she could wrap her brain around that. "Jensen's certainly having a good time."

Samantha followed Todd's nod toward the tent's entrance where the *clang* of castanets clashed with the rhythm of dozens of metallic discs swishing around a belly dancer's hips as she danced inside.

No, the woman wasn't dancing; she was evading. She was evading Mr. Jensen, Dad's attorney.

Robert, as he'd told Samantha to call him once the will had been read and the sucking up had begun, was lurching lopsidedly after the poor woman. Definitely too much *arak*. Most people weren't used to the aniseed aperitif. Samantha wished she hadn't given in to that particular request of Dad's.

She looked around for Albert. Her soon-to-be fiancé was good at these kinds of situations. He was good at a lot of situations, which is why he'd been such a godsend these last six months, handling the company while she'd dealt with Dad's stroke.

But Albert was nowhere to be found, so she was going to have to deal with Robert herself.

Popping the appetizer into her mouth, she excused herself from Todd and Dale and made her way over to Robert. Her hand closed over his fingers before they could make contact with the belly dancer's backside.

"Robert, I'm so glad you're having a good time." Samantha steered him away, years of grabby guys in clubs having given her unwanted expertise in that particular skill.

"Leave it to Monty to throw a bash for his own funeral, costumes and all." Robert waved his drink around. "Though I never did understand why he liked Casablanca. Too damn far to travel to."

"Good memories." Samantha took the drink from him and led him toward a table of food. "Let me make you a platter."

Robert adjusted the fez on his head. "None of that eggplant stuff, Samantha. Never could stand rabbit food. Give me a good cut of steak anytime."

Which she could do since she'd ordered a the table of American fare for those who weren't into being adventurous.

"Oh." Robert fumbled with the side slit in his *djellaba* and pulled a crumpled letter from his pants pocket. "Here. Monty gave me this a long time to go to give to you. He wanted you to have it today. At his, er, party." He exchanged it for the plate she offered him. "Good man, your dad. We're going to miss him. Things just won't be the same."

Samantha pasted a smile on her face, thanked Robert, and managed not to stumble away.

Not be the same? Did he think she didn't know that? Or was he already writing her off as head of the company?

Not that she could blame him, really. She felt a little guilty about that. Okay, a lot guilty. Dad had left her the company and she was letting Albert run it.

She tapped the letter against her palm. She wasn't sure she wanted to read this. Especially tonight. And definitely not without Albert around to pick up the pieces. Speaking of… Where was he?

Tucking the letter into her skirt pocket, Samantha dodged the circle of people around the sword swallower and headed into the kitchen.

"You might want to try upstairs," said Wanda when Samantha asked her if she'd seen Albert. "Maybe he's taking a nap. You know how hard he's been working."

Albert had been at the office almost every night for the past six months, sometimes into the early hours of the morning. Dad had never put that much time in. Maybe it was the learning curve.

She'd been so thankful he'd stepped in and taken charge. She'd been so busy worrying about Dad and keeping up with the charities she was involved with that, frankly, her learning curve would have been steeper than Albert's. At least he knew the mechanics involved with building high-end cars; Samantha only knew how to drive them.

She headed down the guest corridor to the room Albert used when he stayed here. He'd refused it, of course, when she'd first offered it to him. He didn't need the biggest room, he'd said. It'd been one of the things she'd liked best about him. He'd even tried to refuse the wardrobe she'd bought him, and the country club and spa memberships she'd given him on his birthday.

He'd only reluctantly agreed when she'd pointed out that she couldn't authorize a pay raise for him without board approval, but since he was acting the part, he ought to look it, so he ought to take what she offered.

The fact that he'd refused each thing she'd tried to give him or do for him had only endeared him to her. Here was the first guy who wasn't after her money. He wanted her for her.

Maybe someday she'd feel the same way toward him.

Shaking off that thought, Samantha stopped at the door to the suite beside the main staircase and tapped the envelope against her lips. She cared for Albert. He might not be her knight in shining armor, but not every part of the fairy tale could come true. It was enough that he wasn't after anything more from her than making a life together. She might not have what her parents had had, but then, how many people did? She was an adult and well past the age of believing in fairy tales. Albert would be her family now.

Samantha tapped her lip one more time with the envelope and was just about to walk into the room when she heard Albert's voice in a tone she'd never heard before. One that would send shivers down her back if she was the recipient of his conversation. And then she heard her name and shivers did run down her back.

She turned the well-oiled handle—Dad had always made sure everything worked smoothly, both at the company and at home—and tiptoed into the sitting room.

"Trust me, Henley," Albert... sneered. "Daddy's little girl is useless. On all fronts. Run the company? Her old man must have had another stroke back when he had that will drawn up. She's incapable. Inept. Hell, she doesn't even have a clue what I'm up to. She doesn't have a clue about anything, so as soon as this memorial thing is over, I'll get my ring on her finger and my hands on the contents of that safe. Then you'll get your money."

Samantha couldn't breathe.

Useless? Incapable? Inept? *That's* what he thought of her? Where was the undying love? The support? The 'til-death-do-us-part part that he'd been badgering her about?

She jerked the *djellaba*'s hood from her head. Maybe… maybe she'd just misheard him.

Oh, come on, Samantha, misheard*? Do you really need him to spell it out any clearer? The guy's out for your money. Wake up and smell the hookah.*

Samantha shook her head. Hookah?

She shook her head again. Why was she worrying about some random word when Albert was in there… saying… what he was saying…

"Trust me, Henley. I know how the old man did it and I can do it, too. Better. Bigger. You'll get your money, and I'll throw in a one-of-a-kind set of wheels free of charge." Albert laughed a cold, conniving laugh that Samantha would never, in four thousand years, attribute to him. "No, I'm not shitting you. Just sit tight. I'm planning to pop the question when this ridiculous party is over. I'll convince the tub-o-lard to elope. Two days. Three at the most. Then you'll get your money and can get the hell off my back."

Oh. God. Albert was after her money.

She shouldn't be surprised; he certainly wasn't the first. But he should be different. This was the guy who'd been talking marriage and babies and retirement plans.

Oh.

She was Albert's retirement plan.

She couldn't listen anymore. *Ridiculous party? Old man?* Her father had liked Albert. He'd said Albert had a bright future ahead of him at the company so he couldn't be after her money. Not like her other boyfriends. But this... this cut the deepest.

Samantha headed toward the door, thanking her father for his insistence on having the best of everything so her footsteps were muffled in the carpet's thick pile. Albert would never know she'd been there.

She'd gone six steps when she stopped.

How dare he talk about her like that.

How dare he talk about her like that to someone else.

How dare he even *think* about her like that.

And how dare he not know who she really was.

Samantha clutched her stomach, the pain already knotting her insides. How did she not see this? How did she not know?

When would she ever learn?

Sniffing back a sob, she was about to leave when, suddenly, she realized that she *had* learned. She knew how she wanted to be treated—how she deserved to be treated. And this wasn't it.

Albert was not going to get away with treating her this way.

Samantha spun around and tore off the *djellaba*. She was going to face Albert as herself, not hiding behind some stone-like façade as she'd done every other time the truth had come out about a guy she'd been dating.

She didn't have long to wait because Albert almost ran into her coming out of the bedroom.

"Samantha?" He paled a little beneath the tan he refreshed once a week at the spa—using the membership he'd so gallantly tried to refuse. "Darling, I thought you were at the party."

"I'll bet you did." Samantha folded the *djellaba* and laid it on the back of the love seat. Oh, her earring. It must have come off when she'd yanked off the hood.

She picked it up and put it back on. "Who's Henley?"

Albert's poker face slid into place. "I'm sorry. Who?"

"Don't patronize me, Albert. Who's Henley and what deal do you have going with him?"

"Samantha. Darling. You're distraught. It's understandable, given how close you were with your father. You're not thinking clearly. What, did the fortune-teller not show up?"

Samantha cursed. In Sumerian. And she had no idea how she knew the word or that it was Sumerian, but right now, she didn't care. "Don't change the subject, Albert. My thinking is perfectly clear. My hearing's pretty damn good, too. Tub-o-lard? Elope? Does that ring any bells for you?"

She almost wished they *were* engaged so she could throw the ring in his face.

"Samantha, please." He gripped her arm. "Let's sit down and discuss this like rational adults—"

She yanked her arm free. "That would mean I'd have to be rational and you'd have to be an adult, and frankly, I'm not feeling very rational right now, Albert. I'd rather pitch a huge fit and let everyone know what a damned two-faced liar you are. But I have too much respect for my father's memory to do that, so let's keep this between you and me. We're finished. Don't call me, don't try to see me, and consider every membership, credit card, and restaurant table canceled. We're through." She spun around and started to walk away.

"Samantha, darling. You don't mean that—"

"Yes I do." She turned around, strode back across the room, and poked him in the chest. "Oh, and you're fired."

"You can't fire me."

"I most certainly can."

"I don't report to you."

"Um... Owner?"

"Shit." He pinched the bridge of his nose.

"And another thing." She poked him again. "You're a selfish pig of a lover. And not a very good one, either."

Albert was going to have to go to a month's worth of tanning sessions to reclaim the color he lost at her statement—oh, but he couldn't. She grinned. She was canceling his membership.

And she'd let him wonder how she knew about his sexual inadequacies. She'd be wondering that herself, actually.

She stormed out of the room, giving the door a satisfying slam behind her.

"Samantha?" Wanda's voice echoed up the stairs. "There's a problem outside. The caterer needs you."

Great, she didn't even have the chance to deal with *this* situation and now she had another one.

Albert yanked the door open. "Samantha—"

She held up her hand. "I have a party to attend to." At least it gave her something to do other than break down in a puddle of tears in Dad's office.

Patting her pocket where Dad's letter would just have to wait, Samantha took a deep breath and headed down the stairs.

David was waiting for her in the foyer. "Honestly, Samantha, I don't understand it. I don't know where the breakdown in communication happened and no one's admitting to setting it up. And I have *no* idea who the guy is who's taken up shop inside."

"Calm down, David. What are you talking about?"

"There's a tent out there."

"There are a lot of tents out there. That's what I ordered, remember?"

David waved his hands. "I know I know I know. I'm talking about the other tent. The orange one. And the guy inside it is refusing to budge until he speaks to you."

"An orange tent? I thought we agreed on blue?"

"You see my problem." David smoothed the arch of his eyebrow. "You have to speak to him so I can get him to pack up. I'll eat the labor costs, of course."

She patted David's arm. "I'm sure it's just a misunderstanding. I'll handle it."

"Good. Because the acrobats are having issues so I have to deal with them. You're a love, Samantha." David air-kissed her cheeks and was off to put out another fire.

—◊◊◊—

The tent was definitely orange, but it was far enough from the others and behind the copse of pomegranate trees her father had planted in Mom's memory that Samantha realized why she hadn't seen it earlier.

Straightening her shoulders and fortifying herself with a deep breath, Samantha pulled back the fabric that covered the opening.

Brass lanterns hung from the posts, plush rugs covered the floor, and comfortable sofas and cushions were spread throughout the tent, the same as the rest at the party.

The guy standing before her, however, was nothing like anything else at the party.

"Hello, Samantha."

He knew her? Interesting, because she didn't know him and she *definitely* would have remembered meeting him.

"Um, hi?"

"You don't remember me, do you?"

That wasn't a question you could bluff your way out of. "No, I'm sorry. I don't."

He took a step closer. "Yes, you do, Sam. I know you do. You have to. Think, Sam. Really hard."

He was so intent. So intense. So gorgeous.

Samantha scoffed at herself. Was she one to be swayed by a pretty face?

But she *was* swaying. And her hormones were dancing. Her thighs tingling.

Her thighs were tingling?

She looked up at him again. Studied him from his gorgeous wavy hair to his warm, dark, melted-chocolate eyes. His high cheekbones and a perfectly formed set of lips that curved up at the corners. A killer set of abs framed by the open vest he wore, with an orange stone in the shape of an eagle on the chain at the base of his throat…

Wait. She recognized that stone.

Didn't she?

Samantha shook her head. She was being ridiculous. Wishful thinking, that's all. "I'm sorry, but I don't. Where did we meet?"

"Izaaz."

"Is what?"

He smiled then, and if he'd been gorgeous before, now he was devastating. A twinkle in his eye, the dimple in his cheek, the shape of his lips—

"You said that last time."

"Last time?"

He reached for her hand. "You don't remember."

It wasn't a question.

"I'm sorry, but you must have me confused with someone else."

He cupped her cheek. "Someone else named Samantha?" He took a step closer and Samantha's legs wouldn't move to take one back. "With the most gorgeous green eyes on the planet and the hint of lilac clinging to her skin?" He leaned in a little closer, the web his words were weaving making her glad she wasn't moving. "With that sexy beauty mark on her hip?"

Samantha let his words wash over her. She did have green eyes, but gorgeous? That was debatable. And as for the lilac body wash she wore, well, lots of women wore that.

That beauty mark, however…

"Which hip?" she whispered.

He stared at her mouth. "The left one."

Oh, God, she did have a beauty mark on her left hip. How she wanted to be the Samantha this guy knew…

"Come on, Sam. Think. You know me. I know you know it."

But she didn't, and how sad was it that they both wanted her to but she didn't?

Though… *Sam*. There was something about the way he called her that.

Samantha shook her head. Wishful thinking and,

thanks to Albert, self-esteem that could really use this guy's brand of pick-me-up.

She nibbled on her bottom lip, then took a deep breath. And a step to the side. "I'm sorry. I wish I could remember you, but I don't."

"What did you say?"

Samantha cocked her head. "Um, I wish I could remember you?"

When he smiled this time, it transformed his face—

Or maybe that happened when he waved his hand and it was as if a veil had been lifted.

She saw everything so much more clearly.

She saw *Kal* so much more clearly.

Kal. Who'd sent her home just as she'd asked.

Kal, who'd made her forget what had happened just as she'd asked.

Kal, who'd broken her heart.

"Kal." It all came rushing back. Izaaz, Dirham, the leprechauns.

The pain. The disillusionment. The nasty reality.

How much more was she going to have to take today?

"You remember?"

She nodded. Yes, she did. Every single detail.

Why couldn't he have let her forget?

She spun around to leave, but Kal grabbed her wrist— and held out the lantern pendant she'd left behind.

"Please, Sam, let me say this, and then if you still want to leave, I won't stop you."

She shouldn't. She really shouldn't.

But she did.

Because he was him. And because she was in love with him—well, *had been* in love with him.

He turned her hand over and placed his lantern in her palm. "When you picked it up from O'Malley and Paddy, you became my master again. And I can't think of one I'd rather have."

She shoved it back at him. "Take it, Kal. I don't want it and I know you do. There. Be free. I wish it."

Her voice hitched at the end. If only he'd come because he loved her and wanted to spend the rest of *her* life with her, she could have lived with that. But as an obligation?

No way.

Kal looked at the lantern, then at her. "Okay, so now I'm free. But it doesn't matter because I've earned the job I wanted."

"I'm happy for you, Kal. Truly. Enjoy your job and your magic."

"I can't."

"What—"

He cupped her cheek again, and she let herself sink into it for a second.

"Because I love you, Sam."

Those were the words she'd longed to hear but the last ones she thought he'd say. "You do? Why?"

"Why?" Kal looked taken aback, but, hey, if he'd been in her shoes, he'd understand.

She looked down at his feet. The curled slippers they'd both worn in Izaaz.

What had O'Malley said? Samantha didn't have to struggle to remember, not with the way the memories were flooding her. She could see it as if it were yesterday. Actually, it might have been yesterday. Or today.

Samantha shook her head. When it was didn't matter;

the words were as clear as if O'Malley were standing right here, saying them all over again.

Genies cannot love mortals or they'll lose their magic and immortality.

"Yes, Kal. Why? Why would you say that? Doesn't that take your magic away?"

He ran his thumb over her bottom lip. "I don't care."

"But—"

"Sam, I realized something when you made that last wish that I was honor-bound to fulfill. I hated doing it. Hated knowing you'd be back here not remembering anything about me. About us. I didn't want to live the rest of my life knowing that you wouldn't remember."

He brought his other hand to her face, raised her chin, and brought her closer. "Don't you see? For the past two thousand years, I've been driven to clear my name and best Faruq, the guy who'd taken it all from me, to have the highest job in my world.

"Well, I did, and you know what? It's not enough. I thought it would be. I thought it was what I wanted. But I'd forgotten what it was like to be alone. Truly alone. No friends, no family, and now, no master. All I'd have to look forward to was living in my palace and ruling others like me.

"But then you came along and I fell in love with you, Sam. It didn't start out that way, but something about you made me want to be with you. To protect you and take care of you, that had nothing to do with who I was as a genie, but who I am as a man. What you and I have, it's unlike anything I've known. It's real. And I want that, Sam. I want you. I want a life with you. A real one. With real joys and a real relationship. A family, not like

Bart and Maille, but what they could have. Not this mere existence I've been living.

"I want to marry you. I want to live out the rest of my mortal life with you. I want to have children with you. I want to make memories and relive them when we're old and gray. I never want to be alone again, Sam. Having the title means nothing if I don't have you. All the magical powers in the world don't come close to the magic, the wonder, of loving you. Because I can't go—"

Samantha kissed him. He'd said enough.

For now.

A little while later, he pulled back. "Say it, Sam. I need to hear it."

She smiled then and linked her hands behind his neck, pulling him down for another kiss. "As you wish, Kal. I love you."

He kissed her again, a quick hard peck. "No, Sam. As *we* wish."

THE END

النهايه

Author's Note

Djinn are religious figures in Islam, and while I tried to incorporate that history and culture into my world-building, this story is based more on U.S. pop-culture references. No disrespect or insult to anyone's beliefs is intended.

Read on for an excerpt from

I Dream of Genies

Now available from
Sourcebooks Casablanca

SCHEHERAZADE, THE FAMED ARABIAN STORYTELLER, had to come up with a thousand and one nights' worth of tales to save herself.

Eden should have it so easy.

But at least her life wasn't on the line like Scheherazade's, so that was a plus. Her mind, though, was another matter. There was only so much magic a genie could do to pass three thousand years of confinement and not go mad.

Unwilling to succumb to such madness, Eden flicked her wrists and snapped her fingers, her magic sending the butterflies, hummingbirds, and twirling glass balls she'd bewitched toward the ceiling of her bottle so she could have a better view through the hazy saffron glass. The rain of yet another Pacific Northwest storm streaked the storefront display window she'd inhabited for the last forty-five years, two months, and thirteen days. If the Arabian weaver of tales had used Eden's last half century as the basis of the stories that had saved her life, the poor woman would have been dead before her first sunrise.

"Mornin', babe." Obo, the cat she'd been cursed—or blessed, depending on one's viewpoint—to share this latest part of her penance with, leapt onto the shelf

beside her bottle, licking his Egg McMuffin breakfast from his whiskers. The cat was a master forager.
"Whatcha lookin' at?"

"Wilson." Eden nodded to the tree in front of the
store. She'd watched it grow from a sapling to its current
block-the-rest-of-the-world-from-view size for so long
that she'd named it.

"Kind of pitiful that you named a tree after a
volleyball."

"It worked for Tom Hanks."

"Yeah, but he was stranded on a deserted island.
You've got the bustle of the city and hundreds of people
right in front of you to keep you company."

Hundreds of people she couldn't interact with. She
was on the outside looking in—well, actually, she was
on the inside and wanting to *get* out. But the High Master
had sealed her bottle with so much magic that nothing
short of an explosion would set her free.

"And me, of course." The cat winked at her, his yellow eyes against his black fur making the motion notice-
able. "You've always got me. I know I'm the bright spot
in your day."

"In your dreams, Romeo."

"Speaking of lover-boy, has he been by yet?" Obo
nudged the copper ashtray with the mermaid cigarette
holder out of the way and curled his tail around her bottle before plunking himself onto his belly. Mr. Murphy,
the store owner, hadn't shown up yet, so Obo could get
away with hanging out here. Once the man did, however, all bets were off.

It was a sad state of affairs to look forward to these
daily chats with Obo, who was high on her list of Least

Favorite Beings ever since he'd let her take the fall for *his* necklace heist from Ramses II's tomb. It showed just how lonely and bored she was that she even deigned to talk to him, let alone looked forward to it. Other than her thoughts and her magic, she had only him to keep her company.

Oh, and "lover-boy" Matt Ewing. Couldn't forget him. And she didn't. He was pretty unforgettable, and heavens knew, she thought about him more than she should.

"No, he hasn't been by. I guess this weather's keeping him inside." Almost every morning, Matt jogged around the corner of the store in those tight, form-hugging running clothes. The perspiration slicking his face, that sexy curling hair, the controlled, even grace of his movements had fueled her fantasies ever since Mr. Murphy had moved her glass bottle to the front window.

"Or he could have had a hot date last night and it carried over."

Eden curled her legs under her, the curly toes of her slippers catching on the piping around the edge of the new sofa. She propped her elbow on the back cushion and plopped her chin onto her palm. "Thanks, Obo. That's helpful."

The cat licked his paw and swiped it over his ear. "Just callin' it like I see it."

Eden turned to look at him, brushing a wayward hummingbird out of the way, her gold shackle, er, bracelet flashing in the lone weak beam of sunlight that somehow fought its way through Wilson's leaves and the steady rain. "And how *do* you see it, Obo? You've been to his house. What's his world like?"

The cat shuddered and tucked his paws beneath his chest. "A damn sight wetter than yours. You should be thankful you're in this place. It's a monsoon out there."

The cat could be tight-lipped when he wanted to be. Which was often. All she asked for was news of the outside world and its people, descriptions of the smells and sounds, and the general feeling of being free to come and go as she pleased, but other than getting Matt's name out of Obo, the cat barely shared anything else. He had no idea how lucky he was to have the ability to go where and when he wanted.

She definitely didn't understand why he chose to be *here*. In this musty old shop, surrounded by things other people wanted to get rid of. How Mr. Murphy stayed in business was beyond her, because most of the stuff had been here as long as she had, and there certainly hadn't been any runs on antique plant stands or tarnished brass headboards.

Flicking her wrists again with the accompanying finger-snap that completed her Way of doing her magic, Eden arced a rainbow from one side of her bottle to the other, the purple ray disappearing into the shadow of the bottle's neck. The butterflies immediately began flying through it, and the hummingbirds raced along the ribbons of color that matched their wings.

She snapped her fingers again, and Humphrey *poof*ed onto her arm like a trained parrot. The dragonlet, a baby dragon about the size of her palm and her latest "foster child," reminded her of Bogart in his early movies, with a long face, high forehead, and large eyes, hence the name, though the dragon's eyes were blue to Bogart's brown.

In that, Humphrey reminded her of the High Master, but Adham was such a lofty name for such a tiny thing. And besides, like the Humphrey of those on-demand movies, this Humphrey was on loan, too—until he reached unmanageable proportions, which, with a dragon, was usually around the one month mark, meaning she had about five days left with this one before the hormones kicked in.

She stroked Humphrey's golden scales, then pointed to the rainbow. He gave her the tiniest nip on her palm—full blown dragon love could be really painful—then fluttered his little wings, his strength increasing daily. Today was probably the last day he could fly with the butterflies. The hummingbirds were fast enough to evade his beak-like jaws, but the butterflies wouldn't be a match; they'd more likely be lunch. But for today, he could play among the colors with them. Dragons loved rainbows.

She did, too, because of the happiness they innately engendered, especially on dreary days like today. But rainbows were infrequent manifestations for her because, while Mr. Murphy couldn't see in and most things couldn't pass through the magical barrier of her bottle walls without her okay, rainbows required an inordinate amount of light and, therefore, could be seen. Light shining from a dusty, and supposedly empty, old bottle would definitely be noticed.

"Uh, babe?" The gentle *whoosh* of Obo's fur thrummed softly along the ribbed lower portion of her bottle as he brushed his tail against the outside. "The rain might be murder on pedestrian traffic, but it's upped the vehicular kind. And the traffic light is red. A couple of interested kids, and your beacon there is going to get some notice."

Eden sighed, hating that he was right, but flicked her wrists anyway. The rainbow dissipated, leaving traces behind on the winged creatures. Humphrey sported a blue stripe down the ridge of his back and one of the iridescent Blue Morpho butterflies was going to have to change its name to Purple Morpho.

"Why are you here again, Obo? With the free run you have of this town, I'd think this has to be the most boring place you could be."

Obo's tail paused mid-flick and his ear twitched. "Ah, well, you know… I, uh, can't talk to mortals without freaking them out, and none of the animals in this country have been on the planet as long as me. Who else can I share the good ol' days with? You're the closest I get to normal, babe."

Which was sad because nothing in her life had been *normal* from the moment she'd gone to live with the High Master over two thousand years ago following her parents' death.

Eden sighed and gathered her magic to summon a pomegranate smoothie on the teak inlay table next to the lime green sectional she'd ordered last month. The persimmon-colored pillows weren't pulling the whole look together as she'd hoped. While she loved color, the backdrop of the saffron bottle made her art deco a little too avant-garde. Ah, well, she'd do some redecorating today to keep herself occupied. The satellite dish Faruq had given her for her birthday a few years ago came in handy.

Not that she'd ever admit it to Faruq. The High Master's vizier, charged with monitoring Genie

Compliance, already had too much control of—and too much interest in—her life.

She sipped the smoothie. The dish, and the high-def TV that had replaced the antiquated electronics she'd accumulated over the years, were gods-sends. Much easier to shop, teach herself new languages, keep abreast of changing societies and customs, and learn all about new technology and the selling power of J.D. Power and Associates. Not to mention, how to make smoothies.

And with her bottle's magical ability to alter its interior without changing the dimensions on the outside, she could order up a swimming pool and Mr. Murphy would never know the difference.

Actually, maybe she'd do that. She'd like to hear Faruq's comment when he found out he was going to have to magick up a couple thousand gallons of water. And as for getting it through the magic channels to her, well, that ought to give him a few fits.

She took another sip of her smoothie. Such were the pleasures of her life.

"Hey, that looks good." Obo peered into her bottle, the tapered neck distorting his yellow irises until he looked like the Cyclops she'd seen off the coast of Crete that last summer she'd been on the outside. "Can you conjure one up for me?"

Eden set her treat down on the Egyptian brazier topped with a circular mosaic tile platter she called an end table. Nothing like combining Old World and New. "Sorry, Obo, but my magic won't leave the bottle for the mortal world while the stopper's in." Otherwise she would have zapped herself somewhere warm and sandy years ago.

"Well, could you calm the butterflies down then? Their flapping wings are driving me nuts. And the dragon…" He shuddered and dropped his head onto his paws. "I don't get *that* at all."

Humphrey did a loop-the-loop above her head and Eden held out her hand for him to land on as a reward. Baby dragons were so lovable and eager to please. Until they hit that unmanageable milestone—then their fiery heritage took over. It was a treat to be able to enjoy them at this stage, one far too rare for her liking.

As for her other cohabitants, they were the only living things Faruq approved to be in her bottle. She'd tried to talk him into a kitten after a few hundred years of solitude, but he'd refused. Said kittens would grow up to be cats, and cats were sneaky. That any cat he gave her might be able to figure a way out of the bottle.

It didn't speak well to the High Master's magic if his own vizier thought a cat could undo it, but Eden didn't buy Faruq's argument for one minute. Just one more thing he wanted to control about her.

So she'd volunteered to foster orphan dragonlets and hadn't complained when Obo had shown up. Not that the cat had any interest in helping her out of her bottle. Knowing where to find her so he could "share the good ol' days" was incentive enough, apparently, for him to make sure she stayed put. Probably worried what she'd do to him after he'd abandoned her during that necklace fiasco. A few hundred years ago, she might have done something, but nowadays, she was just thankful for the companionship. She'd told him so and had even tried bribing him into tipping the bottle off the shelf with promises of making all his wishes come true, but the cat had turned her down.

She hadn't held out any great hope of a fall breaking her bottle anyway. She'd been dropped many times over the years as her bottle had changed hands—sometimes on purpose—but nothing had budged that stopper.

She conjured up an acacia seedpod for Humphrey and his blue tongue flicked out to taste it. A bunch of cooing ensued, complete with little claw marks on her arm as he hunched into his "don't take my food" position over the pod. He happily munched away on the outer casing. Nothing like the throaty rumblings of a contented dragonlet. "What time is it, Obo?"

Obo didn't even look at the cuckoo clock hanging on the wall by the shop's door. "Matt's not coming, Eden. You wore your sexy little outfit for nothing." He opened one eye and the black slit of pupil thinned even more. "Thinking of auditioning for a TV show, are we?"

Eden shrugged. The costumes hadn't been purchased specifically with Matt in mind, but if the opportunity ever presented itself, well, hey. She had urges just as much as the next person. And after being cooped up so long with only Obo and Faruq to talk to, those urges were teetering on the brink of meltdown.

But she'd just *had* to buy the harem girl outfits, one in every color, after watching that genie on the television show. She didn't know who'd ratted out her race, but that Mr. Sidney Sheldon had gotten almost every detail right. Except the costume. No self-respecting genie would be caught dead in this little get-up while in The Service. But it was comfortable and it was colorful. And there was no one but her to see her in it.

"I wonder where Mr. Murphy is? He's usually here by now."

Obo sighed and rolled onto his side, his tail whispering along her bottle again. "Probably rowing his canoe in. I'm beginning to wonder if Noah's up to his old tricks."

Eden smiled. Crotchety and full of complaints—and a liar and a thief—Obo might be, but he was right; they didn't have anyone but each other to share the old times with. Unless she counted Faruq. And she wasn't about to.

But then the bells over the service door jingled, and Obo jumped to his paws so fast it was a wonder he *didn't* knock her bottle over. He ducked behind the black marble obelisk on the shelf next to her.

"If you're counting on the lack of sunlight to hide you, it's not working," she whispered, flicking the butterflies and hummingbirds onto the gardenia and honeysuckle bushes in her flower garden and Humphrey onto the mini acacia tree he used as a perch when she let him fly around. The twirling glass balls went into the padded box that prevented them from breaking whenever someone moved the bottle. "You better get out of here, Obo."

"Tell me something I don't know." The cat wiggled his butt trying to shrink into the shadows. "I have to go out the way he's coming in, so we'll need to distract him."

"Keep talking and that ought to do it," she whispered, using her magic to clean up a spot of yellow the rainbow had left behind.

Mr. Murphy walked into the room, but didn't flip over the OPEN sign like usual. Instead, he went behind a French Provincial sideboard beneath a Baroque mirror and brought out a large cardboard box—an empty one— that he soon started filling with every knickknack from the top of the sideboard. And from the bookcase next to that. And the top of the retro refrigerator next to that.

Eden ducked behind the big stone marker Hadrian had given her as thanks for the carpet ride all those years ago when he'd surveyed the land for his wall. True, Mr. Murphy wouldn't be able to see her spying on him, but years of habits weren't so easily forgotten, no matter how rarely utilized those habits were. "This doesn't look good."

"Gee, ya think?" Obo muttered, his back end tiptoeing toward the edge of the shelf. "I'm outta here, babe." With that, Obo executed the perfect stealthy leap cats were known for, hit the floor running, and was into the back room before Mr. Murphy heard anything.

Lucky Obo. Eden could only sit and worry.

⸺⁂⸺

Obo nudged his way out of the back of the shop. Skulking in the shadows again. Story of his life—and one he was heartily sick of.

For years, over two thousand of them, he'd been hiding. First from the assassins, then from tomb raiders, then from anyone who wanted a "pet kitty." He'd lived a life of luxury before being on the run, and while pâté and room service were heavenly, the plotting and backstabbing by usurpers was anything but. He'd been done with that life when his mistress had ended hers, and he hadn't looked back. Obo looked out for one thing and one thing only: his own life.

With the end of it approaching—nine magical lives could only take a cat so far—he had to look out for his *After*life now.

Walking along the back of the store, Obo tried to keep

his paws out of the puddles. Futile, but worth a shot because nothing was worse than soggy paws. Well, except burning ones. He might complain about the weather here, but it definitely beat the hot sands of the desert. If he never saw a desert again, it'd be too soon.

Getting out of that part of the world had been an added bonus to Bastet's offer: keep an eye on Eden and balance the heavenly scales for a good number of his transgressions. He had a *lot* of transgressions to make up for, so this seemed to be a simple enough task.

All he'd had to do was pack up his meager belongings and get himself to this part of the world, then provide monthly reports via the mockingbird the goddess had sent to, well, *mock* him. A bird was her messenger? Seriously? Bastet was a cat goddess and she sent a *bird* to collect her reports? There was probably some sort of test in that, too: don't kill the messenger and knock off two extra bad deeds from his celestial tally.

However the goddess was keeping tabs, Obo was in.

A gutter groaned overhead, and its contents gushed down in front of him, a good portion splashing off the concrete and soaking his fur. He wouldn't mind being *in* right now, but any of his regulars—mortals who took in stray cats—lived far enough from Eden's store that he'd be just as soaked anyway.

Obo shook the rain water off and rounded the end of the building. Maybe Wilson would provide some cover. At least he could hang out in the branches to keep his paws somewhat dry.

He dragged himself into the crook of Wilson's lowest branch just as Mr. Murphy walked out of his store and dumped that cardboard box on top of a garbage can by the curb, then ran back inside and adjusted the CLOSED sign.

What was the mortal up to? Why was he tossing things he'd been trying to sell? Cardboard dissolved in this much rain. It didn't make any sense.

Then a trash truck turned the corner and it suddenly did.

Except—

Son-of-a-bichon! The top of Eden's bottle was sticking out of that box!

Acknowledgments

Once again, a huge, heartfelt thank-you to my Egyptian friend, Tarek Amer, for all of his help with the Arabic, customs, references, and sayings, and for giving his time. Any mistakes are all mine. And to Valerie Amer for the fabulous dinner at Little Marakesh. (And our great concert tickets!)

To the owners and staff at Little Marakesh, in particular, Alycea Moss, whose knowledge was incredibly helpful, thank you for a delicious evening, amazing ambiance, and wonderful entertainment.

To Deb Werksman, my editor. I can't say thank you enough for making my stories so much better. Congratulations on being named editor of the year!

To my agent, Jennifer Schober, for all you do.

To Sue Grimshaw, for all you've done.

To Steph for walking me through it. Over and over. I can't tell you how much it means to me. You are worth more than any goddess's amulet. ;)

To The Wisdom, my Writing Wombats, possessors of all types of information, who so amazingly and generously share their time and expertise, in particular, beta readers and grammarians extraordinaire: Beth Hill, Wanda Hughes, Jill Lynn Anderson, Olivia Cunning, and Wendy Christy. Thank you for your help, speedy reads, and great insight!

And especially to my readers. Thank you for coming on this (magic carpet) ride with me—it's because of you that I can do this.

About the Author

Judi Fennell has had her nose in a book and her head in some celestial realm all her life, including those early years when her mom would exhort her to "get outside!" instead of watching *Bewitched* or *I Dream of Jeannie* on television. So she did—right into Dad's hammock with her Nancy Drew books.

These days she's more likely to have her nose in her laptop and her head (and the rest of her body) at her favorite writing spot, but she's still reading, whether it be her latest manuscript or friends' books.

A PRISM-Award winner, Golden Leaf award winner, and author of the Mer series: *In Over Her Head*, *Wild Blue Under*, and *Catch of a Lifetime*, and Book 1 of the Bottled Magic series, *I Dream of Genies,* Judi enjoys hearing from her readers. Check out on her website at www.JudiFennell.com for excerpts, deleted scenes, reviews, contests, and pictures from reader and writer conferences, as well as the chance to discover a whole new world!